Louisa May Alcott's
CIVIL WAR

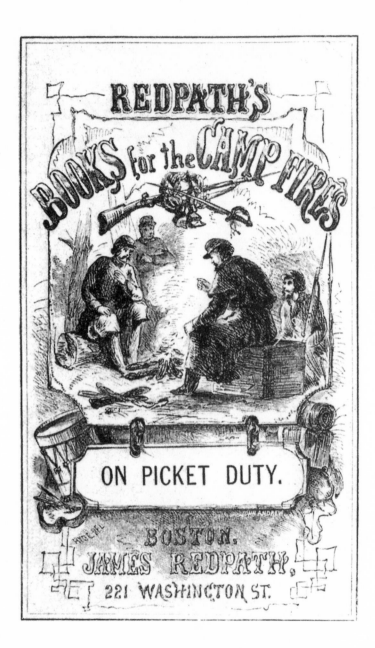

REDPATH'S

BOOKS for the CAMP FIRES

ON PICKET DUTY.

BOSTON.
JAMES REDPATH,
221 WASHINGTON ST.

Louisa May Alcott's CIVIL WAR

Louisa May Alcott

with an introduction by Jan Turnquist

Edinborough Press
Roseville, Minnesota

Edinborough Press
www.edinborough.com

LIBRARY OF CONGRESS CATALOGING-IN-PUBLICATION DATA

Alcott, Louisa May, 1832-1888.
Louisa May Alcott's Civil War / Louisa May Alcott ; introduction by Jan Turnquist.
   p. cm.
      ISBN-13: 978-1-889020-10-5 (alk. paper)
      ISBN-10: 1-889020-10-9 (alk. paper)
      1. Alcott, Louisa May, 1832-1888—Diaries. 2. United States—History—Civil
War, 1861-1865—Fiction. 3. United States—History—Civil War, 1861-1865—Personal
narratives. 4. United States—History—Civil War, 1861-1865—Hospitals. 5. Authors,
American—19th century—Diaries. I. Title.
PS1018.A4 2003
813'.4—dc21

                              2002155843

The text is set in Adobe Garamond and printed on acid-free paper.

FRONT COVER: Louisa May Alcott, 1862. *National Library of Medicine*
BACK COVER: A Ward in Armory Square Hospital, Washington, D.C. *Library of Congress*

CONTENTS

Introduction

I

Civil War Journals

13

Hospital Sketches

Civil War Stories

Credits

265

HOSPITAL SKETCHES.

BY

L. M. ALCOTT.

"Which, naming no names, no offence could be took."—*Sairy Gamp.*

BOSTON:

JAMES REDPATH, Publisher,

221 Washington Street.

1863.

Hospital Sketches, *title page, first edition, 1863*

INTRODUCTION

Jan Turnquist

"WAR DECLARED WITH THE SOUTH, and our Concord company went to Washington," wrote Louisa May Alcott in her April 1861 journal. "At the station the scene was very dramatic, as the brave boys went away perhaps never to come back again. I've often longed to see a war, and now I have my wish." More than year later, ready to head to Washington, D.C. to begin service as a nurse, she remained ardent in her devotion to the Union, writing, "I like the stir in the air, and long for battle like a warhorse when he smells powder. The blood of the Mays is up!"[1]

In her autobiographical classic, *Little Women,* Miss Alcott's alter ego, Jo March announces, "Don't I wish I could go as a drummer . . . or a nurse."[2] The novel's heroine is based closely on the author, and to many people, Jo and Louisa May Alcott are one and the same; but there is much more to this complicated, passionate woman than the character portrayed in *Little Women.* This volume, containing ten Civil War pieces written by Alcott, reveals her views and war experiences. The stories should be understood in light of her complexity, resisting the temptation to view her only as Jo March.

I stand at the small, half-round desk where Louisa May Alcott set *Little Women* in the time of the Civil War, looking out the window onto Lexington Road, where she saw, "All the young men and boys drill with all their might."[3] She knew full well the solemnity of the occasion, as she wrote in her journal, "In a little town like this, we all seem like one family in times like these."[4] Seeing her neighbors as an extended family, she could describe them with warm humor, as in a letter to a friend, explaining that Ralph Waldo Emerson's young son:

Edward Emerson has a company of 'Concord Cadets' who poke each others eyes out, bang their heads & blow themselves up with gunpowder most valiantly & will do good service by & by. I've no doubt if there is anything left of them when ordered to the field.[5]

The Alcott family raised their daughters to think more independently than many families of that era dared to raise their sons. The bold, independent attitudes of her parents, who were involved in every major reform movement of the day, allowed Louisa to develop into a complex person. She consistently saw poignancy and humor in the same moment.

I am privileged to live a mile from the Alcotts' home, Orchard House, where I have worked since 1977 in varying capacities, and now as executive director. Through these years, I developed an original one-woman show, in which I portray Louisa May Alcott in as much depth as I can to show this woman's intricacies. In fact, I was asked to write this introduction because the editor of this volume felt that "figuratively standing in her shoes brings a special insight" into her life.

Louisa May Alcott has ignited passion in scholars and captured the attention of modern day readers because of her multifaceted personality. Today, she is portrayed more as a strong-minded feminist, proud spinster, independent thinker, and rebel than as a dutiful daughter who wrote optimistic children's literature. Indeed, she was independent, proud, and strong-minded. In her November 1862 journal she wrote,

Thirty years old. Decided to go to Washington as a nurse. . . . I love nursing and must let out my pent up energy in some new way . . . I want new experiences, and am sure to get 'em if I go.[6]

Who was the young woman who wrote those words in 1862? At age thirty, *she* did not think herself to be young. On the surface, one might say she did not think much of herself at all. Continually self-effacing, Louisa did not consider herself attractive, socially adept or a great writer. Rather, she considered herself a workhorse who had the harder road, at least compared to her youngest sister. In one journal entry, she wrote, "She (sister May) is one of the fortunate ones, and gets what she wants easily. I have to grub for my help, or go without it. Good for me . . . cheer up, Louisa, and grind away."[7]

Louisa routinely identified with the outsider and wistfully acknowledged what she could not have. The reader of Alcott's journals may conclude that Louisa was jealous of her sister, but should also note numerous passages such as, "On the 17th go to B[oston] and see our youngest [May] start on her first little flight alone into the world, full of hope and courage. May all go well with her!"[8] Keeping the whole person in mind as I portray Louisa, I take the view that her sibling envy is on the surface, and that, underneath, the soul is strong and positive.

One must look beneath that surface in order to understand her. Who was Louisa? Was she a strong-minded feminist? An independent thinker? A dutiful daughter? A humorist at the core? An actress at heart? A preacher? A repressed soul, frustrated not to be in the traditional role of wife and mother? A proud, independent spinster? A jealous outsider? A proud rebel? An optimist? A pessimist?

Louisa was all of these, and reflected them in her writing. She was, after all, a product of her age. Women were strongly admonished everywhere in the Victorian culture to prepare themselves to fulfill their sacred duty to be wife and mother. The story, *On Picket Duty,* repeatedly reveals the attributes of a good wife. As the men on picket duty tell "how we found our wives," the women left behind are described as capable of "the good-naturedest gale of laughin' you ever heard in your life," and "tip-top" and "fust-rate," and "a right noble woman" — except for the wife who fell back into her theatrical days. After her husband rescued her from a homeless life and wed her, she abandons him and returns to "her dancing in Philadelphia, with paint on her cheeks, trinkets on her neck and arms, handsome woman twirling there before the footlights."[9]

In this story, Louisa allowed the conventional, proper Victorian woman to win. One must remember, however, that the same author wrote a number of thriller tales uncovered by foremost Alcott scholars Leona Rostenberg and Madeleine Stern. Rostenberg and Stern have become good friends with whom I frequently discuss Alcott. At our first meeting, I was extremely nervous, knowing they were about to see me perform my characterization for the first time. After the performance, Miss Stern told me, "You are Louisa May Alcott. Louisa would have loved this!" As our friendship grew, I learned more about their thoughts of Alcott, finding out that it was the depth of the characterization, the attempt to bring in the conflicts and divergent aspects of Louisa's personality, that drew Miss Stern's compliment (which I shame-lessly treasure to this day).

In tale after tale, with titles such as *Behind a Mask, or the Story of a Woman's Power,* Louisa celebrated strong women who are every bit as bold as the dancer in *On Picket Duty.* These feminist literary thrillers are very much a part of Louisa May Alcott, even when she wrote in other genres. Picture, if you will, the femme fatale heroine of *Behind a Mask*, Miss Jean Muir, charming the family who hired her to be their governess. They think her to be a fresh, innocent seventeen-year-old, yet, as Alcott wrote,

> When alone Miss Muir's conduct was decidedly peculiar. Her first act was to clench her hands and mutter between her teeth, with passionate force, "I'll not fail again if there is power in a woman's wit and will!" She . . . shook her clenched hand as if menacing some unseen enemy.

Later in the story, the façade is broken. Miss Muir enjoys "a glass of some ardent cordial" and speaks to it, saying, "*Merci*, old friend. You put heart and courage into me . . . Come the curtain is down, so I may be myself for a few hours, if actresses ever are themselves." Alcott continued,

> She unbound and removed the long abundant braids from her head, wiped the pink from her face, took out several pearly teeth, and . . . appeared herself indeed, a haggard, worn, and moody woman of thirty at least. The metamorphosis was wonderful, but the disguise was more in the expression she assumed than in any art of costume or false adornment . . . At last she rose and crept to bed, like one worn out with weariness and mental pain.[10]

As you read *On Picket Duty*, remember that Louisa had another side!

Louisa was also a product of her unique reformer parents and their illus-trious friends who stood boldly for their beliefs—often unpopular. She used to say, "In the army of reform, I never knew less than a General." She sometimes signed letters: "Yours for reforms of all kinds, L. M. Alcott."

Louisa was raised in an abolitionist household full of "hopers," and was one of those who early on *did* see the Civil War as a way to end slavery. In *The Colored Soldiers' Letters,* the reader sees Louisa's concern for black-white equality—rare even among many abolitionists of the day. She learned this

view from her parents, founding members of both male and female abolitionist societies and activists in the Underground Railroad. Louisa wrote, "Let
us hope that both [colored soldiers] may prosper in the double battle they
must fight against treason and ignorance." The term "colored" is no longer
considered "correct," but in Louisa's time, it was common. Less common was
Louisa's concern that a college "refused to grant a colored student the honors
he had won." Louisa repeatedly expressed a desire to go to Port Royal to teach
the newly-freed slaves to read. Although circumstances conspired to block
that path, that dream expressed her true concern for others — regardless of
race or creed.

In the bosom of a family who practiced what they preached, she learned
to value people more than things and independent thinking over material
possessions and social position. She greatly admired her mother whom she
called, "The best woman in the world." Well-born Abigail May was a true
philanthropist who gave out of her own need, when she could not give out of
abundance. She truly was the Marmee of *Little Women*, with more dimension
in real life.

Her mother's cheerful nature, and its influence on Louisa, is seen in *The
Brothers,* when Nurse Dane recalls a humorous moment,

> We both laughed, though the Doctor was on his way to the deadhouse and
> I held a shroud on my lap. But, in a hospital, one learns that cheerfulness
> is one's salvation; for, in an atmosphere of suffering and death, heaviness of
> heart would soon paralyze usefulness of hand, if the blessed gift of smiles
> had been denied us.[11]

Indeed, the good cheer of Mrs. Alcott and daughter was often in the midst
of suffering and death. The Alcotts repeatedly made an intentional choice to
search for joy in hard times. Louisa loved finding or making fun everywhere.
Humor gives perspective. Perspective gives health. In my opinion, Louisa had
a very healthy perspective on her life and life around her.

She was ready to test her strong, healthy being in the strange new setting
of a Union army hospital. Humor abounds in the midst of serious stories.
Often it is subtle, as her descriptions of an attempt at Christmas decorating,
in *A Hospital Christmas:*

"Look at de neatness of dat job, gen'l'men," — at which point the whole thing tumbled down about his ears, — how they all shouted but Pneumonia Ned, who, having lost his voice, could only make ecstatic demonstrations with his legs. . . . Miss Hale, stepping into a chair, pounded stoutly at the traitorous nail and performed some miracle with a bit of string.[12]

Other times the humor is whimsical as in *Nelly's Hospital*. First, we meet Nelly, who announces to her mother that,

Since brother Will came home with his lame foot, and I've helped you tend him, I've heard a great deal about hospitals, and liked it very much. To-day I said I wanted to go and be a nurse, like Aunt Mercy; but Will laughed and told me I'd better begin by nursing sick birds and butterflies and pussies before I tried to take care of men.

Soon the reader is delighted with charming, humorous images of "an invalid butterfly carried in a tiny litter by long-legged spiders and a fat frog with gouty feet hopping upon crutches."[13]

At other times, Louisa's humor reflects her determination to make the best of difficulties. In *Hospital Sketches* she wrote,

The sight of several stretchers, each with its legless, armless, or desperately wounded occupant, entering my ward, admonished me that I was there to work, not to wonder or weep; so I corked up my feelings and returned to duty . . . Round the great stove was gathered the dreariest group I ever saw ragged, gaunt and pale, mud to the knees, with bloody bandages untouched since put on days before . . . I pitied them so much, I dared not speak to them though . . . I yearned to serve the dreariest of them all. Presently, Miss Blank tore me from my refuge behind piles of one-sleeved shirts . . . put basin, sponge, towels, and a block of brown soap into my hands, with these appalling directions: "Come, my dear, begin to wash as fast as you can. Tell them to take off socks, coats and shirts, scrub them well, put on clean shirts, and the attendants will finish them off, and lay them in bed" . . . to scrub some dozen lords of creation at a moment's notice, was really — really —.

However, there was no time for nonsense. . . . I drowned my scruples in my washbowl, clutched my soap manfully, and assuming a businesslike air, made a dab at the first dirty specimen I saw . . . a withered old Irishman, wounded in the head, which caused that portion of his frame to be tastefully laid out like a garden, the bandages being the walks, his hair the shrubbery. He was so overpowered by the honor of having a lady wash him, as he expressed it, that he did nothing but roll up his eyes, and bless me, in an irresistible style which was too much for my sense of the ludicrous; so we laughed together. . . . This comical tableau produced a general grin, at which propitious beginning I took heart and scrubbed away like any tidy parent on a Saturday night.[14]

Louisa dearly loved her philosopher father. Bronson Alcott did not provide well materially, but gave strong nurture to her inner being. Instead of mourning his lack of sons, he celebrated his daughters as equally viable movers and shakers. In an era when it was considered unlady-like for a woman to have a desk of her own, Mr. Alcott built his budding authoress her own desk. Louisa enjoyed this personal encouragement, love and support.

Like any young woman, however, she found coming to terms with familial oddities a challenge. Louisa openly expressed the two sides of her dilemma. She said of her father's philosophical bent, "Why try to know the unknowable when there are still poor to be fed?" Yet she also wrote, "I wish the stupid would wake up and pay him what he is worth." She knew that as a lecturer, he was not always paid what was promised, even though his "conversations" had been characterized as going "to heaven in a swing." The philosopher's struggle to find enlightenment — or the light — seems to be portrayed in *The Hospital Lamp*. Louisa introduced the main character of this short piece by saying, "On one of these beds lay the watcher of the light." This "watcher" is a soldier coming to terms with physical pain and guilt over the price others paid on his behalf. [15]

During the darkest period in the Alcott family's life, after a failed utopian experiment, Fruitlands, when Louisa was eleven years old, she observed her father temporarily incapacitated by the failure of his dream. Eventually, he saw the figurative light and raised up from bed to say the single word, "hope," which signaled his return to vigor. Louisa's soldier in *The Hospital Lamp* is awake in the night, when his nurse asks, "I am afraid it [the light] keeps you awake. . . . What are you so busy about all night, when the other men are dreaming?" "Thinking ma'am." He reveals his suffering and adds, "I didn't know a man could bear so much and live."[16]

Although he is speaking of his physical pain, psychic pain creates such agony, too. Louisa's symbolic answer to both kinds of pain is light and hope. Her soldier suffers survivor's guilt. He stays awake thinking about it and staring at the hospital lamp. His nurse understands his staring at the light to be leading him to "a clearer knowledge of himself, bringing from the painful present the promise of a nobler future." This phrase certainly describes Louisa's father, when he reflected on the material lack that his family endured while striving for higher philosophical goals. Louisa, her mother, and sisters understood Bronson Alcott, as did his good friend Ralph Waldo Emerson, in a way few others could. This understanding informs Louisa's writing in *The Hospital Lamp.*[17]

In *Hospital Sketches,* we see Louisa's vibrant connection with the war experience because it is so highly autobiographical, based on letters written during her actual experience as a nurse at the Union Hotel Hospital in Georgetown (dubbed "Hurley Burley House" by Louisa). On her way to Georgetown, she described looking out her train window, "Military washes flapped and futtered on the fences . . . everywhere the boys threw up their caps and cut capers as we passed."

From childhood, Louisa loved the exuberance of "her boys." Her affection and empathetic nature show repeatedly in passages from *Hospital Sketches,* such as,

> A slight wound in the knee brought him there; but his mind had suffered more than his body . . . As I sat by him, endeavoring to soothe his poor distracted brain. . . . I saw a one-legged phantom hopping nimbly down the room . . . toward home, as he blandly informed me, touching the military cap which formed a striking contrast to the severe simplicity of the rest of his decidedly *undress* uniform.[18]

After "the lively monoped" was settled, Nurse and "a big Prussian who spoke no English" noticed "the echo of a sob" from a twelve-year-old drummer boy who was having a nightmare. In response, her original patient began to stir, as did "the lively monoped!" Then, "the Prussian, with a nod and a smile, took the lad away to his own bed, and lulled him to sleep with a soothing murmur."[19] The horror, humor, and tender side of war mix with Louisa's obvious love of her patients to bring her reader into the complex reality of that hospital ward.

When preparing to take on the role of playing Louisa May Alcott, I try to be honest and take her as a whole being. I endeavor to take conflicting feelings and let them coexist in one person. Indeed, we are all made up of contradictory parts, which we frequently do not see very clearly in ourselves. Yet, as a whole, these diverse pieces come together to create a vital interesting person. A problem with intelligent, complex historic people, such as Louisa May Alcott, is that when dissected in a purely academic light, one loses that sense of the whole. For Alcott, as for others, like a pointillist painting, close inspection of the tiny pieces means loss of the whole where one sees the true character.

A strong part of the popular culture, Louisa's book, *Little Women,* is a useful reference point for understanding Alcott—to a degree. When reading the novel, readers are not called upon to dissect and scrutinize tiny pieces of her conflicting nature. They understand her conflict to be a normal part of an interestingly complex real person. One of Jo's most endearing qualities is that she is *not* perfect, yet she goes on loving, living, and doing her best to make a real difference in the world.

In this way, I believe *Little Women* is an aid in understanding the young woman who stood at the brink of war and wished to plunge in! Louisa was strong, independent, brave, and ready to make a real difference in the world, even as she was self-effacing. To some degree, that modesty was a façade, fulfilling society's expectation of a woman, yet the side of her that went forth and *acted boldly* anyway always won out over any doubts. Such bold action is a sign of healthy esteem, even if you also look wistfully to what might have been, as Louisa sometimes did. The imaginative and creative soul can envision oneself on the path not taken, feel a sense of loss, but refuse to dwell in regrets.

To really understand Alcott as she enters the Civil War years, I suggest, therefore, that one stand back as much as possible and see her as a whole. See her as a young woman who feels mature and ready to *give* even as her philan-thropist mother gave. See her as a young woman, supported by her father, who *can* do important work, despite society's strictures that such is reserved for the male sex. See her as an active tom-boy who longs for adventure and excitement as she always had been encouraged to find it—even though a female. Understand that like the rest of her society in 1861, she did not grasp the horrors of war and could only see its glories.

To know Alcott as a whole person and as author of the remarkable Civil War pieces in this volume, one final look at *Little Women* may be useful. Louisa May Alcott was both a product of her times and a challenge to them. Her autobiographical character, Jo March, has been hailed as a role model for women for over a century now and inspires people from all walks of life and all parts of the globe. Women in particular draw inspiration from strong-minded Jo. Yet, it is unfortunate that the very title, *Little Women*, creates a certain reluctance in some males to reading the book. I am convinced that Louisa's experiences in life and in the Civil War allowed her to cut through gender roles and convey the inspiration and attraction of her family experience to male and female alike.

She begins this classic during the dark days of the Civil War. To make her book more socially acceptable, the pragmatic author gave many of her own Civil War experiences to Mr. March. The similarities are unmistakable: A telegram brings the family the dreaded news that Mr. March is in a Union Army Hospital. Mother leaves immediately for Washington, "praying that she is not too late." In reality, Louisa was the subject of just such a telegram and her father traveled to the Union Hotel Hospital, hoping that he may see his second born alive.[20]

Familiarity with the story of *Little Women* reminds us of the warmth and support from home that provides strength for Louisa, so far from away and in such trying circumstances. In each of the stories in this volume, the reader will find strength exuding from the pages. With remarkable straight-forward simplicity, Miss Alcott shares what she experienced, but also what she imparted. The strength of a good family is a constant presence. As she expressed in *Hospital Sketches,* it is the love of family "which makes life beautiful and outlives death."[21]

In my role as performer, as well as in my job as executive director of her home, Orchard House, I meet literally hundreds of her readers every month. I have been truly astounded by her impact on lives. I am often asked to explain phenomena such as the hundreds of thousands of Japanese visitors who flock to Orchard House, brimming with enthusiasm. I have come to believe that the fact that Jo March displays strength and independence, while maintaining absolute respect for all members of her family and championing the value of family and people over material possessions and social standing, makes her a universal role model. Humans the world over long to find ways to maintain their inner spirit, while sustaining connections to those who really matter in life.

Of all the statements that I have heard, however, a recent one really gave me pause. A woman, who saw my Louisa May Alcott performance, told me that her fifteen-year-old grandson's favorite book was *Little Women*. She told me that he would not admit to his friends that he had even read it, much less what he thought of it. I asked her if he had given her a reason for his fondness of the book. She told me that he said it was because the March family was so weird in a cool way. I have turned this idea over in my mind a great deal since then: "Weird in a cool way."

That pretty well sums it up, I guess. In the midst of people who are afraid to be themselves, whether the year is 1861 or 2061, it can seem weird to be oneself with all of one's conflicts and inconsistencies showing. It can definitely seem weird to stand up for one's unpopular beliefs and to act in ways that do not "fit" with everyone else. And in today's vernacular, where "cool" means admirable, it is cool to see the bravery and integrity it takes to do these things. Do I hero-worship Louisa May Alcott? No. Do I admire her? Yes. Her writings in this volume come from the heart and intellect of a person of tremendous integrity and spirit. They accurately record events of the time, but from a unique perspective of a person whose family nurtured her with independence and integrity—a person most definitely flawed, but definitely "cool."

Endnotes

1 See page 21. The text for the Alcott's journals comes from Louisa May Alcott, *Louisa May Alcott, Her Life and Letters, and Journals*, ed. Ednah Cheney (Boston, Roberts Brothers, 1889).

2 Louisa May Alcott, *Little Women* (New York: Barnes & Noble, Inc., 2000), 9.

3 LMA to Alfred Whiteman, Concord, 19 May 1861, *The Selected Letters of Louisa May Alcott*, ed. Joel Myerson and Daniel Shealy (Boston: Little, Brown and Company, 1987), 64.

4 See page 19.

[5] LMA to Alfred Whiteman, Concord, 19 May 1861, *The Selected Letters of Louisa May Alcott*, ed. Joel Myerson and Daniel Shealy, (Boston: Little, Brown and Company, 1987), 64.

[6] See page 21.

[7] See page 15.

[8] See page 15.

[9] See pages 136, 142.

[10] Louisa May Alcott, *Modern Magic: Five Stories by Louisa May Alcott* (New York: The Modern Library, 1995), 119-120.

[11] See page 114.

[12] See page 155.

[13] See page 235.

[14] See page 60-61.

[15] See page 172.

[16] See page 173.

[17] See page 178.

[18] See page 73.

[19] See page 73-74.

[20] See page 25.

[21] See page 83.

Civil War Journals

November 1860

Father sixty-one; L. aged twenty-eight. Our birthday. Gave Father a ream of paper, and he gave me Emerson's picture; so both were happy.

Wrote little, being busy with visitors. The John Brown Association asked me for a poem, which I wrote.

Kind Miss R. sent May $30 for lessons, so she went to B. to take some of Johnstone. She is one of the fortunate ones, and gets what she wants easily. I have to grub for my help, or go without it. Good for me, doubtless, or it wouldn't be so; so cheer up, Louisa, and grind away!

December

More luck for May. She wanted to go to Syracuse and teach, and Dr. W. sends for her, thanks to Uncle S. J. May. I sew like a steam-engine for a week, and get her ready. On the 17th go to B. and see our youngest start on her first little flight alone into the world, full of hope and courage. May all go well with her!

Mr. Emerson invited me to his class when they meet to talk on Genius; a great honor, as all the learned ladies go.

Sent "Debby's Debit" to the "Atlantic," and they took it. Asked to the John Brown meeting, but had no "good gown," so didn't go; but my "pome" did, and came out in the paper. Not good. I'm a better patriot than poet, and couldn't say what I felt.

A quiet Christmas; no presents but apples and flowers. No merry-making; for Nan and May were gone, and Betty under the snow. But we are used to hard times, and, as Mother says, "while there is a famine in Kansas we mustn't ask for sugarplums."

All the philosophy in our house is not in the study; a good deal is in the kitchen, where a fine old lady thinks high thoughts and does kind deeds while she cooks and scrubs.

January 1861

Twenty-eight; received thirteen New Year's gifts. A most uncommon fit of generosity seemed to seize people on my behalf, and I was blessed with all manner of nice things, from a gold and ivory pen to a mince-pie and a bonnet.

Wrote on a new book—"Success" ["Work"]—till Mother fell ill, when I corked up my inkstand and turned nurse. The dear woman was very ill, but rose up like a phoenix from her ashes after what she gayly called "the irrepressible conflict between sickness and the May constitution."

Father had four talks at Emerson's; good people came, and he enjoyed them much; made $30. R. W. E. probably put in $20. He has a sweet way of bestowing gifts on the table under a book or behind a candle-stick, when he thinks Father wants a little money, and no one will help him earn. A true friend is this tender and illustrious man.

Wrote a tale and put it away,—to be sent when "Debby" comes out. "F. T." appeared, and I got a dress, having mended my six-year old silk till it is more patch and tear than gown. Made the claret merino myself, and enjoyed it, as I do anything bought with my "head-money."

February

Another turn at "Moods," which I remodelled. From the 2d to the 25th I sat writing, with a run at dusk; could not sleep, and for three days was so full of it I could not stop to get up. Mother made me a green silk cap with a red bow, to match the old green and red party wrap, which I wore as a "glory cloak." Thus arrayed I sat in groves of manuscripts, "living for immortality," as May said. Mother wandered in and out with cordial cups of tea, worried because I couldn't eat. Father thought it fine, and brought his reddest apples and hardest cider for my Pegasus to feed upon. All sorts of fun was going on; but I didn't care if the world returned to chaos if I and my inkstand only "lit" in the same place.

It was very pleasant and queer while it lasted; but after three weeks of it I found that my mind was too rampant for my body, as my head was dizzy, legs shaky, and no sleep would come. So I dropped the pen, and took long walks, cold baths, and had Nan up to frolic with me. Read all I had done to my family; and Father said: "Emerson must see this. Where did you get your metaphysics?" Mother pronounced it wonderful, and Anna laughed and cried, as she always does, over my works, saying, "My dear, I'm proud of you."

So I had a good time, even if it never comes to anything; for it was worth something to have my three dearest sit up till midnight listening with wide-open eyes to Lu's first novel.

I planned it some time ago, and have had it in my mind ever so long; but now it begins to take shape.

Father had his usual school festival, and Emerson asked me to write a song, which I did. On the 16th the schools all met in the hall (four hundred),—a pretty posy bed, with a border of proud parents and friends. Some of the fogies objected to the names Phillips and John Brown. But Emerson said: "Give it up? No, no; I will read it." Which he did, to my great contentment; for when the great man of the town says "Do it," the thing is done. So the choir warbled, and the Alcotts were uplifted in their vain minds.

Father was in glory, like a happy shepherd with a large flock of sportive lambs; for all did something. Each school had its badge,—one pink ribbons, one green shoulder-knots, and one wreaths of pop-corn on the curly pates. One school to whom Father had read Pilgrim's Progress told the story, one child after the other popping up to say his or her part; and at the end a little tot walked forward, saying with a pretty air of wonder, — "And behold it was all a dream."

When all was over, and Father about to dismiss them, F. H., a tall, handsome lad came to him, and looking up confidingly to the benign old face, asked "our dear friend Mr. Alcott to accept of Pilgrim's Progress and George Herbert's Poems from the children of Concord, as a token of their love and respect."

Father was much touched and surprised, and blushed and stammered like a boy, hugging the fine books while the children cheered till the roof rung.

His report was much admired, and a thousand copies printed to supply the demand; for it was a new thing to have a report, neither dry nor dull; and teachers were glad of the hints given, making education a part of religion, not a mere bread-making grind for teacher and an irksome cram for children.

April

War declared with the South, and our Concord company went to Washington. A busy time getting them ready, and sad day seeing them off; for in a little town like this we all seem like one family in times like these. At the station the scene was very dramatic, as the brave boys went away perhaps never to come back again.

I've often longed to see a war, and now I have my wish. I long to be a man; but as I can't fight, I will content myself with working for those who can.

Sewed a good deal getting May's summer things in order, as she sent for me to make and mend and buy and send her outfit. Stories simmered in my brain, demanding to be writ; but I let them simmer, knowing that the longer the divine afflatus was bottled up the better it would be.

John Brown's daughters came to board, and upset my plans of rest and writing when the report and the sewing were done. I had my fit of woe up garret on the fat rag-bag, and then put my papers away, and fell to work at housekeeping. I think disappointment must be good for me, I get so much of it; and the constant thumping Fate gives me may be a mellowing process; so I shall be a ripe and sweet old pippin before I die.

May

Spent our May-day working for our men,—three hundred women all sewing together at the hall for two days.

May will not return to S[yracuse]. after her vacation in July; and being a lucky puss, just as she wants something to do, F. B. S[anborn]. needs a drawing teacher in his school and offers her the place.

Nan found that I was wearing all the old clothes she and May left; so the two dear souls clubbed together and got me some new ones; and the great parcel, with a loving letter, came to me as a beautiful surprise.

Nan and John walked up from Cambridge for a day, and we all walked back. Took a sail to the forts, and saw our men on guard there. Felt very martial and Joan-of-Arc-y as I stood on the walls with the flag flying over me and cannon all about.

June

Read a good deal; grubbed in my garden, and made the old house pretty for May. Enjoyed Carlyle's French Revolution very much. His earthquaky style suits me.

"Charles Auchester" is charming,—a sort of fairy tale for grown people. Dear old "Evelina," as a change, was pleasant. Emerson recommended Hodson's

India, and I got it, and liked it; also read Sir Thomas More's Life. I read Fielding's "Amelia," and thought it coarse and queer. The heroine having "her lovely nose smashed all to bits falling from a post shay" was a new idea. What some one says of Richardson applies to Fielding, "The virtues of his heroes are the vices of decent men."

July

Spent a month at the White Mountains with L[ouisa]. W[illis]., a lovely time, and it did me much good. Mountains are restful and uplifting to my mind. Lived in the woods, and revelled in brooks, birds, pines, and peace.

August

May came home very tired, but satisfied with her first attempt, which has been very successful in every way. She is quite a belle now, and much improved,—a tall blond lass, full of grace and spirit.

September

Ticknor sent $50. Wrote a story for C[lapp]., as Plato needs new shirts, and Minerva a pair of boots, and Hebe a fall hat.

October

All together on Marmee's birthday. Sewing and knitting for "our boys" all the time. It seems as if a few energetic women could carry on the war better than the men do it so far.

A week with Nan in the dove-cot. As happy as ever.

November and December

Wrote, read, sewed, and wanted something to do.

January 1862

E. P. Peabody wanted me to open a Kindergarten, and Mr. Barnard gave a room at the Warren Street Chapel. Don't like to teach, but take what comes; so when Mr. F. offered $40 to fit up with, twelve pupils, and his patronage, I began.

Saw many great people, and found them no bigger than the rest of the world,—often not half so good as some humble soul who made no noise. I learned a good deal in my way, and am not half so much impressed by society as before I got a peep at it. Having known Emerson, Parker, Phillips, and that set of really great and good men and women living for the world's work and service of God, the mere show people seem rather small and silly, though they shine well, and feel that they are stars.

February

Visited about, as my school did not bring enough to pay board and the assistant I was made to have, though I didn't want her.

Went to lectures; saw Booth at the Goulds',—a handsome, shy man, glooming in a corner.

Very tired of this wandering life and distasteful work; but kept my word and tugged on.

Hate to visit people who only ask me to help amuse others, and often longed for a crust in a garret with freedom and pen. I never knew before what insolent things a hostess can do, nor what false positions poverty can push one into.

April

Went to and from C[oncord]. every day that I might be at home. Forty miles a day is dull work; but I have my dear people at night, and am not a beggar.

Wrote "King of Clubs,"—$30. The school having no real foundation (as the people who sent didn't care for Kindergartens, and Miss P[eabody]. wanted me to take pupils for nothing, to try the new system), I gave it up, as I could do much better at something else. May took my place for a month, that I might keep my part of the bargain; and I cleaned house, and wrote a story which made more than all my months of teaching. They ended in a wasted winter and a debt of $40,—to be paid if I sell my hair to do it.

May

School finished for me, and I paid Miss N. by giving her all the furniture, and leaving her to do as she liked; while I went back to my writing, which pays much better, though Mr. F[ields]. did say, "Stick to your teaching; you can't write." Being wilful, I said, "I won't teach; and I can write, and I'll prove it."

Saw Miss Rebecca Harding, author of "Margaret Howth," which has made a stir, and is very good. A handsome, fresh, quiet woman, who says she never had any troubles, though she writes about woes. I told her I had had lots of troubles; so I write jolly tales; and we wondered why we each did so.

June, July, August

Wrote a tale for B., and he lost it, and wouldn't pay.

Wrote two tales for L. I enjoy romancing to suit myself; and though my tales are silly, they are not bad; and my sinners always have a good spot somewhere. I hope it is good drill for fancy and language, for I can do it fast; and Mr. L. says my tales are so "dramatic, vivid, and full of plot," they are just what he wants.

September, October

Sewing Bees and Lint Picks for "our boys" kept us busy, and the prospect of the first grandchild rejoiced the hearts of the family.

Wrote much; for brain was lively, and work paid for readily. Rewrote the last story, and sent it to L[eslie]., who wants more than I can send him. So, between blue flannel jackets for "our boys" and dainty slips for Louisa Caroline or John B., Jr., as the case may be, I reel off my "thrilling" tales, and mess up my work in a queer but interesting way.

War news bad. Anxious faces, beating hearts, and busy minds. I like the stir in the air, and long for battle like a warhorse when he smells powder. The blood of the Mays is up!

Journal kept at the Hospital, Georgetown, D. C., 1862

November

Thirty years old. Decided to go to Washington as nurse if I could find a place. Help needed, and I love nursing, and must let out my pent-up energy in some new way. Winter is always a hard and a dull time, and if I am away there is one less to feed and warm and worry over.

I want new experiences, and am sure to get 'em if I go. So I've sent in my name, and bide my time writing tales, to leave all snug behind me, and mending up my old clothes,—for nurses don't need nice things, thank Heaven!

December

On the 11th I received a note from Miss H[annah]. M. Stevenson telling me to start for Georgetown next day to fill a place in the Union Hotel Hospital. Mrs. Ropes of Boston was matron, and Miss Kendall of Plymouth was a nurse there, and though a hard place, help was needed. I was ready, and when my commander said "March!" I marched. Packed my trunk, and reported in B. that same evening.

We had all been full of courage till the last moment came; then we all broke down. I realized that I had taken my life in my hand, and might never see them all again. I said, "Shall I stay, Mother?" as I hugged her close. "No, go! and the Lord be with you!" answered the Spartan woman; and till I turned the corner she bravely smiled and waved her wet handkerchief on the door-step. Shall I ever see that dear old face again?

So I set forth in the December twilight, with May and Julian Hawthorne as escort, feeling as if I was the son of the house going to war.

Friday, the 12th, was a very memorable day, spent in running all over Boston to get my pass, etc., calling for parcels, getting a tooth filled, and buying a veil,—my only purchase. A. C. gave me some old clothes; the dear Sewalls money for myself and boys, lots of love and help; and at 5 P.M., saying "good-by" to a group of tearful faces at the station, I started on my long journey, full of hope and sorrow, courage and plans.

A most interesting journey into a new world full of stirring sights and sounds, new adventures, and an evergrowing sense of the great task I had undertaken.

I said my prayers as I went rushing through the country white with tents, all alive with patriotism, and already red with blood. A solemn time, but I'm glad to live in it; and am sure it will do me good whether I come out alive or dead.

All went well, and I got to Georgetown one evening very tired. Was kindly welcomed, slept in my narrow bed with two other room-mates, and on the morrow began my new life by seeing a poor man die at dawn, and sitting all day between a boy with pneumonia and a man shot through the lungs. A strange day, but I did my best; and when I put mother's little black shawl round the boy while he sat up panting for breath, he smiled and said, "You are real motherly, ma'am." I felt as if I was getting on. The man only lay and stared with his big black eyes, and made me very nervous. But all were well behaved; and I sat looking at the twenty strong faces as they looked back at me,—the only new thing they had to amuse them,—hoping that I looked "motherly" to them; for my thirty years made me feel old, and the suffering round me made me long to comfort every one.

January 1863

Union Hotel Hospital, Georgetown, D. C.—I never began the year in a stranger place than this: five hundred miles from home, alone, among strangers, doing painful duties all day long, and leading a life of constant excitement in this great house, surrounded by three or four hundred men in all stages of suffering, disease, and death. Though often homesick, heartsick, and worn out, I like it,—find real pleasure in comforting, tending, and cheering these poor souls who seem to love me, to feel my sympathy though unspoken, and acknowledge my hearty good-will, in spite of the ignorance, awkwardness, and bashfulness which I cannot help showing in so new and trying a situation. The men are docile, respectful, and affectionate, with but few exceptions; truly lovable and manly many of them. John Sulie, a Virginia blacksmith, is the prince of patients; and though what we call a common man in education and condition, to me is all I could expect or ask from the first gentleman in the land. Under his plain speech and unpolished manner I seem to see a noble character, a heart as warm and tender as a woman's, a nature fresh and frank as any child's. He is about thirty, I think, tall and handsome, mortally wounded, and dying royally without reproach, repining, or remorse. Mrs. Ropes and myself love him, and feel indignant that such a man should be so early lost; for though he might never distinguish himself before the world, his influence and example cannot be without effect, for real goodness is never wasted.

Monday, 4th—I shall record the events of a day as a sample of the days I spend:—

Up at six, dress by gaslight, run through my ward and throw up the windows, though the men grumble and shiver; but the air is bad enough to breed a pestilence; and as no notice is taken of our frequent appeals for better ventilation, I must do what I can. Poke up the fire, add blankets, joke, coax, and command; but continue to open doors and windows as if life depended upon it. Mine does, and doubtless many another, for a more perfect pestilence-box than this house I never saw,—cold, damp, dirty, full of vile odors from wounds, kitchens, wash-rooms, and stables. No competent head, male or female, to right matters, and a jumble of good, bad, and indifferent nurses, surgeons, and attendants, to complicate the chaos still more.

After this unwelcome progress through my stifling ward, I go to breakfast with what appetite I may; find the uninvitable fried beef, salt butter, husky bread, and washy coffee; listen to the clack of eight women and a dozen men,—the first silly, stupid, or possessed of one idea; the last absorbed with their breakfast and themselves to a degree that is both ludicrous and provoking, for all the dishes are ordered down the table full and returned empty; the conversation is entirely among themselves, and each announces his opinion with an air of importance that frequently causes me to choke in my cup, or bolt my meals with undignified speed lest a laugh betray to these famous beings that a "child's amang them takin' notes."

Till noon I trot, trot, giving out rations, cutting up food for helpless "boys," washing faces, teaching my attendants how beds are made or floors are swept,. dressing wounds, taking Dr. F[itz]. P[atrick].'s orders (privately wishing all the time that he would be more gentle with my big babies), dusting tables, sewing bandages, keeping my tray tidy, rushing up and down after pillows, bed-linen, sponges, books, and directions, till it seems as if I would joyfully pay down all I possess for fifteen minutes' rest. At twelve the big bell rings, and up comes dinner for the boys, who are always ready for it, and never entirely satisfied. Soup, meat, potatoes, and bread is the bill of fare. Charley Thayer, the attendant, travels up and down the room serving out the rations, saving little for himself, yet always thoughtful of his mates, and patient as a woman with their helplessness. When dinner is over, some sleep, many read, and others want letters written. This I like to do, for they put in such odd things, and express their ideas so comically, I have great fun interiorially, while as grave as possible exteriorially. A few of the men word their paragraphs well. and make excellent letters. John's was the best of all I wrote. The answering of letters from friends after some one had died is the saddest and hardest duty a nurse has to do.

Supper at five sets every one to running that can run; and when that flurry is over, all settle down for the evening amusements, which consist of newspapers, gossip, the doctor's last round, and, for such as need them, the final doses for the night. At nine the bell rings, gas is turned down, and day nurses go to bed. Night nurses go on duty, and sleep and death have the house to themselves.

My work is changed to night watching, or half night and half day,—from twelve to twelve. I like it, as it leaves me time for a morning run, which is what I need to keep well; for bad air, food, and water, work and watching, are getting to be too much for me. I trot up and down the streets in all directions, sometimes to the Heights, then half way to Washington, again to the hill, over which the long trains of army wagons are constantly vanishing and ambulances appearing. That way the fighting lies, and I long to follow.

Ordered to keep [to] my room, being threatened with pneumonia. Sharp pain in the side, cough, fever, and dizziness. A pleasant prospect for a lonely soul five hundred miles from home! Sit and sew on the boys' clothes, write letters, sleep, and read; try to talk and keep merry, but fail decidedly, as day after day goes, and I feel no better. Dream—awfully, and wake unrefreshed, think of home, and wonder if I am to die here, as Mrs. R[opes]., the matron, is likely to do. Feel too miserable to care much what becomes of me. Dr. S[mith]. creaks up twice a day to feel my pulse, gives me doses, and asks if I am at all consumptive, or some other cheering question. Dr. O[tman]. examines my lungs and looks sober. Dr. J[ohn]. haunts the room, coming by day and night with wood, cologne, books, and messes, like a motherly little man as he is. Nurses, fussy and anxious, matron dying, and everything very gloomy. They want me to go home, but I won't yet.

January 16th—Was amazed to see Father enter the room that morning, having been telegraphed to by order of Mrs. R[opes]. without asking leave. I was very angry at first, though glad to see him, because I knew I should have to go. Mrs. D[ana]. and Miss Dix came, and pretty Miss W[ansey]., to take me to Willard's to be cared for by them. I wouldn't go, preferring to keep still, being pretty ill by that time.

On the 21st I suddenly decided to go home, feeling very strangely, and dreading to be worse. Mrs. R[opes]. died, and that frightened the doctors about me; for my trouble was the same,—typhoid pneumonia. Father, Miss K[endal]., and Lizzie T[hurber]. went with me. Miss Dix brought a basket full of bottles of wine, tea, medicine, and cologne, besides a little blanket and pillow, a fan, and a testament. She is a kind old soul, but very queer and arbitrary.

Was very sorry to go, and "my boys" seemed sorry to have me. Quite a flock came to see me off; but I was too sick to have but a dim idea of what was going on.

Had a strange, excited journey of a day and night,—half asleep, half wandering, just conscious that I was going home; and, when I got to Boston, of being taken out of the car, with people looking on as if I was a sight. I daresay I was all blowzed, crazy, and weak. Was too sick to reach Concord that night, though we tried to do so. Spent it at Mr. Sewall's; had a sort of fit; they sent for Dr. H[ay], and I had a dreadful time of it.

Next morning felt better, and at four went home. just remember seeing May's shocked face at the depot, Mother's bewildered one at home, and getting to bed in the firm belief that the house was roofless, and no one wanted to see me.

As I never shall forget the strange fancies that haunted me, I shall amuse myself with recording some of them.

The most vivid and enduring was the conviction that I had married a stout, handsome Spaniard, dressed in black velvet, with very soft hands, and a voice that was continually saying, "Lie still, my dear!" This was Mother, I suspect; but with all the comfort I often found in her presence, there was blended an awful fear of the Spanish spouse who was always coming after me, appearing out of closets, in at windows, or threatening me dreadfully all night long. I appealed to the Pope, and really got up and made a touching plea in something meant for Latin, they tell me. Once I went to heaven, and found it a twilight place, with people darting through the air in a queer way, all very busy, and dismal, and ordinary. Miss Dix, W. H. Channing, and other people were there; but I thought it dark and "slow," and wished I hadn't come.

A mob at Baltimore breaking down the door to get me, being hung for a witch, burned, stoned, and otherwise maltreated, were some of my fancies. Also being tempted to join Dr. W. and two of the nurses in worshipping the Devil. Also tending millions of rich men who never died or got well.

February

Recovered my senses after three weeks of delirium, and was told I had had a very bad typhoid fever, had nearly died, and was still very sick. All of which seemed rather curious, for I remembered nothing of it. Found a queer, thin, big-eyed face when I looked in the glass; didn't know myself at all; and when I tried to walk discovered that I couldn't, and cried because my legs wouldn't go.

Never having been sick before, it was all new and very interesting when I got quiet enough to understand matters. Such long, long nights; such feeble, idle days; dozing, fretting about nothing; longing to eat, and no mouth to do it with,—mine being so sore, and full of all manner of queer sensations, it was nothing but a plague. The old fancies still lingered, seeming so real I believed in them, and deluded Mother and May with the most absurd stories, so soberly told that they thought them true.

Dr. B[artlett]. came every day, and was very kind. Father and Mother were with me night and day, and May sang "Birks of Aberfeldie," or read to me, to wile away the tiresome hours. People sent letters, money, kind inquiries, and goodies for the old "Nuss." I tried to sew, read, and write, and found I had to begin all over again. Received $10 for my labors in Washington. Had all my hair, a yard and a half long, cut off, and went into caps like a grandma. Felt badly about losing my one beauty. Never mind, it might have been my head, and a wig outside is better than a loss of wits inside.

March

Began to get about a little, sitting up nearly all day, eating more regularly, and falling back into my old ways. My first job was characteristic: I cleared out my piece-bags and dusted my books, feeling as tired as if I had cleaned the whole house. Sat up till nine one night, and took no lunch at three A.M.—two facts which I find carefully recorded in my pocket diary in my own shaky handwriting.

Father had two courses of conversations: one at Mr. Quincy's, very select and fine; the other at a hall not so good. He was tired out with taking care of me, poor old gentleman; and typhus was not inspiring.

Read a great deal, being too feeble to do much else. No end of rubbish, with a few good things as ballast. "Titan" was the one I enjoyed the most, though it tired my weak wits to read much at a time. Recalled, and wrote some lines on "Thoreau's Flute," which I composed one night on my watch by little Shaw at the hospital.

On the 28th Father came home from Boston, bringing word that Nan had a fine boy. We all screamed out when he burst in, snowy and beaming; then Mother began to cry, May to laugh, and I to say, like B. Trotwood, "There, I knew it wouldn't be a girl!" We were all so glad it was safely over, and a jolly little lad was added to the feminine family.

Mother went straight down to be sure that "mother and child were doing well," and I fell to cleaning house, as good work for an invalid and a vent for a happy aunt.

April

Had some pleasant walks and drives, and felt as if born again, everything seemed so beautiful and new. I hope I was, and that the Washington experience may do me lasting good. To go very near to death teaches one to value life, and this winter will always be a very memorable one to me.

Sewed on little shirts and gowns for my blessed nephew, who increased rapidly in stature and godliness.

Sanborn asked me to do what Conway suggested before he left for Europe; viz., to arrange my letters in a printable shape, and put them in the "Commonwealth." They thought them witty and pathetic. I didn't; but I wanted money; so I made three hospital sketches. Much to my surprise, they made a great hit; and people bought the paper faster than they could be supplied. The second, "A Night" was much liked, and I was glad; for my beautiful "John Sulie" was the hero, and the praise belonged to him. More were wanted; and I added a postscript in the form of a letter, which finished up, as I then thought.

Received $100 from F[rank]. L[eslie]. for a tale which won the prize last January; paid debts, and was glad that my winter bore visible fruit. Sent L[eslie]. another tale. Went to Boston, and saw "our baby;" thought him ugly, but promising. Got a set of furniture for my room,—a long-talked-of dream of ours.

May

Spent the first week or two in putting the house in order. May painted and papered the parlors. I got a new carpet and rug besides the paper, and put things to rights in a thorough manner. Mother was away with Nan, so we had full sweep; and she came home to a clean, fresh house.

Nan and the Royal infanta came as bright as a whole gross of buttons, and as good as a hairless brown angel. Went to Readville, and saw the 54th Colored Regiment, both there and next day in town as they left for the South. Enjoyed it very much; also the Antislavery meetings.

Had a fresh feather in my cap; for Mrs. Hawthorne showed Fields "Thoreau's Flute," and he desired it for the "Atlantic." Of course I didn't say no. It was printed, copied, praised, and glorified; also paid for, and being a mercenary creature, I liked the $10 nearly as well as the honor, of being "a new star" and "a literary celebrity."

June

Began to write again on "Moods," feeling encouraged by the commendation bestowed on "Hospital Sketches," which were noticed, talked of, and inquired about, much to my surprise and delight. Had a fine letter from Henry James, also one from Wasson, and a request from Redpath to be allowed to print the sketches in a book. Roberts Bros. also asked, but I preferred the Redpath, and said yes; so he fell to work with all his might.

Went to Class Day for the first time; had a pleasant day seeing new sights and old friends.

G[ail]. H[amilton]. came to the H.'s Didn't like her as well as Miss H[arding].; too sharp and full of herself; insisted on talking about religion with Emerson, who glided away from the subject so sweetly, yet resolutely, that the energetic lady gave it up at last.

July

Sanborn asked for more contributions, and I gave him some of my old Mountain Letters vamped up. They were not good, and though they sold the paper, I was heartily ashamed of them, and stopped in the middle, resolving never again to try to be funny, lest I should be rowdy and nothing more. I'm glad of the lesson, and hope it will do me good.

Had some pleasant letters from Sergeant Bain,—one of my boys who has not forgotten me, though safely at home far away in Michigan. It gratified me very much, and brought back the hospital days again. He was a merry, brave little fellow, and I liked him very much. His right arm was amputated after Fredericksburg, and he took it very cheerfully, trying at once to train his left hand to do duty for both, and never complained of his loss. "Baby B."

August

Redpath carried on the publishing of the "Sketches" vigorously, sending letters, proof, and notices daily, and making all manner of offers, suggestions, and prophecies concerning the success of the book and its author.

Wrote a story, "My Contraband," and sent it to Fields, who accepted and paid $50 for it, with much approbation for it and the "Sketches." L[eslie]. sent $40 for a story, and wanted another.

Major M[ansfield]. invited me to Gloucester; but I refused, being too busy and too bashful to be made a lion of, even in a very small way. Letters from Dr. Hyde, Wilkie (home with a wound from Wagner), Charles Sumner, Mr. Hale, and others, all about the little "Sketches," which keep on making friends for me, though I don't get used to the thing at all, and think it must be all a mistake.

On the 25th my first morning-glory bloomed in my room, a hopeful blue,- and at night up came my book in its new dress. I had added several chapters to it, and it was quite a neat little affair. An edition of one thousand, and I to have five cents on each copy.

September

Redpath anxious for another book. Send him a volume of stories and part of a book to look at. He likes both; but I decide on waiting a little, as I'm not satisfied with the stories, and the novel needs time. "Sketches" sell well, and a new edition is called for.

Dear old Grandma died at Aunt Betsey's in her eighty-ninth year,—a good woman, and much beloved by her children. I sent money to help lay her away; for Aunt B. is poor, and it was all I could do for the kind little old lady.

Nan and Freddy made us a visit, and we decided that of all splendid babies he was the king. Such a hearty, happy, funny boy, I could only play with and adore him all the while he stayed, and long for him when he went. Nan and John are very fond of "our son," and well they may be. Grandma and Grandpa think him perfect, and even artistic Aunty May condescends to say he is "a very nice thing."

"My Contraband; or, the Brothers," my story in the "Atlantic," came out, and was liked. Received $40 from Redpath for "Sketches,"—first edition; wanted me to be editor of a paper; was afraid to try, and let it go.

Poor old "Moods" came out for another touching up.

October

Thought much about going to Port Royal to teach contrabands. Fields wanted the letters I should write, and asked if I had no book. Father spoke of "Moods," and he desired to see it. So I fell to work, and finished it off, thinking the world must be coming to an end, and all my dreams getting fulfilled in a most amazing way. If there was ever an astonished young woman, it is myself; for things have gone on so swimmingly of late I don't know who I am. A year ago I had no publisher, and went begging with my wares; now three have asked me for something, several papers are ready to print my contributions, and F. B. S[anborn]. says "any publisher this side of Baltimore would be glad to get a book." There is a sudden hoist for a meek and lowly scribbler, who was told to "stick to her teaching," and never had a literary friend to lend a helping hand! Fifteen years of hard grubbing may be coming to something after all; and I may yet "pay all the debts, fix the house, send May to Italy, and keep the old folks cosey," as I've said I would so long, yet so hopelessly.

May began to take anatomical drawing lessons of Rimmer. I was very glad to be able to pay her expenses up and down and clothe her neatly.

Twenty dollars more from Redpath on account.

December

Earnings 1863, $380.

The principal event of this otherwise quiet month was the Sanitary Fair in Boston, and our part in it. At G. G. B.'s request, I dramatized six scenes from Dickens, and went to town on the 14th to play. Things did not go well for want of a good manager and more time. Our night was not at all satisfactory to us, owing to the falling through of several scenes for want of actors. People seemed to like what there was of it, and after a wearisome week I very gladly came home again. Our six entertainments made twenty-five hundred dollars for the Fair.

Rewrote the fairy tales, one of which was published; but owing to delays it was late for the holidays, and badly bound in the hurry; so the poor "Rose Family" fared badly.

Had a letter from the publisher of a new magazine, called the "Civil Service Magazine," asking for a long tale. Had no time to write one; but will by and by, if the thing is good.

While in town received $10 of F. B. S. and $20 of Redpath, with which I bought May hat, boots, gloves, ribbons, and other little matters, besides furnishing money for her fares up and down to Rimmer.

January 1864

New Year's Day was a very quiet one. Nan and Freddy were here, and in the evening we went to a dance at the hall. A merry time; for all the town was there, as it was for the Soldiers' Aid Society, and every one wanted to help. Nan and I sat in the gallery, and watched the young people dance the old year out, the new year in as the clock struck twelve.

On looking over my accounts, I find I have earned by my writing alone nearly six hundred dollars since last January, and spent less than a hundred for myself, which I am glad to know. May has had $70 for herself, and the rest has paid debts or bought necessary things for the family.

Received from the "Commonwealth" $18 for "A Hospital Christmas." Wrote a fairy tale, "Fairy Pinafores." "Picket Duty" and other tales came out,—first of Redpath's series of books for the "Camp Fires." Richardson sent again for a long story for the "Civil Service Magazine." Tried a war story, but couldn't make it go.

February

Nan quite sick again. Mother passed most of the month with her; so I had to be housekeeper, and let my writing go,—as well perhaps, as my wits are tired, and the "divine afflatus" don't descend as readily as it used to do. Must wait and fill up my idea-box before I begin again. There is nothing like work to set fancy a-going.

Redpath came flying up on the 4th to get "Moods," promising to have it out by May. Gave it to him with many fears, and he departed content. The next day received a telegram to come down at once and see the printers. Went, and was told the story was too long for a single volume, and a two-volume novel was bad to begin with. Would I cut the book down about half? No, I wouldn't, having already shortened it all it would bear. So I took my "opus" and posted home again, promising to try and finish my shorter book in a month.

A dull, heavy month, grubbing in the kitchen, sewing, cleaning house, and trying to like my duty.

Mrs. S[tearnes]. takes a great fancy to May; sends her flowers, offers to pay for her to go to the new Art School, and arranges everything delightfully for her. She is a fortunate girl, and always finds some one to help her as she wants to be helped. Wish I could do the same, but suppose as I never do that it is best for me to work and wait and do all for myself.

Mr. Storrs, D.D., wrote for a sketch for his little paper, "The Drum Beat," to be printed during the Brooklyn Sanitary Fair. A very cordial, pleasant letter, which I answered by a little sketch called "A Hospital Lamp." He sent me another friendly letter, and all the daily, papers as they came out. A very gentlemanly D.D. is Dr. Storrs.

March

A busy month getting settled. Freddy's birthday on the 28th, one year old. He had a dozen nice little presents laid out in a row when he came down to breakfast, and seemed quite overpowered with his riches. On being told to take what he liked best, he chose the picture of little Samuel which Father gave him, and the good pope was much delighted at that.

Was asked for a poem for the great album at the St. Louis Fair, and sent "Thoreau's Flute" as my best. Also received a letter from the Philadelphia managers asking contributions for the paper to be printed at their Fair.

Wrote nothing this month.

April

At Father's request I sent "Moods" to T[icknor]. and got a very friendly note from him, saying they had so many books on hand that they could do nothing about it now. So I put it back on the shelf, and set about my other work. Don't despair, "Moods," we'll try again by and by!

Wrote the first part of a story for Professor C[oppee]. called "Love and Loyalty,"—flat, patriotic, and done to order. Wrote a new fairy tale, "Nelly's Hospital."

May

Had a letter from Mrs. Gildersleeve, asking for my photograph and a sketch of my life, for a book called "Heroic Women" which she was getting up. Respectfully refused. Also a letter and flattering notice from "Ruth Hall," and a notice from a Chicago critic with a long extract from "Rose Family."

My tale "Enigmas" came out, and was much liked by readers of sensation rubbish. Having got my $50, I was resigned.

June

To town with Father on the 3d to a Fraternity Festival to which we were invited. Had a fine time, and was amazed to find my "'umble" self made a lion of, set up among the great ones, stared at, waited upon, complimented, and made to hold a "laynee" whether I would or no; for Mr. S. kept bringing up people to be introduced till I was tired of shaking hands and hearing the words "Hospital Sketches" uttered in every tone of interest, admiration, and respect. Mr. Wasson, Whipple, Alger, Clarke, Calthrop, and Chadwick came to speak to me, and many more whose names I forget. It was a very pleasant surprise and a new experience. I liked it, but think a small dose quite as much as is good for me; for after sitting in a corner and grubbing à la Cinderella, it rather turns one's head to be taken out and treated like a princess all of a sudden.

August

Went to Gloucester for a fortnight with May at the M[ansfield].'s. Found a family of six pretty daughters, a pleasant mother, and a father who was an image of one of the Cheeryble brothers. Had a jolly time boating, driving, charading, dancing, and picnicking. One mild moonlight night a party of us camped out on Norman's Woe, and had a splendid time, lying on the rocks singing, talking, sleeping, and rioting up and down. Had a fine time, and took coffee at all hours. The moon rose and set beautifully, and the sunrise was a picture I never shall forget.

Wrote another fairy tale, "Jamie's Wonder Book," and sent the "Christmas Stories" to W[alker]. & W[ise]., with some lovely illustrations by Miss Greene. They liked the book very much, and said they would consult about publishing it, though their hands were full.

September

Mrs. D[all]. made a visit, and getting hold of my old book of stories liked them, and insisted on taking "Moods" home to read. As she had had experience with publishers, was a good business woman, and an excellent critic, I let her have it, hoping she might be able to give the poor old book the lift it has been waiting for all these years. She took it, read it, and admired it heartily, saying that "no American author had showed so much promise; that the plan was admirable; the execution unequal, but often magnificent; that I had a great field before me, and my book must be got out."

Mrs. D. sent it to L[oring]., who liked it exceedingly, and asked me to shorten it if I could, else it would be too large to sell well. Was much disappointed, said I'd never touch it again, and tossed it into the spidery little cupboard where it had so often returned after fruitless trips.

October

Wrote several chapters of "Work," and was getting on finely, when, as I lay awake one night, a way to shorten and arrange "Moods" came into my head. The whole plan laid itself smoothly out before me, and I slept no more that night, but worked on it as busily as if mind and body had nothing to do with one another. Up early, and began to write it all over again. The fit was on strong, and for a fortnight I hardly ate, slept, or stirred, but wrote, wrote, like a thinking machine in full operation. When it was all rewritten without copying, I found it much improved, though I'd taken out ten chapters, and sacrificed many of my favorite things; but being resolved to make it simple, strong, and short, I let everything else go, and hoped the book would be better for it.

Sent it to L[oring]; and a week after, as I sat hammering away at the parlor carpet,—dusty, dismal, and tired,—a letter came from L. praising the story more enthusiastically than ever, thanking me for the improvements, and proposing to bring out the book at once. Of course we all had a rapture, and I finished my work "double quick," regardless of weariness, toothache, or blue devils.

Next day I went to Boston and saw L. A brisk, business-like man who seemed in earnest and said many complimentary things about "Hospital Sketches" and its author. It was agreed to bring out the book immediately, and Mrs. D[all]. offered to read the proof with me.

Was glad to have the old thing under way again, but didn't quite believe it would ever come out after so many delays and disappointments.

Sewed for Nan and Mary, heard Anna Dickinson and liked her. Read "Emily Chester" and thought it an unnatural story, yet just enough like "Moods" in a few things to make me sorry that it came out now.

On Mother's sixty-fourth birthday I gave her "Moods" with this in-scription,—"To Mother, my earliest patron, kindest critic, dearest reader, I gratefully and affectionately inscribe my first romance."

A letter from T[icknor]. asking me to write for the new magazine "Our Young Folks," and saying that "An Hour" was in the hands of the editors.

November

Proof began to come, and the chapters seemed small, stupid, and no more my own in print. I felt very much afraid that I'd ventured too much and should be sorry for it. But Emerson says "that what is true for your own private heart is true for others." So I wrote from my own consciousness and observation and hope it may suit some one and at least do no harm.

I sent "An Hour" to the "Commonwealth" and it was considered excellent. Also wrote a Christmas Story, "Mrs. Todger's Teapot." T[icknor]. asked to see the other fairy tales and designs and poems, as he liked "Nelly's Hospital" so much.

On my thirty-second birthday received Richter's Life from Nan and enjoyed it so much that I planned a story of two men something like Jean Paul and Goethe, only more every-day people. Don't know what will come of it, but if "Moods" goes well "Success" shall follow.

Sewed for Wheeler's colored company and sent them comfort-bags, towels, books, and bed-sacks. Mr. W. sent me some relics from Point Look Out and a pleasant letter.

December

Earnings, 1864,—$476.

On Christmas Eve received ten copies of "Moods" and a friendly note from L[oring]. The book was hastily got out, but on the whole suited me, and as the inside was considered good I let the outside go. For a week wherever I went I saw, heard, and talked "Moods;" found people laughing or crying over it, and was continually told how well it was going, how much it was liked, how fine a thing I'd done. I was glad but not proud, I think, for it has always seemed as if "Moods" grew in spite of me, and that I had little to do with it except to put into words the thoughts that would not let me rest until I had. Don't know why.

By Saturday the first edition was gone and the second ready. Several booksellers ordered a second hundred, the first went so fast, and friends could not get it but had to wait till more were ready.

Spent a fortnight in town at Mary's, shopping, helping Nan, and having plays. Heard Emerson once. Gave C[lapp]. "Mrs. Todger's Teapot," which was much liked. Sent L[eslie]. the rest of his story and got $50. S[lack]. paid $35 for "An Hour." R[ichardson]. promised $100 for "Love and Loyalty," so my year closes with a novel well-launched and about $300 to pay debts and make the family happy and comfortable till spring. Thank God for the success of the old year, the promise of the new!

January 1865

The month began with some plays at the town hall to raise funds for the Lyceum. We did very well and some Scenes from Dickens were excellent. Father lectured and preached a good deal, being asked like a regular minister and paid like one. He enjoyed it very much and said good things on the new religion which we ought to and shall have. May had orders from Canada and England for her pretty pen-and-ink work and did well in that line.

Notices of "Moods," came from all directions, and though people didn't understand my ideas owing to my shortening the book so much, the notices were mostly favorable and gave quite as much praise as was good for me. I had letters from Mrs. Parker, Chadwick, Sanborn, E. B. Greene, the artist, T. W. Higginson and some others. All friendly and flattering.

February

Saw more notices of "Moods" and received more letters, several from strangers and some very funny. People seemed to think the book finely written, very promising, wise, and interesting; but some fear it isn't moral, because it speaks freely of marriage.

Wrote a little on poor old "Work" but being tired of novels, I soon dropped it and fell back on rubbishy tales, for they pay best, and I can't afford to starve on praise, when sensation stories are written in half the time and keep the family cosey.

Earned $75 this month.

March

I went to Boston and heard Father lecture before the Fraternity. Met Henry James, Sr., there, and he asked me to come and dine, also called upon me with Mrs. James. I went, and was treated like the Queen of Sheba. Henry Jr. wrote a notice of "Moods" for the "North American," and was very friendly. Being a literary youth he gave me advice, as if he had been eighty and I a girl. My curly crop made me look young, though thirty-one.

Acted in some public plays for the N. E. Women's Hospital and had a pleasant time.

L[eslie]. asked me to be a regular contributor to his new paper, and I agreed if he'd pay beforehand; he said he would, and bespoke two tales at once, So each, longer ones as often as I could, and whatever else I liked to send. So here's another source of income and Alcott brains seem in demand, whereat I sing "Hallyluyer" and fill up my inkstand.

April

Richmond taken on the 2d. Hurrah! Went to Boston and enjoyed the grand jollification. Saw Booth again in Hamlet and thought him finer than ever. Had a pleasant walk and talk with Phillips.

On the 15th in the midst of the rejoicing came the sad news of the President's assassination, and the city went into mourning. I am glad to have seen such a strange and sudden change in a nation's feelings. Saw the great procession, and though few colored men were in it, one was walking arm in arm with a white gentleman, and I exulted thereat.

Nan went to housekeeping in a pleasant house at Jamaica Plain, and I went to help her move. It was beautiful to see how Freddy enjoyed the freedom, after being cooped up all winter, and how every morning, whether it rained or shone, he looked out and said, with a smile of perfect satisfaction, "Oh, pretty day!"—for all days were pretty to him, dear little soul!

Hospital Sketches

PREFACE

THESE SKETCHES, TAKEN FROM LETTERS hastily written in the few leisure moments of a very busy life, make no pretension to literary merit, but are simply a brief record of one person's hospital experience.

As such, they are republished, with their many faults but partially amended, lest in retouching they should lose whatever force or freshness the inspiration of the time may have given them.

To those who have objected to a "tone of levity" in some portions of the sketches, I desire to say that the wish to make the best of every thing, and send home cheerful reports even from that saddest of scenes, an army hospital, probably produced the impression of levity upon those who have never known the sharp contrasts of the tragic and comic in such a life.

That Nurse Periwinkle gave no account of her religious services, thereby showing a "sad want of *Christian experience*," can only be explained by the fact, that it would have as soon occurred to her to print the letters written for the men, their penitent confidences, or their dying messages, as to mention the prayers she prayed, the hymns she sung, the sacred words she read; while the "Christian experience" she was receiving then and there was far too deep and earnest to be recorded in a newspaper.

The unexpected favor with which the little book was greeted, and the desire for a new edition, increase the author's regret that it is not more worthy such a kind reception.

L. M. A.
Concord, March, 1869.

Hospital Sketches was first published by James Redpath in 1863.

41

CHAPTER ONE

Obtaining Supplies

"I WANT SOMETHING TO DO."

This remark being addressed to the world in general, no one in particular felt it their duty to reply; so I repeated it to the smaller world about me, received the following suggestions, and settled the matter by answering my own inquiry, as people are apt to do when very much in earnest.

"Write a book," quoth the author of my being.

"Don't know enough, sir. First live, then write."

"Try teaching again," suggested my mother.

"No thank you, ma'am, ten years of that is enough."

"Take a husband like my Darby, and fulfill your mission," said sister Joan, home on a visit.

"Can't afford expensive luxuries, Mrs. Coobiddy."

"Turn actress, and immortalize your name," said sister Vashti, striking an attitude.

"I won't."

"Go nurse the soldiers," said my young brother, Tom, panting for "the tented field."

"I will!"

So far, very good. Here was the will—now for the way. At first sight not a foot of it appeared, but that didn't matter, for the Periwinkles are a hopeful race; their crest is an anchor, with three cock-a-doodles crowing atop. They all wear rose-colored spectacles, and are lineal descendants of the inventor of aerial architecture. An hour's conversation on the subject set the whole family in a blaze of enthusiasm. A model hospital was erected, and each member had accepted an honorable post therein. The paternal P. was chaplain, the maternal P. was matron, and all the youthful P.'s filled the pod of futurity with achievements whose brilliancy eclipsed the glories of the present and the past. Arriving at this satisfactory conclusion, the meeting adjourned, and the fact that Miss Tribulation was available as army nurse went abroad on the wings of the wind.

In a few days a townswoman heard of my desire, approved of it, and brought about an interview with one of the sisterhood which I wished to join, who was at home on a furlough, and able and willing to satisfy all inquiries. A morning chat with Miss General S. [Hannah Stevenson, a nurse from Boston] —we hear no end of Mrs. Generals, why not a Miss?—produced three results: I felt that I could do the work, was offered a place, and accepted it, promising not to desert, but stand ready to march on Washington at an hour's notice.

A few days were necessary for the letter containing my request and recommendation to reach headquarters, and another, containing my commission, to return; therefore no time was to be lost; and heartily thanking my pair of friends, I tore home through the December slush as if the rebels were after me, and like many another recruit, burst in upon my family with the announcement—"I've enlisted!"

An impressive silence followed. Tom, the irrepressible, broke it with a slap on the shoulder and the graceful compliment "Old Trib, you're a trump!"

"Thank you; then I'll *take* something," which I did, in the shape of dinner, reeling off my news at the rate of three dozen words to a mouthful; and as every one else talked equally fast, and all together, the scene was most inspiring.

As boys going to sea immediately become nautical in speech, walk as if they already had their "sea legs" on, and shiver their timbers on all possible occasions, so I turned military at once, called my dinner my rations, saluted all new comers, and ordered a dress parade that very afternoon. Having reviewed every rag I possessed, I detailed some for picket duty while airing over the fence; some to the sanitary influences of the wash-tub; others to mount guard in the trunk; while the weak and wounded went to the Work-basket Hospital, to be made ready for active service again. To this squad I devoted myself for a week; but all was done, and I had time to get powerfully impatient before the letter came. It did arrive however, and brought a disappointment along with its good will and friendliness, for it told me that the place in the Armory Hospital that I supposed I was to take, was already filled, and a much less desirable one at Hurly-burly House was offered instead.

"That's just your luck, Trib. I'll tote your trunk up garret for you again; for of course you won't go," Tom remarked, with the disdainful pity which small boys affect when they get into their teens. I was wavering in my secret soul, but that settled the matter, and I crushed him on the spot with martial brevity—

"It is now one; I shall march at six."

I have a confused recollection of spending the afternoon in pervading the house like an executive whirlwind, with my family swarming after me, all working, talking, prophesying and lamenting, while I packed my "go-abroady" possessions, tumbled the rest into two big boxes, danced on the lids till they shut, and gave them in charge, with the direction,—

"If I never come back, make a bonfire of them."

Then I choked down a cup of tea, generously salted instead of sugared, by some agitated relative, shouldered my knapsack—it was only a traveling bag, but do let me preserve the unities—hugged my family three times all round without a vestige of unmanly emotion, till a certain dear old lady broke down upon my neck, with a despairing sort of wail—

"Oh, my dear, my dear, how can I let you go?"

"I'll stay if you say so, mother."

"But I don't; go, and the Lord will take care of you."

Much of the Roman matron's courage had gone into the Yankee matron's composition, and, in spite of her tears, she would have sent ten sons to the war, had she possessed them, as freely as she sent one daughter, smiling and flapping on the door-step till I vanished, though the eyes that followed me were very dim, and the handkerchief she waved was very wet.

My transit from The Gables to the village depot was a funny mixture of good wishes and good byes, mud-puddles and shopping. A December twilight is not the most cheering time to enter upon a somewhat perilous enterprise, and, but for the presence of Vashti and neighbor Thorn, I fear that I might have added a drop of the briny to the native moisture of

"The town I left behind me;"

though I'd no thought of giving out: oh, bless you, no! When the engine screeched "Here we are," I clutched my escort in a fervent embrace, and skipped into the car with as blithe a farewell as if going on a bridal tour—though I believe brides don't usually wear cavernous black bonnets and fuzzy brown coats, with a hair-brush, a pair of rubbers, two books, and a bag of ginger-bread distorting the pockets of the same. If I thought that any one would believe it, I'd boldly state that I slept from C. to B., which would simplify matters immensely; but as I know they wouldn't, I'll confess that the head under the funereal coal-hod fermented with all manner of high thought and heroic purposes "to do or die," — perhaps both; and the heart under the fuzzy brown coat felt very tender with the memory of the dear old lady, probably sobbing over her army socks and the loss of her topsy-turvy Trib. At this juncture I took the veil, and what I did behind it is nobody's business; but I maintain that the soldier who cries when his mother says "Good bye," is the boy to fight best, and die bravest, when the time comes, or go back to her better than he went.

Till nine o'clock I trotted about the city streets, doing those last errands which no woman would even go to heaven without attempting, if she could. Then I went to my usual refuge, and, fully intending to keep awake, as a sort of vigil appropriate to the occasion, fell fast asleep and dreamed propitious dreams till my rosy-faced cousin waked me with a kiss.

A bright day smiled upon my enterprise, and at ten I reported myself to my General, received last instructions and no end of the sympathetic encouragement which women give, in look, touch, and tone more effectually than in words. The next step was to get a free pass to Washington, for I'd no desire to waste my substance on railroad companies when "the boys" needed even a spinster's mite. A friend of mine had procured such a pass, and I was bent on doing likewise, though I had to face the president of the railroad to accomplish it. I'm a bashful individual, though I can't get any one to believe it; so it cost me a great effort to poke about the Worcester depot till the right door appeared, then walk into a room containing several gentlemen, and blunder out my request in a high state of stammer and blush. Nothing could have been more courteous than this dreaded President, but it was evident that I had made as absurd a demand as if I had asked for the nose off his respectable face. He referred me to the Governor at the State House, and I backed out, leaving him no doubt to regret that such mild maniacs were left at large. Here was a Scylla and Charybdis business: as if a President wasn't trying enough, without the Governor of Massachusetts and the hub of the hub piled on top of that. "I never can do it," thought I. "Tom will hoot at you if you don't," whispered the inconvenient little voice that is always goading people to the performance of disagreeable duties, and always appeals to the most effective agent to produce the proper result. The idea of allowing any boy that ever wore a felt basin and a shoddy jacket with a microscopic tail, to crow over me, was preposterous, so giving myself a mental slap for such faint-heartedness, I streamed away across the Common, wondering if I ought to say "your Honor," or simply "Sir," and decided upon the latter, fortifying myself with recollections of an evening in a charming green library, where I beheld the Governor placidly consuming oysters, and laughing as if Massachusetts was a myth, and he had no heavier burden on his shoulders than his host's handsome hands.

Like an energetic fly in a very large cobweb, I struggled through the State House, getting into all the wrong rooms and none of the right, till I turned desperate, and went into one, resolving not to come out till I'd made somebody hear and answer me. I suspect that of all the wrong places I had blundered into, this was the most so. But I didn't care; and, though the apartment was full of soldiers, surgeons, starers, and spittoons, I cornered a perfectly incapable person, and proceeded to pump for information with the following result:

"Was the Governor anywhere about?"

No, he wasn't.

"Could he tell me where to look?"

No, he couldn't.

"Did he know anything about free passes?"

No, he didn't.

"Was there any one there of whom I could inquire?"

Not a person.

"Did he know of any place where information could be obtained?"

Not a place.

"Could he throw the smallest gleam of light upon the matter, in any way?"

Not a ray.

I am naturally irascible, and if I could have shaken this negative gentleman vigorously, the relief would have been immense. The prejudices of society forbidding this mode of redress, I merely glowered at him; and, before my wrath found vent in words, my General appeared, having seen me from an opposite window, and come to know what I was about. At her command the languid gentleman woke up, and troubled himself to remember that Major or Sergeant or something Mc K. knew all about the tickets, and his office was in Milk Street. I perked up instanter, and then, as if the exertion was too much for him, what did this animated wet blanket do but add—

"I think Mc K. may have left Milk Street, now, and I don't know where he has gone."

"Never mind; the new comers will know where he has moved to, my dear, so don't be discouraged; and if you don't succeed, come to me, and we will see what to do next," said my General.

I blessed her in a fervent manner and a cool hall, fluttered round the corner, and bore down upon Milk Street, bent on discovering Mc K. if such a being was to be found. He wasn't, and the ignorance of the neighborhood was really pitiable. Nobody knew anything, and after tumbling over bundles of leather, bumping against big boxes, being nearly annihilated by descending bales, and sworn at by aggravated truckmen, I finally elicited the advice to look for Mc K. in Haymarket Square. Who my informant was I've really forgotten; for, having hailed several busy gentlemen, some one of them fabricated this delusive quietus for the perturbed spirit, who instantly departed to the sequestered locality he named. If I had been in search of the Koh-i-noor diamond I should have been as likely to find it there as any vestige of Mc K. I stared at signs, inquired in shops, invaded an eating house, visited the recruiting tent in the middle of the Square, made myself a nuisance generally, and accumulated mud enough to retard another Nile. All in vain: and I mournfully turned my face toward the General's, feeling that I should be forced to enrich the railroad company after all; when, suddenly, I beheld that admirable young man, brother-in-law Darby Coobiddy, Esq. I arrested him with a burst of news, and wants, and woes, which caused his manly countenance to lose its usual repose.

"Oh, my dear boy, I'm going to Washington at five, and I can't find the free ticket man, and there won't be time to see Joan, and I'm so tired and cross I don't know what to do; and will you help me, like a cherub as you are?"

"Oh, yes, of course. I know a fellow who will set us right," responded Darby, mildly excited, and darting into some kind of an office, held counsel with an invisible angel, who sent him out radiant. "All serene. I've got him. I'll see you through the business, and then get Joan from the Dove Cote in time to see you off."

I'm a woman's rights woman, and if any man had offered help in the morning, I should have condescendingly refused it, sure that I could do everything as well, if not better, myself. My strong-mindedness had rather abated since then, and I was now quite ready to be a "timid trembler," if necessary. Dear me! how easily Darby did it all: he just asked one question, received an answer, tucked me under his arm, and in ten minutes I stood in the presence of Mc K., the Desired.

"Now my troubles are over," thought I, and as usual was direfully mistaken.

"You will have to get a pass from Dr. H., in Temple Place, before I can give you a pass, madam," answered Mc K., as blandly as if he wasn't carrying desolation to my soul. Oh, indeed! why didn't he send me to Dorchester Heights, India Wharf, or Bunker Hill Monument, and done with it? Here I was, after a morning's tramp, down in some place about Dock Square, and was told to step to Temple Place. Nor was that all; he might as well have asked me to catch a humming-bird, toast a salamander, or call on the man in the moon, as find a Doctor at home at the busiest hour of the day. It was a blow but weariness had extinguished enthusiasm, and resignation clothed me as a garment. I sent Darby for Joan, and doggedly paddled off, feeling that mud was my native element, and quite sure that the evening papers would announce the appearance of the Wandering Jew, in feminine habiliments.

"Is Dr. H. [William Hammond, surgeon-general of the Union army] in?"

"No, mum, he aint."

Of course he wasn't; I knew that before I asked: and, considering it all in the light of a hollow mockery, added:

"When will be probably return?"

If the damsel had said, "ten to-night," I should have felt a grim satisfaction, in the fulfillment of my own dark prophecy; but she said, "At two, mum;" and I felt it a personal insult.

"I'll call, then. Tell him my business is important:" with which mysteriously delivered message I departed, hoping that I left her consumed with curiosity; for mud rendered me an object of interest.

By way of resting myself, I crossed the Common, for the third time, bespoke the carriage, got some lunch, packed my purchases, smoothed my plumage, and was back again, as the clock struck two. The Doctor hadn't come yet; and I was morally certain that he would not, till, having waited till the last minute, I was driven to buy a ticket, and, five minutes after the irrevocable deed was done, he would be at my service, with all manner of helpful documents and directions. Everything goes by contraries with me; so, having made up my mind to be disappointed, of course I wasn't; for, presently, in walked Dr. H., and no sooner had he heard my errand, and glanced at my credentials, than he said, with the most engaging readiness:

"I will give you the order, with pleasure, madam."

Words cannot express how soothing and delightful it was to find, at last, somebody who could do what I wanted, without sending me from Dan to Beersheba, for a dozen other bodies to do something else first. Peace descended, like oil, upon the ruffled waters of my being, as I sat listening to the busy scratch of his pen; and, when he turned about, giving me not only the order, but a paper of directions wherewith to smooth away all difficulties between Boston and Washington, I felt as did poor Christian [reference to John Bunyan's *Pilgrim's Progress*] when the Evangelist gave him the scroll, on the safe side of the Slough of Despond. I've no doubt many dismal nurses have inflicted themselves upon the worthy gentleman since then; but I am sure none have been more kindly helped, or are more grateful, than T. P.; for that short interview added another to the many pleasant associations that already surround his name.

Feeling myself no longer a "Martha Struggles," but a comfortable young woman, with plain sailing before her, and the worst of the voyage well over, I once more presented myself to the valuable Mc K. The order was read, and certain printed papers, necessary to be filled out, were given a young gentleman—no, I prefer to say Boy, with a scornful emphasis upon the word, as the only means of revenge now left me. This Boy, instead of doing his duty with the diligence so charming in the young, loitered and lounged, in a manner which proved his education to have been sadly neglected in the—

"How doth the little busy bee,"

direction. He stared at me, gaped out of the window, ate peanuts, and gossiped with his neighbors—Boys, like himself, and all penned in a row, like colts at a Cattle Show. I don't imagine he knew the anguish he was inflicting; for it was nearly three, the train left at five, and I had my ticket to get, my dinner to eat, my blessed sister to see, and the depot to reach, if I didn't die of apoplexy. Meanwhile, Patience certainly had her perfect work that day, and I hope she enjoyed the job more than I did. Having waited some twenty minutes, it pleased this reprehensible Boy to make various marks and blots on my documents, toss them to a venerable creature of sixteen, who delivered them to me with such paternal directions, that it only needed a pat on the head and an encouraging — "Now run home to your Ma, little girl, and mind the crossings, my dear," to make the illusion quite perfect.

Why I was sent to a steamboat office for car tickets, is not for me to say, though I went as meekly as I should have gone to the Probate Court, if sent. A fat, easy gentleman gave me several bits of paper, with coupons attached, with a warning not to separate them, which instantly inspired me with a yearning to pluck them apart, and see what came of it. But, remembering through what fear and tribulation I had obtained them, I curbed Satan's promptings, and, clutching my prize, as if it were my pass to the Elysian Fields, I hurried home. Dinner was rapidly consumed; Joan enlightened, comforted, and kissed; the dearest of apple-faced cousins hugged; the kindest of apple-faced cousins' fathers subjected to the same process; and I mounted the ambulance, baggage-wagon, or anything you please but hack, and drove away, too tired to feel excited, sorry, or glad.

CHAPTER TWO

A Forward Movement

AS TRAVELLERS LIKE TO GIVE their own impressions of a journey, though every inch of the way may have been described a half dozen times before, I add some of the notes made by the way, hoping that they will amuse the reader, and convince the skeptical that such a being as Nurse Periwinkle does exist, that she really did go to Washington, and that these Sketches are not romance.

New York Train—Seven P.M.—Spinning along to take the boat at New London. Very comfortable; munch gingerbread, and Mrs. C.'s fine pear, which deserves honorable mention, because my first loneliness was comforted by it, and pleasant recollections of both kindly sender and bearer. Look much at Dr. H.'s paper of directions—put my tickets in every conceivable place, that they may be get-at-able, and finish by losing them entirely. Suffer agonies till a compassionate neighbor pokes them out of a crack with his pen-knife. Put them in the inmost corner of my purse, that in the deepest recesses of my pocket, pile a collection of miscellaneous articles atop, and pin tip the whole. Just get composed, feeling that I've done my best to keep them safely, when the Conductor appears, and I'm forced to rout them all out again, exposing my precautions, and getting into a flutter at keeping the man waiting. Finally, fasten them on the seat before me, and keep one eye steadily upon the yellow torments, till I forget all about them, in chat with the gentleman who shares my seat. Having heard complaints of the absurd way in which American women become images of petrified propriety, if addressed by strangers, when traveling alone, the inborn perversity of my nature causes me to assume an entirely opposite style of deportment; and, finding my companion hails from Little Athens, is acquainted with several of my three hundred and sixty-five cousins, and in every way a respectable and respectful member of society, I put my bashfulness in my pocket, and plunge into a long conversation on the war, the weather, music, Carlyle, skating, genius, hoops, and the immortality of the soul.

Ten, P.M.—Very sleepy. Nothing to be seen outside, but darkness made visible; nothing inside but every variety of bunch into which the human form can be twisted, rolled, or "massed," as Miss Prescott, says of her jewels [in Harriet Prescott's story, "In a Cellar," diamonds were described as a "mass of white magnificence"]. Every man's legs sprawl drowsily, every woman's head (but mine) nods, till it finally settles on somebody's shoulder, a new proof of the truth of the everlasting oak and vine simile; children fret; lovers whisper; old folks snore, and somebody privately imbibes brandy, when the lamps go out. The penetrating perfume rouses the multitude, causing some to start up, like war horses at the smell of powder. When the lamps are relighted, every one laughs, sniffs, and looks inquiringly at his neighbor—every one but a stout gentleman, who, with well-gloved hands folded upon his broad-cloth rotundity, sleeps on impressively. Had he been innocent, he would have waked up; for, to slumber in that babe-like manner, with a car full of giggling, staring, sniffing humanity, was simply preposterous. Public suspicion was down upon him at once. I doubt if the appearance of a flat black bottle with a label would have settled the matter more effectually than did the over dignified and profound repose of this short-sighted being. His moral neck-cloth, virtuous boots, and pious attitude availed him nothing, and it was well he kept his eyes shut, for "Humbug!" twinkled at him from every window-pane, brass nail and human eye around him.

Eleven, P.M.—In the boat "City of Boston," escorted thither by my car acquaintance, and deposited in the cabin. Trying to look as if the greater portion of my life had been passed on board boats, but painfully conscious that I don't know the first thing; so sit bolt upright, and stare about me till I hear one lady say to another—"We must secure our berths at once;" whereupon I dart at one, and, while leisurely taking off my cloak, wait to discover what the second move may be. Several ladies draw the curtains that hang in a semicircle before each nest—instantly I whisk mine smartly together, and then peep out to see what next. Gradually, on hooks above the blue and yellow drapery, appear the coats and bonnets of my neighbors, while their boots and shoes, in every imaginable attitude, assert themselves below, as if their owners had committed suicide in a body. A violent creaking, scrambling, and fussing, causes the fact that people are going regularly to bed to dawn upon my mind. Of course they are! and so am I—but pause at the seventh pin, remembering that, as I was born to be drowned, an eligible opportunity now presents itself; and, having twice escaped a watery grave, the third immersion will certainly extinguish my vital spark. The boat is new, but if it ever intends to blow up, spring a leak, catch afire, or be run into, it will do the deed tonight, because I'm here to fulfill my destiny. With tragic calmness I resign myself, replace my pins, lash my purse and papers together with my handkerchief, examine the saving circumference of my hoop, and look about me for any means of deliverance when the moist moment shall arrive; for I've no intention folding my hands and bubbling to death without an energetic splashing first. Barrels, hen-coops, portable settees, and life-preservers do not adorn the cabin, as they should; and, roving wildly to and fro, my eye sees no ray of hope till it falls upon a plump old lady, devoutly reading in the cabin Bible, and a voluminous night-cap. I remember that, at the swimming school fat girls always floated best, and in an instant my plan is laid. At the first alarm I firmly attach myself to the plump lady, I cling to her through fire and water; for I feel that my old enemy, the cramp, will seize me by the foot, if I attempt to swim; and, though I can hardly expect to reach Jersey City with myself and my baggage in as good condition as I hoped, I might manage to get picked up by holding to my fat friend; if not it will be a comfort to feel that I've made an effort and shall die in good society. Poor dear woman! how little she dreamed, as she read and rocked, with her cap in a high state of starch, and her feet comfortably cooking at the register, what fell designs were hovering about her, and how intently a small but determined eye watched her, till it suddenly closed.

Sleep got the better of fear to such an extent that my boots appeared to gape, and my bonnet nodded on its peg, before I gave in. Having piled my cloak, bag, rubbers, books and umbrella on the lower shelf, I drowsily swarmed onto the upper one, tumbling down a few times, and excoriating the knobby portions of my frame in the act. A very brief nap on the upper roost was enough to set me gasping as if a dozen feather beds and the whole boat were laid over me. Out I turned; and, after a series of convulsions, which caused my neighbor to ask if I wanted the stewardess, I managed to get my luggage up and myself down. But even in the lower berth, my rest was not unbroken, for various articles kept dropping off the little shelf at the bottom of the bed, and every time I flew up, thinking my hour had come, I bumped my head severely against the little shelf at the top, evidently put there for that express purpose. At last, after listening to the swash of the waves outside, wondering if the machinery usually creaked in that way, and watching a knot-hole in the side of my berth, sure that death would creep in there as soon as I took my eye from it, I dropped asleep, and dreamed of muffins.

Five, A.M.—On deck, trying to wake up and enjoy an east wind and a morning fog, and a twilight sort of view of something on the shore. Rapidly achieve my purpose, and do enjoy every moment, as we go rushing through the Sound, with steamboats passing up and down, lights dancing on the shore, mist wreaths slowly furling off, and a pale pink sky above us, as the sun comes up.

Seven, A.M.—In the cars, at Jersey City. Much fuss with tickets, which one man scribbles over, another snips, and a third "makes note on." Partake of refreshment, in the gloom of a very large and dirty depot. Think that my sandwiches would be more relishing without so strong a flavor of napkin, and my gingerbread more easy of consumption if it had not been pulverized by being sat upon. People act as if early travelling didn't agree with them. Children scream and scamper; men smoke and growl; women shiver and fret; porters swear; great truck horses pace up and down with loads of baggage; and every one seems to get into the wrong car, and come tumbling out again. One man, with three children, a dog, a bird-cage, and several bundles, puts himself and his possessions into every possible place where a man, three children, dog, bird-cage and bundles could be got, and is satisfied with none of them. I follow their movements, with an interest that is really exhausting, and, as they vanish, hope for rest, but don't get it. A strong-minded woman, with a tumbler in her hand, and no cloak or shawl on, comes rushing through the car, talking loudly to a small porter, who lugs a folding bed after her, and looks as if life were a burden to him.

"You promised to have it ready. It is not ready. It must be a car with a water jar, the windows must be shut, the fire must be kept up, the blinds must be down. No, this won't do. I shall go through the whole train, and suit myself, for you promised to have it ready. It is not ready," &c., all through again, like a hand-organ. She haunted the cars, the depot, the office and baggage-room, with her bed, her tumbler, and her tongue, till the train started; and a sense of fervent gratitude filled my soul, when I found that she and her unknown invalid were not to share our car.

Philadelphia.—An old place, full of Dutch women, in "bellus top" bonnets, selling vegetables, in long, open markets. Every one seems to be scrubbing their white steps. All the houses look like tidy jails, with their outside shutters. Several have crape on the door-handles, and many have flags flying from roof or balcony. Few men appear, and the women seem to do the business, which, perhaps, accounts for its being so well done. Pass fine buildings, but don't know what they are. Would like to stop and see my native city; for, having left it at the tender age of two, my recollections are not vivid.

Baltimore.—A big, dirty, shippy, shiftless place, full of goats, geese, colored people, and coal, at least the part of it I see. Pass near the spot where the riot took place, and feel as if I should enjoy throwing a stone at somebody, hard [the attack on the Sixth Massachusetts Regiment on 16 April 1861]. Find a guard at the ferry, the depot, and here and there, along the road. A camp whitens one hill-side, and a cavalry training school, or whatever it should be called, is a very interesting sight, with quantities of horses and riders galloping, marching, leaping, and skirmishing, over all manner of break-neck places. A party of English people get in—the men, with sandy hair and red whiskers, all trimmed alike, to a hair; rough grey coats, very rosy, clean faces, and a fine, full way of speaking, which is particularly agreeable, after our slip-shod American gabble. The two ladies wear funny velvet fur-trimmed hoods; are done up, like compact bundles, in tartan shawls; and look as if bent on seeing everything thoroughly. The devotion of one elderly John Bull to his red-nosed spouse was really beautiful to behold. She was plain and cross, and fussy and stupid, but J. B., Esq., read no papers when she was awake, turned no cold shoulder when she wished to sleep, and cheerfully said, "Yes, me dear," to every wish or want the wife of his bosom expressed. I quite warmed to the excellent man, and asked a question or two, as the only means of expressing my good will. He answered very civilly, but evidently hadn't been used to being addressed by strange women in public conveyances; and Mrs. B. fixed her green eyes upon me, as if she thought me a forward huzzy, or whatever is good English for a presuming young woman. The pair left their friends before we reached Washington; and the last I saw of them was a vision of a large plaid lady, stalking grimly away, on the arm of a rosy, stout gentleman, loaded with rugs, bags, and books, but still devoted, still smiling, and waving a hearty "Fare ye well! We'll meet ye at Willard's on Chusday."

Soon after their departure we had an accident; for no long journey in America would be complete without one. A coupling iron broke; and, after leaving the last car behind us, we waited for it to come up, which it did, with a crash that knocked every one forward on their faces, and caused several old ladies to screech dismally. Hats flew off, bonnets were flattened, the stove skipped, the lamps fell down, the water jar turned a somersault, and the wheel just over which I sat received some damage. Of course, it became necessary for all the men to get out, and stand about in everybody's way, while repairs were made; and for the women to wrestle their heads out of the windows, asking ninety-nine foolish questions to one sensible one. A few wise females seized this favorable moment to better their seats, well knowing that few men can face the wooden stare with which they regard the former possessors of the places they have invaded.

The country through which we passed did not seem so very unlike that which I had left, except that it was more level and less wintry. In summer time the wide fields would have shown me new sights, and the way-side hedges blossomed with new flowers; now, everything was sere and sodden, and a general air of shiftlessness prevailed, which would have caused a New England farmer much disgust, and a strong desire to "buckle to," and "right up" things. Dreary little houses, with chimneys built outside, with clay and rough sticks piled cross wise, as we used to build cob towers, stood in barren looking fields, with cow, pig, or mule lounging about the door. We often passed colored people, looking as if they had come out of a picture book, or off the stage, but not at all the sort of people I'd been accustomed to see at the North.

Way-side encampments made the fields and lanes gay with blue coats and the glitter of buttons. Military washes flapped and fluttered on the fences; pots were steaming in the open air; all sorts of tableaux seen through the openings of tents, and everywhere the boys threw up their caps and cut capers as we passed.

Washington.—It was dark when we arrived; and, but for the presence of another friendly gentleman, I should have yielded myself a helpless prey to the first overpowering hackman, who insisted that I wanted to go just where I didn't. Putting me into the conveyance I belonged in, my escort added to the obligation by pointing out the objects of interest which we passed in our long drive. Though I'd often been told that Washington was a spacious place, its visible magnitude quite took my breath away, and of course I quoted Randolph's expression, "a city of magnificent distances," as I suppose every one does when they see it. The Capitol was so like the pictures that hang opposite the staring Father of his Country, in boarding-houses and hotels, that it did not impress me, except to recall the time when I was sure that Cinderella went to housekeeping in just such a place, after she had married the inflammable Prince; though, even at that early period, I had my doubts as to the wisdom of a match whose foundation was of glass.

The White House was lighted up, and carriages were rolling in and out of the great gate. I stared hard at the famous East Room, and would have like a peep through the crack of the door. My old gentleman was indefatigable in his attentions, and I said "Splendid!" to everything he pointed out, though I suspect I often admired the wrong place, and missed the right. Pennsylvania Avenue, with its bustle, lights, music, and military, made me feel as if I'd crossed the water and landed somewhere in Carnival time. Coming to less noticeable parts of the city, my companion fell silent, and I meditated upon the perfection which Art had attained in America having just passed a bronze statue of some hero, who looked like a black Methodist minister, in a cocked hat, above the gist, and a tipsy squire below; while his horse stood like an opera dancer, on one leg, in a high, but somewhat remarkable wind, which blew his mane one way and his massive tail the other.

"Hurly-burly House, ma'am!" called a voice, startling me from my reverie, as we stopped before a great pile of buildings, with a flag flying before it, sentinels at the door, and a very trying quantity of men lounging about. My heart beat rather faster than usual, and it suddenly struck me that I was very far from home; but I descended with dignity, wondering whether I should be stopped for want of a countersign, and forced to pass the night in the street. Marching boldly up the steps, I found that no form was necessary, for the men fell back, the guard touched their caps, a boy opened the door, and, as it closed behind me, I felt that I was fairly started, and Nurse Periwinkle's Mission was begun.

CHAPTER THREE

A Day

"THEY'VE COME! THEY'VE COME! hurry up, ladies—you're wanted."

"Who have come? the rebels?"

This sudden summons in the gray dawn was somewhat startling to a three days' nurse like myself, and, as the thundering knock came at our door, I sprang up in my bed, prepared

"To gird my woman's form,
And on the ramparts die,"

if necessary, but my room-mate took it more coolly, and, as she began a rapid toilet, answered my bewildered question,—

"Bless you, no child; it's the wounded from Fredericksburg; forty ambulances are at the door, and we shall have our hands full in fifteen minutes."

"What shall we have to do?"

"Wash, dress, feed, warm and nurse them for the next three months, I dare say. Eighty beds are ready, and we were getting impatient for the men to come. Now you will begin to see hospital life in earnest, for you won't probably find time to sit down all day, and may think yourself fortunate if you get to bed by midnight. Come to me in the ball-room when you are ready; the worst cases are always carried there, and I shall need your help."

So saying, the energetic little woman twirled her hair into a button at the back of her head, in a "cleared for action" sort of style, and vanished, wrestling her way into a feminine kind of pea-jacket as she went.

I am free to confess that I had a realizing sense of the fact that my hospital bed was not a bed of roses just then, or the prospect before me one of unmingled rapture. My three days' experiences had begun with a death, and, owing to the defalcation of another nurse, a somewhat abrupt plunge into the superintendence of a ward containing forty beds, where I spent my shining hours washing faces, serving rations, giving medicine, and sitting in a very hard chair, with pneumonia on one side, diptheria on the other, five typhoids on the opposite, and a dozen dilapidated patriots, hopping, lying, and lounging about, all staring more or less at the new "nuss," who suffered untold agonies, but concealed them under as matronly an aspect as a spinster could assume, and blundered through her trying labors with a Spartan firmness, which I hope they appreciated, but am afraid they didn't. Having a taste for "ghastliness," I had rather longed for the wounded to arrive, for rheumatism wasn't heroic, neither was liver complaint, or measles; even fever had lost its charms since "bathing burning brows" had been used up in romances, real and ideal; but when I peeped into the dusky street lined with what I at first had innocently called market carts, now unloading their sad freight at our door, I recalled sundry reminiscences I had heard from nurses of longer standing, my ardor experienced a sudden chill, and I indulged in a most unpatriotic wish that I was safe at home again, with a quiet day before me, and no necessity for being hustled up, as if I were a hen and had only to hop off my roost, give my plumage a peck, and be ready for action. A second bang at the door sent this recreant desire to the right about, as a little woolly head popped in, and Joey, (a six years' old contraband,) announced—

"Miss Blank is jes' wild fer ye, and says fly round right away. They's comin' in, I tell yer, heaps on 'em—one was took out dead, and I see him,—ky! warn't he a goner!"

With which cheerful intelligence the imp scuttled away. singing like a blackbird, and I followed, feeling that Richard was *not* himself again, and wouldn't be for a long time to come.

The first thing I met was a regiment of the vilest odors that ever assaulted the human nose, and took it by storm. Cologne, with its seven and seventy evil savors, was a posy-bed to it; and the worst of this affliction was, every one had assured me, that it was a chronic weakness of all hospitals, and I must bear it. I did, armed with lavender water, with which I so besprinkled myself and premises, that, like my friend, Sairy [Sairy Gamp, the nurse in Charles Dickens's *Martin Chuzzlewit*]. I was soon known among my patients as "the nurse with the bottle." Having been run over by three excited surgeons, bumped against by migratory coal-hods, water-pails, and small boys; nearly scalded by an avalanche of newly-filled tea-pots, and hopelessly entangled in a knot of colored sisters coming to wash, I progressed by slow stages up stairs and down, till the main hall was reached, and I paused to take breath and a survey. There they were! "our brave boys," as the papers justly call them, for cowards could hardly have been so riddled with shot and shell, so torn and shattered, nor have borne suffering for which we have no name, with an uncomplaining fortitude, which made one glad to cherish each as a brother. In they came, some on stretchers, some in men's arms, some feebly staggering along propped on rude crutches, and one lay stark and still with covered face, as a comrade gave his name to be recorded before they carried him away to the dead house. All was hurry and confusion; the hall was full of these wrecks of humanity, for the most exhausted could not reach a bed till duly ticketed and registered; the walls were lined with rows of such as could sit, the floor covered with the more disabled, the steps and doorways filled with helpers and lookers on; the sound of many feet and voices made that usually quiet hour as noisy as noon; and, in the midst of it all, the matron's motherly face brought more comfort to many a poor soul, than the cordial draughts she administered, or the cheery words that welcomed all, making of the hospital a home.

The sight of several stretchers, each with its legless, armless, or desperately wounded occupant, entering my ward, admonished me that I was there to work, not to wonder or weep; so I corked up my feelings, and returned to the path of duty, which was rather "a hard road to travel" just then. The house had been a hotel before hospitals were needed, and many of the doors still bore their old names; some not so inappropriate as might be imagined, for my ward was in truth a ball-room, if gun-shot wounds could christen it. Forty beds were prepared, many already tenanted by tired men who fell down anywhere, and drowsed till the smell of food roused them. Round the great stove was gathered the dreariest group I ever saw ragged, gaunt and pale, mud to the knees, with bloody bandages untouched since put on days before; many bundled up in blankets, coats being lost or useless; and all wearing that disheartened look which proclaimed defeat, more plainly than any telegram of the Burnside blunder. I pitied them so much, I dared not speak to them, though, remembering all they had been through since the route at Fredericksburg, I yearned to serve the dreariest of them all. Presently, Miss Blank tore me from my refuge behind piles of one-sleeved shirts, odd socks, bandages and lint; put basin, sponge, towels, and a block of brown soap into my hands, with these appalling directions:

"Come, my dear, begin to wash as fast as you can. Tell them to take off socks, coats and shirts, scrub them well, put on clean shirts, and the attendants will finish them off, and lay them in bed."

If she had requested me to shave them all, or dance a hornpipe on the stove funnel, I should have been less staggered; but to scrub some dozen lords of creation at a moment's notice, was really—really—. However, there was no time for nonsense, and, having resolved when I came to do everything I was bid, I drowned my scruples in my washbowl, clutched my soap manfully, and, assuming a businesslike air, made a dab at the first dirty specimen I saw, bent on performing my task *vi et armis* if necessary. I chanced to light on a withered old Irishman, wounded in the head, which caused that portion of his frame to be tastefully laid out like a garden, the bandages being the walks, his hair the shrubbery. He was so overpowered by the honor of having a lady wash him, as he expressed it, that he did nothing but roll up his eyes, and bless me, in an irresistible style which was too much for my sense of the ludicrous; so we laughed together, and when I knelt down to take off his shoes, he "flopped" also and wouldn't hear of my touching "them dirty craters. May your bed above be aisy darlin', for the day's work ye are doon!—Woosh! there ye are, and bedad, it's hard tellin' which is the dirtiest, the fut or the shoe." It was; and if he hadn't been to the fore, I should have gone on pulling, under the impression that the "fut" was a boot, for trousers, socks, shoes and legs were a mass of mud. This comical tableau produced a general grin, at which propitious beginning I took heart and scrubbed away like any tidy parent on a Saturday night. Some of them took the performance like sleepy children, leaning their tired heads against me as I worked, others looked grimly scandalized, and several of the roughest colored like bashful girls. One wore a soiled little bag about his neck, and, as I moved it, to bathe his wounded breast, I said,

"Your talisman didn't save you, did it?"

"Well, I reckon it did, marm, for that shot would a gone a couple a inches deeper but for my old mammy's camphor bag," answered the cheerful philosopher.

Another, with a gun-shot wound through the cheek, asked for a looking-glass, and when I brought one, regarded his swollen face with a dolorous expression, as he muttered—

"I vow to gosh, that's too bad! I warn't a bad looking chap before, and now I'm done for; won't there be a thunderin' scar? and what on earth will Josephine Skinner say?"

He looked up at me with his one eye so appealingly, that I controlled my risibles, and assured him that if Josephine was a girl of sense, she would admire the honorable scar, as a lasting proof that he had faced the enemy, for all women thought a wound the best decoration a brave soldier could wear. I hope Miss Skinner verified the good opinion I so rashly expressed of her, but I shall never know.

The next scrubbee was a nice looking lad, with a curly brown mane, and a budding trace of gingerbread over the lip, which he called his beard, and defended stoutly, when the barber jocosely suggested its immolation. He lay on a bed, with one leg gone, and the right arm so shattered that it must evidently follow; yet the little Sergeant was as merry as if his afflictions were not worth lamenting over, and when a drop or two of salt water mingled with my suds at the sight of this strong young body, so marred and maimed, the boy looked up, with a brave smile, though there was a little quiver of the lips, as he said,

"Now don't you fret yourself about me, miss; I'm first rate here, for it's nuts to lie still on this bed, after knocking about in those confounded ambulances, that shake what there is left of a fellow to jelly. I never was in one of these places before, and think this cleaning up a jolly thing for us, though I'm afraid it isn't for you ladies."

"Is this your first battle, Sergeant?"

"No, miss; I've been in six scrimmages, and never got a scratch till this last one; but it's done the business pretty thoroughly for me, I should say. Lord! what a scramble there'll be for arms and legs, when we old boys come out of our graves, on the Judgment Day: wonder if we shall get our own again? If we do, my leg will have to tramp from Fredericksburg, my arm from here, I suppose, and meet my body, wherever it may be.

The fancy seemed to tickle him mightily, for he laughed blithely, and so did I; which, no doubt, caused the new nurse to be regarded as a light-minded sinner by the Chaplain, who roamed vaguely about, informing the men that they were all worms, corrupt of heart, with perishable bodies, and souls only to be saved by a diligent perusal of certain tracts, and other equally cheering bits of spiritual consolation, when spirituous ditto would have been preferred.

"I say, Mrs.!" called a voice behind me; and, turning, I saw a rough Michigander, with an arm blown off at the shoulder, and two or three bullets still in him—as he afterwards mentioned, as carelessly as if gentlemen were in the habit of carrying such trifles about with them. I went to him, and, while administering a dose of soap and water, he whispered, irefully:

"That red-headed devil, over yonder, is a reb, damn him! You'll agree to that, I'll bet? He's got shet of a foot, or he'd a cut like the rest of the lot. Don't you wash him, nor feed him, but jest let him holler till he's tired. It's a blasted shame to fetch them fellers in here, along side of us; and so I'll tell the chap that bosses this concern; cuss me if I don't."

I regret to say that I did not deliver a moral sermon upon the duty of forgiving our enemies, and the sin of profanity, then and there; but, being a red-hot Abolitionist, stared fixedly at the tall rebel, who was a copperhead, in every sense of the word, and privately resolved to put soap in his eyes, rub his nose the wrong way, and excoriate his cuticle generally, if I had the washing of him.

My amiable intentions, however, were frustrated; for, when I approached, with as Christian an expression as my principles would allow, and asked the question—"Shall I try to make you more comfortable, sir?" all I got for my pains was a gruff "No; I'll do it myself."

"Here's your Southern chivalry, with a witness," thought I, dumping the basin down before him, thereby quenching a strong desire to give him a summary baptism, in return for his ungraciousness; for my angry passions rose, at this rebuff, in a way that would have scandalized good Dr. Watts. He was a disappointment in all respects, (the rebel, not the blessed Doctor,) for he was neither fiendish, romantic, pathetic, or anything interesting; but a long, fat man, with a head like a burning bush, and a perfectly expressionless face: so I could hate him without the slightest drawback, and ignored his existence from that day forth. One redeeming trait he certainly did possess, as the floor speedily testified; for his ablutions were so vigorously performed, that his bed soon stood like an isolated island, in a sea of soap-suds, and he resembled a dripping merman, suffering from the loss of a fin. If cleanliness is a near neighbor to godliness, then was the big rebel the godliest man in my ward that day.

Having done up our human wash, and laid it out to dry, the second syllable of our version of the word war-fare was enacted with much success. Great trays of bread, meat, soup and coffee appeared; and both nurses and attendants turned waiters, serving bountiful rations to all who could eat. I can call my pinafore to testify to my good will in the work, for in ten minutes it was reduced to a perambulating bill of fare, presenting samples of all the refreshments going or gone. It was a lively scene; the long room lined with rows of beds, each filled by an occupant, whom water, shears, and clean raiment, had transformed from a dismal ragamuffin into a recumbent hero, with a cropped head. To and fro rushed matrons, maids, and convalescent "boys," skirmishing with knives and forks; retreating with empty plates; marching and counter-marching, with unvaried success, while the clash of busy spoons made most inspiring music for the charge of our Light Brigade:

Beds to the front of them,
Beds to the right of them
Beds to the left of them,
Nobody blundered.
Beamed at by hungry souls,
Screamed at with brimming bowls,
Steamed at by army rolls,
Buttered and sundered.
With coffee not cannon plied,
Each must be satisfied,
Whether they lived or died;
All the men wondered.

Very welcome seemed the generous meal, after a week of suffering, exposure, and short commons; soon the brown faces began to smile, as food, warmth, and rest, did their pleasant work; and the grateful "Thankee's" were followed by more graphic accounts of the battle and retreat, than any paid reporter could have given us. Curious contrasts of the tragic and comic met one everywhere; and some touching as well as ludicrous episodes, might have been recorded that day. A six foot New Hampshire man, with a leg broken and perforated by a piece of shell, so large that, had I not seen the wound, I should have regarded the story as a Munchausenism, beckoned me to come and help him, as he could not sit up, and both his bed and beard were getting plentifully anointed with soup. As I fed my big nestling with corresponding mouthfuls, I asked him how he felt during the battle.

"Well, 'twas my fust, you see, so I aint ashamed to say I was a trifle flustered in the beginnin', there was such an all-fired racket; for ef there's anything I do spleen agin, it's noise. But when my mate, Eph Sylvester, caved, with a bullet through his head, I got mad, and pitched in, licketty cut. Our part of the fight didn't last long; so a lot of us larked round Fredericksburg, and give some of them houses a pretty consid'able of a rummage, till we was ordered out of the mess. Some of our fellows cut like time; but I warn't a-goin to run for nobody; and, fust thing I knew, a shell bust, right in front of us, and I keeled over, feelin' as if I was blowed higher'n a kite. I sung out, and the boys come back for me, double quick; but the way they chucked me over them fences was a caution, I tell you. Next day I was most as black as that darkey yonder, lickin' plates on the sly. This is bully coffee, ain't it? Give us another pull at it, and I'll be obleeged to you."

I did; and, as the last gulp subsided, he said, with a rub of his old handkerchief over eyes as well as mouth:

"Look a here; I've got a pair a earbobs and a handkercher pin I'm a goin' to give you, if you'll have them; for you're the very moral o' Lizy Sylvester, poor Eph's wife: that's why I signalled you to come over here. They aint much, I guess, but they'll do to memorize the rebs by."

Burrowing under his pillow, he produced a little bundle of what he called "truck," and gallantly presented me with a pair of earrings, each representing a cluster of corpulent grapes, and the pin a basket of astonishing fruit, the whole large and coppery enough for a small warming-pan. Feeling delicate about depriving him of such valuable relics, I accepted the earrings alone, and was obliged to depart, somewhat abruptly, when my friend stuck the warming-pan in the bosom of his night-gown, viewing it with much complacency, and, perhaps, some tender memory, in that rough heart of his, for the comrade he had lost.

Observing that the man next him had left his meal untouched, I offered the same service I had performed for his neighbor, but he shook his head.

"Thank you, ma'am; I don't think I'll ever eat again, for I'm shot in the stomach. But I'd like a drink of water, if you aint too busy.

I rushed away, but the water-pails were gone to be refilled, and it was some time before they reappeared. I did not forget my patient patient, meanwhile, and, with the first mugful, hurried back to him. He seemed asleep; but something in the tired white face caused me to listen at his lips for a breath. None came. I touched his forehead; it was cold: and then I knew that, while he waited, a better nurse than I had given him a cooler draught, and healed him with a touch. I laid the sheet over the quiet sleeper, whom no noise could now disturb; and, half an hour later, the bed was empty. It seemed a poor requital for all he had sacrificed and suffered,—that hospital bed, lonely even in a crowd; for there was no familiar face for him to look his last upon; no friendly voice to say, Good bye; no hand to lead him gently down into the Valley of the Shadow; and he vanished, like a drop in that red sea upon whose shores so many women stand lamenting. For a moment I felt bitterly indignant at this seeming carelessness of the value of life, the sanctity of death; then consoled myself with the thought that, when the great muster roll was called, these nameless men might be promoted above many whose tall monuments record the barren honors they have won.

All having eaten, drank, and rested, the surgeons began their rounds; and I took my first lesson in the art of dressing wounds. It wasn't a festive scene, by any means; for Dr. P., whose Aid I constituted myself, fell to work with a vigor which soon convinced me that I was a weaker vessel, though nothing would have induced me to confess it then. He had served in the Crimea, and seemed to regard a dilapidated body very much as I should have regarded a damaged garment; and, turning up his cuffs, whipped out a very unpleasant looking housewife, cutting, sawing, patching and piecing, with the enthusiasm of an accomplished surgical seamstress; explaining the process, in scientific terms, to the patient, meantime; which, of course, was immensely cheering and comfortable. There was an uncanny sort of fascination in watching him, as he peered and probed into the mechanism of those wonderful bodies, whose mysteries he understood so well. The more intricate the wound, the better he liked it. A poor private, with both legs off, and shot through the lungs, possessed more attractions for him than a dozen generals, slightly scratched in some "masterly retreat;" and had any one appeared in small pieces, requesting to be put together again, he would have considered it a special dispensation.

The amputations were reserved till the morrow, and the merciful magic of ether was not thought necessary that day, so the poor souls had to bear their pains as best they might. It is all very well to talk of the patience of woman;

and far be it from me to pluck that feather from her cap, for, heaven knows, she isn't allowed to wear many; but the patient endurance of these men, under trials of the flesh, was truly wonderful; their fortitude seemed contagious, and scarcely a cry escaped them, though I often longed to groan for them, when pride kept their white lips shut, while great drops stood upon their foreheads, and the bed shook with the irrepressible tremor of their tortured bodies. One or two Irishmen anathematized the doctors with the frankness of their nation, and ordered the Virgin to stand by them, as if she had been the wedded Biddy to whom they could administer the poker, if she didn't; but, as a general thing, the work went on in silence, broken only by some quiet request for roller, instruments, or plaster, a sigh from the patient, or a sympathizing murmur from the nurse.

It was long past noon before these repairs were even partially made; and, having got the bodies of my boys into something like order, the next task was to minister to their minds, by writing letters to the anxious souls at home; answering questions, reading papers, taking possession of money and valuables; for the eighth commandment was reduced to a very fragmentary condition, both by the blacks and whites, who ornamented our hospital with their presence. Pocket books, purses, miniatures, and watches, were sealed up, labelled, and handed over to the matron, till such times as the owners thereof were ready to depart homeward or campward again. The letters dictated to me, and revised by me, that afternoon, would have made an excellent chapter for some future history of the war; for, like that which Thackeray's "Ensign Spooney" [a character in Thackeray's *Vanity Fair*] wrote his mother just before Waterloo, they were "full of affection, pluck, and bad spelling;" nearly all giving lively accounts of the battle, and ending with a somewhat sudden plunge from patriotism to provender, desiring "Marm," "Mary Ann," or "Aunt Peters," to send along some pies, pickles, sweet stuff, and apples, "to yourn in haste," Joe, Sam, or Ned, as the case might be.

My little Sergeant insisted on trying to scribble something with his left hand, and patiently accomplished some half dozen lines of hieroglyphics, which he gave me to fold and direct, with a boyish blush, that rendered a glimpse of "My Dearest Jane," unnecessary, to assure me that the heroic lad had been more successful in the service of Commander-in-Chief Cupid than that of Gen. Mars; and a charming little romance blossomed instanter in Nurse Periwinkle's romantic fancy, though no further confidences were made that day, for Sergeant fell asleep, and, judging from his tranquil face, visited his absent sweetheart in the pleasant land of dreams.

At five o'clock a great bell rang, and the attendants flew, not to arms, but to their trays, to bring up supper, when a second uproar announced that it was ready. The new comers woke at the sound; and I presently discovered that it took a very bad wound to incapacitate the defenders of the faith for the consumption of their rations; the amount that some of them sequestered was amazing; but when I suggested the probability of a famine hereafter, to the matron, that motherly lady cried out: "Bless their hearts, why shouldn't they eat? It's their only amusement; so fill every one, and, if there's not enough ready to-night, I'll lend my share to the Lord by giving it to the boys." And, whipping up her coffee-pot and plate of toast, she gladdened the eyes and stomachs of two or three dissatisfied heroes, by serving them with a liberal hand; and I haven't the slightest doubt that, having cast her bread upon the waters, it came back buttered, as another large-hearted old lady was wont to say.

Then came the doctor's evening visit; the administration of medicines; washing feverish faces; smoothing tumbled beds; wetting wounds; singing lullabies; and preparations for the night. By eleven, the last labor of love was done; the last "good night" spoken; and, if any needed a reward for that day's work, they surely received it, in the silent eloquence of those long lines of faces, showing pale and peaceful in the shaded rooms, as we quitted them, followed by grateful glances that lighted us to bed, where rest, the sweetest, made our pillows soft, while Night and Nature took our places, filling that great house of pain with the healing miracles of Sleep, and his diviner brother, Death.

CHAPTER FOUR

A Night

BEING FOND OF THE NIGHT SIDE OF NATURE I was soon promoted to the post of night nurse, with every facility for indulging in my favorite pastime of "owling." My colleague, a black-eyed widow, relieved me at dawn, we two taking care of the ward, between us, like the immortal Sairy and Betsey, "turn and turn about." I usually found my boys in the jolliest state of mind their condition allowed; for it was a known fact that Nurse Periwinkle objected to blue devils, and entertained a belief that he who laughed most was surest of recovery. At the beginning of my reign, dumps and dismals prevailed; the nurses looked anxious and tired, the men gloomy or sad; and a general "Hark!-from-the-tombs-a-doleful-sound" style of conversation seemed to be the fashion: a state of things which caused one coming from a merry, social New England town, to feel as if she had got into an exhausted receiver; and the instinct of self-preservation, to say nothing of a philanthropic desire to serve the race, caused a speedy change in Ward No. 1.

More flattering than the most gracefully turned compliment, more grateful than the most admiring glance, was the sight of those rows of faces, all strange to me a little while ago, now lighting up, with smiles of welcome, as I came among them, enjoying that moment heartily, with a womanly pride in their regard, a motherly affection for them all. The evenings were spent in reading aloud, writing letters, waiting on and amusing the men, going the rounds with Dr. P., as he made his second daily survey, dressing my dozen wounds afresh, giving last doses, and making them cozy for the long hours to come, till the nine o'clock bell rang, the gas was turned down, the day nurses went off duty, the night watch came on, and my nocturnal adventure began.

My ward was now divided into three rooms; and, under favor of the matron, I had managed to sort out the patients in such a way that I had what I called, "my duty room," my "pleasure room," and my "pathetic room," and worked for each in a different way. One, I visited, armed with a dressing tray, full of rollers, plasters, and pins; another, with books, flowers, games, and gossip; a third, with teapots, lullabies, consolation, and, sometimes, a shroud.

Wherever the sickest or most helpless man chanced to be, there I held my watch, often visiting the other rooms, to see that the general watchman of the ward did his duty by the fires and the wounds, the latter needing constant wetting. Not only on this account did I meander, but also to get fresher air than the close rooms afforded; for, owing to the stupidity of that mysterious "somebody" who does all the damage in the world, the windows had been carefully nailed down above, and the lower sashes could only be raised in the mildest weather, for the men lay just below. I had suggested a summary smashing of a few panes here and there, when frequent appeals to headquarters had proved unavailing, and daily orders to lazy attendants had come to nothing. No one seconded the motion, however, and the nails were far beyond my reach; for, though belonging to the sisterhood of "ministering angels," I had no wings, and might as well have asked for Jacob's ladder, as a pair of steps, in that charitable chaos.

One of the harmless ghosts who bore me company during the haunted hours, was Dan, the watchman, whom I regarded with a certain awe; for, though so much together, I never fairly saw his face, and, but for his legs, should never have recognized him, as we seldom met by day. These legs were remarkable, as was his whole figure, for his body was short, rotund, and done up in a big jacket, and muffler; his beard hid the lower part of his face, his hat-brim the upper; and all I ever discovered was a pair of sleepy eyes, and a very mild voice. But the legs!—very long, very thin, very crooked and feeble, looking like grey sausages in their tight coverings, without a ray of pegto-pishness about them, and finished off with a pair of expansive, green cloth shoes, very like Chinese junks, with the sails down. This figure, gliding noise-lessly about the dimly lighted rooms, was strongly suggestive of the spirit of a beer barrel mounted on cork-screws, haunting the old hotel in search of its lost mates, emptied and staved in long ago.

Another goblin who frequently appeared to me, was the attendant of the pathetic room, who, being a faithful soul, was often up to tend two or three men, weak and wandering as babies, after the fever had gone. The amiable creature beguiled the watches of the night by brewing jorums of a fearful beverage, which he called coffee, and insisted on sharing with me; coming in with a great bowl of something like mud soup, scalding hot, guiltless of cream, rich in an all-pervading flavor of molasses, scorch and tin pot. Such an amount of good will and neighborly kindness also went into the mess, that I never could find the heart to refuse, but always received it with thanks, sipped it with hypocritical relish while he remained, and whipped it into the slop-jar the instant he departed, thereby gratifying him, securing one rousing laugh in the doziest hour of the night, and no one was the worse for the transaction but the pigs. Whether they were "cut off untimely in their sins," or not, I carefully abstained from inquiring.

It was a strange life—asleep half the day, exploring Washington the other half, and all night hovering, like a massive cherubim, in a red rigolette, over the slumbering sons of man. I liked it, and found many things to amuse, instruct, and interest me. The snores alone were quite a study, varying from the mild sniff to the stentorian snort, which startled the echoes and hoisted the performer erect to accuse his neighbor of the deed, magnanimously forgive him, and, wrapping the drapery of his couch about him, lie down to vocal slumber. After listening for a week to this band of wind instruments, I indulged in the belief that I could recognize each by the snore alone, and was tempted to join the chorus by breaking out with John Brown's favorite hymn:

"Blow ye the trumpet, blow!"

I would have given much to have possessed the art of sketching, for many of the faces became wonderfully interesting when unconscious. Some grew stern and grim, the men evidently dreaming of war, as they gave orders, groaned over their wounds, or damned the rebels vigorously; some grew sad and infinitely pathetic, as if the pain borne silently all day, revenged itself by now betraying what the man's pride had concealed so well. Often the roughest grew young and pleasant when sleep smoothed the hard lines away, letting the real nature assert itself; many almost seemed to speak, and I learned to know these men better by night than through any intercourse by day. Sometimes they disappointed me, for faces that looked merry and good in the light, grew bad and sly when the shadows came; and though they made no confidences in words, I read their lives, leaving them to wonder at the change of manner this midnight magic wrought in their nurse. A few talked busily; one drummer boy sang sweetly, though no persuasions could win a note from him by day; and several depended on being told what they had talked of in the morning.

Even my constitutionals in the chilly halls, possessed a certain charm, for the house was never still. Sentinels tramped round it all night long, their muskets glittering in the wintry moonlight as they walked, or stood before the doors, straight and silent, as figures of stone, causing one to conjure up romantic visions of guarded forts, sudden surprises, and daring deeds; for in these war times the hum drum life of Yankeedom has vanished, and the most prosaic feel some thrill of that excitement which stirs the nation's heart, and makes its capital a camp of hospitals. Wandering up and down these lower halls, I often heard cries from above, steps hurrying to and fro, saw surgeons passing up, or men coming down carrying a stretcher, where lay a long white figure, whose face was shrouded and whose fight was done. Sometimes I stopped to watch the passers in the street, the moonlight shining on the spire opposite, or the gleam of some vessel floating, like a white-winged sea-gull, down the broad Potomac, whose fullest flow can never wash away the red stain of the land.

The night whose events I have a fancy to record, opened with a little comedy, and closed with a great tragedy; for a virtuous and useful life untimely ended is always tragical to those who see not as God sees. My headquarters were beside the bed of a New Jersey boy, crazed by the horrors of that dreadful Saturday. A slight wound in the knee brought him there; but his mind had suffered more than his body; some string of that delicate machine was over strained, and, for days, he had been reliving, in imagination, the scenes he could not forget, till his distress broke out in incoherent ravings, pitiful to hear. As I sat by him, endeavoring to soothe his poor distracted brain by the constant touch of wet hands over his hot forehead, he lay cheering his comrades on, hurrying them back, then counting them as they fell around him, often clutching my arm, to drag me from the vicinity of a bursting shell, or covering up his head to screen himself from a shower of shot; his face brilliant with fever; his eyes restless; his head never still; every muscle strained and rigid; while an incessant stream of defiant shouts, whispered warnings, and broken laments, poured from his lips with that forceful bewilderment which makes such wanderings so hard to overhear.

It was past eleven, and my patient was slowly wearying himself into fitful intervals of quietude, when, in one of these pauses, a curious sound arrested my attention. Looking over my shoulder, I saw a one-legged phantom hopping nimbly down the room; and, going to meet it, recognized a certain Pennsylvania gentleman, whose wound-fever had taken a turn for the worse, and, depriving him of the few wits a drunken campaign had left him, set him literally tripping on the light, fantastic toe "toward home," as he blandly informed me, touching the military cap which formed a striking contrast to the severe simplicity of the rest of his decidedly *undress* uniform. When sane, the least movement produced a roar of pain or a volley of oaths; but the departure of reason seemed to have wrought an agreeable change, both in the man and his manners; for, balancing himself on one leg, like a meditative stork, he plunged into an animated discussion of the war, the President, lager beer, and Enfield rifles, regardless of any suggestions of mine as to the propriety of returning to bed, lest he be court-martialed for desertion.

Anything more supremely ridiculous can hardly be imagined than this figure, scantily draped in white, its one foot covered with a big blue sock, a dingy cap set rakingly askew on its shaven head, and placid satisfaction beaming in its broad red face, as it flourished a mug in one hand, an old boot in the other, calling them canteen and knapsack, while it skipped and fluttered in the most unearthly fashion. What to do with the creature I didn't know; Dan was absent, and if I went to find him, the perambulator might festoon himself out of the window, set his toga on fire, or do some of his neighbors a mischief. The attendant of the room was sleeping like a near relative of the celebrated Seven [According to tradition, the Seven Sleepers were seven young men of Ephesus who fled persecution and slept in a cave for several hundred years until Christianity became the accepted religion of the empire.], and nothing short of pins would rouse him; for he had been out that day, and whiskey asserted its supremacy in balmy whiffs. Still declaiming, in a fine flow of eloquence, the demented gentleman hopped on, blind and deaf to my graspings and entreaties; and I was about to slam the door in his face, and run for help, when a second and saner phantom, "all in white," came to the rescue, in the likeness of a big Prussian, who spoke no English, but divined the crisis, and put an end to it, by bundling the lively monoped into his bed, like a baby, with an authoritative command to "stay put," which received added weight from being delivered in an odd conglomeration of French and German, accompanied by warning wags of a head decorated with a yellow cotton night cap, rendered most imposing by a tassel like a bell-pull. Rather exhausted by his excursion, the member from Pennsylvania subsided; and, after an irrepressible laugh together, my Prussian ally and myself were returning to our places, when the echo of a sob caused us to glance along the beds. It came from one in the corner such a little bed!—and such a tearful little face looked up at us, as we stopped beside it! The twelve years old drummer boy was not singing now, but sobbing, with a manly effort all the while to stifle the distressful sounds that would break out.

"What is it, Teddy?" I asked, as he rubbed the tears away, and checked himself in the middle of a great sob to answer plaintively: "I've got a chill, ma'am, but I aint cryin' for that, 'cause I'm used to it. I dreamed Kit was here, and when I waked up he wasn't, and I couldn't help it, then."

The boy came in with the rest, and the man who was taken dead from the ambulance was the Kit he mourned. Well he might; for, when the wounded were brought from Fredericksburg, the child lay in one of the camps there-about, and this good friend, though sorely hurt himself, would not leave him to the exposure and neglect of such a time and place; but, wrapping him in his own blanket, carried him in his arms to the transport, tended him during the passage, and only yielded up his charge when Death met him at the door of the hospital which promised care and comfort for the boy. For ten days, Teddy had shivered or burned with fever and ague, pining the while for Kit, and refusing to be comforted, because he had not been able to thank him for the generous protection, which, perhaps, had cost the giver's life. The vivid dream had wrung the childish heart with a fresh pang, and when I tried the solace fitted for his years, the remorseful fear that haunted him found vent in a fresh burst of tears, as he looked at the wasted hands I was endeavoring to warm:

"Oh! if I'd only been as thin when Kit carried me as I am now, maybe he wouldn't have died; but I was heavy, he was hurt worser than we knew, and so it killed him; and I didn't see him, to say good bye."

This thought had troubled him in secret; and my assurances that his friend would probably have died at all events, hardly assuaged the bitterness of his regretful grief.

At this juncture, the delirious man began to shout; the one-legged rose up in his bed, as if preparing for another dart; Teddy bewailed himself more piteously than before: and if ever a woman was at her wit's end, that distracted female was Nurse Periwinkle, during the space of two or three minutes, as she vibrated between the three beds, like an agitated pendulum. Like a most opportune reinforcement, Dan, the bandy, appeared, and devoted himself to the lively party, leaving me free to return to my post; for the Prussian, with a nod and a smile, took the lad away to his own bed, and lulled him to sleep with a soothing murmur, like a mammoth humble bee. I liked that in Fritz, and if he ever wondered afterward at the dainties which sometimes found their way into his rations, or the extra comforts of his bed, he might have found a solution of the mystery in sundry persons' knowledge of the fatherly action of that night.

Hardly was I settled again, when the inevitable bowl appeared, and its bearer delivered a message I had expected, yet dreaded to receive:

"John is going, ma'am, and wants to see you, if you can come."

"The moment this boy is asleep; tell him so, and let me know if I am in danger of being too late."

My, Ganymede departed, and while I quieted poor Shaw, I thought of John. He came in a day or two after the others; and, one evening, when I entered my "pathetic room," I found a lately emptied bed occupied by a large, fair man, with a fine face, and the serenest eyes I ever met. One of the earlier comers had often spoken of a friend, who had remained behind, that those apparently worse wounded than himself might reach a shelter first. It seemed a David and Jonathan sort of friendship. The man fretted for his mate, and was never tired of praising John—his courage, sobriety, self-denial, and unfailing kindliness of heart; always winding up with: "He's an out an' out fine feller, ma'am; you see if he aint."

I had some curiosity to behold this piece of excellence, and when he came, watched him for a night or two, before I made friends with him; for, to tell the truth, I was a little afraid of the stately looking man, whose bed had to be lengthened to accommodate his commanding stature; who seldom spoke, uttered no complaint, asked no sympathy, but tranquilly observed what went on about him; and, as he lay high upon his pillows, no picture of dying statesman or warrior was ever fuller of real dignity than this Virginia black-smith. A most attractive face he had, framed in brown hair and beard, comely featured and full of vigor, as yet unsubdued by pain; thoughtful and often beautifully mild while watching the afflictions of others, as if entirely forgetful of his own. His mouth was grave and firm, with plenty of will and courage in its lines, but a smile could make it as sweet as any woman's; and his eyes were child's eyes, looking one fairly in the face, with a clear, straightforward glance, which promised well for such as placed their faith in him. He seemed to cling to life, as if it were rich in duties and delights, and he had learned the secret of content. The only time I saw his composure disturbed was when my surgeon brought another to examine John, who scrutinized their faces with an anxious look, asking of the elder: "Do you think I shall pull through, sir?" "I hope so, my man." And, as the two passed on, John's eye still followed them, with an intentness which would have won a clearer answer from them, had they seen it. A momentary shadow flitted over his face; then came the usual serenity, as if, in that brief eclipse, he had acknowledged the existence of some hard possibility, and, asking nothing yet hoping all things, left the issue in God's hands, with that submission which is true piety.

The next night, as I went my rounds with Dr. P., I happened to ask which man in the room probably suffered most; and, to my great surprise, he glanced at John:

"Every breath he draws is like a stab; for the ball pierced the left lung, broke a rib, and did no end of damage here and there; so the poor lad can find neither forgetfulness nor ease, because he must lie on his wounded back or suffocate. It will be a hard struggle, and a long one, for he possesses great vitality; but even his temperate life can't save him; I wish it could."

"You don't mean he must die, Doctor?"

"Bless you, there's not the slightest hope for him; and you'd better tell him so before long; women have a way of doing such things comfortably, so I leave it to you. He won't last more than a day or two, at furthest."

I could have sat down on the spot and cried heartily, if I had not learned the wisdom of bottling up one's tears for leisure moments. Such an end seemed very hard for such a man, when half a dozen worn out, worthless bodies round him, were gathering up the remnants of wasted lives, to linger on for years perhaps, burdens to others, daily reproaches to themselves. The army needed men like John, earnest, brave, and faithful; fighting for liberty and justice with both heart and hand, true soldiers of the Lord. I could not give him up so soon, or think with any patience of so excellent a nature robbed of its fulfilment, and blundered into eternity by the rashness or stupidity of those at whose hands so many lives may be required. It was an easy thing for Dr. P. to say: "Tell him he must die," but a cruelly hard thing to do, and by no means as "comfortable" as he politely suggested. I had not the heart to do it then, and privately indulged the hope that some change for the better might take place, in spite of gloomy prophesies; so, rendering my task unnecessary.

A few minutes later, as I came in again, with fresh rollers, I saw John sitting erect, with no one to support him, while the surgeon dressed his back. I had never hitherto seen it done; for, having simpler wounds to attend to, and knowing the fidelity of the attendant, I had left John to him, thinking it might be more agreeable and safe; for both strength and experience were needed in his case. I had forgotten that the strong man might long for the gentler tendance of a woman's hands, the sympathetic magnetism of a woman's presence, as well as the feebler souls about him. The Doctor's words caused me to reproach myself with neglect, not of any real duty perhaps, but of those little cares and kindnesses that solace homesick spirits, and make the heavy hours pass easier. John looked lonely and forsaken just then, as he sat with bent head, hands folded on his knee, and no outward sign of suffering, till, looking nearer, I saw great tears roll down and drop upon the floor. It was a new sight there; for, though I had seen many suffer, some swore, some groaned, most endured silently, but none wept. Yet it did not seem weak, only very touching, and straightway my fear vanished, my heart opened wide and took him in, as, gathering the bent head in my arms, as freely as if he had been a little child, I said, "Let me help you bear it, John."

Never, on any human countenance, have I seen so swift and beautiful a look of gratitude, surprise and comfort, as that which answered me more eloquently than the whispered—

"Thank you, ma'am, this is right good! this is what I wanted!"

"Then why not ask for it before?"

"I didn't like to be a trouble; you seemed so busy, and I could manage to get on alone."

"You shall not want it any more, John."

Nor did he; for now I understood the wistful look that sometimes followed me, as I went out, after a brief pause beside his bed, or merely a passing nod, while busied with those who seemed to need me more than he, because more urgent in their demands; now I knew that to him, as to so many, I was the poor substitute for mother, wife, or sister, and in his eyes no stranger, but a friend who hitherto had seemed neglectful; for, in his modesty, he had never guessed the truth. This was changed now; and, through the tedious operation of probing, bathing, and dressing his wounds, he leaned against me, holding my hand fast, and, if pain wrung further tears from him, no one saw them fall but me. When he was laid down again, I hovered about him, in a remorseful state of mind that would not let me rest, till I had bathed his face, brushed his "bonny brown hair," set all things smooth about him, and laid a knot of heath and heliotrope on his clean pillow. While doing this, he watched me with the satisfied expression I so liked to see; and when I offered the little nosegay, held it carefully in his great hand, smoothed a ruffled leaf or two, surveyed and smelt it with an air of genuine delight, and lay contentedly regarding the glimmer of the sunshine on the green. Although the manliest man among my forty, he said, "Yes, ma'am," like a little boy; received suggestions for his comfort with the quick smile that brightened his whole face; and now and then, as I stood tidying the table by his bed, I felt him softly touch my gown, as if to assure himself that I was there. Anything more natural and frank I never saw, and found this brave John as bashful as brave, yet full of excellencies and fine aspirations, which, having no power to express themselves in words, seemed to have bloomed into his character and made him what he was.

After that night, an hour of each evening that remained to him was devoted to his ease or pleasure. He could not talk much, for breath was precious, and he spoke in whispers; but from occasional conversations, I gleaned scraps of private history which only added to the affection and respect I felt for him. Once he asked me to write a letter, and as I settled pen and paper, I said, with an irrepressible glimmer of feminine curiosity, "Shall it be addressed to wife, or mother, John?"

"Neither, ma'am; I've got no wife, and will write to mother myself when I get better. Did you think I was married because of this?" he asked, touching a plain ring he wore, and often turned thoughtfully on his finger when he lay alone.

"Partly that, but more from a settled sort of look you have, a look which young men seldom get until they marry."

"I don't know that; but I'm not so very young, ma'am, thirty in May, and have been what you might call settled this ten years; for mother's a widow, I'm the oldest child she has, and it wouldn't do for me to marry until Lizzy has a home of her own, and Laurie's learned his trade; for we're not rich, and I must be father to the children and husband to the dear old woman, if I can."

"No doubt but you are both, John; yet how came you to go to war, if you felt so? Wasn't enlisting as bad as marrying?"

"No, ma'am, not as I see it, for one is helping my neighbor, the other pleasing myself. I went because I couldn't help it. I didn't want the glory or

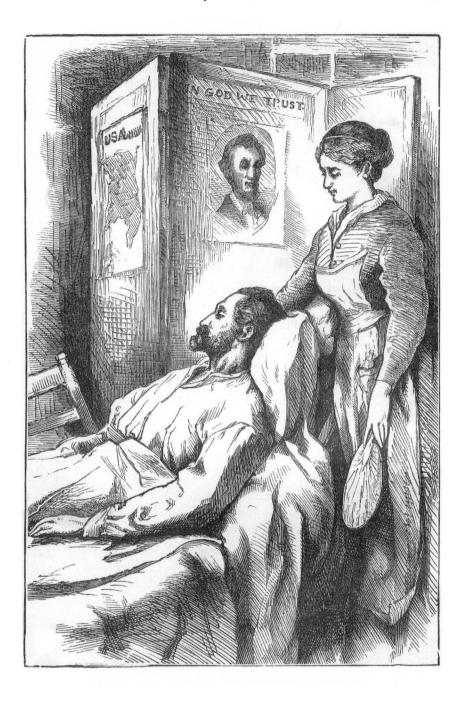

the pay; I wanted the right thing done, and people kept saying the men who were in earnest ought to fight. I was in earnest, the Lord knows! but I held off as long as I could, not knowing which was my duty; mother saw the case, gave me her ring to keep me steady, and said 'Go,' so I went."

A short story and a simple one, but the man and the mother were portrayed better than pages of fine writing could have done it.

"Do you ever regret that you came, when you lie here suffering so much?"

"Never, ma'am; I haven't helped a great deal, but I've shown I was willing to give my life, and perhaps I've got to; but I don't blame anybody, and if it was to do over again, I'd do it. I'm a little sorry I wasn't wounded in front; it looks cowardly to be hit in the back, but I obeyed orders, and it don't matter in the end, I know."

Poor John! it did not matter now, except that a shot in front might have spared the long agony in store for him. He seemed to read the thought that troubled me, as he spoke so hopefully when there was no hope, for he suddenly added:

"This is my first battle; do they think it's going to be my last?"

"I'm afraid they do, John."

It was the hardest question I had ever been called upon to answer; doubly hard with those clear eyes fixed on mine, forcing a truthful answer by their own truth. He seemed a little startled at first, pondered over the fateful fact a moment then shook his head, with a glance at the broad chest and muscular limbs stretched out before him:

"I'm not afraid, but it's difficult to believe all at once. I'm so strong it don't seem possible for such a little wound to kill me."

Merry Mercutio's dying words glanced through my memory as he spoke: "'Tis not so deep as a well, nor so wide as a church door, but 'tis enough." And John would have said the same could he have seen the ominous black holes between his shoulders, he never had; and, seeing the ghastly sights about him, could not believe his own wound more fatal than these, for all the suffering it caused him.

"Shall I write to your mother, now?" I asked, thinking that these sudden tidings might change all plans and purposes; but they did not; for the man received the order of the Divine Commander to march with the same unquestioning obedience with which the soldier had received that of the human one, doubtless remembering that the first led him to life, and the last to death.

"No, ma'am; to Laurie just the same; he'll break it to her best, and I'll add a line to her myself when you get done."

So I wrote the letter which he dictated, finding it better than any I had sent; for, though here and there a little ungrammatical or inelegant, each sentence came to me briefly worded, but most expressive; full of excellent counsel to the boy, tenderly bequeathing "mother and Lizzie" to his care, and bidding him good bye in words the sadder for their simplicity. He added a few lines, with steady hand, and, as I sealed it, said, with a patient sort of sigh, "I hope the answer will come in time for me to see it;" then, turning away his face, laid the flowers against his lips, as if to hide some quiver of emotion at the thought of such a sudden sundering of all the dear home ties.

These things had happened two days before; now John was dying, and the letter had not come. I had been summoned to many death beds in my life, but to none that made my heart ache as it did then, since my mother called me to watch the departure of a spirit akin to this in its gentleness and patient strength. As I went in, John stretched out both hands:

"I knew you'd come! I guess I'm moving on, ma'am."

He was; and so rapidly that, even while he spoke, over his face I saw the grey veil falling that no human hand can lift. I sat down by him, wiped the drops from his forehead, stirred the air about him with the slow wave of a fan, and waited to help him die. He stood in sore need of help—and I could do so little; for, as the doctor had foretold, the strong body rebelled against death, and fought every inch of the way, forcing him to draw each breath with a spasm, and clench his hands with an imploring look, as if he asked, "How long must I endure this, and be still!" For hours he suffered dumbly, without a moment's respite, or a moment's murmuring; his limbs grew cold, his face damp, his lips white, and, again and again, he tore the covering off his breast, as if the lightest weight added to his agony; yet through it all, his eyes never lost their perfect serenity, and the man's soul seemed to sit therein, undaunted by the ills that vexed his flesh.

One by one, the men woke, and round the room appeared a circle of pale faces and watchful eyes, full of awe and pity; for, though a stranger, John was beloved by all. Each man there had wondered at his patience, respected his piety, admired his fortitude, and now lamented his hard death; for the influence of an upright nature had made itself deeply felt, even in one little week. Presently, the Jonathan who so loved this comely David, came creeping from his bed for a last look and word. The kind soul was full of trouble, as the choke in his voice, the grasp of his hand, betrayed; but there were no tears, and the farewell of the friends was the more touching for its brevity.

"Old boy, how are you?" faltered the one.

"Most through, thank heaven!" whispered the other.

"Can I say or do anything for you anywheres?"

"Take my things home, and tell them that I did my best."

"I will! I will!"

"Good bye, Ned."

"Good bye, John, good bye!"

They kissed each other, tenderly as women, and so parted, for poor Ned could not stay to see his comrade die. For a little while, there was no sound in the room but the drip of water, from a stump or two, and John's distressful gasps, as he slowly breathed his life away. I thought him nearly gone, and had just laid down the fan, believing its help to be no longer needed, when suddenly he rose up in his bed, and cried out with a bitter cry that broke the silence, sharply startling every one with its agonized appeal:

"For God's sake, give me air!"

It was the only cry pain or death had wrung from him, the only boon he had asked; and none of us could grant it, for all the airs that blew were useless now. Dan flung up the window. The first red streak of dawn was warming the grey east, a herald of the coming sun; John saw it, and with the love of light which lingers in us to the end, seemed to read in it a sign of hope of help, for, over his whole face there broke that mysterious expression, brighter than any smile, which often comes to eyes that look their last. He laid himself gently down; and, stretching out his strong right arm, as if to grasp and bring the blessed air to his lips in a fuller flow, lapsed into a merciful unconsciousness, which assured us that for him suffering was forever past. He died then; for, though the heavy breaths still tore their way up for a little longer, they were but the waves of an ebbing tide that beat unfelt against the wreck, which an immortal voyager had deserted with a smile. He never spoke again, but to the end held my hand close, so close that when he was asleep at last, I could not draw it away. Dan helped me, warning me as he did so that it was unsafe for dead and living flesh to lie so long together; but though my hand was strangely cold and stiff, and four white marks remained across its back, even when warmth and color had returned elsewhere, I could not but be glad that, through its touch, the presence of human sympathy, perhaps, had lightened that hard hour.

When they had made him ready for the grave, John lay in state for half an hour, a thing which seldom happened in that busy place; but a universal sentiment of reverence and affection seemed to fill the hearts of all who had known or heard of him; and when the rumor of his death went through the house, always astir, many came to see him, and I felt a tender sort of pride in my lost patient; for he looked a most heroic figure, lying there stately and still as the statue of some young knight asleep upon his tomb. The lovely expression which so often beautifies dead faces, soon replaced the marks of pain, and I longed for those who loved him best to see him when half an hour's acquaintance with Death had made them friends. As we stood looking at him, the ward master handed me a letter, saying it had been forgotten the night before. It was John's letter, come just an hour too late to gladden the eyes that had longed and looked for it so eagerly! yet he had it; for, after I had cut some brown locks for his mother, and taken off the ring to send her, telling how well the talisman had done its work, I kissed this good son for her sake, and laid the letter in his hand, still folded as when I drew my own away, feeling that its place was there, and making myself happy with the thought, that, even in his solitary place in the "Government Lot," he would not be without some token of the love which makes life beautiful and outlives death. Then I left him, glad to have known so genuine a man, and carrying with me an enduring memory of the brave Virginia blacksmith, as he lay serenely waiting for the dawn of that long day which knows no night.

CHAPTER FIVE

Off–Duty

"MY DEAR GIRL, WE SHALL have you sick in your bed, unless you keep yourself warm and quiet for a few days. Widow Wadman can take care of the ward alone, now the men are so comfortable, and have her vacation when you are about again. Now do be prudent in time, and don't let me have to add a Periwinkle to my bouquet of patients."

This advice was delivered, in a paternal manner, by the youngest surgeon in the hospital, a kind-hearted little gentleman, who seemed to consider me a frail young blossom, that needed much cherishing, instead of a tough old spinster, who had been knocking about the world for thirty years. At the time I write of, he discovered me sitting on the stairs, with a nice cloud of unwholesome steam rising from the washroom; a party of January breezes disporting themselves in the halls; and perfumes, by no means from "Araby the blest," keeping them company; while I enjoyed a fit of coughing, which caused my head to spin in a way that made the application of a cool banister both necessary and agreeable, as I waited for the frolicsome wind to restore the breath I'd lost; cheering myself, meantime, with a secret conviction that pneumonia was waiting for me round the corner. This piece of advice had been offered by several persons for a week, and refused by me with the obstinacy with which my sex is so richly gifted. But the last few hours had developed several surprising internal and external phenomena, which impressed upon me the fact that if I didn't make a masterly retreat very soon, I should tumble down somewhere, and have to be borne ignominiously from the field. My head felt like a cannon ball; my feet had a tendency to cleave to the floor; the walls at times undulated in a most disagreeable manner; people looked unnaturally big; and the "very bottles on the mankle shelf" appeared to dance derisively before my eyes. Taking these things into consideration, while blinking stupidly at Dr. Z., I resolved to retire gracefully, if I must;

84

so, with a valedictory to my boys, a private lecture to Mrs. Wadman, and a fervent wish that I could take off my body and work in my soul, I mournfully ascended to my apartment, and Nurse P. was reported off duty.

For the benefit of any ardent damsel whose patriotic fancy may have surrounded hospital life with a halo of charms, I will briefly describe the bower to which I retired, in a somewhat ruinous condition. It was well ventilated, for five panes of glass had suffered compound fractures, which all the surgeons and nurses had failed to heal; the two windows were draped with sheets, the church hospital opposite being a brick and mortar Argus, and the female mind cherishing a prejudice in favor of retiracy during the night-capped periods of existence. A bare floor supported two narrow iron beds, spread with thin mattresses like plasters, furnished with pillows in the last stages of consumption. In a fire place, guiltless of shovel, tongs, andirons, or grate, burned a log, inch by inch, being too long to go on all at once; so, while the fire blazed away at one end, I did the same at the other, as I tripped over it a dozen times a day, and flew up to poke it a dozen times at night. A mirror (let us be elegant!) of the dimensions of a muffin, and about as reflective, hung over a tin basin, blue pitcher, and a brace of yellow mugs. Two invalid tables, ditto chairs, wandered here and there, and the closet contained a varied collection of bonnets, bottles, bags, boots, bread and butter, boxes and bugs. The closet was a regular Blue Beard cupboard to me; I always opened it with fear and trembling, owing to rats, and shut it in anguish of spirit; for time and space were not to be had, and chaos reigned along with the rats. Our chimney-piece was decorated with a flat-iron, a Bible, a candle minus stick, a lavender bottle, a new tin pan, so brilliant that it served nicely for a pier-glass, and such of the portly black bugs as preferred a warmer climate than the rubbish hole afforded. Two arks, commonly called trunks, lurked behind the door, containing the worldly goods of the twain who laughed and cried, slept and scrambled, in this refuge; while from the white-washed walls above either bed, looked down the pictured faces of those whose memory can make for us—

"One little room an everywhere."

For a day or two I managed to appear at meals; for the human grub must eat till the butterfly is ready to break loose, and no one had time to come up two flights while it was possible for me to come down. Far be it from me to add another affliction or reproach to that enduring man, the steward; for, compared with his predecessor, he was a horn of plenty; but—I put it to any candid mind—is not the following bill of fare susceptible of improvement, without plunging the nation madly into debt? The three meals were "pretty much of a muchness," and consisted of beef, evidently put down for the men of '76; pork, just in from the street; army bread, composed of saw-dust and saleratus; butter, salt as if churned by Lot's wife; stewed blackberries, so much like preserved cockroaches, that only those devoid of imagination could partake thereof with relish; coffee, mild and muddy; tea, three dried huckleberry leaves to a quart of water—flavored with lime—also animated and unconscious of any approach to clearness. Variety being the spice of life, a small pinch of the article would have been appreciated by the hungry, hard-working sisterhood, one of whom, though accustomed to plain fare, soon found herself reduced to bread and water; having an inborn repugnance to the fat of the land, and the salt of the earth.

Another peculiarity of these hospital meals was the rapidity with which the edibles vanished, and the impossibility of getting a drop or crumb after the usual time. At the first ring of the bell, a general stampede took place; some twenty hungry souls rushed to the dining-room, swept over the table like a swarm of locusts, and left no fragment for any tardy creature who arrived fifteen minutes late. Thinking it of more importance that the patients should be well and comfortably fed, I took my time about my own meals for the first day or two after I came, but was speedily enlightened by Isaac, the black waiter, who bore with me a few times, and then informed me, looking as stern as fate:

"I say, mam, ef you comes so late you can't have no vittles,—'cause I'm 'bleeged fer ter git things ready fer de doctors 'mazin' spry arter you nusses and folks is done. De gen'lemen don't kere fer ter wait, no more does I; so you jes' please ter come at de time, and dere won't be no frettin' nowheres."

It was a new sensation to stand looking at a full table, painfully conscious of one of the vacuums which Nature abhors, and receive orders to right about face, without partaking of the nourishment which your inner woman clamorously demanded. The doctors always fared better than we; and for a moment a desperate impulse prompted me to give them a hint, by walking off with the mutton, or confiscating the pie. But Ike's eye was on me, and, to my shame be it spoken, I walked meekly away; went dinnerless that day, and that evening went to market, laying in a small stock of crackers, cheese and apples, that my boys might not be neglected, nor myself obliged to bolt solid and liquid dyspepsias, or starve. This plan would have succeeded admirably had not the evil star under which I was born, been in the ascendant during that month, and cast its malign influences even into my "'umble" larder; for the rats had their dessert off my cheese, the bugs set up house keeping in my cracker-bag, and the apples like all worldly riches, took to themselves wings and flew away; whither no man could tell, though certain black imps might have thrown light upon the matter, had not the plaintiff in the case been loth to add another to the many trials of long-suffering Africa. After this failure I resigned myself to fate, and, remembering that bread was called the staff of life, leaned pretty exclusively upon it; but it proved a broken reed, and I came to the ground after a few weeks of prison fare, varied by an occasional potato or surreptitious sip of milk.

Very soon after leaving the care of my ward, I discovered that I had no appetite, and cut the bread and butter interests almost entirely, trying the exercise and sun cure instead. Flattering myself that I had plenty of time, and could see all that was to be seen, so far as a lone lorn female could venture in a city, one-half of whose male population seemed to be taking the other half to the guard-house,—every morning I took a brisk run in one direction or another; for the January days were as mild as Spring. A rollicking north wind and occasional snow storm would have been more to my taste, for the one would have braced and refreshed tired body and soul, the other have purified the air, and spread a clean coverlid over the bed, wherein the capital of these United States appeared to be dozing pretty soundly just then.

One of these trips was to the Armory Hospital, the neatness, comfort, and convenience of which makes it an honor to its presiding genius, and arouses all the covetous propensities of such nurses as came from other hospitals to visit it.

The long, clean, warm, and airy wards, built barrack-fashion, with the nurse's room at the end, were fully appreciated by Nurse Periwinkle, whose ward and private bower were cold, dirty, inconvenient, up stairs and down stairs, and in everybody's chamber. At the Armory, in ward K, I found a cheery, bright-eyed, white-aproned little lady, reading at her post near the stove; matting under her feet; a draft of fresh air flowing in above her head; a table full of trays, glasses, and such matters, on one side, a large, well-stocked medicine chest on the other; and all her duty seemed to be going about now and then to give doses, issue orders, which well-trained attendants executed, and pet, advise, or comfort Tom, Dick, or Harry, as she found best. As I watched the proceedings, I recalled my own tribulations, and contrasted the two hospitals in a way that would have caused my summary dismissal, could it have been reported at headquarters. Here, order, method, common sense and liberality reigned and ruled, in a style that did one's heart good to see; at the Hurly-burly Hotel, disorder, discomfort, bad management, and no visible head, reduced things to a condition which I despair of describing. The circumlocution fashion prevailed, forms and fusses tormented our souls, and unnecessary strictness in one place was counterbalanced by unpardonable laxity in another. Here is a sample: I am dressing Sam Dammer's shoulder; and, having cleansed the wound, look about for some strips of adhesive plaster to hold on the little square of wet linen which is to cover the gunshot wound; the case is not in the tray; Frank, the sleepy, half-sick attendant, knows nothing of it; we rummage high and low; Sam is tired, and fumes; Frank dawdles and yawns; the men advise and laugh at the flurry; I feel like a boiling teakettle, with the lid ready to fly off and damage somebody.

"Go and borrow some from the next ward, and spend the rest of the day in finding ours," I finally command. A pause; then Frank scuffles back with the message: "Miss Peppercorn ain't got none, and says you ain't no business to lose your own duds and go borrowin' other folkses." I say nothing, for fear of saying too much, but fly to the surgery. Mr. Toddypestle informs me that I can't have anything without an order from the surgeon of my ward. Great heavens! where is he? and away I rush, up and down, here and there, till at last I find him, in a state of bliss over a complicated amputation, in the fourth story. I make my demand; he answers: "In five minutes," and works away, with his head upside down, as he ties an artery, saws a bone, or does a little needle-work, with a visible relish and very sanguinary pair of hands. The five minutes grow to fifteen, and Frank appears, with the remark that, "Dammer wants to know what in thunder you are keeping him there with his finger on a wet rag for?" Dr. P. tears himself away long enough to scribble the order, with which I plunge downward to the surgery again, find the door locked, and, while hammering away on it, am told that two friends are waiting to see me in the hall. The matron being away, her parlor is locked, and there is no where to see my guests but in my own room, and no time to enjoy them till the plaster is found. I settle this matter, and circulate through the house to find Toddypestle, who has no right to leave the surgery till night. He is discovered in the dead house, smoking a cigar, and very much the worse for his researches among the spirituous preparations that fill the surgery shelves. He is inclined to be gallant, and puts the finishing blow to the fire of my wrath; for the tea-kettle lid flies off, and driving him before me to his post, I fling down the order, take what I choose; and, leaving the absurd incapable kissing his hand to me, depart, feeling as Grandma Riglesty [a character in *Neighbor Jackwood,* an anti-slavery novel by J. T. Trowbridge] is reported to have done, when she vainly sought for chips, in Bimleck Jackwood's "shifless paster."

I find Dammer a well acted charade of his own name, and, just as I get him done, struggling the while with a burning desire to clap an adhesive strip across his mouth, full of heaven-defying oaths, Frank takes up his boot to put it on, and exclaims,

"I'm blest ef here ain't that case now! I recollect seeing it pitch in this mornin', but forgot all about it, till my heel went smash inter it. Here, ma'am, ketch hold on it, and give the boys a sheet on't all round, 'gainst it tumbles inter t'other boot next time yer want it."

If a look could annihilate, Francis Saucebox would have ceased to exist, but it couldn't; therefore, he yet lives, to aggravate some unhappy woman's soul, and wax fat in some equally congenial situation.

Now, while I'm freeing my mind, I should like to enter my protest against employing convalescents as attendants, instead of strong, properly trained, and cheerful men. How it may be in other places I cannot say; but here it was a source of constant trouble and confusion, these feeble, ignorant men trying to sweep, scrub, lift, and wait upon their sicker comrades. One, with a diseased heart, was expected to run up and down stairs, carry heavy trays, and move helpless men; he tried it, and grew rapidly worse than when he first came: and, when he was ordered out to march away to the convalescent hospital, fell, in a sort of fit, before he turned the corner, and was brought back to die.

Another, hurt by a fall from his horse, endeavored to do his duty, but failed entirely, and the wrath of the ward master fell upon the nurse, who must either scrub the rooms herself, or take the lecture; for the boy looked stout and well, and the master never happened to see him turn white with pain, or hear him groan in his sleep when an involuntary motion strained

his poor back. Constant complaints were being made of incompetent attendants, and some dozen women did double duty, and then were blamed for
breaking down. If any hospital director fancies this a good and economical
arrangement, allow one used up nurse to tell him it isn't, and beg him to
spare the sisterhood, who sometimes, in their sympathy, forget that they are
mortal, and run the risk of being made immortal, sooner than is agreeable to
their partial friends.

Another of my few rambles took me to the Senate Chamber, hoping to
hear and see if this large machine was run any better than some small ones I
knew of. I was too late, and found the Speaker's chair occupied by a colored
gentleman of ten; while two others were "on their legs," having a hot debate
on the cornball question, as they gathered the waste paper strewn about the
floor into bags; and several white members played leap-frog over the desks, a
much wholesomer relaxation than some of the older Senators indulge in, I
fancy. Finding the coast clear, I likewise gambolled up and down, from gallery
to gallery; sat in Sumner's chair, and cudgelled an imaginary Brooks within
an inch of his life; examined Wilson's books [Massachusetts Senator Henry
Wilson] in the coolest possible manner; warmed my feet at one of the national
registers; read people's names on scattered envelopes, and pocketed a cast-
away autograph or two; watched the somewhat unparliamentary proceedings
going on about me, and wondered who in the world all the sedate gentlemen
were, who kept popping out of odd doors here and there, like respectable
jacks-in-the-box. Then I wandered over the "palatial residence" of Mrs.
Columbia, and examined its many beauties, though I can't say I thought her
a tidy housekeeper, and didn't admire her taste in pictures; for the eye of this
humble individual soon wearied of expiring patriots, who all appeared to be
quitting their earthly tabernacles in convulsious, ruffled shirts, and a whirl of
torn banners, bomb shells, and buff and blue arms and legs.

The statuary also was massive and concrete, but rather wearying to examine;
for the colossal ladies and gentlemen, carried no cards of introduction in face
or figure; so, whether the meditative party in a kilt, with well-developed legs,
shoes like army slippers, and a ponderous nose, was Columbus, Cato, or
Cockelorum Tibby, the tragedian, was more than I could tell. Several robust
ladies attracted me, as I felt particularly "wimbly" myself, as old country
women say; but which was America and which Pocahontas was a mystery,
for all affected much looseness of costume, dishevelment of hair, swords,

arrows, lances, scales, and other ornaments quite passé with damsels of our day, whose effigies should go down to posterity armed with fans, crochet needles, riding whips, and parasols, with here and there one holding pen or pencil, rolling-pin or broom. The statue of Liberty I recognized at once, for it had no pedestal as yet, but stood flat in the mud, with Young America most symbolically making dirt pies, and chip forts, in its shadow. But high above the squabbling little throng and their petty plans, the sun shone full on Liberty's broad forehead, and, in her hand, some summer bird had built its nest. I accepted the good omen then, and, on the first of January, the Emancipation Act gave the statue a nobler and more enduring pedestal than any marble or granite ever carved and quarried by human hands.

One trip to Georgetown Heights, where cedars sighed overhead, dead leaves rustled underfoot, pleasant paths led up and down, and a brook wound like a silver snake by the blackened ruins of some French Minister's house, through the poor gardens of the black washerwomen who congregated there, and, passing the cemetery with a murmurous lullaby, rolled away to pay its little tribute to the river. This breezy run was the last I took; for, on the morrow, came rain and wind: and confinement soon proved a powerful reinforcement to the enemy, who was quietly preparing to spring a mine, and blow me five hundred miles from the position I had taken in what I called my Chickahominy Swamp.

Shut up in my room, with no voice, spirits, or books, that week was not a holiday, by any means. Finding meals a humbug, I stopped away altogether, trusting that if this sparrow was of any worth, the Lord would not let it fall to the ground. Like a flock of friendly ravens, my sister nurses fed me, not only with food for the body, but kind words for the mind; and soon, from being half starved, I found myself so beteaed and betoasted, petted and served, that I was quite "in the lap of luxury," in spite of cough, headache, a painful consciousness of my pleura, and a realizing sense of bones in the human frame. From the pleasant house on the hill, the home in the heart of Washington, and the Willard caravansary, came friends new and old, with bottles, baskets, carriages and invitations for the invalid; and daily our Florence Nightingale climbed the steep stairs, stealing a moment from her busy life, to watch over the stranger, of whom she was as thoughtfully tender as any mother. Long may she wave! Whatever others may think or say, Nurse Periwinkle is forever grateful; and among her relics of that Washington defeat, none is more valued than the little book which appeared on her pillow, one dreary day; for the D. D. [Dorothea Dix, Superintendent of Women Nurses for the Union army] written in it means to her far more than Doctor of Divinity.

Being forbidden to meddle with fleshly arms and legs, I solaced myself by mending cotton ones, and, as I sat sewing at my window, watched the moving panorama that passed below; amusing myself with taking notes of the most striking figures in it. Long trains of army wagons kept up a perpetual rumble from morning till night; ambulances rattled to and fro with busy surgeons, nurses taking an airing, or convalescents going in parties to be fitted to artificial limbs. Strings of sorry looking horses passed, saying as plainly as dumb creatures could, "Why, in a city full of them, is there no *horse*pital for us?" Often a cart came by, with several rough coffins in it, and no mourners following; barouches, with invalid officers, rolled round the corner, and carriage loads of pretty children, with black coachmen, footmen, and maids. The women who took their walks abroad, were so extinguished in three story bonnets, with overhanging balconies of flowers, that their charms were obscured; and all I can say of them is, that they dressed in the worst possible taste, and walked like ducks.

The men did the picturesque, and did it so well that Washington looked like a mammoth masquerade. Spanish hats, scarlet lined riding cloaks, swords and sashes, high boots and bright spurs, beards and mustaches, which made plain faces comely, and comely faces heroic; these vanities of the flesh transformed our butchers, bakers, and candlestick makers into gallant riders of gaily caparisoned horses, much handsomer than themselves; and dozens of such figures were constantly prancing by, with private prickings of spurs, for the benefit of the perambulating flower-bed. Some of these gentlemen affected painfully tight uniforms, and little caps, kept on by some new law of gravitation, as they covered only the bridge of the nose, yet never fell off; the men looked like stuffed fowls, and rode as if the safety of the nation depended on their speed alone. The fattest, greyest officers dressed most, and ambled statelily along, with orderlies behind, trying to look as if they didn't know the stout party in front, and doing much caracoling on their own account.

The mules were my especial delight; and an hour's study of a constant succession of them introduced me to many of their characteristics; for six of these odd little beasts drew each army wagon, and went hopping like frogs through the stream of mud that gently rolled along the street. The coquettish mule had small feet, a nicely trimmed tassel of a tail, perked up ears, and seemed much given to little tosses of the head, affected skips and prances; and, if he wore the bells, or were bedizzened with a bit of finery, put on as many airs as any belle. The moral mule was a stout, hard-working creature, always tugging with all his might; often pulling away after the rest had stopped, laboring under the conscientious delusion that food for the entire army depended upon his private exertions. I respected this style of mule; and, had I possessed a juicy cabbage, would have pressed it upon him, with thanks for his excellent example. The historical mule was a melodramatic quadruped, prone to startling humanity by erratic leaps, and wild plunges, much shaking of his stubborn head, and lashing out of his vicious heels; now and then falling flat, and apparently dying *à la* Forrest: a gasp—a squirm—a flop, and so on, till the street was well blocked up, the drivers all swearing like demons in bad hats, and the chief actor's circulation decidedly quickened by every variety of kick, cuff, jerk and haul. When the last breath seemed to have left his body, and "Doctors were in vain," a sudden resurrection took place; and if ever a mule laughed with scornful triumph, that was the beast, as he leisurely rose, gave a comfortable shake; and, calmly regarding the excited crowd seemed to say—"A hit! a decided hit! for the stupidest of animals has bamboozled a dozen men. Now, then! what are you stopping the way for?" The pathetic mule was, perhaps, the most interesting of all; for, though he always seemed to be the smallest, thinnest, weakest of the six, the postillion, with big boots, long-tailed coat, and heavy whip, was sure to bestride this one, who struggled feebly along, head down, coat muddy and rough, eye spiritless and sad, his very tail a mortified stump, and the whole beast a picture of meek misery, fit to touch a heart of stone. The jovial mule was a roly poly, happy-go-lucky little piece of horse-flesh, taking everything easily, from cudgeling to caressing; strolling along with a roguish twinkle of the eye, and, if the thing were possible, would have had his hands in his pockets, and whistled as he went. If there ever chanced to be an apple core, a stray turnip, or wisp of hay, in the gutter, this Mark Tapley [a character in Dickens' *Cricket on the Hearth*] was sure to find it, and none of his mates seemed to begrudge him his bite. I suspected this fellow was the peacemaker, confidant and friend of all the others, for he had a sort of "Cheer-up,-old-boy,-I'll-pull-you-through" look, which was exceedingly engaging.

Pigs also possessed attractions for me, never having had an opportunity of observing their graces of mind and manner, till I came to Washington, whose porcine citizens appeared to enjoy a larger liberty than many of its human ones. Stout, sedate looking pigs, hurried by each morning to their places of business, with a preoccupied air, and sonorous greeting to their friends. Genteel pigs, with an extra curl to their tails, promenaded in pairs, lunching here and there, like gentlemen of leisure. Rowdy pigs pushed the passers by off the side walk; tipsy pigs hiccoughed their version of "We won't go home till morning," from the gutter; and delicate young pigs tripped daintily through the mud, as if, like "Mrs. Peerybingle," they plumed themselves upon their ankles, and kept themselves particularly neat in point of stockings. Maternal pigs, with their interesting families, strolled by in the sun; and often the pink, babylike squealers lay down for a nap, with a trust in Providence worthy of human imitation.

But more interesting than officers, ladies, mules, or pigs, were my colored brothers and sisters, because so unlike the respectable members of society I'd known in moral Boston.

Here was the genuine article—no, not the genuine article at all, we must go to Africa for that—but the sort of creatures generations of slavery have made them: obsequious, trickish, lazy and ignorant, yet kind-hearted, merry-tempered, quick to feel and accept the least token of the brotherly love which is slowly teaching the white hand to grasp the black, in this great struggle for the liberty of both the races.

Having been warned not to be too rampant on the subject of slavery, as secesh principles flourished even under the respectable nose of Father Abraham, I had endeavored to walk discreetly, and curb my unruly member; looking about me with all my eyes, the while, and saving up the result of my observations for future use. I had not been there a week, before the neglected, devil-may care expression in many of the faces about me, seemed an urgent appeal to leave nursing white bodies, and take some care for these black souls. Much as the lazy boys and saucy girls tormented me, I liked them, and found that any show of interest or friendliness brought out the better traits which live in the most degraded and forsaken of us all. I liked their cheerfulness, for the dreariest old hag, who scrubbed all day in that pestilential steam, gossiped and grinned all the way out, when night set her free from drudgery. The girls romped with their dusky sweethearts, or tossed their babies, with the tender pride that makes motherlove a beautifier to the homeliest face. The men and boys sang and whistled all day long; and often, as I held my watch, the silence of the night was sweetly broken by some chorus from the street, full of real melody, whether the song was of heaven, or of hoe-cakes; and, as I listened, I felt that we never should doubt nor despair concerning a race which, through such griefs and wrongs, still clings to this good gift, and seems to solace with it the patient hearts that wait and watch and hope until the end.

I expected to have to defend myself from accusations of a prejudice against color; but was surprised to find things just the other way, and daily shocked some neighbor by treating the blacks as I did the whites. The men *would* swear at the "darkies," would put two *g*s into negro, and scoff at the idea of any good coming from such trash. The nurses were willing to be served by the colored people, but seldom thanked them, never praised, and scarcely recognized them in the street; whereat the blood of two generations of abolitionists waxed hot in my veins, and, at the first opportunity, proclaimed itself, and asserted the right of free speech as doggedly as the irrepressible Folsom herself.

Happening to catch up a funny little black baby, who was toddling about the nurses' kitchen, one day, when I went down to make a mess for some of my men, a Virginia woman standing by elevated her most prominent features, with a sniff of disapprobation, exclaiming:

"Gracious, Miss P.! how can you? I've been here six months, and never so much as touched the little toad with a poker."

"More shame for you, ma'am," responded Miss P.; and, with the natural perversity of a Yankee, followed up the blow by kissing "the toad," with ardor. His face was providentially as clean and shiny as if his mamma had just polished it up with a corner of her apron and a drop from the tea-kettle spout, like old Aunt Chloe [Uncle Tom's wife in Harriet Beecher Stowe's novel]. This rash act, and the anti-slavery lecture that followed, while one hand stirred gruel for sick America, and the other hugged baby Africa, did not produce the cheering result which I fondly expected; for my comrade henceforth regarded me as a dangerous fanatic, and my protegé nearly came to his death by insisting on swarming up stairs to my room, on all occasions, and being walked on like a little black spider.

I waited for New Year's day with more eagerness than I had ever known before; and, though it brought me no gift, I felt rich in the act of justice so

tardily performed toward some of those about me. As the bells rung midnight, I electrified my room-mate by dancing out of bed, throwing up the window, and flapping my handkerchief, with a feeble cheer, in answer to the shout of a group of colored men in the street below. All night they tooted and tramped, fired crackers, sung "Glory, Hallelujah," and took comfort, poor souls! in their own way. The sky was clear, the moon shone benignly, a mild wind blew across the river, and all good omens seemed to usher in the dawn of the day whose noontide cannot now be long in coming. If the colored people had taken hands and danced around the White House, with a few cheers for the much abused gentleman who has immortalized himself by one just act, no President could have had a finer levee, or one to be prouder of.

While these sights and sounds were going on without, curious scenes were passing within, and I was learning that one of the best methods of fitting oneself to be a nurse in a hospital, is to be a patient there; for then only can one wholly realize what the men suffer and sigh for; how acts of kindness touch and win; how much or little we are to those about us; and for the first time really see that in coming there we have taken our lives in our hands, and may have to pay dearly for a brief experience. Every one was very kind; the attendants of my ward often came up to report progress, to fill my woodbox, or bring messages and presents from my boys. The nurses took many steps with those tired feet of theirs, and several came each evening, to chat over my fire and make things cosy for the night. The doctors paid daily visits, tapped at my lungs to see if pneumonia was within, left doses without names, and went away, leaving me as ignorant, and much more uncomfortable than when they came. Hours began to get confused; people looked odd; queer faces haunted the room, and the nights were one long fight with weariness and pain. Letters from home grew anxious; the doctors lifted their eyebrows, and nodded ominously; friends said "Don't stay," and an internal rebellion seconded the advice; but the three months were not out, and the idea of giving up so soon was proclaiming a defeat before I was fairly routed; so to all "Don't stays" I opposed "I wills," till, one fine morning, a grey-headed gentlemen rose like a welcome ghost on my hearth; and, at the sight of him, my resolution melted away, my heart turned traitor to my boys, and, when he said, "Come home," I answered, "Yes, father;" and so ended my career as an army nurse.

I never shall regret the going, though a sharp tussle with typhoid, ten dollars, and a wig, are all the visible results of the experiment; for one may live and learn much in a month. A good fit of illness proves the value of health; real danger tries one's mettle; and self-sacrifice sweetens character. Let no one who sincerely desires to help the work on in this way, delay going through any fear; for the worth of life lies in the experiences that fill it, and this is one which cannot be forgotten. All that is best and bravest in the hearts of men and women, comes out in scenes like these; and, though a hospital is a rough school, its lessons are both stern and salutary; and the humblest of pupils there, in proportion to his faithfulness, learns a deeper faith in God and in himself. I, for one, would return tomorrow, on the "up-again,-and-take-another" principle, if I could; for the amount of pleasure and profit I got out of that month compensates for all after pangs; and, though a sadly womanish feeling, I take some satisfaction in the thought that, if I could not lay my head on the altar of my country, I have my hair; and that is more than handsome Helen did for her dead husband, when she sacrificed only the ends of her ringlets on his urn. Therefore, I close this little chapter of hospital experiences, with the regret that they were no better worth recording; and add the poetical gem with which I console myself for the untimely demise of "Nurse Periwinkle:"

> *Oh, lay her in a little pit,*
> *With a marble stone to cover it;*
> *And carve thereon a gruel spoon,*
> *To show a "nuss" has died too soon.*

CHAPTER SIX

A Postscript

My Dear S.:—AS INQUIRIES LIKE your own have come to me from various friendly readers of the Sketches, I will answer them *en masse,* and in printed form, as a sort of postscript to what has gone before. One of these questions was, "Are there no services by hospital death-beds, or on Sundays?"

In most Hospitals I hope there are; in ours, the men died, and were carried away, with as little ceremony as on a battlefield. The first event of this kind which I witnessed was so very brief, and bare of anything like reverence, sorrow, or pious consolation, that I heartily agreed with the bluntly expressed opinion of a Maine man lying next his comrade, who died with no visible help near him, but a compassionate woman and a tender-hearted Irishman, who dropped upon his knees, and told his beads, with Catholic fervor, for the good of his Protestant brother's parting soul:

"If, after gettin' all the hard knocks, we are left to die this way, with nothing but a Paddy's prayers to help us, I guess Christians are rather scarce round Washington."

I thought so too; but though Miss Blank, one of my mates, anxious that souls should be ministered to, as well as bodies, spoke more than once to the Chaplain, nothing ever came of it. Unlike another Shepherd, whose earnest piety weekly purified the Senate Chamber, this man did not feed as well as fold his flock, nor make himself a human symbol of the Divine Samaritan, who never passes by on the other side.

I have since learned that our non-committal Chaplain [William Henry Channing] had been a Professor in some Southern College; and, though he maintained that he had no secesh proclivities, I can testify that he seceded from his ministerial duties, I may say, skedaddled; for, being one of his own words, it is as appropriate as inelegant. He read Emerson, quoted Carlyle, and tried to be a Chaplain; but judging from his success, I am afraid he still hankered after the hominy pots of Rebeldom.

Occasionally, on a Sunday afternoon, such of the nurses, officers, attendants, and patients as could avail themselves of it, were gathered in the Ball Room, for an hour's service, of which the singing was the better part. To me it seemed that if ever strong, wise, and loving words were needed, it was then; if ever mortal man had living texts before his eyes to illustrate and illuminate his thought, it was there; and if ever hearts were prompted to devoutest self-abnegation, it was in the work which brought us to anything but a Chapel of Ease. But some spiritual paralysis seemed to have befallen our pastor; for, though many faces turned toward him, full of the dumb hunger that often comes to men when suffering or danger brings them nearer to the heart of things, they were offered the chaff of divinity, and its wheat was left for less needy gleaners, who knew where to look. Even the fine old Bible stories, which may be made as lifelike as any history of our day, by a vivid fancy and pictorial diction, were robbed of all their charms by dry explanations and literal applications, instead of being useful and pleasant lessons to those men, whom weakness had rendered as docile as children in a father's hands.

I watched the listless countenances all about me, while a mild Daniel was moralizing in a den of utterly uninteresting lions; while Shadrach, Meshech, and Abednego were leisurely passing through the fiery furnace, where, I sadly feared, some of us sincerely wished they had remained as permanencies; while the Temple of Solomon was laboriously erected, with minute descriptions of the process, and any quantity of bells and pomegranates on the raiment of the priests. Listless they were at the beginning, and listless at the end; but the instant some stirring old hymn was given out, sleepy eyes brightened, lounging figures sat erect, and many a poor lad rose up in his bed, or stretched an eager hand for the book, while all broke out with a heartiness that proved that somewhere at the core of even the most abandoned, there still glowed some remnant of the native piety that flows in music from the heart of every little child. Even the big rebel joined, and boomed away in a thunderous bass, singing,

"Salvation! let the echoes fly,"

as energetically as if he felt the need of a speedy execution of the command.

That was the pleasantest moment of the hour, for then it seemed a homelike and happy spot; the groups of men looking over one another's shoulders as they sang; the few silent figures in the beds; here and there a woman noiselessly performing some necessary duty, and singing as she worked; while in the arm chair standing in the midst, I placed, for my own satisfaction, the imaginary likeness of a certain faithful pastor, who took all outcasts by the hand, smote the devil in whatever guise he came, and comforted the indigent in spirit with the best wisdom of a great and tender heart, which still speaks to us from its Italian grave. With that addition, my picture was complete; and I often longed to take a veritable sketch of a Hospital Sunday, for, despite its drawbacks, consisting of continued labor, the want of proper books, the barren preaching that bore no fruit, this day was never like the other six.

True to their home training, our New England boys did their best to make it what it should be. With many, there was much reading of Testaments, humming over of favorite hymns, and looking at such books as I could cull from a miscellaneous library. Some lay idle, slept, or gossiped; yet, when I came to them for a quiet evening chat, they often talked freely and well of themselves; would blunder out some timid hope that their troubles might "do 'em good, and keep 'em stiddy;" would choke a little, as they said good night, and turned their faces to the wall to think of mother, wife, or home, these human ties seeming to be the most vital religion which they yet knew. I observed that some of them did not wear their caps on this day, though at other times they clung to them like Quakers; wearing them in bed, putting them on to read the paper, eat an apple, or write a letter, as if, like a new sort of Samson, their strength lay, not in their hair, but in their hats. Many read no novels, swore less, were more silent, orderly, and cheerful, as if the Lord were an invisible Ward-master, who went his rounds but once a week, and must find all things at their best. I liked all this in the poor, rough boys, and could have found it in my heart to put down sponge and tea-pot, and preach a little sermon then and there, while homesickness and pain had made these natures soft, that some good seed might be cast therein, to blossom and bear fruit here or hereafter.

Regarding the admission of friends to nurse their sick, I can only say, it was not allowed at Hurly-burly House; though one indomitable parent took my ward by storm, and held her position, in spite of doctors, matron, and Nurse Periwinkle. Though it was against the rules, though the culprit was an acid, frost-bitten female, though the young man would have done quite as well without her anxious fussiness, and the whole room-full been much more comfortable, there was something so irresistible in this persistent devotion, that no one had the heart to oust her from her post. She slept on the floor, without uttering a complaint; bore jokes somewhat of the rudest; fared scantily, though her basket was daily filled with luxuries for her boy; and tended that petulant personage with a never-failing patience beautiful to see.

I feel a glow of moral rectitude in saying this of her; for, though a perfect pelican to her young, she pecked and cackled (I don't know that pelicans usually express their emotions in that manner,) most obstreperously, when others invaded her premises; and led me a weary life, with "George's tea-rusks," "George's foot-bath," "George's measles," and "George's mother;" till, after a sharp passage of arms and tongues with the matron, she wrathfully packed up her rusks, her son, and herself, and departed, in an ambulance, scolding to the very last.

This is the comic side of the matter. The serious one is harder to describe; for the presence, however brief, of relations and friends by the bedsides of the dead or dying, is always a trial to the bystanders. They are not near enough to know how best to comfort, yet too near to turn their backs upon the sorrow that finds its only solace in listening to recitals of last words, breathed into nurse's ears, or receiving the tender legacies of love and longing bequeathed through them.

To me, the saddest sight I saw in that sad place, was the spectacle of a grey-haired father, sitting hour after hour by his son, dying from the poison of his wound. The old father, hale and hearty; the young son, past all help, though one could scarcely believe it; for the subtle fever, burning his strength away, flushed his cheeks with color, filled his eyes with lustre, and lent a mournful mockery of health to face and figure, making the poor lad comelier in death than in life. His bed was not in my ward; but I was often in and out, and, for a day or two, the pair were much together, saying little, but looking much. The old man tried to busy himself with book or pen, that his presence might not be a burden; and once, when he sat writing, to the anxious mother at home, doubtless, I saw the son's eyes fixed upon his face, with a look of mingled resignation and regret, as if endeavoring to teach himself to say cheerfully the long good bye. And again, when the son slept, the father watched him, as he had himself been watched; and though no feature of his grave countenance changed, the rough hand, smoothing the lock of hair upon the pillow, the bowed attitude of the grey head, were more pathetic than the loudest lamentations. The son died; and the father took home the pale relic of the life he gave, offering a little money to the nurse, as the only visible return it was in his power to make her; for, though very grateful, he was poor. Of course, she did not take it, but found a richer compensation in the old man's earnest declaration:

"My boy couldn't have been better cared for if he'd been at home; and God will reward you for it, though I can't."

My own experiences of this sort began when my first man died. He had scarcely been removed, when his wife came in. Her eye went straight to the well-known bed; it was empty; and feeling, yet not believing the hard truth, she cried out, with a look I never shall forget:

"Why, where's Emanuel?"

I had never seen her before, did not know her relationship to the man whom I had only nursed for a day, and was about to tell her he was gone, when McGee, the tender-hearted Irishman before mentioned, brushed by me with a cheerful "It's shifted to a better bed he is, Mrs. Connel. Come out, dear, till I show ye;" and, taking her gently by the arm, he led her to the matron, who broke the heavy tidings to the wife, and comforted the widow.

Another day, running up to my room for a breath of fresh air and a five minutes' rest after a disagreeable task, I found a stout young woman sitting on my bed, wearing the miserable look which I had learned to know by that time. Seeing her, reminded me that I had heard of some one's dying in the night, and his sister's arriving in the morning. This must be she, I thought. I pitied her with all my heart. What could I say or do? Words always seem impertinent at such times; I did not know the man; the woman was neither interesting in herself nor graceful in her grief; yet, having known a sister's sorrow myself, I could not leave her alone with her trouble in that strange place, without a word. So, feeling heart-sick, home-sick, and not knowing what else to do, I just put my arms about her, and began to cry in a very helpless but hearty way; for, as I seldom indulge in this moist luxury, I like to enjoy it with all my might, when I do.

It so happened I could not have done a better thing; for, though not a word was spoken, each felt the other's sympathy; and, in the silence, our handker-chiefs were more eloquent than words. She soon sobbed herself quiet; and, leaving her on my bed, I went back to work, feeling much refreshed by the shower, though I'd forgotten to rest, and had washed my face instead of my hands. I mention this successful experiment as a receipt proved and approved, for the use of any nurse who may find herself called upon to minister to these wounds of the heart. They will find it more efficacious than cups of tea, smelling-bottles, psalms, or sermons; for a friendly touch and a companionable cry, unite the consolations of all the rest for womankind; and, if genuine, will be found a sovereign cure for the first sharp pang so many suffer in these heavy times.

I am gratified to find that my little Sergeant has found favor in several quarters, and gladly respond to sundry calls for news of him, though my personal knowledge ended five months ago. Next to my good John—I hope the grass is green above him, far away there in Virginia!—I placed the Sergeant on my list of worthy boys; and many a jovial chat have I enjoyed with the merry-hearted lad, who had a fancy for fun, when his poor arm was dressed. While Dr. P. poked and strapped, I brushed the remains of the Sergeant's brown mane—shorn sorely against his will—and gossiped with all my might, the boy making odd faces, exclamations, and appeals, when nerves got the better of nonsense, as they sometimes did

"I'd rather laugh than cry, when I must sing out anyhow, so just say that bit from Dickens again, please, and I'll stand it like a man." He did; for "Mrs. Cluppins," "Chadband," and "Sam Weller," [Characters from Dickens's *The Pickwick Papers* and *Bleak House*] always helped him through; thereby causing me to lay another offering of love and admiration on the shrine of the god of my idolatry, though he does wear too much jewelry and talk slang.

The Sergeant also originated, I believe, the fashion of calling his neighbors by their afflictions instead of their names; and I was rather taken aback by hearing them bandy remarks of this sort, with perfect good humor and much enjoyment of the new game.

"Hallo, old Fits is off again!" "How are you, Rheumatiz?" "Will you trade apples, Ribs?" "I say, Miss P., may I give Typhus a drink of this?" "Look here, No Toes, lend us a stamp, there's a good feller," etc. He himself was christened "Baby B.," because he tended his arm on a little pillow, and called it his infant.

Very fussy about his grub was Sergeant B., and much trotting of attendants was necessary when he partook of nourishment. Anything more irresistibly wheedlesome I never saw, and constantly found myself indulging him, like the most weak-minded parent, merely for the pleasure of seeing his brown eyes twinkle, his merry mouth break into a smile, and his one hand execute a jaunty little salute that was entirely captivating. I am afraid that Nurse P. damaged her dignity, frolicking with this persuasive young gentleman, though done for his well-being. But "boys will be boys," is perfectly applicable to the case; for, in spite of years, sex, and the "prunes-and-prisms" doctrine laid down for our use, I have a fellow feeling for lads, and always owed Fate a grudge because I wasn't a lord of creation instead of a lady.

Since I left, I have heard, from a reliable source, that my Sergeant has gone home; therefore, the small romance that budded the first day I saw him, has blossomed into its second chapter; and I now imagine "dearest Jane" filling my place, tending the wounds I tended, brushing the curly jungle I brushed, loving the excellent little youth I loved, and eventually walking altarward, with the Sergeant stumping gallantly at her side. If she doesn't do all this, and no end more, I'll never forgive her; and sincerely pray to the guardian saint of lovers, that "Baby B." may prosper in his wooing, and his name be long in the land.

One of the lively episodes of hospital life, is the frequent marching away of such as are well enough to rejoin their regiments, or betake themselves to some convalescent camp. The ward master comes to the door of each room that is to be thinned, reads off a list of names, bids their owners look sharp and be ready when called for; and, as he vanishes, the rooms fall into an indescribable state of topsy-turvyness, as the boys begin to black their boots, brighten spurs, if they have them, overhaul knapsacks, make presents; are fitted out with needfuls, and—well, why not?—kissed sometimes, as they say, good bye; for in all human probability we shall never meet again, and a woman's heart yearns over anything that has clung to her for help and comfort. I never liked these breakings-up of my little household; though my short stay showed me but three. I was immensely gratified by the hand shakes I got, for their somewhat painful cordiality assured me that I had not tried in vain. The big Prussian rumbled out his unintelligible *adieux,* with a grateful face and a premonitory smooth of his yellow moustache, but got no farther, for some one else stepped up, with a large brown hand extended, and this recommendation of our very faulty establishment:

"We're off, ma'am, and I'm powerful sorry, for I'd no idea a 'orspittle was such a jolly place. Hope I'll git another ball somewheres easy, so I'll come back, and be took care on again. Mean, ain't it?"

I didn't think so, but the doctrine of inglorious ease was not the right one to preach up, so I tried to look shocked, failed signally, and consoled myself by giving him the fat pincushion he had admired as the "cutest little machine agoin." Then they fell into line in front of the house, looking rather wan and feeble, some of them, but trying to step out smartly and march in good order, though half the knapsacks were carried by the guard, and several leaned on sticks instead of shouldering guns. All looked up and smiled, or waved their hands and touched their caps, as they passed under our windows down the long street, and so away, some to their homes in this world, and some to that in the next; and, for the rest of the day, I felt like Rachel mourning for her children, when I saw the empty beds and missed the familiar faces.

You ask if nurses are obliged to witness amputations and such matters, as a part of their duty? I think not, unless they wish; for the patient is under the effects of ether, and needs no care but such as the surgeons can best give. Our work begins afterward, when the poor soul comes to himself, sick, faint, and wandering; full of strange pains and confused visions, of disagreeable sensations and sights. Then we must sooth and sustain, tend and watch; preaching and practicing patience, till sleep and time have restored courage and self-control.

I witnessed several operations; for the height of my ambition was to go to the front after a battle, and feeling that the sooner I inured myself to trying sights, the more useful I should be. Several of my mates shrunk from such things; for though the spirit was wholly willing, the flesh was inconveniently weak. One funereal lady came to try her powers as a nurse; but, a brief conversation eliciting the facts that she fainted at the sight of blood, was afraid to watch alone, couldn't possibly take care of delirious persons, was nervous about infections, and unable to bear much fatigue, she was mildly dismissed. I hope she found her sphere, but fancy a comfortable bandbox on a high shelf would best meet the requirements of her case.

Dr. Z. [Dr. John Winslow] suggested that I should witness a dissection; but I never accepted his invitations, thinking that my nerves belonged to the living, not to the dead, and I had better finish my education as a nurse before I began that of a surgeon. But I never met the little man skipping through the hall, with oddly shaped cases in his hand, and an absorbed expression of countenance, without being sure that a select party of surgeons were at work in the dead house, which idea was a rather trying one, when I knew the subject was some person whom I had nursed and cared for.

But this must not lead any one to suppose that the surgeons were willfully hard or cruel, though one of them remorsefully confided to me that he feared his profession blunted his sensibilities, and, perhaps, rendered him indifferent to the sight of pain.

I am inclined to think that in some cases it does; for, though a capital surgeon and a kindly man, Dr. P., through long acquaintance with many of the ills flesh is heir to, had acquired a somewhat trying habit of regarding a man and his wound as separate institutions, and seemed rather annoyed that the former should express any opinion upon the latter, or claim any right in it, while under his care. He had a way of twitching off a bandage, and giving a limb a comprehensive sort of clutch, which, though no doubt entirely scientific, was rather startling than soothing, and highly objectionable as a means of preparing nerves for any fresh trial. He also expected the patient to assist in small operations, as he considered them, and to restrain all demonstrations during the process.

"Here, my man, just hold it this way, while I look into it a bit," he said one day to Fitz G., putting a wounded arm into the keeping of a sound one, and proceeding to poke about among bits of bone and visible muscles, in a red and black chasm made by some infernal machine of the shot or shell description. Poor Fitz held on like grim Death, ashamed to show fear before a woman, till it grew more than he could bear in silence; and, after a few smothered groans, he looked at me imploringly, as if he said, "I wouldn't, ma'am, if I could help it," and fainted quietly away.

Dr. P. looked up, gave a compassionate sort of cluck, and poked away more busily than ever, with a nod at me and a brief—"Never mind; be so good as to hold this till I finish."

I obeyed, cherishing the while a strong desire to insinuate a few of his own disagreeable knives and scissors into him, and see how he liked it. A very disrespectful and ridiculous fancy, of course; for he was doing all that could be done, and the arm prospered finely in his hands. But the human mind is prone to prejudice; and, though a personable man, speaking French like a born "Parley voo," and whipping off legs like an animated guillotine, I must confess to a sense of relief when he was ordered elsewhere; and suspect that several of the men would have faced a rebel battery with less trepidation than they did Dr. P., when he came briskly in on his morning round.

As if to give us the pleasures of contrast, Dr. Z. succeeded him, who, I think, suffered more in giving pain than did his patients in enduring it; for he often paused to ask: "Do I hurt you?" and, seeing his solicitude, the boys invariably answered: "Not much; go ahead, Doctor," though the lips that uttered this amiable fib might be white with pain as they spoke. Over the dressing of some of the wounds, we used to carry on conversations upon subjects foreign to the work in hand, that the patient might forget himself in the charms of our discourse. Christmas eve was spent in this way; the Doctor strapping the little Sergeant's arm, I holding the lamp, while all three laughed and talked, as if anywhere but in a hospital ward; except when the chat was broken by a long-drawn "Oh!" from "Baby B.," an abrupt request from the Doctor to "Hold the lamp a little higher, please," or an encouraging, "Most through, Sergeant," from Nurse P.

The chief Surgeon, Dr. O., I was told, refused the higher salary, greater honor, and less labor, of an appointment to the Officer's Hospital, round the corner, that he might serve the poor fellows at Hurly-burly House, or go to the front, working there day and night, among the horrors that succeed the glories of a battle. I liked that so much, that the quiet, brown-eyed Doctor was my especial admiration; and when my own turn came, had more faith in him than in all the rest put together, although he did advise me to go home, and authorize the consumption of blue pills.

Speaking of the surgeons reminds me that, having found all manner of fault, it becomes me to celebrate the redeeming feature of Hurly-burly House. I had been prepared by the accounts of others, to expect much humiliation of spirit from the surgeons, and to be treated by them like a door-mat, a worm, or any other meek and lowly article, whose mission it is to be put down and walked upon; nurses being considered as mere servants, receiving the lowest pay, and, it's my private opinion, doing the hardest work of any part of the army, except the mules. Great, therefore, was my surprise, when I found myself treated with the utmost courtesy and kindness. Very soon my carefully prepared meekness was laid upon the shelf; and, going from one extreme to the other, I more than once expressed a difference of opinion regarding sundry messes it was my painful duty to administer.

As eight of us nurses chanced to be off duty at once, we had an excellent opportunity of trying the virtues of these gentlemen; and I am bound to say they stood the test admirably, as far as my personal observation went. Dr. O.'s stethescope was unremitting in its attentions; Dr. S. brought his buttons into my room twice a day, with the regularity of a medical clock; while Dr. Z. filled my table with neat little bottles, which I never emptied, prescribed Browning, bedewed me with Cologne, and kept my fire going, as if, like the candles in St. Peter's, it must never be permitted to die out. Waking, one cold night, with the certainty that my last spark had pined away and died, and consequently hours of coughing were in store for me, I was much amazed to see a ruddy light dancing on the wall, a jolly blaze roaring up the chimney, and, down upon his knees before it, Dr. Z., whittling shavings. I ought to have risen up and thanked him on the spot; but, knowing that he was one of those who liked to do good by stealth, I only peeped at him as if he were a friendly ghost; till, having made things as cozy as the most motherly of nurses could have done, he crept away, leaving me to feel, as somebody says, "as if angels were a watching of me in my sleep;" though that species of wild fowl do not usually descend in broadcloth and glasses. I afterwards discovered that he split the wood himself on that cool January midnight, and went about making or mending fires for the poor old ladies in their dismal dens; thus causing himself to be felt—a bright and shining light in more ways than one. I never thanked him as I ought; therefore, I publicly make a note of it, and further aggravate that modest M.D. by saying that if this was not being the best of doctors and the gentlest of gentlemen, I shall be happy to see any improvement upon it.

To such as wish to know where these scenes took place, I must respectfully decline to answer; for Hurly-burly House has ceased to exist as a hospital; so let it rest, with all its sins upon its head,—perhaps I should say chimney top. When the nurses felt ill, the doctors departed, and the patients got well, I believe the concern gently faded from existence, or was merged into some other and better establishment, where I hope the washing of three hundred sick people is done out of the house, the food is eatable, and mortal women are not expected to possess an angelic exemption from all wants, and the endurance of truck horses.

Since the appearance of these hasty Sketches, I have heard from several of my comrades at the Hospital; and their approval assures me that I have not let sympathy and fancy run away with me, as that lively team is apt to do when harnessed to a pen. As no two persons see the same thing with the same eyes, my view of hospital life must be taken through my glass, and held for what it is worth. Certainly, nothing was set down in malice, and to the serious-minded party who objected to a tone of levity in some portions of the Sketches, I can only say that it is a part of my religion to look well after the cheerfulnesses of life, and let the dismals shift for themselves; believing, with good Sir Thomas More, that it is wise to "be merrie in God."

The next hospital I enter will, I hope, be one for the colored regiments, as they seem to be proving their right to the admiration and kind offices of their white relations, who owe them so large a debt, a little part of which I shall be so proud to pay.

Yours,

With a firm faith
In the good time coming,
Tribulation Periwinkle.

Civil War Stories

The Brothers

DOCTOR FRANCK CAME IN AS I sat sewing up the rents in an old shirt, that Tom might go tidily to his grave. New shirts were needed for living, and there was no wife or mother to "dress him handsome when he went to meet the Lord," as one woman said, describing the fine funeral she had pinched herself to give her son.

"Miss Dane, I'm in a quandary," began the Doctor, with that expression of countenance which says as plainly as words, "I want to ask a favor, but I wish you'd save me the trouble."

"Can I help you out of it?"

"Faith! I don't like to propose it, but you certainly can, if you please."

"Then name it, I beg."

"You see a Reb has just been brought in crazy with typhoid; a bad case every way; a drunken, rascally little captain somebody took the trouble to capture, but whom nobody wants to take the trouble to cure. The wards are full, the ladies worked to death, and willing to be for our own boys, but rather slow to risk their lives for a Reb. Now, you've had the fever, you like queer patients, your mate will see to your ward for a while, and I will find you a good attendant. The fellow won't last long, I fancy; but he can't die without some sort of care, you know. I've put him in the fourth story of the west wing, away from the rest. It is airy, quiet, and comfortable there. I'm on that ward, and will do my best for you in every way. Now, then, will you go?"

"Of course I will, out of perversity, if not common charity; for some of these people think that because I'm an abolitionist I am also a heathen, and I should rather like to show them that, though I cannot quite love my enemies, I am willing to take care of them."

First published in *The Atlantic Monthly*, 12, (November 1863).

"Very good; I thought you'd go; and speaking of abolition reminds me that you can have a contraband for servant, if you like. It is that fine mulatto fellow who was found burying his rebel master after the fight, and, being badly cut over the head, our boys brought him along. Will you have him?"

"By all means,—for I'll stand to my guns on that point, as on the other; these black boys are far more faithful and handy than some of the white scamps given me to serve, instead of being served by. But is this man well enough?"

"Yes, for that sort of work, and I think you'll like him. He must have been a handsome fellow before he got his face slashed; not much darker than myself; his master's son, I dare say, and the white blood makes him rather high and haughty about some things. He was in a bad way when he came in, but vowed he'd die in the street rather than turn in with the black fellows below; so I put him up in the west wing, to be out of the way, and he's seen to the captain all the morning. When can you go up?"

"As soon as Tom is laid out, Skinner moved, Haywood washed, Marble dressed, Charley rubbed, Downs taken up, Upham laid down, and the whole forty fed."

We both laughed, though the Doctor was on his way to the deadhouse and I held a shroud on my lap. But in a hospital one learns that cheerfulness is one's salvation; for, in an atmosphere of suffering and death, heaviness of heart would soon paralyze usefulness of hand, if the blessed gift of smiles had been denied us.

In an hour I took possession of my new charge, finding a dissipated-looking boy of nineteen or twenty raving in the solitary little room, with no one near him but the contraband in the room adjoining. Feeling decidedly more interest in the black man than in the white, yet remembering the Doctor's hint of his being "high and haughty," I glanced furtively at him as I scattered chloride of lime about the room to purify the air, and settled matters to suit myself. I had seen many contrabands, but never one so attractive as this. All colored men are called "boys," even if their heads are white; this boy was five-and-twenty at least, strong-limbed and manly, and had the look of one who never had been cowed by abuse or worn with oppressive labor. He sat on his bed doing nothing; no book, no pipe, no pen or paper anywhere appeared, yet anything less indolent or listless than his attitude and expression I never saw. Erect he sat, with a hand on either knee, and eyes fixed on the bare wall opposite, so rapt in some absorbing thought as to be unconscious of my presence, though the door stood wide open and my movements were by no means noiseless. His face was half averted, but I instantly approved the Doctor's taste, for the profile which I saw possessed all the attributes of comeliness belonging to his mixed race. He was more quadroon than mulatto, with Saxon features, Spanish complexion darkened by exposure, color in lips and cheek, waving hair, and an eye full of the passionate melancholy which in such men always seems to utter a mute protest against the broken law that doomed them at their birth. What could he be thinking of? The sick boy cursed and raved, I rustled to and fro, steps passed the door, bells rang, and the steady rumble of army-wagons came up from the street, still he never stirred. I had seen colored people in what they call "the black sulks," when, for days, they neither smiled nor spoke, and scarcely ate. But this was something more than that; for the man was not dully brooding over some small grievance; he seemed to see an all-absorbing fact or fancy recorded on the wall, which was a blank to me. I wondered if it were some deep wrong or sorrow, kept alive by memory and impotent regret; if he mourned for the dead master to whom he had been faithful to the end; or if the liberty now his were robbed of half its sweetness by the knowledge that some one near and dear to him still languished in the hell from which he had escaped. My heart quite warmed to him at that idea; I wanted to know and comfort him; and, following the impulse of the moment, I went in and touched him on the shoulder.

In an instant the man vanished and the slave appeared. Freedom was too new a boon to have wrought its blessed changes yet; and as he started up, with his hand at his temple, and an obsequious "Yes, Missis," any romance that had gathered round him fled away, leaving the saddest of all sad facts in living guise before me. Not only did the manhood seem to die out of him, but the comeliness that first attracted me; for, as he turned, I saw the ghastly wound that had laid open cheek and forehead. Being partly healed, it was no longer bandaged, but held together with strips of that transparent plaster which I never see without a shiver, and swift recollections of the scenes with which it is associated in my mind. Part of his black hair had been shorn away, and one eye was nearly closed; pain so distorted, and the cruel sabre-cut so marred that portion of his face, that, when I saw it, I felt as if a fine medal had been suddenly reversed, showing me a far more striking type of human suffering and wrong than Michael Angelo's bronze prisoner. By one of those inexplicable processes that often teach us how little we understand ourselves, my purpose was suddenly changed; and, though I went in to offer comfort as a friend, I merely gave an order as a mistress.

"Will you open these windows? this man needs more air."

He obeyed at once, and, as he slowly urged up the unruly sash, the handsome profile was again turned toward me, and again I was possessed by my first impression so strongly that I involuntarily said,

"Thank you."

Perhaps it was fancy, but I thought that in the look of mingled surprise and something like reproach which he gave me, there was also a trace of grateful pleasure. But he said, in that tone of spiritless humility these poor souls learn so soon,—

"I isn't a white man, Missis, I'se a contraband."

"Yes, I know it; but a contraband is a free man, and I heartily congratulate you."

He liked that; his face shone, he squared his shoulders, lifted his head, and looked me full in the eye with a brisk,

"Thank ye, Missis; anything more to do fer yer?"

"Doctor Franck thought you would help me with this man, as there are many patients and few nurses or attendants. Have you had the fever?"

"No, Missis."

"They should have thought of that when they put him here; wounds and fevers should not be together. I'll try to get you moved."

He laughed a sudden laugh: if he had been a white man, should have called it scornful; as he was a few shades darker than myself, I suppose it must be considered an insolent, or at least an unmannerly one.

"It don't matter, Missis. I'd rather be up here with the fever than down with those niggers; and there isn't no other place fer me."

Poor fellow! that was true. No ward in all the hospital would take him in to lie side by side with the most miserable white wreck there. Like the bat in Aesop's fable, he belonged to neither race; and the pride of one and the helplessness of the other, kept him hovering alone in the twilight a great sin has brought to overshadow the whole land.

"You shall stay, then; for I would far rather have you than my lazy Jack. But are you well and strong enough?"

"I guess I'll do, Missis."

He spoke with a passive sort of acquiescence,—as if it did not much matter if he were not able, and no one would particularly rejoice if he were.

"Yes, I think you will. By what name shall I call you?"

"Bob, Missis."

Every woman has her pet whim; one of mine was to teach the men self-respect by treating them respectfully. Tom, Dick, and Harry would pass, when lads rejoiced in those familiar abbreviations; but to address men often old enough to be my father in that style did not suit my old-fashioned ideas of propriety. This "Bob" would never do; I should have found it as easy to call the chaplain "Gus" as my tragical-looking contraband by a title so strongly associated with the tail of a kite.

"What is your other name?" I asked. "I like to call my attendants by their last names rather than by their first."

"I'se got no other, Missis; we has our masters' names, or do without. Mine's dead, and I won't have anything of his 'bout me."

"Well, I'll call you Robert, then, and you may fill this pitcher for me, if you will be so kind."

He went; but, through all the tame obedience years of servitude had taught him, I could see that the proud spirit his father gave him was not yet subdued, for the look and gesture with which he repudiated his master's name were a more effective declaration of independence than any Fourth-of-July orator could have prepared.

We spent a curious week together. Robert seldom left his room, except upon my errands; and I was a prisoner all day, often all night, by the bedside of the rebel. The fever burned itself rapidly away, for there seemed little vitality to feed it in the feeble frame of this old young man, whose life had been none of the most righteous, judging from the revelations made by his unconscious lips; since more than once Robert authoritatively silenced him, when my gentler bushings were of no avail, and blasphemous wanderings or ribald camp-songs made my checks burn and Robert's face assume an aspect of disgust. The captain was the gentleman in the world's eye, but the contraband was the gentleman in mine;—I was a fanatic, and that accounts for such depravity of taste, I hope. I never asked Robert of himself, feeling that somewhere there was a spot still too sore to bear the lightest touch; but, from his language, manner, and intelligence, I inferred that his color had procured for him the few advantages within the reach of a quick-witted, kindly-treated slave. Silent, grave, and thoughtful, but most serviceable, was my contraband; glad of the books I brought him, faithful in the performance of the duties I assigned to him, grateful for the friendliness I could not but feel and show toward him. Often I longed to ask what purpose was so visibly altering his aspect with such daily deepening gloom. But I never dared, and no one else had either time or desire to pry into the past of this specimen of one branch of the chivalrous "F. F. Vs."

On the seventh night, Dr. Franck suggested that it would be well for some one, besides the general watchman of the ward, to be with the captain, as it might be his last. Although the greater part of the two preceding nights had been spent there, of course I offered to remain,—for there is a strange fascination in these scenes, which renders one careless of fatigue and unconscious of fear until the crisis is past.

"Give him water as long as he can drink, and if he drops into a natural sleep, it may save him. I'll look in at midnight, when some change will probably take place. Nothing but sleep or a miracle will keep him now. Good-night."

Away went the Doctor; and, devouring a whole mouthful of grapes, I lowered the lamp, wet the captain's head, and sat down on a hard stool to begin my watch. The captain lay with his hot, haggard face turned toward me, filling the air with his poisonous breath, and feebly muttering, with lips and tongue so parched that the sanest speech would have been difficult to understand. Robert was stretched on his bed in the inner room, the door of which stood ajar, that a fresh draught from his open window might carry the fever-fumes away through mine. I could just see a long, dark figure, with the lighter outline of a face, and, having little else to do just then, I fell to thinking of this curious contraband, who evidently prized his freedom highly, yet seemed in no haste to enjoy it. Dr. Franck had offered to send him on to safer quarters, but he had said, "No, thank yer, sir, not yet," and then had gone away to fall into one of those black moods of his, which began to disturb me, because I had no power to lighten them. As I sat listening to the clocks from the steeples all about us, I amused myself with planning Robert's future, as I often did my own, and had dealt out to him a generous hand of trumps wherewith to play this game of life which hitherto had gone so cruelly against him, when a harsh choked voice called,

"Lucy!"

It was the captain, and some new terror seemed to have gifted him with momentary strength.

"Yes, here's Lucy," I answered, hoping that by following the fancy I might quiet him,—for his face was damp with the clammy moisture, and his frame shaken with the nervous tremor that so often precedes death. His dull eye fixed upon me, dilating with a bewildered look of incredulity and wrath, till he broke out fiercely,

"That's a lie! she's dead,—and so's Bob, damn him!"

Finding speech a failure, I began to sing the quiet tune that had often soothed delirium like this; but hardly had the line,—

"See gentle patience smile on pain,"

passed my lips, when he clutched me by the wrist, whispering like one in mortal fear,

"Hush! she used to sing that way to Bob, but she never would to me. I swore I'd whip the devil out of her, and I did; but you know before she cut her throat she said she'd haunt me, and there she is!"

He pointed behind me with an aspect of such pale dismay, that I involuntarily glanced over my shoulder and started as if I had seen a veritable ghost; for, peering from the gloom of that inner room, I saw a shadowy face, with dark hair all about it, and a glimpse of scarlet at the throat. An instant showed me that it was only Robert leaning from his bed's foot, wrapped in a gray army-blanket, with his red shirt just visible above it, and his long hair disordered by sleep. But what a strange expression was on his face! The unmarred side was toward me, fixed and motionless as when I first observed it,—less absorbed now, but more intent. His eye glittered, his lips were apart like one who listened with every sense, and his whole aspect reminded me of a hound to which some wind had brought the scent of unsuspected prey.

"Do you know him, Robert? Does he mean you?"

"Laws, no, Missis; they all own half-a-dozen Bobs: but hearin' my name woke me; that's all."

He spoke quite naturally, and lay down again, while I returned to my charge, thinking that this paroxysm was probably his last. But by another hour I perceived a hopeful change; for the tremor had subsided, the cold dew was gone, his breathing was more regular, and Sleep, the healer, had descended to save or take him gently away. Doctor Franck looked in at midnight, bade me keep all cool and quiet, and not fail to administer a certain draught as soon as the captain woke. Very much relieved, I laid my head on my arms, uncomfortably folded on the little table, and fancied I was about to perform one of the feats which practice renders possible, "sleeping with one eye open," as we say, a half-and-half doze, for all senses sleep but that of hearing; the faintest murmur, sigh, or motion will break it, and give one back one's wits much brightened by the brief permission to "stand at ease." On this night the experiment was a failure, for previous vigils, confinement, and much care had rendered naps a dangerous indulgence. Having roused half-a-dozen times in an hour to find all quiet, I dropped my heavy head on my arms, and, drowsily resolving to look up again in fifteen minutes, fell fast asleep.

The striking of deep-voiced clock awoke me with a start. "That is one," thought I; but to my dismay, two more strokes followed, and in remorseful haste I sprang up to see what harm my long oblivion had done. A strong hand put me back into my seat, and held me there. It was Robert. The instant my eye met his my heart began to beat, and all along my nerves tingled that electric flash which foretells a danger that we cannot see. He was very pale, his mouth grim, and both eyes full of sombre fire; for even the wounded one was open now, all the more sinister for the deep scar above and below. But his touch was steady, his voice quiet, as he said, "Sit still, Missis; I won't hurt yer, nor scare yer, ef I can help it, but yer waked too soon."

"Let me go, Robert,—the captain is stirring,—I must give him something."

"No, Missis, yer can't stir an inch. Look here!"

Holding me with one hand, with the other he took up the glass in which I had left the draught, and showed me it was empty.

"Has he taken it?" I asked, more and more bewildered.

"I flung it out o' winder, Missis; he'll have to do without."

"But why, Robert? why did you do it?"

"'Kase I hate him!"

Impossible to doubt the truth of that; his whole face showed it, as he spoke through his set teeth, and launched a fiery glance at the unconscious captain. I could only hold my breath and stare blankly at him, wondering what mad act was coming next. I suppose I shook and turned white, as women have a foolish habit of doing when sudden danger daunts them; for Robert released my arm, sat down upon the bedside just in front of me, and said, with the ominous quietude that made me cold to see and hear,

"Don't yer be frightened, Missis; don't try to run away, fer the door's locked and the key in my pocket; don't yer cry out, fer yer'd have to scream a long while, with my hand on yer mouth, 'efore yer was heard. Be still, an' I'll tell yer what I'm gwine to do."

"Lord help us! he has taken the fever in some sudden, violent way, and is out of his head. I must humor him till some one comes"; in pursuance of which swift determination, I tried to say, quite composedly,

"I will be still and hear you; but open the window. Why did you shut it?"

"I'm sorry I can't do it, Missis; but yer'd jump out, or call, if I did, an' I'm not ready yet. I shut it to make yer sleep, an' heat would do it quicker'n anything else I could do."

The captain moved, and feebly muttered "Water!" Instinctively I rose to give it to him, but the heavy hand came down upon my shoulder, and in the same decided tone Robert said,

"The water went with the physic; let him call."

"Do let me go to him! he'll die without care!"

"I mean he shall; don't yer meddle, if yer please, Missis."

In spite of his quiet tone and respectful manner, I saw murder in his eyes, and turned faint with fear; yet the fear excited me, and, hardly knowing what I did, I seized the hands that had seized me, crying,

"No, no; you shall not kill him! It is base to hurt a helpless man. Why do you hate him? He is not your master."

"He's my brother."

I felt that answer from head to foot, and seemed to fathom what was coming, with a prescience vague, but unmistakable. One appeal was left to me, and I made it.

"Robert, tell me what it means? Do not commit a crime and make me accessory to it. There is a better way of righting wrong than by violence;—let me help you find it."

My voice trembled as I spoke, and I heard the frightened flutter of my heart; so did he, and if any little act of mine had ever won affection or respect from him, the memory of it served me then. He looked down, and seemed to put some question to himself; whatever it was, the answer was in my favor, for when his eyes rose again, they were gloomy, but not desperate.

"I *will* tell yer, Missis; but mind, this makes no difference; the boy is mine. I'll give the Lord a chance to take him fust: if He don't, I shall."

"Oh, no! remember he is your brother."

An unwise speech; I felt it as it passed my lips, for a black frown gathered on Robert's face, and his strong hands closed with an ugly sort of grip. But he did not touch the poor soul gasping there behind him, and seemed content to let the slow suffocation of that stifling room end his frail life. "I'm not like to forget dat, Missis, when I've been thinkin' of it all this week. I knew him when they fetched him in, an' would 'a' done it long 'fore this, but I wanted to ask where Lucy was; he knows,—he told to-night,—an' now he's done for."

"Who is Lucy?" I asked hurriedly, intent on keeping his mind busy with any thought but murder.

With one of the swift transitions of a mixed temperament like this, at my question Robert's deep eyes filled, the clenched hands were spread before his face, and all I heard were the broken words,

"My wife,—he took her—"

In that instant every thought of fear was swallowed up in burning indignation for the wrong, and a perfect passion of pity for the desperate man so tempted to avenge an injury for which there seemed no redress but this. He was no longer slave or contraband, no drop of black blood marred him in my sight, but an infinite compassion yearned to save, to help, to comfort him. Words seemed so powerless I offered none, only put my hand on his poor head, wounded, homeless, bowed down with grief for which I had no cure, and softly smoothed the long, neglected hair, pitifully wondering the while where was the wife who must have loved this tenderhearted man so well.

The captain moaned again, and faintly whispered, "Air!" but I never stirred. God forgive me! just then I hated him as only a woman thinking of a sister woman's wrong could hate. Robert looked up; his eyes were dry again, his mouth grim. I saw that, said, "Tell me more," and he did; for sympathy is a gift the poorest may give, the proudest stoop to receive.

"Yer see, Missis, his father,—I might say ours, ef I warn't ashamed of both of 'em,—his father died two years ago, an' left us all to Marster Ned,—that's him here, eighteen then. He always hated me, I looked so like old Marster: he don't,—only the light skin an' hair. Old Marster was kind to all of us, me 'specially, an' bought Lucy off the next plantation down there in South Carolina, when he found I liked her. I married her, all I could; it warn't much, but we was true to one another till Marster Ned come home a year after an' made hell fer both of us. He sent my old mother to be used up in his rice-swamp in Georgy; he found me with my pretty Lucy, an' though young Miss cried, an' I prayed to him on my knees, an' Lucy run away, he wouldn't have no mercy; he brought her back, an'—took her."

"Oh, what did you do?" I cried, hot with helpless pain and passion.

How the man's outraged heart sent the blood flaming up into his face and deepened the tones of his impetuous voice, as he stretched his arm across the bed, saying, with a terribly expressive gesture,—

"I half murdered him, an' to-night I'll finish."

"Yes, yes—but go on now; what came next?"

He gave me a look that showed no white man could have felt a deeper degradation in remembering and confessing these last acts of brotherly oppression.

"They whipped me till I couldn't stand, an' then they sold me further South. Yer thought I was a white man once,—look here!"

With a sudden wrench he tore the shirt from neck to waist, and on his strong, brown shoulders showed me furrows deeply ploughed, wounds which, though healed, were ghastlier to me than any in that house. I could not speak to him, and, with the pathetic dignity a great grief lends the humblest sufferer, he ended his brief tragedy by simply saying,

"That's all, Missis. I'se never seen her since, an' now I never shall in this world,—maybe not in t'other."

"But, Robert, why think her dead? The captain was wandering when he said those sad things; perhaps he will retract them when he is sane. Don't despair; don't give up yet."

"No, Missis, I 'spect he's right; she was too proud to bear that long. It's like her to kill herself. I told her to, if there was no other way; an' she always minded me, Lucy did. My poor girl! Oh, it warn't right! No, by God, it warn't!"

As the memory of this bitter wrong, this double bereavement, burned in his sore heart, the devil that lurks in every strong man's blood leaped up; he put his hand upon his brother's throat, and, watching the white face before him, muttered low between his teeth,

"I'm lettin' him go too easy; there' no pain in this; we a'n't even yet. I wish he knew me. Marster Ned! it's Bob; where's Lucy?"

From the captain's lips there came a long faint sigh, and nothing but a flutter of the eyelids showed that he still lived. A strange stillness filled the room as the elder brother held the younger's life suspended in his hand, while wavering between a dim hope and a deadly hate. In the whirl of thoughts that went on in my brain, only one was clear enough to act upon. I must prevent murder, if I could,—but how? What could I do up there alone, locked in with a dying man and a lunatic?—for any mind yielded utterly to any unrighteous impulse is mad while the impulse rules it. Strength I had not, nor much courage, neither time nor will for stratagem, and chance only could bring me help before it was too late. But one weapon I possesed,—a tongue,—often a woman's best defence; and sympathy, stronger than fear, gave me power to use it. What I said Heaven only knows, but surely Heaven helped me; words burned on my lips, tears streamed from my eyes, and some good angel prompted me to use the one name that had power to arrest my hearer's hand and touch his heart. For at that moment I heartily believed that Lucy lived, and this earnest faith roused in him a like belief.

He listened with the lowering look of one in whom brute instinct was sovereign for the time,—a look that makes the noblest countenance base. He was but a man,—a poor, untaught, outcast, outraged man. Life had few joys for him; the world offered him no honors, no success, no home, no love. What future would this crime mar? and why should he deny himself that sweet, yet bitter morsel called revenge? How many white men, with all New England's freedom, culture, Christianity, would not have felt as he felt then? Should I have reproached him for a human anguish, a human longing for redress, all now left him from the ruin of his few poor hopes? Who had taught him that self-control, self-sacrifice, are attributes that make men masters of the earth, and lift them nearer heaven? Should I have urged the beauty of forgiveness, the duty of devout submission? He had no religion, for he was no saintly "Uncle Tom," and Slavery's black shadow seemed to darken all the world to him, and shut out God. Should I have warned him of penalties, of judgments, and the potency of law? What did he know of justice, or the mercy that should temper that stern virtue, when every law, human and divine, had been broken on his hearthstone? Should I have tried to touch him by appeals to filial duty, to brotherly love? How had his appeals been answered? What memories had father and brother stored up in his heart to plead for either now? No,—all these influences, these associations, would have proved worse than useless, had I been calm enough to try them. I was not; but instinct, subtler than reason, showed me the one safe clue by which to lead this troubled soul from the labyrinth in which it groped and nearly fell. When I paused, breathless, Robert turned to me, asking, as if human assurances could strengthen his faith in Divine Omnipotence,

"Do you believe, if I let Marster Ned live, the Lord will give me back my Lucy?"

"As surely as there is a Lord, you will find her here or in the beautiful hereafter, where there is no black or white, no master and no slave."

He took his hand from his brother's throat, lifted his eyes from my face to the wintry sky beyond, as if searching for that blessed country, happier even than the happy North. Alas, it was the darkest hour before the dawn!—there was no star above, no light below but the pale glimmer of the lamp that showed the brother who had made him desolate. Like a blind man who believes there is a sun, yet cannot see it, he shook his head, let his arms drop nervelessly upon his knees, and sat there dumbly asking that question which many a soul whose faith is firmer fixed than his has asked in hours less dark than this,—"Where is God?" I saw the tide had turned, and strenuously tried to keep this rudderless life-boat from slipping back into the whirlpool wherein it had been so nearly lost.

"I have listened to you, Robert; now hear me, and heed what I say, because my heart is full of pity for you, full of hope for your future, and a desire to help you now. I want you to go away from here, from the temptation of this place, and the sad thoughts that haunt it. You have conquered yourself once, and I honor you for it, because, the harder the battle, the more glorious the victory; but it is safer to put a greater distance between you and this man. I will write you letters, give you money, and send you to good old Massachusetts to begin your new life a freeman,—yes, and a happy man; for when the captain is himself again, I will learn where Lucy is, and move heaven and earth to find and give her back to you. Will you do this, Robert?"

Slowly, very slowly, the answer came; for the purpose of a week, perhaps a year, was hard to relinquish in an hour.

"Yes, Missis, I will."

"Good! Now you are the man I thought you, and I'll work for you with all my heart. You need sleep, my poor fellow; go, and try to forget. The captain is alive, and as yet you are spared that sin. No, don't look there; I'll care for him. Come, Robert, for Lucy's sake."

Thank Heaven for the immortality of love! for when all other means of salvation failed, a spark of this vital fire softened the man's iron will, until a woman's hand could bend it. He let me take from him the key, let me draw him gently away, and lead him to the solitude which now was the most healing balm I could bestow. Once in his little room, he fell down on his bed and lay there, as if spent with the sharpest conflict of his life. I slipped the bolt across his door, and unlocked my own, flung up the window, steadied myself with a breath of air, then rushed to Doctor Franck. He came; and till dawn we worked together, saving one brother's life, and taking earnest thought how best to secure the other's liberty. When the sun came up as blithely as if it shone only upon happy homes, the Doctor went to Robert. For an hour I heard the murmur of their voices; once I caught the sound of heavy sobs, and for a time a reverent hush, as if in the silence that good man were ministering to soul as well as body. When he departed he took Robert with him, pausing to tell me he should get him off as soon as possible, but not before we met again.

Nothing more was seen of them all day; another surgeon came to see the captain, and another attendant came to fill the empty place. I tried to rest, but could not, with the thought of poor Lucy tugging at my heart, and was soon back at my post again, anxiously hoping that my contraband had not been too hastily spirited away. Just as night fell there came a tap, and, opening, I saw Robert literally "clothed, and in his right mind." The Doctor had replaced the ragged suit with tidy garments, and no trace of the tempestuous night remained but deeper lines upon the forehead, and the docile look of a repentant child. He did not cross the threshold, did not offer me his hand,—only took off his cap, saying, with a traitorous falter in his voice,

"God bless yer, Missis! I'm gwine."

I put out both my hands, and held his fast.

"Good-by, Robert! Keep up good heart, and when I come home to Massachusetts we'll meet in a happier place than this. Are you quite ready, quite comfortable for your journey?"

"Yes, Missis, yes; the Doctor's fixed everything! I'se gwine with a friend of his; my papers are all right, an' I'm as happy as I can be till I find"—

He stopped there; then went on, with a glance into the room,—

"I'm glad I didn't do it, an' I thank yer, Missis, fer hinderin' me—thank yer hearty; but I'm afraid I hate him jest the same."

Of course he did; and so did I; for these faulty hearts of ours cannot turn perfect in a night, but need frost and fire, wind and rain, to ripen and make them ready for the great harvest-home. Wishing to divert his mind, I put my poor mite into his hand, and, remembering the magic of a certain little book, I gave him mine, on whose dark cover whitely shone the Virgin Mother and the Child, the grand history of whose life the book contained. The money went into Robert's pocket with a grateful murmur, the book into his bosom, with a long look and a tremulous—

"I never saw *my* baby, Missis."

I broke down then; and though my eyes were too dim to see, I felt the touch of lips upon my hands, heard the sound of departing feet, and knew my contraband was gone.

WHEN ONE FEELS AN INTENSE DISLIKE, the less one says about the subject of it the better; therefore I shall merely record that the captain lived,—in time was exchanged; and that, whoever the other party was, I am convinced the Government got the best of the bargain. But long before this occurred, I had fulfilled my promise to Robert; for as soon as my patient recovered strength of memory enough to make his answer trustworthy, I asked, without any circumlocution,

"Captain Fairfax, where is Lucy?"

And too feeble to be angry, surprised, or insincere, he straightway answered,

"Dead, Miss Dane."

"And she killed herself when you sold Bob?"

"How the devil did you know that?" he muttered, with an expression half-remorseful, half-amazed; but I was satisfied, and said no more.

Of course this went to Robert, waiting far away there in a lonely home,—waiting, working, hoping for his Lucy. It almost broke my heart to do it; but delay was weak, deceit was wicked; so I sent the heavy tidings, and very soon the answer came,—only three lines; but I felt that the sustaining power of the man's life was gone.

"I thought I'd never see her any more; I'm glad to know she's out of trouble. I thank yer, Missis; an' if they let us, I'll fight fer yer till I'm killed, which I hope will be 'fore long."

Six months later he had his wish, and kept his word.

Every one knows the story of the attack on Fort Wagner; but we should not tire yet of recalling how our Fifty-Fourth, spent with three sleepless nights, a day's fast, and a march under the July sun, stormed the fort as night fell, facing death in many shapes, following their brave leaders through a fiery rain of shot and shell, fighting valiantly for "God and Governor Andrew,"—how the regiment that went into action seven hundred strong, came out having had nearly half its number captured, killed, or wounded, leaving their young commander to be buried, like a chief of earlier times, with his body-guard around him, faithful to the death. Surely, the insult turns to honor, and the wide grave needs no monument but the heroism that consecrates it in our sight; surely, the hearts that held him nearest, see through their tears a noble victory in the seeming sad defeat; and surely, God's benediction was bestowed, when this loyal soul answered, as Death called the roll, "Lord, here am I, with the brothers Thou hast given me!"

The future must show how well that fight was fought; for though Fort Wagner once defied us, public prejudice is down; and through the cannon-smoke of that black night, the manhood of the colored race shines before many eyes that would not see, rings in many ears that would not hear, wins many hearts that would not hitherto believe.

When the news came that we were needed, there was none so glad as I to leave teaching contrabands, the new work I had taken up, and go to nurse "our boys," as my dusky flock so proudly called the wounded of the Fifty-Fourth. Feeling more satisfaction, as I assumed my big apron and turned up my cuffs, than if dressing for the President's levee, I fell to work in Hospital No. 10 at Beaufort. The scene was most familiar, and yet strange; for only dark faces looked up at me from the pallets so thickly laid along the floor, and I missed the sharp accent of my Yankee boys in the slower, softer voices calling cheerily to one another, or answering my questions with a stout, "We'll never give it up, Missis, till the last Reb's dead," or, "If our people's free, we can afford to die."

Passing from bed to bed, intent on making one pair of hands do the work of three, at least, I gradually washed, fed, and bandaged my way down the long line of sable heroes, and coming to the very last, found that he was my contraband. So old, so worn, so deathly weak and wan, I never should have known him but for the deep scar on his cheek. That side lay uppermost, and caught my eye at once; but even then I doubted, such an awful change had come upon him, when, turning to the ticket just above his head, I saw the name, "Robert Dane." That both assured and touched me, for, remembering that he had no name, I knew that he had taken mine. I longed for him to speak to me, to tell how he had fared since I lost sight of him, and let me perform some little service for him in return for many he had done for me; but he seemed asleep; and as I stood re-living that strange night again, a bright lad, who lay next him softly waving an old fan across both beds, looked up and said,

"I guess you know him, Missis?"

"You are right. Do you?"

"As much as any one was able to, Missis."

"Why do you say 'was,' as if the man were dead and gone?"

"I s'pose because I know he'll have to go. He's got a bad jab in the breast, an' is bleedin' inside, the Doctor says. He don't suffer any, only gets weaker 'n' weaker every minute. I've been fannin' him this long while, an' he's talked a little; but he don't know me now, so he's most gone, I guess."

There was so much sorrow and affection in the boy's face, that I remembered something, and asked, with redoubled interest,—

"Are you the one that brought him off? I was told about a boy who nearly lost his life in saving that of his mate."

I dare say the young fellow blushed, as any modest lad might have done; I could not see it, but I heard the chuckle of satisfaction that escaped him, as he glanced from his shattered arm and bandaged side to the pale figure opposite.

"Lord, Missis, that's nothin'; we boys always stan' by one another, an' I warn't goin' to leave him to be tormented any more by them cussed Rebs. He's been a slave once, though he don't look half so much like it as me, an' I was born in Boston."

He did not; for the speaker was as black as the ace of spades,—being a sturdy specimen, the knave of clubs would perhaps be a fitter representative,—but the dark freeman looked at the white slave with the pitiful, yet puzzled expression

I have so often seen on the faces of our wisest men, when this tangled question of Slavery presented itself, asking to be cut or patiently undone.

"Tell me what you know of this man; for, even if he were awake, he is too weak to talk."

"I never saw him till I joined the regiment, an' no one 'peared to have got much out of him. He was a shut-up sort of feller, an' didn't seem to care for anything but gettin' at the Rebs. Some say he was the fust man of us that enlisted; I know he fretted till we were off, an' when we pitched into Old Wagner, he fought like the devil."

"Were you with him when he was wounded? How was it?"

"Yes, Missis. There was somethin' queer about it; for he 'peared to know the chap that killed him, an' the chap knew him. I don't dare to ask, but I rather guess one owned the other some time; for, when they clinched, the chap sung out, 'Bob!' an' Dane, 'Marster Ned!'—then they went at it."

I sat down suddenly, for the old anger and compassion struggled in my heart, and I both longed and feared to hear what was to follow.

"You see, when the Colonel,—Lord keep an' send him back to us!—it a'n't certain yet, you know, Missis, though it's two days ago we lost him,—well, when the Colonel shouted, 'Rush on, boys, rush on!' Dane tore away as if he was goin' to take the fort alone; I was next him, an' kept close as we went through the ditch an' up the wall. Hi! warn't that a rusher!" and the boy flung up his well arm with a whoop, as if the mere memory of that stirring moment came over him in a gust of irrepressible excitement.

"Were you afraid?" I said, asking the question women often put, and receiving the answer they seldom fail to get.

"No, Missis!"—emphasis on the "Missis"—"I never thought of anything but the damn' Rebs, that scalp, slash, an' cut our ears off, when they git us. I was bound to let daylight into one of 'em at least, an' I did. Hope he liked it!"

"It is evident that you did. Now go on about Robert, for I should be at work."

"He was one of the fust up; I was just behind, an' though the whole thing happened in a minute, I remember how it was, for all I was yellin' an' knockin' round like mad. Just where we were, some sort of an officer was wavin' his sword an' cheerin' on his men; Dane saw him by a big flash that come by; he flung away his gun, give a leap, an' went at that feller as if he was Jeff,

Beauregard, an' Lee, all in one. I scrabbled after as quick as I could, but was only up in time to see him git the sword straight through him an' drop into the ditch. You needn't ask what I did next, Missis, for I don't quite know myself; all I'm clear about is, that I managed somehow to pitch that Reb into the fort as dead as Moses, git hold of Dane, an' bring him off. Poor old feller! we said we went in to live or die; he said he went in to die, an' he's done it."

I had been intently watching the excited speaker; but as he regretfully added those last words I turned again, and Robert's eyes met mine,—those melancholy eyes, so full of an intelligence that proved he had heard, remembered, and reflected with that preternatural power which often outlives all other faculties. He knew me, yet gave no greeting; was glad to see a woman's face, yet had no smile wherewith to welcome it; felt that he was dying, yet uttered no farewell. He was too far across the river to return or linger now; departing thought, strength, breath, were spent in one grateful look, one murmur of submission to the last pang he could ever feel. His lips moved, and, bending to them, a whisper chilled my cheek, as it shaped the broken words,

"I'd 'a' done it,—but it's better so,—I'm satisfied."

Ah! well he might be,—for, as he turned his face from the shadow of the life that was, the sunshine of the life to be touched it with a beautiful content, and in the drawing of a breath my contraband found wife and home, eternal liberty and God.

On Picket Duty

"WHAT AIR YOU THINKIN' OF, PHIL?"

"My wife, Dick."

"So was I! Aint it odd how fellers fall to thinkin' of thar little women, when they get a quiet spell like this?"

"Fortunate for us that we do get it, and have such gentle bosom guests to keep us brave and honest through the trials and temptations of a life like ours."

October moonlight shone clearly on the solitary tree, draped with gray moss, scarred by lightning and warped by wind, looking like a venerable warrior, whose long campaign was nearly done; and underneath was posted the guard of four. Behind them twinkled many camp-fires on a distant plain, before them wound a road ploughed by the passage of an army, strewn with the relics of a rout. On the right, a sluggish river glided, like a serpent, stealthy, sinuous, and dark, into a seemingly impervious jungle; on the left, a Southern swamp filled the air with malarial damps, swarms of noisome life, and discordant sounds that robbed the hour of its repose. The men were friends as well as comrades, for though gathered from the four quarters of the Union, and dissimilar in education, character, and tastes, the same spirit animated all; the routine of camp life threw them much together, and mutual esteem soon grew into a bond of mutual good fellowship.

Thorn was a Massachusetts volunteer; a man who seemed too early old, too early embittered by some cross, for though grim of countenance, rough of speech, cold of manner, a keen observer would have soon discovered traces of a deeper, warmer nature hidden behind the repellent front he turned upon the world. A true New Englander, thoughtful, acute, reticent, and opinionated;

On Picket Duty was first published in December 1863.

yet earnest withal, intensely patriotic, and often humorous, despite a touch of Puritan austerity.

Phil, the "romantic chap," as he was called, looked his character to the life. Slender, swarthy, melancholy eyed, and darkly bearded; with feminine features, mellow voice, and alternately languid or vivacious manners. A child of the South in nature as in aspect, ardent, impressible, and proud; fitfully aspiring and despairing; without the native energy which moulds character and ennobles life. Months of discipline and devotion had done much for him, and some deep experience was fast ripening the youth into a man.

Flint, the long-limbed lumberman, from the wilds of Maine, was a conscript who, when government demanded his money or his life, calculated the cost, and decided that the cash would be a dead loss and the claim might be repeated, whereas the conscript would get both pay and plunder out of government, while taking excellent care that government got precious little out of him. A shrewd, slow-spoken, self-reliant specimen, was Flint; yet something of the fresh flavor of the backwoods lingered in him still, as if Nature were loath to give him up, and left the mark of her motherly hand upon him, as she leaves it in a dry, pale lichen, on the bosom of the roughest stone.

Dick "hailed" from Illinois, and was a comely young fellow, full of dash and daring; rough and rowdy, generous and jolly, overflowing with spirits and ready for a free fight with all the world.

Silence followed the last words, while the friendly moon climbed up the sky. Each man's eye followed it, and each man's heart was busy with remembrances of other eyes and hearts that might be watching and wishing as theirs watched and wished. In the silence, each shaped for himself that vision of home that brightens so many campfires, haunts so many dreamers under canvas roofs, and keeps so many turbulent natures tender by memories which often are both solace and salvation.

Thorn paced to and fro, his rifle on his shoulder, vigilant and soldierly, however soft his heart might be. Phil leaned against the tree, one band in the breast of his blue jacket, on the painted presentment of the face his fancy was picturing in the golden circle of the moon. Flint lounged on the sward, whistling softly as he whittled at a fallen bough. Dick was flat on his back, heels in air, cigar in mouth, and some hilarious notion in his mind, for suddenly he broke into a laugh.

"What is it, lad?" asked Thorn, pausing in his tramp, as if willing to be drawn from the disturbing thought that made his black brows lower and his mouth look grim.

"Thinkin' of my wife, and wishin' she was here, bless her heart! set me rememberin' how I see her fust, and so I roared, as I always do when it comes into my head."

"How was it? Come, reel off a yarn and let's hear houw yeou hitched teams," said Flint, always glad to get information concerning his neighbors, if it could be cheaply done.

"Tellin' how we found our wives wouldn't be a bad game, would it, Phil?"

"I'm agreeable; but let us have your romance first."

"Devilish little of that about me or any of my doin's. I hate sentimental bosh as much as you hate slang, and should have been a bachelor to this day if I hadn't seen Kitty jest as I did. You see, I'd been too busy larkin' round to get time for marryin', till a couple of years ago, when I did up the job double-quick, as I'd like to do this thunderin' slow one, hang it all!"

"Halt a minute till I give a look, for this picket isn't going to be driven in or taken while I'm on guard."

Down his beat went Thorn, reconnoitring river, road, and swamp, as thoroughly as one pair of keen eyes could do it, and came back satisfied, but still growling like a faithful mastiff on the watch; performances which he repeated at intervals till his own turn came.

"I didn't have to go out of my own State for a wife, you'd better believe," began Dick, with a boast, as usual; "for we raise as fine a crop of girls thar as any State in or out of the Union, and don't mind raisin' Cain with any man who denies it. I was out on a gunnin' tramp with Joe Partridge, a cousin of mine,—poor old chap! he fired his last shot at Gettysburg, and died game in a way he didn't dream of the day we popped off the birds together. It ain't right to joke that way; I won't if I can help it; but a feller gets awfully kind of heathenish these times, don't he?"

"Settle up them scores byme-by; fightin' Christians is scurse raound here. Fire away, Dick."

"Well, we got as hungry as hounds half a dozen mile from home, and when a farm-house hove in sight, Joe said he'd ask for a bite and leave some of the plunder for pay. I was visitin' Joe, didn't know folks round, and backed out of the beggin' part of the job; so he went ahead alone. We'd come up the woods behind the house, and while Joe was foragin', I took are connoissance. The view was fust-rate, for the main part of it was a girl airin' beds on the roof of a stoop. Now, jest about that time, havin' a leisure spell, I'd begun to think of marryin', and took a look at all the girls I met, with an eye to business. I s'pose every man has some sort of an idee or pattern of the wife he wants; pretty and plucky, good and gay was mine, but I'd never found it till I see Kitty; and as she didn't see me, I had the advantage and took an extra long stare."

"What was her good pints, hey?"

"Oh, well, she had a wide-awake pair of eyes, a bright, jolly sort of a face, lots of curly hair tumblin' out of her net, a trig little figger, and a pair of the neatest feet and ankles that ever stepped. 'Pretty,' thinks I; 'so far so good.' The way she whacked the pillers, shooked the blankets, and pitched into the beds was a caution; specially one blunderin' old featherbed that wouldn't do nothin' but sag round in a pig-headed sort of way, that would have made most girls get mad and give up. Kitty didn't, but just wrastled with it like a good one, till she got it turned, banged, and spread to suit her; then she plumped down in the middle of it, with a sarcy little nod and chuckle to herself, that tickled me mightily. 'Plucky,' thinks I, 'better 'n' better.' Jest then an old woman came flyin' out the back-door, callin', 'Kitty! Kitty! Squire Partridge's son's here, 'long with a friend; been gunnin', want luncheon, and I'm all in the suds; do come down and see to 'em.'

"'Where are they?' says Kitty, scrambling up her hair and settlin' her gown in a jiffy, as women have a knack of doin', you know.

"'Mr. Joe's in the front entry; the other man's somewheres round, Billy says, waitin' till I send word whether they can stop. I darsn't till I'd seen you, for I can't do nothin', I'm in such a mess,' says the old lady.

"'So am I, for I can't get in except by the the entry window, and he'll see me,' says Kitty, gigglin' at the thoughts of Joe.

"'Come down the ladder, there's a dear. I'll pull it round and keep it stiddy,' says her mother.

"'Oh, ma, don't ask me!' says Kitty, with a shiver. 'I'm dreadfully seared of ladders since I broke my arm off this very one. It's so high, it makes me dizzy jest to think of.'

"'Well, then, I'll do the best I can; but I wish them boys was to Jericho!' says the old lady, with a groan, for she was fat and hot, had her gown pinned up, and was in a fluster generally. She was goin' off rather huffy, when Kitty called out,—

"'Stop, ma! I'll come down and help you, only ketch me if I tumble.'

"She looked scared but stiddy, and I'll bet it took as much grit for her to do it as for one of us to face a battery. It don't seem much to tell of, but I wish I may be hit if it wasn't a right down dutiful and clever thing to see done. When the old lady took her off at the bottom, with a good motherly hug, I found myself huggin' my rifle like a fool, but whether I thought it was the ladder, or Kitty, I ain't clear about. 'Good,' thinks I; 'what more do you want?'

"A snug little property wouldn't a ben bad, I reckon. Well she had it, old skin-flint, though I didn't know or care about it then. What a jolly row she'd make if she knew I was tellin' the ladder part of the story! She always does when I get to it, and makes believe cry, with her head in my breast-pocket, or any such bandy place, till I take it out and swear I'll never do so ag'in. Poor little Kit, I wonder what she's doin' now. Thinkin' of me, I'll bet."

Dick paused, pitched his cap lower over his eyes, and smoked a minute with more energy than enjoyment, for his cigar was out and he did not perceive it.

"That's not all, is it?" asked Thorn, taking a fatherly interest in the younger man's love passages.

"Not quite. 'Fore long, Joe whistled, and as I always take short cuts everywhar, I put in at the back-door, jest as Kitty come trottin' out of the pantry with a big berry-pie in her hand. I startled her, she tripped over the sill and down she come; the dish flew one way, the pie flopped into her lap, the juice spatterin' my boots and her clean gown. I thought she'd cry, scold, have hysterics, or some confounded thing or other; but she jest sat still a minute, then looked up at me with a great blue splosh on her face, and went off into the good-naturedest gale of laughin' you ever heard in your life. That finished me. 'Gay.' thinks I; 'go in and win.' So I did; made love hand over hand, while I stayed with Joe; pupposed a fortnight after, married her in three months, and there she is, a tip-top little woman, with a pair of stunnin' boys in her arms!"

Out came a well-worn case, and Dick proudly displayed the likeness of a stout, much bejewelled young woman, with two staring infants on her knee. In his sight, the poor picture was a more perfect work of art than any of Sir Joshua's baby-beauties, or Raphael's Madonnas, and the little story needed no letter sequel than the young father's praises of his twins, the covert kiss he gave their mother when he turned as if to get a clearer light upon the face. Ashamed to show the tenderness that filled his honest heart, he hummed "Kingdom Coming," while relighting his cigar, and presently began to talk again.

"Now, then, Flint, it's your turn to keep guard, and Thorn's to tell his romance. Come, don't try to shirk; it does a man good to talk of such things, and we're all mates here."

"In some cases it don't do any good to talk of such things; better let 'em alone," muttered Thorn, as he reluctantly sat down, while Flint as reluctantly departed.

With a glance and gesture of real affection, Phil laid his hand upon his comrade's knee, saying, in his persuasive voice, "Old fellow, it *will* do you good, because I know you often long to speak of something that weighs upon you. You've kept us steady many a time, and done us no end of kindnesses; why be too proud to let us give our sympathy in return, if nothing more?"

Thorn's big hand closed over the slender one upon his knee, and the mild expression, so rarely seen upon his face, passed over it as he replied, "I think I could tell you almost anything if you asked me that way, my boy. It isn't that I'm too proud,—and you're right about my sometimes wanting to free my mind,—but it's because a man of forty don't just like to open out to young fellows, if there is any danger of their laughing at him, though he may deserve it. I guess there isn't now, and I'll tell you how I found my wife."

Dick sat up, and Phil drew nearer, for the earnestness that was in the man dignified his plain speech, and inspired an interest in his history, even before it was begun. Looking gravely at the river and never at his hearers, as if still a little shy of confidants, yet grateful for the relief of words, Thorn began abruptly, "I never hear the number eighty-four without clapping my band to my left breast and missing my badge. You know I was on the police in New York, before the war, and that's about all you do know yet. One bitter cold night, I was going my rounds for the last time, when, as I turned a corner, I saw there was a trifle of work to be done. It was a bad part of the city, full of dirt and deviltry; one of the streets led to a ferry, and at the corner an old woman had an apple-stall. The poor soul had dropped asleep, word out with the cold, and there were her goods left, with no one to watch 'em. Somebody was watching 'em, however; a girl, with a ragged shawl over her head, stood at the mouth of an alley close by, waiting for a chance to grab something. I'd seen her there when I went by before, and mistrusted she was up to some mischief; as I turned the corner, she put out her hand and cribbed an apple. She saw me the minute she did it, but neither dropped it nor ran, only stood stock still with the apple in her hand till came up.

"'This won't do, my girl,' said I. I never could be harsh with 'em, poor things! She laid it back and looked up at me with a miserable sort of a smile, that made me put my hand in my pocket to fish for a ninepence before she spoke.

"'I know it won't,' she says. 'I didn't—want to do it, it's so mean, but I'm awful hungry, sir.'

"'Better run home and get your supper then.'

"'I've got no home.'

"'Where do you live?'

"'In the street.'

"'Where do you sleep?'

"'Anywhere; last night in the lock-up, and I thought I'd get in there again, if I did that when you saw me. I like to go there, it's warm and safe.'

"'If I don't take you there, what will you do?'

"'Don't know. I want to go over there and dance again, as I used to; but being sick has made me ugly, so they won't have me, and no one else will take me because I have been there once.'

"I looked where she pointed, and thanked the Lord that they wouldn't take her. It was one of those low theatres that do so much damage to the like of her; there was a gambling den one side of it, an eating saloon the other, and at the door of it lounged a scamp I knew very well, looking like a big spider watching for a fly. I longed to fling my billy at him; but as I couldn't, I held on to the girl. I was new to the thing then, but though I'd heard about hunger and homelessness often enough, I'd never had this sort of thing, nor seen that look on a girl's face. A white, pinched face hers was, with frightened, tired-looking eyes, but so innocent; she wasn't more than sixteen, had been pretty once I saw, looked sick and starved now, and seemed just the most helpless, hopeless little thing that ever was.

"'You'd better come to the Station for to-night, and we'll see to you to-morrow,' says I.

"'Thank you, sir,' says she, looking as grateful as if I'd asked her home. I suppose I did speak kind of fatherly. I ain't ashamed to say I felt so, seeing what a child she was; nor to own that when she put her little hand in mine, it hurt me to feel how thin and cold it was. We passed the eatinghouse where the red lights made her face as rosy as it ought to have been; there was meat and pies in the window, and the poor thing stopped to look. It was too much for her; off came her shawl, and she said in that coaxing way of hers, "'I wish you'd let me stop at the place close by and sell this; they'll give a little for it, and I'll get some supper. I've had nothing since yesterday morning, and maybe cold is easier to bear than hunger.'

"'Have you nothing better than that to sell?' I says, not quite sure that she wasn't all a humbug, like so many of 'em. She seemed to see that, and looked up at me again with such innocent eyes, I couldn't doubt her when she said, shivering with something beside the cold, "'Nothing but myself.' Then the tears came, and she laid her head down on my arm, sobbing, — 'Keep me! oh, do keep me safe somewhere!'"

Thorn choked here, steadied his voice with a resolute hem! but could only add one sentence more:

"That's how I found my wife."

"Come, don't stop thar? I told the whole o' mine, you do the same. Whar did you take her? how'd it all come round?" .

"Please tell us, Thorn."

The gentler request was answered presently, very steadily, very quietly.

"I was always a soft-hearted fellow, though you wouldn't think it now, and when that little girl asked me to keep her safe, I just did it. I took her to a good woman whom I knew, for I hadn't any women belonging to me, nor any place but that to put her in. She stayed there till spring working for her keep, growing brighter, prettier, every day, and fonder of me I thought. If I believed in witchcraft, I shouldn't think myself such a cursed fool as I do now, but I don't believe in it, and to this day I can't understand how I came to do it. To be sure I was a lonely man, without kith or kin, had never had a sweetheart in my life, or been much with women since my mother died. Maybe that's why I was so bewitched with Mary, for she had little ways with her that took your fancy and made you love her whether you would or no. I found her father was an honest fellow enough, a fiddler in some theatre, that he'd taken good care of Mary till he died, leaving precious little but advice for her to live on. She'd tried to get work, failed, spent all she had, got sick, and was going to the devil, as the poor souls can hardly help doing with so many ready to give them a shove. It's no use trying to make a bad job better; so the long and short of it was. I thought she loved me; God knows I loved her, and I married her before the year was out."

"Show us her picture; I know you've got one; all the fellows have, though half of 'em won't own up."

"I've only got part of one. I once saved my little girl, and her picture once saved me."

From an inner pocket Thorn produced a woman's housewife, carefully untied it, though all its implements were missing but a little thimble, and from one of its compartments took a flattened bullet and the remnants of a picture.

"I gave her that the first Christmas after I found her. She wasn't as tidy about her clothes as I liked to see, and I thought if I gave her a handy thing like this, she'd be willing to sew. But she only made one shirt for me, and then got tired, so I keep it like an old fool, as I am. Yes, that's the bit of lead that would have done for me, if Mary's likeness hadn't been just where it was."

"You'll like to show her this when you go home, won't you?" said Dick, as he took up the bullet, while Phil examined the marred picture, and Thorn poised the little thimble on his big finger, with a sigh.

"How can I, when I don't know where she is, and camp is all the home I've got?"

The words broke from him like a sudden cry, when some old wound is rudely touched. Both of the young men started, both laid back the relics they had taken up, and turned their eyes from Thorn's face, across which swept a look of shame and sorrow, too significant to be misunderstood. Their silence assured him of their sympathy, and, as if that touch of friendlessness unlocked his heavy heart, he eased it by a full confession. When he spoke again, it was with the calmness of repressed emotion; and calmness more touching to his mates than the most passionate outbreak, the most pathetic lamentation; for the coarse camp-phrases seemed to drop from his vocabulary; more than once his softened voice grew tremulous, and to the words "my little girl," there went a tenderness that proved how dear a place she still retained in that deep heart of his.

"Boys, I've gone so far; I may as well finish; and you'll see I'm not without some cause for my stern looks and ways; you'll pity me, and from you I'll take the comfort of it. It's only the old story,—I married her, worked for her, lived for her, and kept my little girl like a lady. I should have known that I was too old, too sober, for a young thing like that; the life she led before the pinch came just suited her. She liked to be admired, to dress and dance and make herself pretty for all the world to see; not to keep house for a quiet man like me. Idleness wasn't good for her, it bred discontent; then some of her old friends, who'd left her in her trouble, found her out when better times came round, and tried to get her back again. I was away all day, I didn't know how things were going, and she wasn't open with me, afraid, she said; I was so grave, and hated theatres so. She got courage, finally, to tell me that she wasn't happy; that she wanted to dance again, and asked me if she mightn't. I'd rather have had her ask me to put her in a fire, for I did hate theatres, and was bred to; others think they're no harm. I do; and knew it was a bad life for a girl like mine, It pampers vanity, and vanity is the Devil's help with such; so I said No, kindly at first, sharp and stern when she kept on teasing. That roused her spirit. 'I will go!' she said, one day. 'Not while you're my wife,' I answered back; and neither said any more, but she gave me a look I didn't think she could, and I resolved to take her away from temptation before worse came of it.

"I didn't tell her my plan; but I resigned my place, spent a week or more finding and fixing a little home for her out in the wholesome country, where she'd be safe from theatres and disreputable friends, and maybe learn to love me better when she saw how much she was to me. It was coming summer, and I made things look as home-like and as pretty as I could. She liked flowers, and I fixed a garden for her; she was fond of pets, and I got her a bird, a kitten, and a dog to play with her; she fancied gay colors and tasty little matters, so I filled her rooms with all the handsome things I could afford, and when it was done, I was as pleased as any boy, thinking what happy times we'd have together and how pleased she'd be. Boys, when I went to tell her and to take her to her little home, she was gone."

"Who with?"

"With those cursed friends of hers; a party of them left the city just then; she was wild to go; she had money now, and all her good looks back again. They teased and tempted her; I wasn't there to keep her, and she went, leaving a line behind to tell me that she loved the old life more than the new; that my house was a prison, and she hoped I'd let her go in peace. That almost killed me; but I managed to bear it, for I knew most of the fault was mine; but it was awful bitter to think I hadn't saved her, after all."

"Oh, Thorn! what did you do?"

"Went straight after her; found her dancing in Philadelphia, with paint on her cheeks, trinkets on her neck and arms, looking prettier than ever; but the innocent eyes were gone, and I couldn't see my little girl in the bold, handsome woman twirling there before the footlights. She saw me, looked seared at first, then smiled, and danced on with her eyes upon me, as if she said,—

"'See! I'm happy now; go away and let me be.'

"I couldn't stand that, and got out somehow. People thought me mad, or drunk; I didn't care, I only wanted to see her once in quiet and try to get her home. I couldn't do it then nor afterwards by fair means, and I wouldn't try force. I wrote to her, promised to forgive her, begged her to come back, or let me keep her honestly somewhere away from me. But she never answered, never came, and I have never tried again."

"She wasn't worthy of you, Thorn; you jest forget her."

"I wish I could! I wish I could! "in his voice quivered an almost passionate regret, and a great sob heaved his chest, as be turned his face away to hide the love and longing, still so tender and so strong.

"Don't say that, Dick; such fidelity should make us charitable for its own sake. There is always time for penitence, always certainty of pardon. Take heart, Thorn, you may not wait in vain, and she may yet return to you."

"I know she will! I've dreamed of it, I've prayed for it; every battle I come out of safe makes me surer that I was kept for that, and when I've borne enough to atone for my part of the fault, I'll be repaid for all my patience, all my pain, by finding her again. She knows how well I love her still, and if there comes a time when she is sick and poor and all alone again, then she'll remember her old John, then she'll come home and let me take her in."

Hope shone in Thorn's melancholy eyes, and long-suffering all-forgiving love beautified the rough, brown face, as he folded his arms and bent his gray head on his breast, as if the wanderer were already come.

The emotion which Dick scorned to show on his own account was freely manifested for another, as he sniffed audibly, and, boy-like, drew his sleeve across his eyes. But Phil, with the delicate perception of a finer nature, felt that the truest kindness he could show his friend was to distract his thoughts from himself, to spare him any comments, and lessen the embarrassment which would surely follow such unwonted confidence.

"Now I'll relieve Flint, and he will give you a laugh. Come on Hiram and tell us about your Beulah."

The gentleman addressed had performed his duty by sitting on a fence and "righting up" his pockets, to beguile the tedium of his exile. Before his multitudinous possessions could be restored to their native sphere, Thorn was himself again, and on his feet.

"Stay where you are Phil; I like to tramp, it seems like old times, and I know you're tired. Just forget all this I've been saying, and go on as before. Thank you, boys! thank you!" and with a grasp of the two hands extended to him, he strode away along the path already worn by his own restless feet.

"It's done him good, and I'm glad of that; but I'd like to see the little baggage that bewitched the poor old boy, wouldn't you, Phil? "

"Hush! here's Flint."

"What's up naow? want me tow address the meetin', hey? I'm willin', only the laugh's ruther ag'inst me, ef I tell that story; expect you'll like it all the better for that." Flint coiled up his long limbs, put his hands in his pockets, chewed meditatively for a moment, and then began with his slowest drawl:—

"Waal, sir, it's pretty nigh ten year ago, I was damster daown tew Oldtaown, clos't tew Banggore. My folks lived tew Bethel; there was only the old man, and Aunt Sloam, keepin' house for him, seein' as I was the only chick he hed. I hedn't heared from 'em for a long spell, when there come a letter sayin' the old man was breakin' up. He'd said it every spring for a number er years, and I didn't mind it no more'n the breakin' up er the river; not so much jest then; for the gret spring drive was comin' on, and my hands was tew full to quit work all tew oncet. I sent word I'd be 'long fore a gret while, and bymeby I went. I ought tew hev gone at fust; but they'd sung aout 'Wolf!' so often I warn't scared; an' sure 'nuff the wolf did come at last. Father hed been dead an' berried a week when I got there, and aunt was so mad she wouldn't write, nor scurcely speak tew me for a consider'ble spell. I didn't blame her a mite, and felt jest the wust kind; so I give in every way, and fetched her raound. Yeou see I hed a cousin who'd kind er took my place tew hum while I was off, an' the old man bed left him a good slice or his money, an' me the farm, hopin' to keep me there. He'd never liked the lumberin' bizness, an' hankered arfter me a sight, I faound. Waal, seein' haow 'twas, I tried tew please him, late as it was; but ef there was ennything I did spleen ag'inst, it was farmin, 'specially arfter the smart times I'd ben hevin, up Oldtaown way. Yeou don't know nothin' abaout it; but ef yeou want tew see high dewin's, jest hitch onto a timber-drive an' go it daown along them lakes and rivers, say from Kaumchenungamooth tew Punnobscot Bay. Guess yeou'd see a thing or tew, an' find livin' on a log come as handy as ef yeou was born a turtle.

"Waal, I stood it one summer; but it was the longest kind of a job. Come fall I turned contrary, darned the farm, and vaowed I'd go back tew loggin'. Aunt hed got fond er me by that time, and felt dreadful bad abaout my leavin' on her. Cousin Siah, as we called Josiah, didn't cotton tew the old woman, though he did tew her cash; but we hitched along fust-rate. She was 'tached tew the place, hated tew hev it let or sold, thought I'd go to everlastin' rewin of I took tew lumberin' ag'in, an' hevin' a tidy little sum er money all her own, she took a notion tew buy me off. 'Hiram,' sez she, 'ef yeou'll stay tew hum, merry some smart gal, an' kerry on the farm, I'll leave yeou the hull er my fortin. Ef yeou don't, I'll leave every cent on't tew Siah, though he ain't done as waal by me as yeou hev. Come,' sez she, 'I'm breakin' up like brother; I shan't wurry any one a gret while, and 'fore spring I dessay you'll hev cause tew rejice that yeou done as Aunt Si counselled yeou.'

"Now, that idee kinder took me, seein' I hedn't no overpaourin' love fer cousin; but I brewdid over it a spell 'fore I 'greed. Fin'lly, I said I'd dew it, as it warn't a hard nor a bad trade; and begun to look raound fer Mis Flint, Jr. Aunt was dreadf'l pleased; but 'mazin pertickler as tew who was goan tew stan' in her shoes, when she was fetched up ag'inst the etarnal hoom. There was a sight er lovely women-folks raound taown; but aunt she set her foot daown that Mis Flint must be smart, pious, an' good-natered; harnsome she didn't say nothin' abaout, bein' the humliest woman in the State er Maine. I hed my own calk'lations on that pint, an' went sparkin' two or three er the pootiest gals, all that winter. I warn't in no hurry, fer merryin' is an awful resky bizness; an' I warn't goan to be took in by nobuddy. Some haouw I couldn't make up my mind which I'd hev, and kept dodgin', all ready to slew raound, an' hitch on tew ary one that seemed likeliest. 'Long in March, aunt, she ketched cold, took tew her bed, got wuss, an' told me tew 'hurry up, fer nary red should I hev, ef I warn't safely merrier 'fore she stepped out. I thought that was rather craoudin' a feller; but I see she was goan sure, an' I'd got intew a way er considerin' the cash mine, so that it come hard to hear abaout givin' on't up. Off I went that evenin' an' asked Almiry Nash ef she'd hev me. No, she wouldn't; I'd shilly-shallyed so long, she'd got tired er waitin' and took tew keepin' company with a doctor daown tew Banggore, where she'd ben visitin' a spell. I didn't find that as hard a rub to swaller, as I'd a thought I would, though Almiry was the richest, pootiest, and good-naterest of the lot. Aunt larfed waal, an' told me tew try agin; so a couple er nights arfter, I spruced up, an' went over to Car'line Miles's; she was as smart as old cheese, an' waal off intew the barg'in. I was just as sure she'd hev me, as I be that I'm gittin' the rewmatiz a settin' in this ma'sh. But that minx, Almiry, hed ben and let on abaout her own sarsy way er servin' on me, an' Car'line jest up an' said she warn't goan to hev annybuddy's leavin's; so daown I come ag'in.

"Things was gettin' desper't by that time; fer aunt was failin' rapid, an' the story hed leaked aout some way, so the hull taown was gigglin' over it. I thought I'd better quit them parts; but aunt she showed me her will all done complete, 'sceptin' the fust name er the legatee. 'There,' sez she, 'it all depends on yeou, whether that place is took by Hiram or Josiah. It's easy done, an' so it's goan tew stan' till the last minnit.' That riled me consid'able, an' I streaked off tew May Jane Simlin's. She want very waal off; nor extra harnsome, but she was pious the wust kind, an' dreadf'l clever to them she fancied. But I was daown on my luck agin; fer at the fust word I spoke of merryin', she showed me the door, an' give me to understan' that she couldn't think er hevin' a man that warn't a church-member, that hadn't experienced religion, or even ben struck with conviction, an' all the rest on't. Ef anny one her a wanted tew hev seen a walkin' hornet's nest, they could hev done it cheap that night, as I went hum. I jest stramed intew the kitchen, chucked my hat intew one corner, my coat intew 'nother, kicked the cat, cussed the fire, drawed up a chair, and set scaoulin' like sixty, bein' tew mad fer talkin'. The young woman that was nussin' aunt,—Bewlab Blish, by name,—was a cookin' grewel on the coals, and 'peared tew understan' the mess I was in; but she didn't say nothin', only blowed up the fire, fetched me a mug er cider, an' went raound so kinder quiet, and sympathizin', that I faound the wrinkles in my temper gettin' smoothed aout 'mazin' quick; an' 'fore long I made a clean breast or the hull thing. Bewlah larfed, but I didn't mind her doin' on't, for she sez, sez she, real sort o' cunnin',— "'Poor Hiram! they didn't use yeou waal. Yeou ought to hev tried some er the poor an' humly girls; they'd a' been glad an' grateful for such a sweetheart as yeou be.'

"I was good-natered agin by that time, an' I sez, larfin' along with her, 'Waal I've got three mittens, but I guess I might's waal hev 'nother, and that will make two pair complete. Say, Bewlah, will yeou hev me?'

"'Yes, I will,' sez she.

"'Reelly?' sez I.

"'Solemn trew,' sez she.

"Ef she'd up an' slapped me in the face, I shouldn't hev ben more throwed aback, for I never mistrusted she cared two chips for me. I jest set an' gawped; fer she was solemn trew, I see that with half an eye, an' it kinder took my breath away. Bewlah drawed the grewel off the fire, wiped her hands, an' stood lookin' at me a minnet, then she sez, slow an' quiet, but tremblin' a little, as women hev a way er doin', when they've consid'able steam aboard,—

"'Hiram, other folks think lumberin' has spilt yeou; I don't; they call yeou rough an' rewd; I know you've got a real kind heart for them as knows haow tew find it. Them girls give yeou up so easy, 'cause they never loved yeou, an' yeou give them up 'cause yeou only thought abaout their looks an' money. I'm humly, an' I'm poor; but I've loved yeou ever sence we went a-nuttin' years ago, an' yeou shook daown fer me, kerried my bag, and kissed me tew the gate, when all the others shunned me, 'cause my father drank an' I was shably dressed, ugly, an' shy. Yeou asked me in sport, I answered in airnest; but I don't expect nothin' unless yeou mean as I mean. Like me, Hiram, or leave me, it won't make no odds in my lovin' or yeou, nor helpin' er yeou, of I kin.'

"'Tain't easy tew say haouw I felt, while she was goin' on that way; but my idees was tumblin' raound inside er me, as of half a dozen dams was broke loose all tew oncet. One thing was ruther stiddier 'n the rest, an' that was that I liked Bewlah morn'n I knew. I begun tew see what kep me loopin' tew hum so much, sence aunt was took daown; why I want in no hurry tew git them other gals, an' haow I come tew pocket my mittens so easy arfter the fast rile was over. Bewlah was humly, poor in flesh, dreadful freckled, hed red hair, black eyes, an' a gret mold side er her nose. But I'd got wonted tew her; she knowed my ways, was a fust rate housekeeper, real good-tempered, and pious without flingin' on't in yer face. She was a lonely creeter,—her folks bein' all dead but one sister, who didn't use her waal, an' somehow I kinder yearned over her, as they say in Scripter. For all I set an' gawped, I was coming raound fast, though I felt as I used tew, when I was goin' to shoot the rapids, kinder breathless an' oncertin, whether I'd come aout right side up or not. Queer, warn't it?"

"Love, Flint; that was a sure symptom of it."

"Waal, guess 'twas; anyway I jumped up all er a sudden, ketched Bewlah raound the neck, give her a hearty kiss, and sung aout, 'I'll dew it sure's my name's Hi Flint!' The words was scurcely aout er my maouth, 'fore daown come Dr. Parr. He'd ben up tew see aunt, an' said she wouldn't last the night threw, prob'ly. That give me a scare or the wust kind; an' when I told doctor haow things was, he sez, kinder jokin',—

"'Better git married right away, then. Parson Dill is tew come an' see the old lady, an' he'll dew both jobs tew oncet.'

"'Will yeou, Bewlah?' sez I.

"'Yes, Hiram, to 'blige yeou,' sez she.

"With that, I put it fer the parson and the license; got 'em both, an' was back in less'n half an haour, most tuckered aout with the flurry er the hull concern. Quick as I'd been, Bewlah hed faound time tew whip on her best gaoun, fix up her hair, and put a couple or white chrissanthymums intew her hank'chif pin. For the fust time in her life, she looked harnsome,—leastways I thought so,—with a pretty color in her cheeks, somethin' brighter'n a larf shinin' in her eyes, an' her lips smilin' an' tremblin', as she come to me an' whispered so's't none er the rest could hear, "'Hiram, don't yeou dew it, ef yeou'd ruther not. I've stood it a gret while alone, an' I guess I can ag'in.'

"Never yeou mind what I said or done abaout that; but we was married ten minutes arfter, 'fore the kitchen fire, with Dr. Parr an' oaur hired man, fer witnesses; an' then we all went up tew aunt. She was goan fast, but she under-stood what I told her, hed strength tew fill up the hole in the will, an' to say, a-kissin' Bewlah, 'Yeou'll be a good wife, an' naouw yeou ain't a poor one.'

"I couldn't help givin' a peek tew the will, and there I see not Hiram Flint, nor Josiah Flint, but Bewlah Flint, wrote every which way, but as plain as the nose on yer face. 'It won't make no odds dear,' whispered my wife, peekin' over my shoulder. 'Guess it won't!' sez I, aout laoud; 'I'm glad on't, and it ain't a cent more'n yeou derserve.'

"That pleased aunt. 'Riz me, Hiram,' sez she; an' when I'd got her easy, she put her old arms raound my neck, an' tried to say, 'God bless you, dear—,' but died a doin' of it; an' I ain't ashamed tew say I boo-hooed real hearty, when I, laid her daown, fer she was dreadf'l good tew me, an' I don't forget her in a hurry."

"How's Bewlah?" asked Dick, after the little tribute of respect all paid to Aunt Siloam's memory, by a momentary silence.

"Fust-rate! that harum scarum venter er mine was the best I ever made. She's done waal by me, es Bewlah; ben a grand good haousekeeper, kin kerry on the farm better'n me, any time, an' is as dutif'l an' lovin' a wife as,—waal as annything that is extra dutif'l and lovin'."

"Got any boys to brag of?"

"We don't think much o' boys daown aour way; they're 'mazin resky stock to fetch up,—alluz breakin' baounds, gittin' intew the paound, and wurry your life aout somehaow 'nother. Gals naow does waal; I got six o' the likeliest the is goin', every one on 'em is the very moral of Bewlah,—red hair, black eyes, quiet ways, an' a mold side the nose. Baby's ain't growed yet; but I expect tew see it in a consid'able state o' forrardness, when I git hum, an' wouldn't miss it fer the world."

The droll expressions of Flint's face, and the satisfied twang of his last words, were irresistable. Dick and Phil went off into a shout of laughter; and even Thorn's grave lips relapsed into a smile at the vision of six little Flints with their six little moles. As if the act were an established ceremony, the "paternal head" produced his pocket-book, selected a worn, black and white paper, which be spread in his broad palm, and displayed with the air of a connoisseur.

"There, thets Bewlah! we call it a cuttin'; but the proper name's a silly-hoot I b'leeve. I've got a harnsome big degarrytype tew hum but the heft on't makes it bad tew kerry raound, so I took this. I don't tote it abaout inside my shirt as some dew,—it aint my way; but I keep it in my puss long with my other valleu'bles, and guess I set as much store by it as ef it was all painted up, and done off to keell."

The "silly-hoot" was examined with interest, and carefully stowed away again in the old brown wallet which way settled in its place with a satisfied slap, then Flint said briskly,

"Naouw, Phil, yeou close this interestin' and instructive meeting; and be spry, fer time's most up."

"I haven't much to tell, but must begin with a confession which I have often longed but never dared to make before, because I am a coward."

"Sho! who's goan to b'leeve that o' a man who fit like a wild cat, wuz offered fer permotion on the field, and wuz reported tew headquarters arfter his fust scrimmage. Try ag'in, Phil."

"Physical courage is as plentiful as brass buttons, nowadays, but moral courage is a rarer virtue; and I'm lacking in it, as I'll prove. You think me a Virginian; I'm an Alabamian by birth, and was a reb three months ago."

This confession startled his hearers, as he knew it would, for he had kept his secret well. Thorn laid his hand involuntarily upon his rifle, Dick drew off a little, and Flint illustrated one of his own expressions, for he "gawped." Phil laughed that musical laugh of his, and looked up at them with his dark face waking into sudden life as he went on: —

"There's no treason in the camp, for I'm as fierce a Federalist as any of you now, and you may thank a woman for it. When Lee made his raid into Pennsylvania, I was a lieutenant in the—well, never mind what regiment, it hasn't signalized itself since, and I'd rather not hit my old neighbors when they are down. In one of the skirmishes during our retreat, I got a wound and was left for dead. A kind old Quaker found and took me home; but though I was too weak to talk, I had my senses by that time, and knew what went on about me. Everything was in confusion, even in that well-ordered place; no surgeon could be got at first, and a flock of frightened women thee'd and thou'd one another over me, but hadn't wit enough to see that I was bleeding to death. Among the faces that danced before my dizzy eyes was one that seemed familiar, probably because no cap surrounded it. I was glad to have it bending over me, to hear a steady voice say, 'Give me a bandage, quick! ' and when none was instantly forthcoming to me, the young lady stripped up a little white apron she wore, and stanched the wound in my shoulder. I was not as badly hurt as I supposed, but so worn-out, and faint from loss of blood, they believed me to be dying, and so did I, when the old man took off his hat and said,

"'Friend, if thee has anything to say, thee had better say it, for thee probably has not long to live.'

"I thought of my little sister, far away in Alabama, fancied she came to me, and muttered, 'Amy, kiss me, good-by.' The women sobbed at that; but the girl bent her sweet compassionate face to mine, and kissed me on the forehead. That was my wife."

"So you seceded from Secession right away, to pay for that lip-service, hey?"

"No, Thorn, not right away,—to my shame be it spoken. I'll tell you how it came about. Margaret was not old Bent's daughter, but a Virginia girl on a visit, and a long one it proved, for she couldn't go till things were quieter.

While she waited, she helped take care of me; for the good souls petted me like a baby when they found that a Rebel could be a gentleman. I held my tongue, and behaved my best to prove my gratitude, you know. Of course, I loved Margaret very soon. How could I help it? She was the sweetest woman I had ever seen, tender, frank, and spirited; all I had ever dreamed of and longed for. I did not speak of this, nor hope for a return, because I knew she was a hearty Unionist, and thought she only tended me from pity. But suddenly she decided to go home, and when I ventured to wish she would stay longer, she would not listen, and said, "I must not stay; I should have gone before."

"The words were nothing, but as she uttered them the color came up beautifully over all her face, and her eyes filled as they looked away from mine. Then I knew that she loved me, and my secret broke out half against my will. Margaret was forced to listen, for I would not let her go, but she seemed to harden herself against me, growing colder, stiller, statelier, as I went on, and when I said in my desperate way, "'You should love me, for we are bid to love our enemies,' she flashed an indignant look at me and said, "'I will not love what I cannot respect! Come to me a loyal man, and see what answer I shall give you.'

"Then she went away. It was the wisest thing she could have done, for absence did more to change me than an ocean of tears, a year of exhortations. Lying there, I missed her every hour of the day, recalled every gentle act, kind word, and fair example she had given me. I contrasted my own belief with hers, and found a new significance in the words honesty and honor, and, remembering her fidelity to principle, was ashamed of my own treason to God and to herself. Education, prejudice, and interest, are difficult things to overcome, and that was the hottest fight I ever passed through, for, as I tell you, I was a coward. But love and loyalty won the day, and, asking no quarter, the Rebel surrendered."

"Phil Beaufort, you're a brick!" cried Dick, with a sounding slap on his comrade's shoulder.

"A brand snatched from the burnin'. Hallelujah!" chanted Flint, seesawing with excitement.

"Then you went to find your wife? How? Where?" asked Thorn, forgetting vigilance in interest.

"Friend Bent hated war so heartily that he would have nothing to do with paroles, exchanges, or any martial process whatever, but bade me go when and where I liked, remembering to do by others as I had been done by. Before I was well enough to go, however, I managed, by means of Copperhead influence and returned prisoners, to send a letter to my father and receive an answer. You can imagine what both contained; and so I found myself penniless, but not poor, an outcast, but not alone. Old Bent treated me like a prodigal son, and put money in my purse; his pretty daughters loved me for Margaret's sake, and gave me a patriotic salute all round when I left them, the humblest, happiest man in Pennsylvania. Margaret once said to me that this was the time for deeds, not words; that no man should stand idle, but serve the good cause with head, heart, and hand, no matter in what rank; for in her eyes a private fighting for liberty was nobler than a dozen generals defending slavery. I remembered that, and, not having influential friends to get me a commission, enlisted in one of her own Virginia regiments, knowing that no act of mine would prove my sincerity like that. You should have seen her face when I walked in upon her, as she sat alone, busied with the army work, as I'd so often seen her sitting by my bed; it showed me all she had been suffering in silence, all I should have lost had I chosen darkness instead of light. She hoped and feared so much she could not spears, neither could I, but dropped my cloak, and showed her that, through love of her, I had become a soldier of the Flag. How I love the coarse blue uniform! for when she saw it, she came to me without a word and kept her promise in a month."

"Thunder! what a harnsome woman!" exclaimed Flint, as Phil, opening the golden case that held his talisman, showed them the beautiful, beloved face of which be spoke.

"Yes! and a right noble woman too. I don't deserve her, but I will. We parted on our wedding-day, for orders to be off came suddenly, and she would not let me go until I had given her my name to keep. We were married in the morning, and at noon I had to go. Other women wept as we marched through the town, but my brave Margaret kept her tears till we were gone, smiling, and waving her hand to me,—the hand that wore the wedding-ring,—till I was out of sight. That image of her is before me day and night, and day and night her last words are ringing in my ears,

"'I give you freely, do your best. Better a true man's widow than a traitor's wife.'

"Boys, I've only stood on the right side for a month; I've only fought one battle, earned one honor; but I believe these poor achievements are an earnest of the long atonement I desire to make for five and twenty years of blind transgression. You say I fight well. Have I not cause to dare much?—for in owning many slaves, I too became a slave; in helping to make many freemen, I liberate myself. You wonder why I refused promotion. Have I any right to it yet? Are there not men who never sinned as I have done, and beside whose sacrifices mine look pitifully small? You tell me I have no ambition. I have the highest, for I desire to become God's noblest work,—an honest man, living, to make Margaret happy, in a love that every hour grows worthier of her own,—dying, to make death proud to take me."

Phil had risen while he spoke, as if the enthusiasm of his mood lifted him into the truer manhood he aspired to attain. Straight and strong he stood up in the moonlight, his voice deepened by unwonted energy, his eye clear and steadfast, his whole face ennobled by the regenerating power of this late loyalty to country, wife, and self, and bright against the dark blue of his jacket shone the pictured face, the only medal he was proud to wear.

Ah, brave, brief moment, cancelling years of wrong! Ah, fair and fatal decoration, serving as a mark for a hidden foe! The sharp crack of a rifle broke the stillness of the night, and with those hopeful words upon his lips, the young man sealed his purpose with his life.

A Hospital Christmas

"MERRY CHRISTMAS!" "MERRY CHRISTMAS!" "Merry Christmas, and lots of 'em, ma'am!" echoed from every side, as Miss Hale entered her ward in the gray December dawn. No wonder the greetings were hearty, that thin faces brightened, and eyes watched for the coming of this small luminary more eagerly than for the rising of the sun; for when they woke that morning, each man found that in the silence of the night some friendly hand had laid a little gift beside his bed. Very humble little gifts they were, but well chosen and thoughtfully bestowed by one who made the blithe anniversary pleasant even in a hospital, and sweetly taught the lesson of the hour — Peace on earth, good-will to man.

"I say, ma'am, these are just splendid. I've dreamt about such for a week, but I never thought I'd get 'em," cried one poor fellow, surveying a fine bunch of grapes with as much satisfaction as if he had found a fortune.

"Thank you kindly, Miss, for the paper and the fixing. I hated to keep borrowing, but I hadn't any money," said another, eying his gift with happy anticipations of the home letters with which the generous pages should be filled.

"They are dreadful soft and pretty, but I don't believe I'll ever wear 'em out; my legs are so wimbly there's no go in 'em," whispered a fever patient, looking sorrowfully at the swollen feet ornamented with a pair of carpet slippers gay with roses, and evidently made for his especial need.

"Please hang my posy basket on the gas-burner in the middle of the room, where all the boys can see it. It's too pretty for one alone."

First published in *The Commonwealth*, II, nos. 19, 20, (8, 15 January 1864).

"But then you can't see it yourself, Joe, and you are fonder of such things than the rest," said Miss Hale, taking both the little basket and the hand of her pet patient, a lad of twenty, dying of rapid consumption.

"That's the reason I can spare it for a while, for I shall feel 'em in the room just the same, and they'll do the boys good. You pick out the one you like best, for me to keep, and hang up the rest till by-and-by, please."

She gave him a sprig of mignonette, and he smiled as he took it, for it reminded him of her in her sad-colored gown, as quiet and unobtrusive, but as grateful to the hearts of those about her as was the fresh scent of the flower to the lonely lad who never had known womanly tenderness and care until he found them in a hospital. Joe's prediction was verified; the flowers did do the boys good, for all welcomed them with approving glances, and all felt their refining influence more or less keenly, from cheery Ben, who paused to fill the cup inside with fresher water, to surly Sam, who stopped growling as his eye rested on a geranium very like the one blooming in his sweetheart's window when they parted a long year ago.

"Now, as this is to be a merry day, let us begin to enjoy it at once. Fling up the windows, Ben, and Barney, go for breakfast while I finish washing faces and settling bed-clothes."

With which directions the little woman fell to work with such infectious energy that in fifteen minutes thirty gentlemen with spandy clean faces and hands were partaking of refreshment with as much appetite as their various conditions would permit. Meantime the sun came up, looking bigger, brighter, jollier than usual, as he is apt to do on Christmas days. Not a snow-flake chilled the air that blew in as blandly as if winter had relented, and wished the "boys" the compliments of the season in his mildest mood; while a festival smell pervaded the whole house, and appetizing rumors of turkey, mince-pie, and oysters for dinner, circulated through the wards. When breakfast was done, the wounds dressed, directions for the day delivered, and as many, of the disagreeables as possible well over, the fun began. In any other place that would have been considered a very quiet morning; but to the weary invalids prisoned in that room, it was quite a whirl of excitement. None were dangerously ill but Joe, and all were easily amused, for weakness, homesickness and *ennui* made every trifle a joke or an event.

In came Ben, looking like a "Jack in the Green," with his load of hemlock and holly. Such of the men as could get about and had a hand to lend, lent it, and soon, under Miss Hale's direction, a green bough hung at the head of each bed, depended from the gas-burners, and nodded over the fireplace, while the finishing effect was given by a cross and crown at the top and bottom of the room. Great was the interest, many were the mishaps, and frequent was the laughter which attended this performance; for wounded men, when convalescent, are particularly jovial. When "Daddy Mills," as one venerable volunteer was irreverently christened, expatiated learnedly upon the difference between "sprewce, hemlock and pine," how they all listened, each thinking of some familiar wood still pleasantly haunted by boyish recollections of stolen gunnings, gum-pickings, and bird-nestings. When quiet Hayward amazed the company, by coming out strong in a most unexpected direction, and telling with much effect the story of a certain "fine old gentleman" who supped on hemlock tea and died like a hero, what commendations were bestowed upon the immortal heathen in language more hearty than classical, as a twig of the historical tree was passed round like a new style of refreshment, that inquiring parties might satisfy themselves regarding the flavor of the Socratic draught. When Barney, the colored incapable, essayed a grand ornament above the door, and relying upon one insufficient nail, descended to survey his success with the proud exclamation, "Look at de neatness of dat job, gen'l'men," — at which point the whole thing tumbled down about his ears, — how they all shouted but Pneumonia Ned, who, having lost his voice, could only make ecstatic demonstrations with his legs. When Barney cast himself and his hammer despairingly upon the floor, and Miss Hale, stepping into a chair, pounded stoutly at the traitorous nail and performed some miracle with a bit of string which made all fast, what a burst of applause arose from the beds. When gruff Dr. Bangs came in to see what all the noise was about, and the same intrepid lady not only boldly explained, but stuck a bit of holly in his button-hole, and wished him a merry Christmas with such a face full of smiles that the crabbed old doctor felt himself giving in very fast, and bolted out again, calling Christmas a humbug, and exulting over the thirty emetics he would have to prescribe on the morrow, what indignant denials followed him. And when all was done, how everybody agreed with Joe when he said, "I think we are coming Christmas in great style; things look so green and pretty, I feel as I was settin' in a bower."

Pausing to survey her work, Miss Hale saw Sam looking as black as any thunder-cloud. He bounced over on his bed, the moment he caught her eye, but she followed him up, and gently covering the cold shoulder he evidently meant to show her, peeped over it, asking, with unabated gentleness, —

"What can I do for you, Sam? I want to have all the faces in my ward bright ones to-day."

"My box ain't come; they said I should have it two, three days ago; why don't they do it, then?" growled Ursa Major.

"It is a busy time, you know, but it will come if they promised, and patience won't delay it, I assure you."

"My patience is used up, and they are a mean set of slow coaches. I'd get it fast enough if I wore shoulder straps; as I don't, I'll bet I sha'n't see it till the things ain't fit to eat; the news is old, and I don't care a hang about it."

"I'll see what I can do; perhaps before the hurry of dinner begins some one will have time to go for it."

"Nobody ever does have time here but folks who would give all they are worth to be stirring round. You can't get it, I know; it's my luck, so don't you worry, ma'am."

Miss Hale did not "worry," but worked, and in time a messenger was found, provided with the necessary money, pass and directions, and despatched to hunt up the missing Christmas-box. Then she paused to see what came next, not that it was necessary to look for a task, but to decide which, out of many, was most important to do first.

"Why, Turner, crying again so soon? What is it now? the light head or the heavy feet?"

"It's my bones, ma'am. They ache so I can't lay easy any way, and I'm so tired I just wish I could die and be out of this misery," sobbed the poor ghost of a once strong and cheery fellow, as the kind hand wiped his tears away, and gently rubbed the weary shoulders.

"Don't wish that Turner, for the worst is over now, and all you need is to get your strength again. Make an effort to sit up a little; it is quite time you tried; a change of posture will help the ache wonderfully, and make this 'dreadful bed,' as you call it, seem very comfortable when you come back to it."

"I can't, ma'am, my legs ain't a bit of use, and I ain't strong enough even to try."

"You never will be if you don't try. Never mind the poor legs, Ben will carry you. I've got the matron's easy-chair all ready, and can make you very cosy by the fire. It's Christmas-day, you know; why not celebrate it by overcoming the despondency which retards your recovery, and prove that illness has not taken all the manhood out of you?"

"It has, though, I'll never be the man I was, and may as well lay here till spring, for I shall be no use if I do get up. "

If Sam was a growler, this man was a whiner, and few hospital wards are without both. But knowing that much suffering had soured the former and pitifully weakened the latter, their nurse had patience with them, and still hoped to bring them round again. As Turner whimpered out his last dismal speech she bethought herself of something which, in the hurry of the morning, had slipped her mind till now.

"By the way, I've got another present for you. The doctor thought I'd better not give it yet, lest it should excite you too much; but I think you need excitement to make you forget yourself, and that when you find how many blessings you have to be grateful for, you will make an effort to enjoy them."

"Blessings, ma'am? I don't see 'em."

"Don't you see one now?" and drawing a letter from her pocket she held it before his eyes. His listless face brightened a little as he took it, but gloomed over again as he said fretfully, "It's from wife, I guess. I like to get her letters, but they are always full of grievings and groanings over me, so they don't do me much good."

"She does not grieve and groan in this one. She is too happy to do that, and so will you be when you read it."

"I don't see why, — hey? — why you don't mean —"

"Yes I do!" cried the little woman, clapping her hands, and laughing so delightedly that the Knight of the Rueful Countenance was betrayed into a broad smile for the first time in many weeks. "Is not a splendid little daughter a present to rejoice over and be grateful for?"

"Hooray! hold on a bit, — it's all right, — I'll be out again in a minute."

After which remarkably spirited burst, Turner vanished under the bed-clothes, letter and all. Whether he read, laughed or cried, in the seclusion of that cotton grotto was unknown; but his nurse suspected that he did all three, for when he reappeared he looked as if during that pause he had dived into his sea of troubles," and fished up his old self, again:

"What *will* I name her?" was his first remark, delivered with such vivacity that his neighbors began to think he was getting delirious again.

"What is your wife's name?" asked Miss Hale, gladly entering into the domesticities which were producing such a salutary effect.

"Her name's Ann, but neither of us like it. I'd fixed on George, for I wanted my boy called after me; and now you see I ain't a bit prepared for this young woman." Very proud of the young woman he seemed, nevertheless, and perfectly resigned to the loss of the expected son and heir.

"Why not call her Georgiana then? That combines both her parents' names, and is not a bad one in itself."

"Now that's just the brightest thing I ever heard in my life!" cried Turner, sitting bolt upright in his excitement, though half an hour before he would have considered it an utterly impossible feat. "Georgiana Butterfield Turner, — it's a tip-top name, ma'am, and we can call her Georgie just the same. Ann will like that, it's so genteel. Bless 'em both! don't I wish I was at home." And down he lay again, despairing.

"You can be before long, if you choose. Get your strength up, and off you go. Come, begin at once, drink your beef-tea, and sit up for a few minutes, just in honor of the good news, you know."

"I will, by George! — no, by Georgiana! That's a good one, ain't it?" and the whole ward was electrified by hearing a genuine giggle from the "Blueing-bag."

Down went the detested beef-tea, and up scrambled the determined drinker with many groans, and a curious jumble of chuckles, staggers, and fragmentary repetitions of his first, last, and only joke. But when fairly settled in the great rocking-chair, with the gray flannel gown comfortably on, and the new slippers getting their inaugural scorch, Turner forgot his bones, and swung to and fro before the fire, feeling amazingly well, and looking very like a trussed fowl being roasted in the primitive fashion. The languid importance of the man, and the irrepressible satisfaction of the parent, were both laughable and touching things to see, for the happy soul could not keep the glad tidings to himself. A hospital ward is often a small republic, beautifully governed by pity, patience, and the mutual sympathy which lessens mutual suffering. Turner was no favorite; but more than one honest fellow felt his heart warm towards him as they saw his dismal face kindle with fatherly pride, and heard the querulous quaver of his voice soften with fatherly affection, as he said, "My little Georgie, sir."

"He'll do now, ma'am; this has given him the boost he needed, and in a week or two he'll be off our hands."

Big Ben made the remark with a beaming countenance, and Big Ben deserves a word of praise, because he never said one for himself. An ex-patient, promoted to an attendant's place, which he filled so well that he was regarded as a model for all the rest to copy. Patient, strong, and tender, he seemed to combine many of the best traits of both man and woman; for he appeared to know by instinct where the soft spot was to be found in every heart, and how best to help sick body or sad soul. No one would have guessed this to have seen him lounging in the hall during one of the short rests he allowed himself. A brawny, six-foot fellow, in red shirt, blue trousers tucked into his boots, an old cap, visor always up, and under it a roughly-bearded, coarsely-featured face, whose prevailing expression was one of great gravity and kindliness, though a humorous twinkle of the eye at times betrayed the man, whose droll sayings often set the boys in a roar. "A good-natured, clumsy body" would have been the verdict passed upon him by a casual observer; but watch him in his ward, and see how great a wrong that hasty judgment would have done him.

Unlike his predecessor, who helped himself generously when the meals came up, and carelessly served out rations for the rest, leaving even the most helpless to bungle for themselves or wait till he was done, shut himself into his pantry, and there, — to borrow a hospital phrase, — gormed, Ben often left nothing for himself, or took cheerfully such cold bits as remained when all the rest were served; so patiently feeding the weak, being hands and feet to the maimed, and a pleasant provider for all that, as one of the boys said, — "It gives a relish to the vittles to have Ben fetch 'em." If one were restless, Ben carried him in his strong arms; if one were undergoing the sharp torture of the surgeon's knife, Ben held him with a touch as firm as kind; if one were homesick, Ben wrote letters for him with great hearty blots and dashes under all the affectionate or important words. More than one poor fellow read his fate in Ben's pitiful eyes, and breathed his last breath away on Ben's broad breast, — always a quiet pillow till its work was done, then it would heave with genuine grief, as his big hand softly closed the tired eyes, and made another comrade ready for the last review. The war shows us many Bens, — for the same power of human pity which makes women brave also makes men tender; and each is the womanlier, the manlier, for these revelations of unsuspected strength and sympathies.

At twelve o'clock dinner was the prevailing idea in ward No. 3, and when the door opened every man sniffed, for savory odors broke loose from the kitchens and went roaming about the house. Now this Christmas dinner had been much talked of; for certain charitable and patriotic persons had endeavored to provide every hospital in Washington with materials for this time-honored feast. Some mistake in the list sent to head-quarters, some unpardonable neglect of orders, or some premeditated robbery, caused the long-expected dinner in the —— Hospital to prove a dead failure; but to which of these causes it was attributable was never known, for the deepest mystery enveloped that sad transaction. The full weight of the dire disappointment was mercifully lightened by premonitions of the impending blow. Barney was often missing; for the attendants were to dine *en masse* after the patients were done, therefore a speedy banquet for the latter parties was ardently desired and he probably devoted his energies to goading on the cooks. From time to time he appeared in the doorway, flushed and breathless, made some thrilling announcement, and vanished, leaving ever-increasing appetite, impatience and expectation, behind him.

Dinner was to be served at one; at half-past twelve Barney proclaimed, "Dere ain't no vegetables but squash and pitaters." A universal groan arose; and several indignant parties on a short allowance of meat consigned the defaulting cook to a warmer climate than the tropical one he was then enjoying. At twenty minutes to one, Barney increased the excitement by whispering, ominously, "I say, de puddins isn't plummy ones."

"Fling a piller at him and shut the door, Ben," roared one irascible being, while several others *not* fond of puddings received the fact with equanimity. At quarter to one Barney piled up the agony by adding the bitter information, "Dere isn't but two turkeys for dis ward, and dey's little fellers."

Anxiety instantly, appeared in every countenance, and intricate calculations were made as to how far the two fowls would go when divided among thirty men; also friendly warnings were administered to several of the feebler gentlemen not to indulge too freely, if at all, for fear of relapses. Once more did the bird of evil omen return, for at ten minutes to one Barney croaked through the key-hole,

"Only jes half ob de pies has come, gen'l'men." That capped the climax, for the masculine palate has a predilection for pastry, and mince-pie was the sheet-anchor to which all had clung when other hopes went down. Even

Ben looked dismayed; not that he expected anything but the perfume and pickings for his share, but he had set his heart on having the dinner an honor to the institution and a memorable feast for the men, so far away from home, and all that usually makes the day a festival among the poorest. He looked pathetically grave as Turner began to fret, Sam began to swear under his breath, Hayward to sigh; Joe to wish it was all over, and the rest began to vent their emotions with a freedom which was anything but inspiring. At that moment Miss Hale came in with a great basket of apples and oranges in one hand, and several convivial-looking bottles in the other.

"Here is our dessert, boys! A kind friend remembered us, and we will drink her health in her own currant wine."

A feeble smile circulated round the room, and in some sanguine bosoms hope revived again. Ben briskly emptied the basket, while Miss Hale whispered to Joe, —

"I know you would be glad to get away from the confusion of this next hour, to enjoy a breath of fresh air, and dine quietly with Mrs. Burton round the corner, wouldn't you?"

"Oh, ma'am, so much! the noise, the smells, the fret and flurry, make me sick just to think of! But how can I go? that dreadful ambulance 'most killed me last time, and I'm weaker now."

"My dear boy, I have no thought of trying that again till our ambulances are made fit for the use of weak and wounded men. Mrs. Burton's carriage is at the door, with her motherly self inside, and all you have got to do is to let me bundle you up, and Ben carry you out."

With a long sigh of relief Joe submitted to both these processes, and when his nurse watched his happy face as the carriage slowly rolled away, she felt well repaid for the little sacrifice of rest and pleasure so quietly made; for Mrs. Burton came to carry her, not Joe, away.

"Now, Ben, help me to make this unfortunate dinner go off as well as we can," she whispered, "On many accounts it is a mercy that the men are spared the temptations of a more generous meal; pray don't tell them so, but make the best of it, as you know very well how to do."

"I'll try my best, Miss Hale, but I'm no less disappointed, for some of 'em, being no better than children, have been living on the thoughts of it for a week, and it comes hard to give it up."

If Ben had been an old-time patriarch, and the thirty boys his sons, he could not have spoken with a more paternal regret, or gone to work with a better will. Putting several small tables together in the middle of the room, he left Miss Hale to make a judicious display of plates, knives and forks, while he departed for the banquet. Presently he returned, bearing the youthful turkeys and the vegetables in his tray, followed by Barney, looking unutterable things at a plum-pudding baked in a milk-pan, and six very small pies. Miss Hale played a lively tattoo as the procession approached, and, when the viands were arranged, with the red and yellow fruit prettily heaped up in the middle, it really did look like a dinner.

"Here's richness! here's the delicacies of the season and the comforts of life!" said Ben, falling back to survey the table with as much apparent satisfaction as if it had been a lord mayor's feast.

"Come, hurry up, and give us our dinner, what there is of it!" grumbled Sam.

"Boys," continued Ben, beginning to cut up the turkeys, "these noble birds have been sacrificed for the defenders of their country; they will go as far as ever they can, and, when they can't go any farther, we shall endeavor to supply their deficiencies with soup or ham, oysters having given out unexpectedly. Put it to vote; both have been provided on this joyful occasion, and a word will fetch either."

"Ham! ham!" resounded from all sides. Soup was an every-day affair, and therefore repudiated with scorn; but ham, being a rarity, was accepted as a proper reward of merit and a tacit acknowledgment of their wrongs.

The "noble birds" did go as far as possible, and were handsomely assisted by their fellow martyr. The pudding was not as plummy as could have been desired, but a slight exertion of fancy made the crusty knobs do duty for raisins. The pies were small, yet a laugh added flavor to the mouthful apiece, for, when Miss Hale asked Ben to cut them up, that individual regarded her with an inquiring aspect as he said, in his drollest tone, —

"I wouldn't wish to appear stupid, ma'am, but, when you mention 'pies,' I presume you allude to these trifles. 'Tarts,' or 'patties,' would meet my views better, in speaking of the third course of this lavish dinner. As such I will do my duty by 'em, hoping that the appetites is to match."

Carefully dividing the six pies into twenty-nine diminutive wedges, he placed each in the middle of a large clean plate, and handed them about with the gravity of an undertaker. Dinner had restored good humor to many; this hit at the pies put the finishing touch to it, and from that moment as atmosphere of jollity prevailed. Healths were drunk in currant wine, apples and oranges flew about as an impromptu game of ball was got up, Miss Hale sang a Christmas carol, and Ben gambolled like a sportive giant as he cleared away. Pausing in one of his prances to and fro, he beckoned the nurse out, and, when she followed, handed her a plate heaped up with good things from a better table than she ever sat at now.

"From the matron, ma'am. Come right in here and eat it while it's hot; they are most through in the dining room, and you'll get nothing half so nice," said Ben, leading the way into his pantry and pointing to a sunny window-seat.

"Are you sure she meant it for me, and not for yourself, Ben?"

"Of course she did! Why, what should I do with it, when I've just been feastin' sumptuous in this very room?"

"I don't exactly see what you have been feasting on," said Miss Hale, glancing round the tidy pantry as she sat down.

"Havin' eat up the food and washed up the dishes, it naturally follows that you don't see, ma'am. But if I go off in a fit by-and-by you'll know what it's owin' to," answered Ben, vainly endeavoring to look like a man suffering from repletion.

"Such kind fibs are not set down against one, Ben, so I will eat your dinner, for if I don't, I know you will throw it out of the window to prove that you can't eat it."

"Thankee ma'am, I'm afraid I should; for, at the rate he's going on, Barney wouldn't be equal to it," said Ben, looking very much relieved, as he polished his last pewter, fork and hung his towels up to dry.

A pretty general siesta followed the excitement of dinner, but by three o'clock the public mind was ready for amusement, and the arrival of Sam's box provided it, He was asleep when it was brought in and quietly deposited at his bed's foot, ready to surprise him on awaking. The advent of a box was a great event, for the fortunate receiver seldom failed to "stand treat," and next best to getting things from one's own home was the getting them from some other boy's home. This was an unusually, large box, and all felt impatient to have it opened, though Sam's exceeding crustiness prevented the indulgence of great expectations. Presently he roused, and the first thing his eye fell upon was the box, with his own name sprawling over it in big black letters. As if it were merely the continuance of his dream, he stared stupidly at it for a moment, then rubbed his eyes and sat up, exclaiming, —

"Hullo! that's mine!"

"Ah! who said it wouldn't come? who hadn't the faith of a grasshopper? and who don't half deserve it for being a Barker by nater as by name?" cried Ben, emphasizing each question with a bang on the box, as he waited, hammer in hand, for the arrival of the ward-master, whose duty it was to oversee the opening of such matters, lest contraband articles should do mischief to the owner or his neighbors.

"Ain't it a jolly big one? Knock it open, and don't wait for anybody or anything!" cried Sam, tumbling off his bed and beating impatiently on the lid with his one hand.

In came the ward-master, off came the cover, and out came a motley collection of apples, socks, dough-nuts, paper, pickles, photographs, pocket-handker-chiefs, gingerbread, letters, jelly, newspapers, tobacco, and cologne. "All right, glad it's come, — don't kill yourself," said the ward-master, as he took a hasty survey and walked off again. Drawing the box nearer the bed, Ben delicately followed, and Sam was left to brood over his treasures in peace.

At first all the others, following Ben's example, made elaborate pretences of going to sleep, being absorbed in books, or utterly uninterested in the outer world. But very soon curiosity got the better of politeness, and one by one they all turned round and stared. They might have done so from the first, for Sam was perfectly unconscious of everything but his own affairs, and, having read the letters, looked at the pictures, unfolded the bundles, turned every-thing inside out and upside down, tasted all the eatables and made a spectacle of himself with jelly, he paused to get his breath and find his way out of the confusion he had created. Presently he called out,—

"Miss Hale, will you come and right up my duds for me?" adding, as her woman's hands began to bring matters straight, "I don't know what to do with 'em all, for some won't keep long, and it will take pretty steady eating to get through 'em in time, supposin' appetite holds out."

"How do the others manage with their things?"

"You know they give 'em away; but I'll be hanged if I do, for they are always callin' names and pokin' fun at me. Guess they won't get anything out of me now."

The old morose look came back as be spoke, for it had disappeared while reading the home letters, touching the home gifts. Still busily folding and arranging, Miss Hale asked,—

"You know the story of the Three Cakes; which are you going to be —Harry, Peter, or Billy?"

Sam began to laugh at this sudden application of the nursery legend; and, seeing her advantage, Miss Hale pursued it:

"We all know how much you have suffered, and all respect you for the courage with which you have borne your long confinement and your loss; but don't you think you have given the boys some cause for making fun of you, as you say? You used to be a favorite, and can be again, if you will only put off these crusty ways, which will grow upon you faster than you think. Better lose both arms than cheerfulness and self-control, Sam."

Pausing to see how her little lecture was received, she saw that Sam's better self was waking up, and added yet another word, hoping to help a mental ailment as she had done so many physical ones. Looking up at him with her kind eyes, she said, in a lowered voice, —

"This day, on which the most perfect life began, is a good day for all of us to set about making ourselves readier to follow that divine example. Troubles are helpers if we take them kindly, and the bitterest may sweeten us for all our lives. Believe and try this, Sam, and when you go, away from us let those who love you find that two battles have been fought, two victories won."

Sam made no answer, but sat thoughtfully picking at the half-eaten cookey in his hand. Presently he stole a glance about the room, and, as if all helps were waiting for him, his eye met Joe's. From his solitary corner by the fire and the bed he would seldom leave again until he went into his grave, the boy smiled back at him so heartily, so happily, that something gushed warm across Sam's heart as he looked down upon the faces of mother, sister, sweet-heart, scattered round him, and remembered how poor his comrade was in all such tender ties, and yet how rich in that beautiful content, which, "having nothing, yet hath all." The man had no words in which to express this feeling, but it came to him and did him good, as he proved in his own way. "Miss Hale," he said, a little awkwardly, "I wish you'd pick out what you think each would like, and give 'em to the boys."

He got a smile in answer that drove him to his cookey as a refuge, for his lips would tremble, and he felt half proud, half ashamed to have earned such bright approval.

"Let Ben help you, — he knows better than I. But you must give them all yourself, it will so surprise and please the boys; and then to-morrow we will write a capital letter home, telling what a jubilee we made over their fine box."

At this proposal Sam half repented; but, as Ben came lumbering up at Miss Hale's summons, he laid hold of his new resolution as if it was a sort of shower-bath and he held the string, one pull of which would finish the baptism. Dividing his most cherished possession, which (alas for romance!) was the tobacco, he bundled the larger half into a paper, whispering to Miss Hale, —

"Ben ain't exactly what you'd call a ministerin' angel to look at, but he is amazin' near one in his ways, so I'm goin' to begin with him."

Up came the "ministering angel," in red flannel and cow-hide boots; and Sam tucked the little parcel into his pocket, saying, as he began to rummage violently in the box, —

"Now jest hold your tongue, and lend a hand here about these things."

Ben was so taken aback by this proceeding that he stared blankly, till a look from Miss Hale enlightened him; and, taking his cue, he played his part as well as could be expected on so short a notice. Clapping Sam on the shoulder, —not the bad one, Ben was always thoughtful of those things, — he exclaimed heartily, —

"I always said you'd come round when this poor arm of yours got a good start, and here you are jollier'n ever. Lend a hand! so I will, a pair of 'em. What's to do? Pack these traps up again."

"No; I want you to tell what *you'd* do with 'em if they were yours. Free, you know, — as free as if they really was."

Ben held on to the box a minute as if this second surprise rather took him off his legs; but another look from the prime mover in this resolution steadied him, and he fell to work as if Sam had been in the habit of being "free."

"Well, let's see. I think I'd put the clothes and sich into this smaller box that the bottles come in, and stan' it under the table, handy. Here's newspapers-pictures in 'em, too! I should make a circulatin' lib'ry of them; they'll be a real treat. Pickles — well, I guess I should keep them on the winder here as a kind of a relish dinner-times, or to pass along to them as longs for 'em. Cologne — that's a dreadful handsome bottle, ain't it?, That, now, would be fust-rate to give away to somebody as was very fond of it, — a kind of a delicate attention, you know, if you happen to meet such a person anywheres."

Ben nodded towards Miss Hale, who was absorbed in folding pocket-hand-kerchiefs. Sam winked expressively, and patted the bottle as if congratulating himself that it was handsome, and that he did know what to do with it. The pantomime was not elegant, but as much real affection and respect went into it as if he had made a set speech, and presented the gift upon his knees.

"The letters and photographs I should probably keep under my piller for a spell; the jelly I'd give to Miss Hale, to use for the sick ones; the cake-stuff and that pot of jam, that's gettin' ready to work, I'd stand treat with for tea, as dinner wasn't all we could have wished. The apples I'd keep to eat, and fling at Joe when he was too bashful to ask for one, and the *tobaccer* I would *not* go lavishin' on folks that have no business to be enjoyin' luxuries when many a poor feller is dyin' of want down to Charlestown. There, sir! that's what *I'd* do if any one was so clever as to send me a jolly box like this."

Sam was enjoying the full glow of his shower-bath by this time. As Ben designated the various articles, he set them apart; and when the inventory ended, he marched away with the first instalment: two of the biggest, rosiest apples for Joe, and all the pictorial papers. Pickles are not usually regarded as tokens of regard, but as Sam dealt them out one at a time, — for he would let nobody help him, and his single hand being the left, was as awkward as it was willing, — the boys' faces brightened; for a friendly word accompanied each, which made the sour gherkins as welcome as sweetmeats. With every trip the donor's spirits rose; for Ben circulated freely between whiles, and, thanks to him, not an allusion to the past marred the satisfaction of the present. Jam, soda-biscuits, and cake were such welcome additions to the usual bill of fare, that when supper was over a vote of thanks was passed, and speeches were made; for, being true Americans, the ruling passion found vent in the usual "Fellow-citizens!" and allusions to the "Star-spangled Banner." After which Sam subsided, feeling himself a public benefactor, and a man of mark.

A perfectly easy, pleasant day throughout would be almost an impossibility in any hospital, and this one was no exception to the general rule; for, at the usual time, Dr. Bangs went his rounds, leaving the customary amount of discomfort, discontent and dismay behind him. A skilful surgeon and an excellent man was Dr. Bangs, but not a sanguine or conciliatory individual; many cares and crosses caused him to regard the world as one large hospital, and his fellow-beings all more or less dangerously wounded patients in it. He saw life through the bluest of blue spectacles, and seemed to think that the sooner people quitted it the happier for them. He did his duty by the men, but if they recovered he looked half disappointed, and congratulated them with cheerful prophecies that there would come a time when they would wish they hadn't. If one died he seemed relieved, and surveyed him with pensive satisfaction, saying heartily, —

"He's comfortable, now, poor soul, and well out of this miserable world, thank God!"

But for Ben the sanitary influences of the doctor's ward would have been small, and Dante's doleful line might: have been written on the threshold of the door,

"Who enters here leaves hope behind."

Ben and the doctor perfectly understood and liked each other, but never agreed, and always skirmished over the boys as if manful cheerfulness and medical despair were fighting for the soul and body of each one.

"Well," began the doctor, looking at Sam's arm, or, rather, all that was left of that member after two amputations, "we shall be ready for another turn at this in a day or two if it don't mend faster. Tetanus sometimes follows such cases; but that is soon over, and I should not object to a case of it, by way of variety." Sam's hopeful face fell, and he set his teeth as if the fatal symptoms were already felt.

"If one kind of lockjaw was more prevailing than 'tis, it wouldn't be a bad thing for some folks I could mention," observed Ben, covering the well-healed stump as carefully as if it were a sleeping baby; adding, as the doctor walked away, "There's a sanguinary old sawbones for you! Why, bless your buttons, Sam, you are doing splendid, and he goes on that way because there's no chance of his having another cut at you! Now he's squenchin' Turner, jest as we've blowed a spark of spirit into him. If ever there was a born extinguisher its Bangs!"

Ben rushed to the rescue, and not a minute too soon; for Turner, — who now labored under the delusion that his recovery depended solely upon his getting out of bed every fifteen minutes, was sitting by the fire, looking up at the doctor, who pleasantly observed, while feeling his pulse, —

"So you are getting ready for another fever, are you? Well, we've grown rather fond of you, and will keep you six weeks longer if you have set your heart on it." Turner looked nervous, for the doctor's jokes were always grim ones; but Ben took the other hand in his, and gently rocked the chair as he replied, with great politeness, —

"This robust convalescent of ourn would be happy to oblige you, sir, but he has a pressin' engagement up to Jersey for next week, and couldn't stop on no account. You see Miss Turner wants a careful nuss for little Georgie, and he's a goin' to take the place."

Feeling himself an the brink of a laugh as Turner simpered with a ludicrous mixture of pride in his baby and fear for himself, Dr. Bangs said, with unusual sternness and a glance at Ben, —

"You take the responsibility of this step upon yourself, do you? Very well; then I wash my hands of Turner; only, if that bed is empty in a week, don't lay the blame of it at my door."

"Nothing shall induce me to do it, sir," briskly responded Ben. "Now then, turn in my boy, and sleep your prettiest, for I wouldn't but disappoint that cheerfulest of men for a month's wages; and that's liberal, as I ain't likely to get it."

"How is this young man after the rash dissipations of the day?" asked the doctor, pausing at the bed in the corner, after he had made a lively progress down the room, hotly followed by Ben.

"I'm first-rate, sir," panted Joe, who always said so, though each day found him feebler than the last. Every one was kind to Joe, even the gruff doctor, whose man. manner softened, and who was forced to frown heavily to hide the pity in his eyes.

"How's the cough?"

"Better, sir; being weaker, I can't fight against it as I used to do, so it comes rather easier."

"Sleep any last night?"

"Not much; but it's very pleasant laying here when the room is still, and no light but the fire. Ben keeps it bright; and, when I fret, he talks to me, and makes the time go telling stories till he gets so sleepy he can hardly speak.

Dear old Ben! I hope he'll have some one as kind to him, when he needs it as I do now."

"He will get what he deserves by-and-by, you maybe sure of that," said the doctor, as severely as if Ben merited eternal condemnation.

A great drop splashed down upon the hearth, as Joe spoke; but Ben put his foot on it, and turned about as if defying any one to say he shed it.

"Of all the perverse and reckless women whom I have known in the course of a forty years' practice, this one is the most perverse and reckless," said the doctor, abruptly addressing Miss Hale, who just then appeared, bringing Joe's "posy-basket" back. "You will oblige me, ma'am, by sitting in this chair with your hands folded for twenty minutes; the clock will then strike nine, and you will go straight up to your bed."

Miss Hale demurely sat down, and the doctor ponderously departed, sighing regretfully as he went through the room, as if disappointed that the whole thirty were not lying at death's door; but on the threshold he turned about, exclaimed:

"Good-night, boys! God bless you!" and vanished as precipitately as if a trap-door had swallowed him up.

Miss Hale was a perverse woman in some things; for, instead of folding her tired hands, she took a rusty-covered volume from the mantle-piece, and, sitting by Joe's bed, began to read aloud. One by one all other sounds grew still; one by one the men composed themselves to listen; and one by one the words of the sweet old Christmas story came to them, as the woman's quiet voice went reading on. If any wounded spirit needed balm, if any hungry heart asked food, if any upright purpose, newborn aspiration, or sincere repentance wavered for want of human strength, all found help, hope, and consolation in the beautiful and blessed influences of the book, the reader, and the hour.

The bells rung nine, the lights grew dim, the day's work was done; but Miss Hale lingered beside Joe's bed, for his face wore a wistful look, and he seemed loath to have her go.

"What is it, dear?" she said; "what can I do for you before I leave you to Ben's care?"

He drew her nearer, and whispered earnestly, —

"It's something that I know you'll do for me, because I can't do it for myself, not as I want it done, and you can. I'm going pretty fast now, ma'am; and when some one else is laying here, I want you to tell the boys, — every one, from Ben to Barney, — how much I thanked 'em, how much I loved 'em, and how glad I was that I had known 'em, even for such a little while."

"Yes, Joe, I'll tell them all. What else can I do, my boy?"

"Only let me say to you what no one else must say for me, that all I want to live for is to try and do something in my poor way to show you how I thank you, ma'am. It isn't what you've said to me, it isn't what you've done for me alone, that makes me grateful; it's because you've learned me many things without knowing it, showed me what I ought to have been before, if I'd had any one to tell me how, and made this such a happy, home-like place, I shall be sorry when I have to go."

Poor Joe! it must have fared hardly with him all those twenty years, if a hospital seemed home-like, and a little sympathy, a little care, could fill him with such earnest gratitude. He stopped a moment to lay his cheek upon the hand he held in both of his, then hurried on as if he felt his breath beginning to give out:

"I dare say many boys have said this to you, ma'am, better than I can, for I don't say half I feel; but I know that none of 'em ever thanked you as I thank you in my heart, or ever loved you as I'll love you all my life. To-day I hadn't anything to give you, I'm so poor; but I wanted to tell you this, on the last Christmas I shall ever see."

It was a very humble kiss he gave that hand; but the fervor of a first love warmed it, and the sincerity of a great gratitude made it both a precious and pathetic gift to one who, half unconsciously, had made this brief and barren life so rich and happy at its close. Always womanly and tender, Miss Hale's face was doubly so, as she leaned over him, whispering, —

"I have had my present, now. Good-night, Joe."

The Hospital Lamp

IT WAS A VERY DULL LAMP; the only one that burned in that sad place. The others were extinguished as the bell rung nine, and this central one was lowered till it became a pale star in the twilight of the room. All night it burned above the motley sleepers, showing the sights only to be seen in a hospital ward; and all night one pair of eyes seemed to watch it, with a wistful constancy which caused me to wonder what thought or purpose was illuminated by that feeble ray.

Wearied with a long watch by a fever-patient's bed, I took advantage of the heavy sleep that fell upon him to rest and refresh myself by pacing, noise-lessly, up and down the aisle, on either side of which stretched the long rows of beds covered with grey army-blankets, and looking in the dusk as narrow, dark, and still, as new-made graves. On one of these beds lay the watcher of the light—a rough, dark man, with keen eyes, and a mane of long black hair, which he never would have cut, although it caused him to be christened "Absalom Tenser" by his mates. Stern and silent was this Hunt, showing a grim, sort of fortitude and patience under great suffering, which won respect but not affection; for lie also possessed gruff mariners, and a decidedly "let-me-alone" expression of countenance. Very short answers were all any questioner received, and an absent "Thanky, ma'am" was the only acknowl-edgment of the daily cares it was my duty to bestow, upon him.

Though the most ungracious and unpromising of all my boys, that one habit of his made him interesting to me, and for several days I had been taking reconnoissances and preparing to steal a march upon him, fancying that he had something on his mind, and would be the easier for telling it.

First published in *The Daily Morning Drum-Beat*, newsletter of the Brooklyn and Long Island Fair (February 1864).

By day he slept much, or appeared to do so, for turning his face to the wall he drew his long hair over his eyes, and either shut out the world entirely or viewed it stealthily from behind that screen. But at night, when the room was still, and no one stirring but myself, he emerged from his covers, folded his grins under his head, and lay staring fixedly at the light as if it had some irresistible fascination for him. He took no heed of me, and I seldom spoke; but while apparently unmindful of him, I watched the varying expression of his face; some, times gloomy and despondent, sometimes restless and eager, but of late grave and steady, as if the dull lamp had shed a comfortable gleam upon some anxious thought of his. His face wore that expression then, and as I paused to wet the stump of the leg left at Fredericksburg, I could not resist speaking to him, though I only, put the question often asked,

"Are you in pain, Hunt?"

He slowly turned his glance from the lamp to me, paused a moment to recall and comprehend the half-heard words, then answered with his usual brevity:

"Not more'n common."

"Doesn't the light trouble you?"

"No, ma'am; I like it."

"I am afraid it keeps you awake. Your bed can be turned, or the lamp shaded, if it is so."

"Don't put out the light, or move me anywheres; I'm easiest so."

He spoke eagerly; and curious to discover the cause of his whim, I said:

"Time enough for that, by and by. I got something! I better 'n sleep these times."

"What are you so busy about all night, when the other men, are dreaming?"

"Thinking, ma'am."

"Well, don't think too much; and if there is anything you wish to have written or attended to, remember I am here, and glad to do it for you;"

"Thank ye, ma'am. I guess I shall have to study this out single-handed; if I can't, I'll let you know."

Still hoping to win the confidence which sooner or later was pretty sure to be bestowed, I dropped that subject and took up another, which usually proved an agreeable one, to the boys, because so full of personal interest, anxiety, or pride.

"Your wound is getting on bravely. Do you know Dr. Cutter says you won't have to lose the knee joint after all, you have kept so quiet and been so patient."

There was a flash of pleasure in Hunt's face, but he seemed more intent upon some happier fact than the preservation of the joint, the loss of which would have entailed greater suffering, danger and helplessness. "He thinks it's owing to my being still and so on, does he?" was all the answer Hunt made me.

"Yes, he says that when you came he was afraid you were going to have a bad time of it, because your leg was not well amputated and you were a restless, excitable person. But you very pleasantly disappointed him and here you are doing well, thanks to your self-control, or to the subject that seems to absorb your mind, and keep your thoughts from your wound."

He drew a long breath, gave a satisfied little nod, and said as if to himself "I guess the thinking did it."

Seeing signs of promise in the half smile that seemed to break out against his will, and the nod, so strongly suggestive of contentment and relief, I pursued the propitious topic.

"I like to hear the men tell about their wounds, but you never told me how you lost your leg."

"Shouldn't think that sort of thing would be interesting to a lady."

He looked gratified, for all his gruff way of speaking, and I replied with as much enthusiasm as a very drowsy voice and countenance could express.

"It is very interesting to me; and as we are the only wakeful ones, let us have a sociable little chat about it."

"I ain't much given to that kind of thing, by nature or by grace neither. Must be lonesome here for you, though."

He seemed to add the last sentence, as if to atone for the bluntness of the preceding one, and looked as if he would like to be sociable if he only knew how.

"Yes, it is lonely sometimes; but you can make it pleasanter by talking a little, and perhaps the sound of your own voice, and the cool trickle of the water will make you sleepy after a while."

"Don't the water make your hands dreadful cold, ma'am?" he asked, as I began on a fresh basinful.

It did; but I could have, clapped them both warm again at that speech, for it was the first sign of friendliness the man had ever shown. I only gave the big sponge a grateful squeeze, however, and answered soberly:

"I rather like to splash about in this way, particularly if I have stories told me at the same time."

"There isn't much to tell, any way," he began, after a pause of recollection. "You've heard enough about our battle to know how things were, so I needn't stop for that. We were doing our best, after we got over the bridge, when there came a shell and scattered half a dozen of us pretty lively. I was pitched flat, but I didn't feel hurt—only mad—and jumped up to hit 'em again but just tumbled over with an awful wrench, and a still awfuller feeling that both my legs were gone."

"Did no one stop to help you?"

"Too busy for that, ma'am; the boys can't stop to pick up their mates when there are Rebs ahead to be knocked down. I knew there was no more fighting for me, and just laid still with the balls singing round me, wondering where they'd hit next."

"How did you feel?"

"Dreadful busy, at first; for everything I'd ever said, seen, or done seemed to go spinning through my head, till I got so dizzy trying to keep my wits stiddy that I lost 'em altogether. I didn't find 'em again till somebody laid hold of me. Two of our boys were lugging me along back, but they had to dodge behind walls, and cut up and down, for the scrimmage was going on all round us. One of 'em was hit in the side, the other in the face, but not bad, and they managed to get me into a little rayvine sort of a place out of danger. There I begged 'em to lay me down and let me be, for I couldn't go any further. Believed I was bleeding to death, rapid, but it wasn't hard, and I only wanted to drop off easy, if I could."

"Did you want to die, Hunt?"

"Didn't much care then?"

An unconscious emphasis on the "then" caused me to ask—

"But you do now?"

"Well ain't quite ready yet." As he spoke his eye went back to the light as, if from force of habit; and the anxious, thoughtful look disturbed the composure of his face for a moment. He seemed to forget his story, so I brought him back to it.

"They didn't leave you there, I hope?"

"No ma'am, for, just as they were at their wits-end what to do with me we come upon a surgeon lurking there, either to watch the fight or to hide; don't know which, and never found out who he was or where lie come from. There he was anyway, looking seared enough, and when he saw us would have cut and run if Tom Hyde, one of the chaps carrying me, hadn't made him stop and take a look at me. My leg was smashed, and ought to come off right away, he said. 'Do it then,' says Tom; he was one of your rough and readys, Tom was, but underneath as kind as a—well—as a woman."

I made my best bow over the basin in return for the compliment, and the odd, half shy, half grateful look that accompanied it. At which demonstration Hunt showed symptoms of a desire to wrap himself up in his hair again, but thought better of it and went on.

"The surgeon was young and soared, and out of sorts every way, and said he couldn't do it, hadn't got his things, and soon. 'Yes you have, so out with 'em,' says Tom, rapping on a case he sees in the chap's breast pocket. 'Can't without bandages,' he says next. 'Here they are, and more where they come from,' says Tom; and shedding his coat, off come his shirt-sleeves, and was stripped up in a jiffy. 'I must have help,' says the surgeon, still dawdling round, and me groaning my life out at his feet. 'Here's help—lots of it,' says Tom, taking my head on his arm, while Joel Parkes tied up his bleeding face, and stood ready to lend a hand. Seeing no way out of it, the surgeon turned up his cuffs and went at me as if I'd done it a-purpose, to spite him. Good Lord I but that was awful."

The mere memory of it made him quiver and shut his eyes, as if he felt again the sharp agony of shattered bones, rent flesh, and pitiless knife.

"Never mind that part of the story, Hunt. Tell how you got comfortable again, and forget the rest of it."

"I don't want to forget it," he said decidedly; "it's part of the concern, and makes things easier now. I didn't know a man could bear so much and live. It's bad enough when done well, with chloroform and everything handy; but laying on the wet ground with nothing right, and a beast of a surgeon hackin' away at you, it's torment, and no mistake. It seemed as if he was cutting my heart out, and I never could have stood it if it hadn't been for Tom. He held me close and steady, but he cried like a baby the whole time, and that did me good. Can't say why, but it did. As for Joel, he gave out altogether and went off for help, seeing as he hadn't pluck enough to stay, though he'd fight till he couldn't see. I'll never forget that place if I live to be a hundred! Seems as if I could see the very grass I tore up, the muddy brook they laid me by, the high bank with Joel creeping up it, Tom's face wet and white, the surgeon with his red hands, swearing to himself as he worked, and all the while such a roar of guns in my ears I hardly heard myself crying out for some one to shoot me, and put me out of my misery."

"How did you get to the hospital?" I asked, anxious that he should neither sadden nor excite himself by re-living in imagination the horrors of that hour.

"Don't know, ma'am. There came a time when I couldn't bear any more, and what happened till I got over the river again is more than I can tell. I didn't mind matters much for a day or two, and the first thing that brought me round was being put aboard the transport to come up here. I was packed in with a lot of poor fellows, and was beginning to wish I'd stayed queer, so I shouldn't care where I was, when I heard Tom's voice saying, 'Never mind boys, put me down anywheres, and see to the others first; I can wait.' That set me up; I sung out, and they stowed him alongside of me. It was so dark down there I couldn't see his face, but his voice and ways were just as hearty as ever, and he kept up my spirits wonderful all that day. I was pretty weak and kept dozing off, but whenever I woke I always felt for Tom, and Tom was always there. He told me that when Joel came back with help I was taken off to the field hospital, and he went back for another go at the Rebs, but got a ball in his throat, and was in rather a bad way, but guessed he'd weather it. He couldn't lay down, but sat leaning back with his hand on my pillar where I could find it easy, and talked to me all he could, for he hadn't much voice left, and there was a dismal groaning all round us. Aint you tired, ma'am?"

"No, indeed, do finish, if you are not sleepy." He showed an inclination to stop there, but I wanted the rest, and seeing the sincerity of my desire, he gravely finished his little story.

"That was along, dark day, not like any I'd ever seen before, for some how I seemed out of the world and done with. Come night, I felt so weak and cold I thought I was most over Jordan so I gave my watch to Tom as a keepsake, and told him to say good-bye to the boys for me. I hadn't any folks of my own, Tom had wife; children, father, mother, brothers and sister, and lots of friends everywhere. I, thinking of this, said it was lucky it was me that was going, not him, for no one would care. 'That isn't all;' says he; 'are you ready to go, Charley?' I hadn't thought of that, not being pious, and living a wild, rough-and-tumble sort of a life. 'Are you?' says I, feeling scared all of a sudden, 'Hope so,' says he; 'anyway, I've tried to be, and that, tells, Charley—that tells in the end. I didn't say any more, but dropped off to sleep, wishing I was Tom. In the morning as soon as ever I woke I looked around to thank him, for a great piece of his blanket was over me; There he was, sitting as I left him; his hand on my pillar, his face turned toward me so quiet looking and so happy I couldn't believe he was gone. But he was; and for all he left so many to miss him I couldn't help feeling that he was the one to go, for I—"

Hunt stopped abruptly, laid his arm across his face, and said no more for several minutes. I, too, was silent; reproaching myself for the injustice I had done him, when, underneath his forbidding exterior, he hid so much of the genuine tenderness which few men are without, Now I had found the clue to these wakeful hours of his, and the love he bore the lamp whose little flame lead lighted him to a clearer knowledge of himself, bringing from the painful present the premise of a nobler future. He seemed so unconscious of the revelation he had made to me, and so slow to speak of that which lay nearest to him, that I made no comment on it then, except to ask for the confirmation of my thought:

"And when you be here, looking at the light, you are thinking of that good friend, Tom?"

"Yes, ma'am, and trying to be ready."

As if fearing to betray emotion, he made his mouth grimmer than ever when he spoke, but involuntarily his eyes turned to the lamp shining above there in the gloom, and as he looked his steady gaze flickered suddenly as two lesser lights were reflected in those softened eyes of his. I knew what was coming, and softly laying a clean, cool napkin on his wound, I went away, that nothing should disturb the precious moment that had come to him.

Half an hour later, as I went down the room in search of water for lips too parched to syllable the word, I glanced at Hunt. He was fast asleep, one cheek pillowed on his hand, and in his rough brown face the tranquil expression of a tired child. It was a sight that made the light flicker before my eyes also as I went back to my watch, feeling sure that for this man peace would come out of war; and the flame kindled in the darkness of a transport, red by the pale glimmer of a hospital lamp, would not die out, but brighten this life for him, and make him "ready" for the life to come.

Love and Loyalty

I.

"O YOU MEAN IT, ROSE?"

"Yes."

"You set a high price on your love; I cannot pay it."

"I think you will."

She came a little nearer, this beautiful woman, whom the young man loved with all the ardor of a first affection, she laid her hand upon his arm, and looked up in his face, her own wearing its most persuasive aspect; for tenderness seemed to have conquered pride, and will was concealed under a winning softness which made her doubly dangerous, as she said, in the slow, sweet voice that betrayed her Southern birth, —

"Remember what you ask,—what I offer; then tell me which demands the highest price for love. You would have me give up friends, fortune, home, all the opinions, prejudices, and beliefs of birth and education, all the hopes and purposes of years, for your sake. I ask nothing of you but the relinquishment of a mistaken duty; I offer you all I possess: a life of luxury and power, and, —myself."

She paused there, with a gesture of proud humility, as if she would ignore the fact, yet could not quite conceal the consciousness, that she had much to bestow upon the lover who had far less to offer.

"Oh, Rose, you tempt me terribly," he said; "not with your possessions or a life of luxury, but with yourself, because I love you more than a thousand fortunes or a century of ease and power. Yet, dear as you are to me, and barren as the world will be without you, I dare not turn traitor even for your sake."

First published in *The United States Service Magazine*, II, nos. 1, 2, 3, 5 (1864).

"Yet you would have me do it for yours."

"No: treachery to the wrong is allegiance to the right, and I only ask you to love your country better than yourself, as I try to do."

"Who shall say which is right and which wrong? I am tired of the words. I want to forget the ills I cannot cure, and enjoy life while I may. Youth was made for happiness; why waste it in a quarrel which time alone can end? Robert, I do not ask you to turn traitor. I do not care what you believe. I only ask you to stay with me, now that I have owned how much you are to me."

"God knows I wish I could, Rose; but idleness is treason in times like these. What right have I to think of my own happiness when my country needs me? It is like deserting my old mother in extremest peril to stand idle now; and when you tempt me to forget this, I must deny your prayer, because it is the only one I cannot grant."

"But, Robert, you are little to the rest of the world, and everything to me. Your country does not need you half so much as I, — 'a stranger in a strange land'; for, in a great struggle like this, what can one man do?"

"His duty, Rose."

She pleaded eloquently with voice, and eyes, and hands; but something in the sad gravity of the young man's face was a keener reproach than his words. She felt that she could not win him so, and, with a swift and subtle change of countenance and manner, she put him from her, saying reproachfully, —

"Then do yours, and make some reparation for the peace of mind you have destroyed. I have a right to ask this. I came here as to a refuge, hoping to live unknown till the storm was over. Why did you find me out, protect me by your influence, lighten any exile by your society, and, under the guise of friendship, teach me to love you?"

Robert Stirling watched her with lover's eyes, listened with lover's ears, and answered like a lover, finding her the fairer and dearer for the growing fear that a hard test was in store for him.

"I found you out, because your beauty would not be concealed; I protected you, because you were a woman, and alone; I gave you friendship, because I wished to prove that we of the North hold sacred the faith our enemies place in us by sending to our keeping the treasure they most value; and, Rose, I loved you because I could not help it."

She smiled then, and the color deepened beautifully in the half-averted face, but she did not speak, and Robert took heart from the sign.

"I never meant to tell you this, fearing what has now happened, and I resolved to go away. But, coming here to say good-by, your grief melted my resolve, and I told you what I could no longer bide. Have I been ungenerous and unjust? If you believe so, tell me what reparation I can make, and, if it is anything an honest man may do, I will do it."

She knew that, was glad to know it; yet, with the exacting affection of a selfish woman, she felt a jealous fear that she loved more than she was beloved, and must assure herself by some trial that she was all in all to her young lover. He waited for her answer with such keen anxiety, such wistful tenderness, that she felt confident of success; and, yielding to the love of power so strong within her, she could not resist the desire of exercising it over this new subject, finding her excuse in the fond yet wayward wish to keep from danger that which was now so dear to her.

"I have lost enough by this costly war. I will lose no more," she said. "It is easier to part at once than later, when time has more endeared us to each other. Choose between the country which you love and the woman who loves you, and by that choice we will both abide."

"Rose, this is cruel, this is hard! Let me choose both, and be the better man for that double service."

"It is impossible. No one can serve two mistresses. I will have all or nothing."

As she spoke she gently, but decidedly, freed herself from his detaining hold, and stood away from him, as if to prove both her strength and her sincerity. The act changed the words of separation trembling on Robert's lips to words of entreaty; for, though his upright nature owned the hard duty, his heart clung to its idol, feeling that it must be wrenched away.

"Wait a little, Rose. Give me time to think. Let me prove that I am no coward; then I will serve you, and you alone."

"No, Robert; if you truly loved me, you would be eager and glad to make any sacrifice for me. I would willingly make many for you; but this one I cannot, because it robs me of you in a double sense. If you fall, I lose you; if you come back alive, I lose you no less, for how can I accept a hand reddened with the blood of those I love?"

He had no answer, and stood silent. She saw that this moment of keen suffering and conflicting passions was the turning-point in the young man's life, yet, nothing doubting her power, she hardened herself to his pain that she might gain her point now and repay his submission by greater affection hereafter. Her voice broke the brief silence, steady, sweet, and sad:

"I see that you have chosen; I submit. But go at once, while I can part as I should; and remember, we must never meet again."

He had dropped his face into his hands, struggling dumbly with honest conscience and rebellious heart. Standing so, he felt a light touch on his bent head, heard the sound of a departing step, and looked up to see Rose passing from his sight, perhaps forever. An exclamation of love and longing broke from his lips; at the sound she paused, and, turning, let him see that her face was bathed in tears. At that sight duty seemed doubly stern and cruel, the sacrifice of integrity grew an easy thing, and separation an impossibility. The tender eyes were on him, the imploring hands outstretched to him, and the beloved voice cried, brokenly,

"Oh, Robert, stay!"

"I will!"

He spoke out defiantly, as if to silence the inward monitor that would not yield consent; he offered his hand to seal the promise, and took one step toward the fair temptation,—no more; for, at the instant, up from below rose a voice, clear and mellow as a silver horn, singing, —

> *He has sounded forth the trumpet,*
> *That shall never call retreat;*
> *He is sifting out the hearts of men*
> *Before his judgment-seat;*
> *Oh, be swift, my soul, to answer him;*
> *Be jubilant, my feet!*
> *For God is marching on.*

The song broke the troubled silence with a martial ring that, to one listener, sounded like a bugle-call, banishing with its magic breath the weakness that had nearly made a recreant of him; for the opportune outbreak of the familiar voice, the memories it woke, the nobler spirit it recalled, all made that sweet and stirring strain the young man's salvation. Both stood motionless, and so still that every word came clearly through the sunny hush that filled the room. Rose's face grew anxious, a flash of anger dried the tears, and the expression which had been so tender changed to one of petulant annoyance. But Robert did not see it; he no longer watched her; he had turned towards the open window, and was looking far away into the distance, where seemed to lie the future this moment was to make or mar, while his whole aspect grew calm and steady, as if with the sense of self-control came the power of self-sacrifice.

As the song ended, he turned, gave one parting look at the woman whom he loved, said, "I have chosen! Rose, good-by," and was gone.

Out into the beautiful spring world he went, blind to its beauty, deaf to its music, unconscious of its peace.

Before him went the blithe singer, — a young man, with uncovered head, brown hair blowing in the wind, thoughtful eyes bent on the ground, and lips still softly singing, as he walked. This brother, always just and gentle, always ready with sympathy and counsel, now seemed doubly dear to the sore heart of Robert, as, hurrying to him, he grasped his arm as a drowning man might clutch at sudden help; for, though the victory seemed won, he dared not trust himself alone, with that great longing tugging at his heart.

"Why, Rob! — what is it?" asked his brother, pausing to wonder at the change which had befallen him since they parted but a little while ago.

"Ask no questions, Richard; but sing on, sing on, and, if you love me, keep me fast till we get home," answered Robert, excitedly.

Something in his manner, and the glance he cast over his shoulder, seemed to enlighten his brother. Richard's face darkened ominously for a moment, then softened with sincerest pity as he drew the hand closer through his arm, and answered, with an almost womanly compassion, —

"Poor lad, I knew it would be so! but I had no fear that you would become a slave to that beautiful tyrant. The bitter draught is often more wholesome than the sweet, and you are wise to *let* her go before it is too late. Tell me your trouble, Rob, and let me help you bear it."

"Not now! not here! Sing, Rick, if you would not have me break away and go back to her again."

His brother obeyed him, not with the war-song, but with the simpler air their mother's voice had made a lullaby, beloved by them as babies, boys, and men. Now, as of old, it soothed and comforted; and, though poor Robert turned his face away and let his brother had him where he would, the first sharpness of his pain eras eased by a recollection born of the song; for he remembered that though one woman had failed him, there still remained another whose faithful love would know no shadow of a change.

As they came into the familiar room, where every object spoke of the dear household league lasting unbroken for so many years, a softer mood replaced the pain and passion that had struggled in the lover's heart; and, throwing himself into the ancient chair where so many boyish griefs had been consoled, he laid his head upon his arms, and forgot his manhood for a little while. Richard stood beside him, with a kind hand on his shoulder, to assure him of a sympathy too deep and wise for words, till the fitting moment should appear. It soon came; and when the younger brother had made known his trouble, and the elder given what cheer he could, he tried to lead Robert's thoughts to other things, that he might forget disappointment in action.

"Nothing need detain you now, Rob," he said; "for the loss of one hope opens the way to the attainment of another. You shall enlist at once, and march away to fight the good fight."

"And you, Rick? We have both longed to go, but could not decide which it should be. Why should not you march away and let me stay with mother till my turn comes?"

"Need I tell you why? We did delay at first, because we could not choose which should stay with the dear old lady who has only us left now. But lately you have lingered because of Rose, and I because I would not leave you till I knew how you fared. That is all over now; and surely it is best for you to put States between you, and let absence teach you to forget."

"You are right, and I am a weak fool to dream of staying. I ought to go; but the spirit that once would have made the duty easy has deserted me. Richard, I have lost faith in myself; and am afraid to go alone. Come with me, to comfort and keep me steady, as you have done all my life."

"I wish I could. Never doubt nor despond, no; but remember that *we* trust you, *we* expect great things of you, and are sure you never will disgrace the name father gave into our keeping."

"I'll do any best, Rick; but I shall need you more than ever, and if mother only knew how it is with me, I think she would say, 'Go.'"

"Mother does say it, heartily!"

Both started, and turned to see their mother watching them with an untroubled face. A right noble old woman, carrying her sixty years gracefully and well, — for her tall figure was unbent; below the gray hair shone eyes clear as any girl's, and her voice had a cheery ring to it that roused energy and hope in those who heard it; while the benignant power of her glance, the motherly compassion of her touch, brought confirmation to the wavering resolve and comfort to the wounded heart.

With the filial instinct which outlives childhood, Robert leaned against her as she drew his head to the bosom that could always give it rest, and told his sorrow in one broken exclamation, —

"Oh, mother, I loved her so!"

"I know it, dear: I saw it, and I warned you. But you thought me unjust. I desired to be proved so, and you ended here. You have loved like a man, have withstood temptation like a man; now bear your loss like one, and do not mar your sacrifice to principle by any vain regrets."

"Ah, mother, all the courage, energy, and strength seem to have gone out of me, and I am tired of my life."

"Not yet, Rob; wait a little, and you will find that life has gained a new significance. This trouble will change the boy into a man, braver and better for the past, because, if I know my son, he will never let his life be thwarted by a selfish woman's folly or caprice."

She spoke proudly, and Robert lifted his head with an air as proud.

"You are right. I will not. But you must let me go! I cannot answer for myself if I stay here."

"You shall go, and Rick with you."

"But, mother, can we, — ought we, — to leave you alone?" began Richard, longing, yet loath, to go.

"No, my boys, you neither can nor will; for I go with you."

"With us?" cried both brothers, in a breath.

"Ay, lads, that I will!" she answered, heartily. "There is work for the old hands as well as for the young; and while my boys fight for me, I will both nurse and pray for them."

"But, mother, the distance and danger, the hardships and horrors of such a life, will be too much for you. Let one of us stay, and keep you safely here at home."

"Not while you are needed elsewhere. Other mothers give their boys; why should not I give mine? Other women endure the hardships and horrors of camps and hospitals; can I not do as much? You offer your young lives; surely I may offer the remains of mine. Say no more: I must enlist with my boys. I could never sit with folded hands at home, tormenting myself with fears for you, although God knows I send you willingly."

"You should have been a Roman matron, mother, with many sons to give for your country and few tears for yourself," said Richard, watching the fire of her glance, and listening to the steady voice that talked so cheerfully of danger and of death.

"Ah, Rob, the ancient legends preserved the brave words of the Roman matrons, but they left no record of the Roman mothers' tears, because they kept them for the bitter hours that came when the sacrifice had been made." And, as she spoke, two great drops rolled down to glitter upon Robert's hair.

For a moment no one stirred, as the three looked their new future in the face, and, seeing all its perils, owned its wisdom, accepted its duties, and stood ready to fulfil them to the last.

Mrs. Stirling spoke first,

"My sons, these are times to try the metal of all souls; and if we would have ours ring clear, we must follow with devout obedience the strong convictions that prompt and lead its to the right. Go, lads, and do your best, remembering that mother follows you, to rejoice if you win, to comfort you if you fail, to nurse you if you need it, and if you fall to lay you tenderly into your graves, with the proud thought, 'They did their duty: God will remember that, and comfort me.'"

The faces of the brothers kindled as she spoke; their hearts answered her with a nobler fervor than the chivalrous enthusiasm of young blood, and both made a silent vow of loyalty, to last inviolate through all their lives, as, laying a hand on either head, that brave old mother dedicated sons and self to the service of the liberties she loved.

II.

THE ARMY OF THE POTOMAC was on its march northward, to defeat Lee's daring raid and make a little Pennsylvania village forever memorable. The heights above the town were already darkened by opposing troops; the quiet valley was already tumultuous with the tramp of gathering thousands, and the fruitful fields already reploughed for the awful human harvest soon to be gathered in. Every road swarmed with blue coats, every hill-side was a camp, every grove a bivouac, every wayside stream a fountain of refreshment to hundreds of weary men spent with the privations and fatigues of those forced marches through midsummer heats.

By one of these little brooks a dusty regiment was halted for brief repose. At the welcome order, many of the exhausted men dropped down where they stood, to snatch an hour's sleep; some sought the grateful shade of an orchard already robbed of its early fruit, and ate their scanty fare with a cheerful content that made it sweet; others stretched themselves along the trampled borders of the brook, bathing their swollen feet, or drinking long draughts of the turbid water, which, to their parched lips, was a better cordial than the costliest twine. Apart from all these groups, two comrades lay side by side in the shadow of the orchard-wall. Both were young and comely men, stalwart, keen-eyed, and already bronzed by a Southern sun, although this was their first campaign. Both were silent, yet neither slept, and in their silence there was a marked difference, — one lay looking straight up through the waving boughs at the clear blue overhead, with an expression as serene; the other half leaned on his folded arm, moodily plucking at the turf which was his pillow, with now and then an impatient sigh, a restless gesture. One of these demonstrations of discontent presently roused his comrade from a waking dream. He sat up, laid a cool hand on the other's hot forehead, and said, with brotherly solicitude,

"Not asleep yet, Rob? I hope you've not had a sunstroke, like poor Blake; for, if you are left behind, we shall both lose our share of the fight."

"As well die that way as with a rebel bullet through your head; though, if I had my choice, I'd try the last, as being the quickest," replied the other, gloomily.

"That doesn't sound like you, Rob, — you'll think better of it to-morrow, when you've had a night's sound sleep. This has been a hard march for a young soldier's first."

"How much older are you than I, either as man or soldier, Rick?" asked Robert, half petulantly, half proudly.

"Three hours older as a man, ten minutes as a soldier: you know I enlisted first. Yet I'm much the elder in many things, as you often tell me," said Richard, with the smile that always soothed his brother's more fiery spirit. One of the privileges of my seniority is the care of you; so tell me what harasses you and scares rest away?"

"The old pain, Rick. All these weeks of absence have not lessened it; and the thought of going into a battle out of which I may never come alive, without seeing her once more, makes me almost resolve to desert, and satisfy myself at any cost. You cannot understand this, for you don't know what it is to love — to have a woman's face haunting you day and night, to hear a woman's voice always sounding in your ears with a distinctness that will not let you rest."

"I know it all, Rob!"

The words seemed to slip involuntarily from the young man's lips, for he checked himself sharply, and cast an anxious look at his brother. But Robert was too absorbed in his own emotions to read those of another, and only answered, in a cheerier tone,

"You mean mother. God bless her, wherever she is, and send us safely home to her!"

An almost pathetic patience replaced the momentary agitation Richard's face betrayed, and his eyes turned wistfully towards the green hills that lay between the mother and her boys, as he answered, with a smile of sorrowful significance,

"Every man is better and braver for a woman's love; so, as I have no younger sweetheart, I shall take the dear old lady for my mistress, and try to serve her like a loyal knight."

"Rick!" exclaimed his brother, earnestly, "if the coming battle proves my last as well as my first, promise that for my sake you'll befriend poor Rose, —that you will forgive her, love her, care for her, as if in truth she were my widow."

Richard grasped the hand outstretched to him, and answered, with a fervor that fully satisfied his brother, "I promise, Rob!" then added quickly, "But there will be no need of that; for, if mortal man can do it, I will keep you, to care for Rose yourself."

Through the momentary pause that followed came the pleasant sound of falling water.

"Hark, Rob? do you hear it? Give me your canteen, and I'll bring you a cool draught that shall remind you of the old well at home."

Rising as he spoke, Richard went to the low wall that rose behind them, swung himself over, and, plunging down a ferny slope, found a hidden spring dripping musically from mossy crevices among the rocks into a little pool below. Pausing a moment to let the shadowy solitude of the green nook bathe his weary spirit in its peace, he turned to catch the coolest drops that fell; but, as he bent, the canteen slipped from his hand and splashed unheeded into the pool, for, just opposite, through thickly-growing brakes, he caught the glitter of a pair of human eyes fixed full upon his face. An instant he stood motionless, conscious of that subtle thrill through blood and nerves which sudden danger or surprise can bring to the stoutest heart. Before he could move or speak, the brakes were parted, and the weird, withered face of an old woman — was lifted to the light. One of the despised race, clothed in rags, covered with dust, spent with weariness and pain, she lay there, such a wild and woful object that the lonely spot seemed chosen not as a resting-place, but as a grave. Leaning on one arm, she stretched the other trembling hand towards the young man, whispering, with an assuring nod,

"Don't be skeered, honey; I'se only a pore ole conty ban', gwine up ter de lan' ob freedom, ef I doesn't drap down by de way."

"Are you sick, or hurt, or only tired, my poor soul?" asked Richard, with such visible compassion in his face that the woman's brightened as she answered, with cheerfulness which made her utter destitution more pathetic, —

"I'se all dem, and starved inter de bargain; but, bress yer, chile, I'se done got used ter dat, and don't mind em much of I kin jes git on a piece ter-day. I'se ben porely for a spell, and layin' by; but I'se mendin' fas', and do sight ob de blue-coats and de kine face is mos' as relishin' as vittles."

"You shall have all three, as far as I can give them to you," said Richard, offering the last of his day's ration, and sitting down opposite the poor old creature, who, muttering hasty thanks, seized and devoured the food with an almost animal voracity, which proved how great her need had been. As the last morsel vanished, she drew a long breath, uttered a sigh of satisfaction, and, sitting more erect, said, with a deprecating gesture and a grateful glance, "Massa, I couldn't help forgittin' manners, kase I'se ben widout a mouffle sence yesterday, scept two green apples and de mint growin' ober dar."

"Have you been lying here all night? Where do you come from, and where are you going? Tell me, without fear, and let me help you if I can."

"De Lord lub yer kine heart, chile, and keep yer fer yer mudder. My boys is all gone now; but I knows de feelin', and I'll trus' yer, for's I dares. Yer see, I'se come from Souf Car'liny, and I'se gwine to de bressed Norf to fine my ole man, what missis tuk wid her when she lef' us bery suddin."

"What part of the North do you want to find?" asked Richard, eager to offer the desolate being such help as lay in his power. She saw the friendly impulse, and thanked him for it with a look; but the distrust born of many wrongs was stronger than the desire for sympathy, and cautiously, yet humbly, she said, "Massa mus' please ter 'scuse me ef I doesn't tell jes' whar I'se gwine. My pore old man is all dey's lef me; and ef missis knowed any ways dat I was lookin' for him, she'd tote him some place whar I couldn't come. It's way off bery fur; but de name of de town is wrote down in my heart, and, ef I lives, I'll fine it, shore."

"Where are your boys?" asked Richard, interested in spite of the woman's uninviting aspect.

"I'se had seven chil'en, honey, but dey's beg sent ebery which way, and I doesn't know whar dey is now, scept de dead ones. My darters was sole off years ago; one ob my boys was whipped to def, and one tore so wid de houn's it was a mercy de dear Lord tuk him. Two was put to work on de fortycations down dar; and the las' one, my little Mose, starved in my arms as we was wadin' fru de big swamps, where we runned when word came dat de Yanks was comin' and we'd be free ef we got to um. It was bery hard to leave de pore chile dar, but dere was two or free more little grabes to keep him comp'ny; so I come on alone, and, Glory Halleluyer! here I is."

"Now, how can I help you, ma'am?" said Richard, involuntarily adding respect to pity, as he heard the short, sad story of the losses now past help.

"Ef yer has a bit of money dat yer could spar, Chile, dat would 'sist me a heap. I kin hide it handy, and git vittles or a lif' when de roads is bery bad. I'se mos' wore out, fer I'se beg weeks a comin', kase I dunno de way, and can't trus' folks much. Now the Yanks is gwine my road, I wants to foller fas' as I kin, for I'se shore dey's right."

While she rambled on, Richard had taken out his purse, and halving the small store it contained, offered it, saying, kindly, —

"There old friend; I'd gladly do more for you if I could. I may be going where I shall never need money anymore; and, you know, they who give to the poor lend to the Lord: so this much will be saved up for me."

The woman rose to her knees, and, taking the generous hand in both her dusky ones, kissed it with trembling lips, wet it with grateful tears, as she cried, brokenly, "Bress yer, chile! bress yer! I'se no words white 'nuff to tank yer in, but I'll 'member yer all my days, and pray de Lord to hold yer safe in de holler ob His han'."

"Thank you, ma'am. What else can I do for you before I go?"

"Jes' tell me yer name, honey, so I kin 'mind de Lord ob yer tickerlally; for dere's such a heap ob prayers gwine up to Him dese bitter times, He mightn't mine sech pore ones as ole June's of de good name warn't in um."

"Richard Stirling," answered the young man, smiling at the poor soul's eagerness. "Good-by, old mother. Keep up a stout heart, and trust the blue-coats when you see them, till you find your husband and the happy North."

While he refilled the canteen, the contraband, with the fine sentiment so often found in the least promising of this affectionate race, hastily gathered a delicate fern or two, and, adding the one wild rose that blossomed in that shady spot, offered her little nosegay, with a humility as touching as her earnestness.

"It's a pore give, chile; but I'se nuffin' else sceptin' de wish dat yer'll hab all yer want in dis world and de nex'."

As Richard took it, through his mind flashed the memory of old romantic legends, wherein weird women foretold happy fortunes to young knights pausing at some wayside well, — fortunes to be won only by unshaken loyalty to virtue, love, and honor. Looking down upon the flower, whose name lent it a double charm to him, he said low, to himself, with quickened breath and kindling eyes, "A propitious wish! May it be fulfilled, if I deserve it!"

Then, as the first drum-beat sounded, he pressed the hard hand that gave the gift, and sprang up the bank, little dreaming how well the grateful heart he left behind him would one day remember and repay his charity.

Three days later, the brothers stood side by side in the ranks at Gettysburg, impatiently awaiting their turn to attack a rebel battery that must be silenced. From height to height thundered the cannon; up and down the long slopes surged a sea of struggling humanity; all the air was darkened by wavering clouds of smoke and dust, which lifted only when iron messengers of death tore their way through with deafening reports and sheets of flame; while, in the brief pauses that sometimes fell, the bands crashed out with dance-music, as if the wild excitement of the hour had made them fitting minstrels for an awful "dance of death."

"Remember, Rob, where that goes, we follow while we can," whispered Richard, glancing up at the torn flag streaming overhead.

"I'm ready, Rick," returned his brother, with flashing eyes, set teeth, and in every lineament such visible resolve to do and dare, that one hour seemed to have made the boy a hero and a man.

As the words left his lips, down the long line rang the welcome order, "Forward! charge!" and, with a shout that rose sharp and shrill above the din of arms, the brave —th dashed into the rain of shot and shell. Stirred by one impulse, the brothers followed wherever through the smoke they caught the flutter of the flag, as it was borne before them up the hill. More than once it dropped from a dead hand, to be caught up by a living one before it touched the ground. Robert Stirling's was one of these; and, as he seized the staff, the battle-madness seemed to fall upon him, for, waving the banner, with a ringing shout he sprang upon the wall, behind which rebel riflemen were lying. The sharp sting of a ball in the right arm reminded him that he was mortal, and at the same instant his brother's hand clutched him, his brother's voice called through the din, —

"You're wounded, Rob! For God's sake fall back." But, with a grim smile, Robert passed the banner into the keeping of his other hand, saying, as his arm dropped useless at his side, —

"Not yet. Clear the way for me, Rick, and let the old flag be the first up."

A loyal cheer from behind drowned the rebel yell that rose in front, as a blue wave rolled up and broke over the wall, carrying the brothers with it. Above the deadly conflict that went on below, the Stars and Stripes tossed wildly to and fro; but steadily the color-bearer struggled higher, and steadily his body-guard of one went on before him, forcing a passage through the press, till, in a single instant, there came a hurtling sound, a deafening crash, a fiery rain of death-dealing fragments, and, with an awful vision of dismembered bodies, wrathful faces panic-stricken in the drawing of a breath, and a wide gap in the swaying mass before him, Robert Stirling was flung, stunned and bleeding, against the wall so lately left.

Cries of mortal anguish roused him from a moment's merciful oblivion, and showed him that, for his brother and himself, the battle was already done. Not far away, half hidden under a pile of mingled blue and gray, Richard lay quiet on the bloody grass, and, as Robert's dizzy eyes wandered up and down his own bruised body to discover whence came the sharp agony that wrung his nerves, he saw that but one arm now hung shattered at his side; the left was gone, and a single glance at the ghastly wound sent such a pang of horror through him that. he closed his eyes, muttering, with white lips, —

"Poor mother! it will be hard to lose us both."

Something silken-soft swept across his face, and, looking up, he saw that the flag had fallen with him, and lay half upright against the wall, still fluttering bravely where many eyes could see it, many willing hearts press on to defend it. Faithful to the last, he leaned across the staff, and, making a shield of his maimed body, waited patiently for the coming of friend or foe. How the battle went he no longer knew; he scarcely cared; for now to him the victories and defeats of life seemed over, and Death standing ready to bestow the pale cross of the legion of honor, laid on so many quiet breasts as the loyal souls depart to their reward.

With strange distinctness came the roar of cannon, the sharp, shrill ringing of the minie-balls, the crash of bursting shells, the shouts, the groans, even the slow drip of his blood, as it splashed down upon the stones; yet neither hope nor fear disturbed him now, as all the past flashed through his mind and faded, leaving three memories, — his love for Rose, his brother's death, his mother's desolation, — to embitter the memorable moment when, with a deathly coldness creeping to his heart, he leaned there bleeding his young life away.

To him it seemed hours, yet but a few short minutes passed before he became conscious of a friendly atmosphere about him, and, through the trance of suffering fast reaching its climax, heard a commanding voice exclaim, —

"It is Stirling: I shall remember this. Take him to the rear, and see that he is cared for."

Robert knew his Colonel's voice, and, gathering up both failing strength and sense, he tried to stand erect, tried to salute with his one arm, and, failing, said, with a piteous look at either wound; —

"I have done my best, sir."

"My brave fellow, you have! What more *could* you do for the old flag?"

Something in the glance, the tone, the words of the commander whom he so loved and honored, seemed to send new life through the fainting man. His dim eye kindled, his voice grew strong and steady, as, forgetful of the maimed body it inhabited, the unconquerable spirit answered, fervently, —

"I could die for it."

Then, as if in truth he *had* done his best, *had* died for it, Robert Stirling fell forward in the shadow of the flag, his head upon the same green pillow where his brother's lay.

III.

"HERE'S THE PAPER, AND FISHER to read it for us, boys. Hush, there, and let's hear what's up!"

An instant silence reigned through the crowded ward as the chief attendant entered with the morning sheet that daily went the rounds. The convalescents gathered about him; the least disabled propped themselves upon their arms to listen; even the weakest turned wistful eyes that way, and ceased their moaning, that they might hear, as Fisher slowly read out the brief despatches, and then the mournful lists of wounded, dead, and missing.

Among the many faces in the room, one female one appeared; a strong, calm face, with steadfast eyes, and lips grown infinitely tender with the daily gospel of patience, hope, and consolation which they preached in words of motherly compassion. Still bathing and binding up a shattered limb, she listened to the reading, though her heart stood still to hear, and her face flushed and paled with the rapid alternations of hope and fear. Presently the one audible voice paused suddenly, and a little stir ran through the group as the reader stole an anxious dance at the woman. She saw it, divined its meaning, and in an instant seemed to have nerved herself for anything. Sponge and bandage dropped from her hands, a quick breath escaped her, and an expression of sharp anguish for a moment marred the composure of her countenance; but she fixed a tearless eye on Fisher, asking, steadily, —

"Are my boys' names there?"

"Only one, ma'am, — only one, I do assure your and he's merely lost an arm. That's better luck than half of 'em have; and now it's got to be a kind of an honor to wear an empty sleeve, you know," replied the old man, with a half-encouraging, half-remorseful look, as he considerately omitted to add the words, "and seriously wounded in the right," to the line, "R. Stirling, left arm gone."

A long sigh of thanksgiving left the mother's lips; then, with one of the natural impulses of a strong character, which found relief in action, she took up the roller and resumed her work more tenderly than ever, — for in her sight that shattered arm was her boy's arm now, — only saying, with a face of pale expectancy, —

"Read on, Fisher: I have another son to keep or lose."

So swift, so subtle, is the magnetism of human sympathy, that not a man in all that room but instantly forgot himself, his own anxieties, hopes, fears, and waited breathlessly for the utterance of that other name. Several sat upright in their beds to catch the good or evil tidings in the reader's face; one dying man sighed softly, from the depths of a homesick heart, "Lord, keep him for his mother!" and the standing group drew closer about Fisher, peering, over his shoulder, that younger, keener eyes might read the words, and warn him lest they left his lips too suddenly for one listener's ear.

Slowly name after name was read, and the long list drew near its end. A look of relief already settled upon some countenances, and one friendly fellow had turned to nod reassuringly at the mother, when a hand clutched Fisher's shoulder, and with a start he stopped short in the middle of a word. Mrs. Stirling rose up to receive the coming blow, and stood there mute and motionless, a figure so full of pathetic dignity that many eyes grew very dim. A gesture signified her wish, and, with choked voice and trembling lips, poor Fisher softly read the brief record that one word made so terrible, —

"R. Stirling, dead."

"Give me the paper."

A dozen hands were outstretched to serve her; and, as she took it, trying to teach herself that the heavy tidings ,ere not false, several caps were silently swept off, — an involuntary tribute of respect to that great grief from rough yet tender-hearted men who had no words to offer.

The hurried entrance of a surgeon broke the heavy silence; and his brisk voice jarred on every ear, as he exclaimed,—

"Good-by, boys! I'm off to the front. God bless me! what's the matter?"

"Bad news for Mrs. Stirling, sir. Do speak to her. I can't," whispered Fisher, with two great tears running down his waistcoat.

There was no time to speak; three words had roused her from the first stupor of her sorrow, and down the long room she went, steady and strong again, straight to the surgeon, saying, briefly,—

"To the front? When do you go?"

"In half an hour. What can I do for you?"

"Take me with you."

"Mrs. Stirling, it is impossible," began the astonished gentleman.

"Nothing is impossible to me. I must find my boys, — one living and one dead. For God's sake don't deny me this!"

She stretched her hands to him imploringly; she made as though she would kneel down before him; and her stricken face pleaded for her more eloquently than her broken words.

Dr. Hyde was an army surgeon; but a man's heart beat warm behind his bright buttons, unhardened by all the scenes of suffering, want, and woe through which he had been passing for three memorable years. Now it yearned over this poor mother with an almost filial pity and affection, as he took the trembling hands into his own and answered, earnestly, —

"Heaven knows I would not deny you if it were safe and wise to grant your wish. My dear lady, you have no conception of the horrors of a battle-field, or the awful scenes you must witness in going to the front. These hasty lists are not to be relied upon. Wait a little, and let me look for your sons. On my soul, I promise to do it as faithfully as a brother."

"I cannot wait. Another week of such suspense would kill me. You never saw my boys. I do not even know which is living and which is dead. Then how can you look for them as well as I? You would not know the poor dead face among a hundred; you would not recognize the familiar voice even in the ravings of pain or the din and darkness of those dreadful transports. I can bear anything, do anything, go anywhere, to find my boys. Oh, sir, by the love you bear your mother, I implore you to let me go!"

The look, the tone, the agony of supplication, made her appeal irresistible.

"You shall," replied the doctor, decidedly, putting all objections, obstacles and dangers out of sight.

"I'll delay one hour for you, Mrs. Stirling."

Up she sprang, as if endowed with the spirit and activity of a girl; hope, courage, gratitude, shone in her eyes, flushed warm across her face, and sounded in her eager voice, as she said, hurrying from the room, "Not an instant for me. Go as you first proposed. I shall be ready long before the time."

She was: for all her thought, her care, was for her boys, not for herself; and, when Dr. Hyde went to seek her in the matron's room, that busy woman looked up from the case of stores she was unpacking, and answered, with a sob,—

"Poor soul! she's waiting for you in the hall."

News of her loss and her departure had flown through the house; for no nurse there was so beloved and honored as "Madam Stirling," as the stately old lady was called among the boys; and when the doctor led her to the ambulance, it was through a crowd of wan and crippled creatures gathered there to see her off. Many eyes followed her, many lips blessed her, many hands were outstretched for a farewell grasp; and, as the ambulance went clattering away, old Fisher gave expression to the general feeling, when he said, with an air of solemn conviction in almost ludicrous contrast to the emotional contortions of his brown countenance, —

"She'll find 'em! It's borne in upon me uncommon strong that the Lord won't rob such a woman of her sons, — bless her stout heart! so give her a cheer, boys, and then clear the way!"

They did give her a cheer, a right hearty one, — though the voices were none of the strongest, and nearly as many crutches as caps were waved in answer to the smile she sent them as she passed from sight.

It was not a long journey that lay before her, yet, to Mrs. Stirling it seemed interminable; for a heavy heart went with her, and, through all the hopeful or despondent thoughts that haunted her, one unanswerable question continually sounded, like a sorrowful refrain, — "One killed, one wounded. Which is living? which is dead?"

All along the road they went two streams of life continually flowed, in opposite directions: one, a sad procession of suffering humanity passing hospital, or homeward, to live or die, as Heaven willed; the other, an almost equally sad procession of pilgrims journeying to the battle-field, to find their wounded or to weep their dead, — men and women, old and young, rich and poor, all animated by a spirit which made them as one great family, through the same costly sacrifice, the same sore affliction. It was well for Mrs. Stirling that the weary way was a little shortened, the heavy hours a little lightened, for her by the companionship of others bent on a like errand. In this atmosphere of general anxiety and excitement, accustomed formalities and reserves were forgotten or set aside; strangers spoke freely to each other; women confidingly asked and gratefully received the chivalrous protection of men, and men yearning for sympathy always found it ready in the hearts and eyes of women as they told their sorrows and were comforted. Many brief tragedies were poured into Mrs. Stirling's ear; more than one weaker nature leaned upon her strength; more than one troubled soul felt itself calmed by the pious patience which touched that worn and venerable countenance with an expression which made it an unconscious comfort to many eyes; and in seeing, solacing acing the woes of others, she found fresh courage to sustain her own.

They came at last, with much difficulty and many delays, to the little town in and along which lay nine thousand dead, and nearly twenty thousand wounded men. Although a week had not yet passed since the thunder of the cannon ceased, the place already looked like the vast cemetery which it was soon to become; for, in groves and fields, by the roadside and along the slopes, wherever they fell, lay loyal and rebel soldiers in the shallow graves that now are green. The long labor of interment was but just begun; for the living appealed more urgently to both friend and stranger, and no heart was closed, no hand grew weary, while strength and power to aid remained. All day supply wagons and cars came full and departed empty; all day ambulances rolled to and fro, bringing the wounded from remoter parts of the wide battle-field to the railroad for removal to fixed hospitals elsewhere; all day the relief-stations, bearing the blessed sign, "U. S. San. Com.," received hundreds of sufferers into the shelter of their tents, who must else have laid waiting their turn for transportation in the burning July sun; all day, and far into the night, red-handed surgeons stood at the rude tables, heart-sick and weary with their hard yet merciful labors, as shattered body after body was laid before them, while many more patiently, even cheerfully, awaited their turn; and all day mothers, wives, and widows, fathers, friends, and lovers, roamed the hills and valleys, or haunted the field-hospitals, searching for the loved and lost.

Dr. Hyde was under orders; but for many hours he neglected everything but Mrs. Stirling, going with her from houses, tents, and churches, to barns, streets, and crowded yards; for everywhere the wounded lay thick as autumn leaves, — some on bloody blankets, some on scattered straw, a few in cleanly beds, many on the bare ground; and if anything could have added to the bitter pain of hope deferred, it would have been the wistful glances turned on the new-comers from eyes that, seeing no familiar face, closed again with a pathetic patience that wrung the heart. All day they searched; but nowhere did the mother find her boys, nor any tidings of them; and, as night fell, her companion besought her to rest from the vain search, and accept the hospitality of a friendly citizen.

"Dear Mrs. Stirling, wait here till morning," the doctor said. "I must go to my work, but will not till I know that you are safe; for you can never wander here alone. I will send a faithful messenger far and wide, to make inquiries through the night, and hope to greet you in the, morning with the happiest news."

She scarcely seemed to hear him, so intent was her mind upon the one hope that absorbed it.

"Go to your work, kind friend," she said; "the poor souls need you more than I. Have no fears for me. I want neither rest nor food; I only want my boys; and I must look for them both day and night, lest one hour of idleness should make my coming one hour too late. I shall go back to the station. A constant stream of wounded men is passing there; and, while I help and comfort them, I can see that my boys are not hurried away while I am waiting for them here."

He let her have her will, well knowing that for such as she there was no rest till hope came, or exhausted nature forced her to pause. Back to the relief-station they went, and, while Dr. Hyde dressed wounds, issued orders, and made diligent inquiry among the throngs that came and went, Mrs. Stirling, with other anxious yet hopeful, helpful women, moved about the tents, preparing nourishment for the men, who came in faster titan they could be served. Through the whole night she worked, lifting water to lips too parched to syllable the word, wetting wounds unbandaged for days, feeding famished creatures who had lain suffering in solitary places till some minister of mercy found and succored them, whispering words of good cheer, and, by the cordial comfort of her presence, sending many a poor soul on his way rejoicing. But, while she worked so tirelessly for others, she still hungered for her children, and would not be comforted. No ambulance came rumbling from the field that she did not hurry out to scan the new-comers with an eye that neither darkness nor disguise could deceive; not a stretcher with its helpless burden was brought in that she did not bend over it with the blessed cup of water in her hand, and her poor heart flattering in her breast; and often, among the groups of sleepers that lay everywhere, there went a shadowy figure through the night, turning the lantern's glimmer or each pallid face; but nowhere did Rick or Rob look back at her with the glad cry, "Mother!"

At dawn, Dr. Hyde came to her. With difficulty did he prevail upon her to eat a morsel and rest a little, while he told her of his night's attempts, and spoke cheerfully of the many mishaps, the unavoidable disappointments and delay, of such a quest at such a time and place.

"We have searched the town; and Blake and Snow will see that no Stirling leaves by any of the trains to-day. But the hospitals on the outskirts still remain for us, — besides the heights and hollows; for, on a battle-field like this, many men might lie unfound for days while search was going on about them. I have a wagon here, — a rough affair, but the best I can get; and, if you will not rest, let us go together, and look again for these lost sons of yours."

They went; and for another long, hot, summer day looked on sights that haunted their memories for years, listened to sounds that pierced their souls, and with each hour felt the weight of impotent compassion weigh heavier and heavier upon their hearts. Various and conflicting rumors, conjectures, and relations from the comrades of the brothers perplexed the seekers, and augmented the difficulties of their task. One man affirmed that he saw both Stirlings fall; a second, that both were taken prisoners; a third, that he had seen both march safely away; and a fourth, that Richard was mortally wounded and Robert missing. But all agreed in their admiration for the virtue and the valor of the brothers, heartily wishing their mother success, and unconsciously applying, by their commendations, the only balm that could mitigate her pain. Up and down, from dawn till dusk, went the heavy-hearted pair; but evening came again, and still no sure intelligence, no confirmed fear or happy meeting, lightened the terrible uncertainty that tortured them.

"Dear madam, we have done all that human patience and perseverance can do. Now, leave your boys in God's hand, and let me care for you as if you were my mother," said the compassionate doctor, as they paused, dusty, jaded, and dejected, at the good citizen's hospitable door.

Mrs. Stirling did not answer him. She sat there, an image of maternal desolation, her hands locked together on her knee, her eyes fixed and unseeing, and in her face a still, white anguish piteous to see. With gentlest constraint, her friend led her in, laid the gray head down upon a woman's breast, and left her to the tender care of one who had known a grief like hers.

For hours she lay where kind hands placed her, physically spent, yet mentally alert as ever. No passing face escaped her, no sound fell unheeded on her ear, no movement of those about her was unobserved: yet she neither spoke, nor stirred, nor slept, till midnight gathered cool and dark above a weary world. Then a brief lapse into unconsciousness partially repaired the ravages those two hard days had wrought. But even when the exhausted body rested, the unwearied soul continued its sad quest, and in her dreams the mother found her boys. So vivid was the vision, that she suddenly awoke to find herself thrilled with a strange joy, trembling with a strange expectancy. She rose up in her bed, she put away her fallen hair, fast whitening with sorrow's frost, and held her breath to listen; for a cry, urgent, imploring, distant, yet near, seemed ringing through the room.

From without came the ceaseless rumble of ambulances and the tread of hurrying feet; from within, the sound of women weeping for their dead, and the low moaning of a brave officer fast breathing his life away upon his young wife's bosom. No voice spoke, that human ear could hear; yet through the mysterious hush that fell upon her in that hour, her spirit heard an exceeding bitter cry, "Mother! mother! come to me!" —

Like one possessed by an impulse past control, she left her bed, flung on her garments, seized the little store of comforts untouched till now, and, without sign or sound, glided like a shadow from the house.

The solemn peace of night could not so soon descend upon those hills again; nature's tranquility had been rudely broken; and, like the suffering humanity that cumbered her wounded breast, she seemed to moan in her troubled sleep. Lights flashed from hill and hollow, some fixed, some wandering, — all beacons of hope to the living or funeral torches for the dead. Many feet went to and fro along the newly-trodden paths; dusky figures flitted everywhere, and sounds of suffering filled the night wind with a sad lament. But, upheld by a power beyond herself, led by an instinct in which she placed blind faith, and unconscious of doubt, or weariness, or fear, the solitary woman walked undaunted and unscathed through that Valley of the Shadow of Death.

Out from the crowded town she went, turning neither to the right nor left, up a steep path her feet had trodden once, that day, straight to the ruined breastworks formed of loose fragments of stone, piled there by many hands whose earthly labor was already done. There, gathered from among the thick-ly-strewn dead, and sheltered by an awning till they could be taken lower, lay a score of men, blue coats and gray, side by side on the bare earth, equals now in courage, suffering, and patience. The one faithful attendant who kept his watch alone was gone for water, that first, greatest need and comfort in hours like those, and the dim light of a single lantern flickered through the gloom. Utter silence filled the dreary place, till from the remotest corner came a faint, imploring cry, the more plaintive and piteous for being a man's voice grown childlike in its weak wandering: —

"Mother! mother! come to me!"

"Who spoke?"

A woman's voice, breathless and broken, put the question; a woman's figure stood at the entrance of the rude shelter; and when a wakened sufferer answered, eagerly, "Robert Stirling, just brought in dying. For God's sake help him if you can," — a woman's face, transfigured with a sudden joy, flashed swiftly, silently before his startled eyes, to bend over one low bed, whence came the sound of tender speech, prayerful thanksgiving, and the strong sobbing of a man who in his hour of extremest need found solace and salvation in the dear refuge of his mother's arms.

IV.

THEY WERE ALONE TOGETHER, THE mother and her one son, after weeks of suffering and a long, slow journey, safely at home at last. Poor Rob was a piteous sight now, for both arms were gone, one at the shoulder, the other at the elbow; yet sadder than the maimed body was the altered face, for, though wan and wasted by much suffering, a strong soul seemed to look out at the despairing eyes, as if the captivity of helplessness were more than he could bear. A still deeper grief cast its shadow over him, making the young man old before his time, for day and night his heart cried out for his brother, as if the tie between the twin-born could not be divided even by death. This longing, which the consolations of neither tenderness nor time could appease, was now the only barrier to his recovery. Vainly his mother assured him that Richard's death had been confirmed by more than one account; vainly she tried to comfort him by hopeful reminders of a glad reunion hereafter, and endeavored to rouse him by appeals to his filial love, telling him that he was her all now, and imploring him to live for his old mother's sake. He listened, promised, and tried to be resigned, but still cherished an unconquerable belief that Richard lived, in spite of all reports, appearances, or seeming certainties. Asleep, he dreamed of him; awake, he talked of him; and the hope of seeing him again in this world seemed the only thing that gave Rob patience and courage to sustain the burden which life had now become to him.

"Mother, when shall I be freed from this dreadful bed?" he broke out, suddenly, as she laid down the book she had been reading to deaf ears, and brushed away a lock of hair the wind had blown across his forehead, for her watchful eye and tireless hand spared him the pain of asking any service that recalled his loss.

"Weeks yet, dear. It takes nature long to repair such rents in her fine handiwork; but the wounds are healing rapidly, thanks to your temperate life and hardy frame."

"And your devoted care, most faithful of nurses," added Robert, turning his lips to the hand that had strayed caressingly from forehead to cheek. "Do your best for me, mother, — and you can do more than any other in the world; get me on my feet again as soon as may be, and then, God willing, I'll find Rick if he's above the sod."

Mrs. Stirling opened her lips to remonstrate against the vain purpose, but, seeing the sudden color that lent the wan face a semblance of health, hearing the tone of energy that strengthened the feeble voice, and remembering how deep a root the hope had taken in the brother's heart, she silently resolved to let it sustain him if it could, undisturbed by a look or word of unbelief.

"We will go together, Rob. My first search was successful; Heaven grant my second may be so likewise. I will do my best; and when I see you your old self again I shall be ready to follow anywhere."

"My old self again? I never can be that, and why I was spared to be a burden to you while Rick was taken — no, not taken — I'll neither say nor think that. If he were dead I should either follow him or find comfort in the thought that he was at peace; but he is alive, for day and night his spirit calls to mine, and I must answer it as you answered me when I cried to you in what I thought to be my dying hour. Remember, mother, how many of our men were found after they were believed to have been killed or taken. John King's grave was pointed out to his wife, you know; and, when she had almost broken her poor heart over it, she went, home, to find him waiting for her there. Why should not some such happy chance befall us? Let us believe and hope till we can do so no longer, and then I will learn submission."

His mother only answered with a gentler touch upon his head, for in her heart she believed that her son was dead. Perhaps the great fear of losing both had made the loss seem less when one was spared, or perhaps she thought that if either must go Richard was fittest for the change, and the nearness she still felt to him made the absence of his visible presence less keenly felt than that of Robert would have been; for, though as dear, he was not so spiritually akin to her as that stronger, gentler son.

"Is Rose in town, mother?" was the abrupt question that broke a momentary silence.

"Yes, she is still here."

"Does she know we have come?"

"She cannot help knowing, when half the town has been trooping by with welcomes, messages, and gifts for you."

"Do you think she will come to welcome us?"

"Not yet, dear."

"Ah! her pride will keep her away, you think?"

"Her pity, rather. Rose has generous impulses, and, but for her mistaken education, would have been a right noble woman. She may be yet, if love proves strong enough to teach her the hard, though happy lesson, that shall give her back to you again."

"That can never be, mother. What woman could love such a wreck; and what right have I to expect or hope it, least of all from Rose? No, I am done with love; my dream has had a stern awakening; do not talk of the impossible to me."

His mother smiled the wise smile of one who understood the workings of a woman's heart, and, knowing both its weakness and its strength, believed that all things are possible to love. Perhaps some village gossip had breathed a hint into her ear which confirmed her hope; or, judging another by herself, she ventured to comfort her son by prophesying the return of the dream which he believed forever ended.

"I will leave that theme for a younger, more persuasive woman to discourse upon, when the hour comes in which you find that hearts do not always change with changing fortunes, that affliction often deepens affection, and when one asks a little pity one sometimes receives much love."

"I shall never ask either of Rose."

"If she truly loves you there will be no need of asking, Rob."

His face brightened beautifully as he listened; his eyes shone, and he moved impetuously, as if the mere thought had power to lift and set him on his feet, a hale and happy man again. But weakness and helplessness held him down; and, with a sharper pang than that of the half-healed wounds, he lay back, exclaiming with a bitter sigh, —

"No hope of such a fate for me! I must be content with the fulfilment of my other longing, and think of poor Rick all the more because I must not think of Rose. Oh! if my worst enemy should bring the dear lad home to me, I'd joyfully forgive, love, honor him for that one act."

As Robert spoke with almost passionate earnestness, a shadow that had lain across the sunny threshold of the door vanished as noiselessly as it had come; and unseen, unheard, Rose glided back into the green covert of the lane, saying within herself, as she hurried on, agitated by the mingled pain, pride and passion of the new-born purpose at her heart, —

"Yes, Mrs. Stirling, love *shall* prove strong enough to make me what I should be, and Robert shall yet forgive and honor me; for, if human power can do it, I will bring his brother home to him."

Completely absorbed by the design that had taken possession of her, she hastened back, thinking intently as she went; and, when she called her one faithful servant to her, all her plans were laid, her resolution fixed, and every moment seemed wasted till the first step was taken, for now her impetuous spirit could not brook delay.

"Jupiter, I am going to Washington in the morning, and shall take you with me — so be ready," was the rapid order issued to the astonished old man, who had no answer to make, but the usual obedient — "Yes, missis."

"I am going to look for Mrs. Stirling's son, the one who is supposed to be dead."

"Lors, missis, he is dead, shore, — ain't he?"

"I intend to satisfy myself on that point, if I search the prisons, camps, hospitals, and graveyards, from Gettysburg to Richmond. I have strength, courage, money, and, some power, and what better use can I make of them than to look for this good neighbor, and ease the hearts of those who love him best. Go, Jupe, tell no one of my purpose, make ready in all haste, and be sure I mill reward you well if you serve me faithfully now,"

"Yes, missis, — you may 'pend on me."

At dawn they were away, the young mistress and her old slave. No one knew why they had gone, nor whither; and village rumor said Miss Rose had left so suddenly because young Stirling and his mother had come home. When Mrs. Stirling heard of the departure, her old eyes kindled with indignation, while her voice trembled with grief, as she said to her son, —

"I am bitterly disappointed in her; think of her no more, Rob."

But Robert turned his face to the wall, and neither spoke nor stirred for many hours.

In ancient times, young knights went out to defend distressed dames and free imprisoned damsels; but, in our day, the errantry is reversed, and many a strong-hearted woman goes journeying up and down the land, bent on delivering some beloved hero from a captivity more terrible than any the old legends tell. Rose was now one of these; and, though neither a meek Una nor a dauntless Britomart, she resolutely began the long quest which was to teach her a memorable lesson, and make a loyal woman of the rebel beauty.

At first she haunted hospitals; and, while her heart was wrung by the sight of every form of suffering, she marked many things that sunk deep into her memory, and forced it to bear testimony to the truth. She saw Confederate soldiers lying side by side with Union men, as kindly treated, almost as willingly served, and twice conquered by those who could smite hard like valiant soldiers, and then lift up their fallen enemy like Christian gentlemen. This sight caused her to recall other scenes in other hospitals, where loyal prisoners lay perishing for help, while rebels close by were cherished with every demonstration of indulgent care by men and women, who not only hardened their hearts against the sadder sufferers, but found a cruel pleasure in tormenting them by every deprivation and indignity their hatred could devise. She had seen a woman, beautiful and young, go through a ward leaving fruit, flowers, delicate food and kind words behind her, for every Southern man that lay there; then offer a cup of water to a Northern soldier, and as the parched lips opened eagerly to receive the blessed draught, she flung it on the ground and went her way with a scornful taunt. This picture was in Rose's mind as she stood in a Washington hospital, by the death-bed of a former neighbor of her own, hearing the fervent thanks uttered with the last breath he drew, watching the sweet-faced nurse close the weary eyes, fold the pale hands, and then forgetting everything but the one fact, that some woman loved and mourned the lost rebel, she "kissed him for his mother," while Rose turned away with full heart and eyes, never again to speak contemptuously of Northern men and women.

She visited many battle-fields and graveyards, where the low mounds rose thickly everywhere, and an army of brave sleepers lay awaiting the call to God's great review. Here, too, despite the dreary task before her, and the daily disappointment that befell her, she could not but contrast the decent burial given to dead enemies with the sacrilegious brutality with which her friends often tried to rob death of its sanctity by mutilation, burning, butchery, and the denial of a few feet of earth to cover some poor body which a brave soul had ennobled by its martyrdom. Seeing these things, she could not but blush for those whom she once had blindly honored; could not but heartily respect those whom she once had as blindly distrusted and despised.

She searched many prisons; for, when neither eloquence nor beauty could win its way, money proved a golden key, and let her in. Here, as elsewhere, the same strong contrast was forced upon her; for, while one side fed, clothed, and treated their conquered with courteous forbearance, often sending them back the richer and better for their sojourn, the other side robbed, starved, tormented, and often wantonly murdered the helpless victims of the chances of war, or returned them worn out with privation and neglect to die at home, or to endure the longer captivity of strong souls pent in ruined bodies. And Rose felt her heart swell with indignant grief and shame, as she came out into the free world again, finding the shadow of prison-bars across its sunshine, hearing the sighs of long-suffering men in every summer wind, and fully seeing at last how black a blight slavery and treason had brought upon the land she loved.

She went to Hospital Directories, those kindly instituted intelligence offices for anxious hearts, and there she saw such sorrowful scenes, yet heard such cheerful, courageous words, that sympathy and admiration contended for the mastery in the Southern woman's breast. She heard an old mother say proudly, as she applied for a pass, "I have had seven sons in the army; three are dead, and two are wounded, but I'm glad my boys went." She saw a young wife come to meet her husband, and learn that he was waiting for her in his coffin; but though her heart was broken, there was no murmuring at the heavy loss, no bitter denunciation of those who had made her life so desolate, only a sweet submission, and sustaining consolation in the knowledge that the great sacrifice had been freely made, and the legacy of an honorable name had been bequeathed to the baby at her breast. Lads came asking for fathers, and whether they found them dead or wounded, the spirit of patriotism burned undiminished in their enthusiastic hearts, and each was eager to fill the empty place, undaunted by pain and peril of the life. Old men mingled, with their tearless lamentations for lost sons, their own regrets that they too could not shoulder guns, and fight the good fight to the end.

All these loyal demonstrations sunk deeply into Rose's softened heart, and in good time bore fruit; for now she began to think within herself, "Surely, a war which does so much for a people, making women glad to give their best and dearest, men eager to lay down their lives, strengthening purifying, and sustaining all, must be a holy war, approved by God, and sure of victory in the end." The last touch needed to complete the work of regeneration was yet to come; but slowly, surely this long discipline made her ready to receive it.

Her search, meanwhile, had not proved fruitless, for after many disappointments one fact was established beyond doubt: Richard Stirling was not killed at Gettysburg. By the merest chance she met, in one of the Union hospitals which she visited, a rebel lieutenant who told her that the same shell wounded both Stirling and himself, and when the first attack was repulsed, that Richard was taken prisoner, and sent to the rear with others of his regiment. An hour later, the lieutenant himself was taken by our men when they returned to the charge; but whether Stirling lived or died he could not tell: probably the latter, being severely wounded in head and chest.

The smile, the thanks Rose gave in return for these good tidings, and the comforts she gratefully provided, would have made captivity dangerously alluring to the young lieutenant had she remained. But armed with this intelligence she went on her way rejoicing, eager to trace and follow the army of prisoners that had gone southward. Weeks had been consumed in her search, and already rumors of the horrors of the Libby Prison-house and Belle Island had disturbed and shocked the North. Haunted with woful recollections of all the varied sufferings she had seen, her imagination pictured Richard weak and wounded, shivering and starving, while she waited with full hands and eager heart to save, and heal, and lead him home. Intent on reaching Richmond, she besieged officials in high places as well as low, money flowed like water, and every faculty was given to the work. It seemed as if she had undertaken an impossibility; for though all pitied, tried to help, and heartily admired the beautiful brave woman, no one could serve her as she would be served; and she began to exercise her fertile wit in devising some way in which she could attain her object by stratagem, if all other means should fail.

Waiting in her carriage, one day, at the door of a helpful friend's office, while Jupe carried up a message, she was startled from an anxious reverie by the sudden appearance of an agitated black countenance at the window, and the sound of an incoherent voice, exclaiming, between laughter and tears, —

"Oh, bress de Lord, and sing hallyluyer! I'se foun' her! I'se foun' her! Doesn't yer know me, Missy Rose? I'se old June, and I'se run away; but I doesn't kere nuffin what comes ob me of missy'll jes' lem me see my pore ole man once more."

To Juno's infinite surprise, no frown appeared upon the face of her young mistress, and no haughty reprimand followed the recognition of the half-ludicrous, half-pathetic tatterdemalion who addressed her, but a white hand was put forth to draw the new-comer in, and the familiar voice answered with a friendliness never heard before, —

"Jupe is safe, and you shall see him soon. Come in, you poor old soul, come in."

In bundled the delighted creature, and began to tell her story, but stopped in the middle to dart out again, and fall upon the neck of the bewildered Jupiter, as he came soberly up to deliver his message. Fortunately it was as a quiet street, else that tumultuous meeting might have been productive of discomfort to all parties; for the old couple wept, laughed, and sung, — went down upon their knees to thank Heaven, — got up to embrace, and dance, and weep again, in a perfect abandonment of gratitude, affection and delight. When Rose could make herself heard, she bade them both enter the carriage; then drawing down the curtains, and ordering the coachman to drive slowly round the square, she let the reunited husband and wife give free vent to their emotions, till from sheer weariness they grew calm again.

"We hopes missis will 'scuse us actin' so wild, but 'pears like we couldn't help it, comin' so bery sudden an' undispected," apologized Jupe, wiping away the last of his own and Juno's tears with the same handkerchief, which, very properly, was a miniature star-spangled banner.

But Rose's own eyes were wet; and in her sight there was nothing unlovely or unmannerly in that natural outbreak of affection, for she had learned to feel for others now, and the same stern discipline which made her both strong and humble, taught her to see much that was true and touching in the spectacle of the gray heads bent towards each other; the wrinkled faces shining with joy; the hard hands locked together, as the childless, friendless old pair found freedom, happiness, and rest for a moment in each other's arms. Like a true woman, Juno calmed herself first, that she might talk; and, emboldened by the gracious change in her once imperious mistress, she told the story of her wanderings at length, not forgetting the chief incident of her long and lonely flight, the meeting with Robert Stirling. At the sound of his name, both Rose and Jupe exclaimed, and Juno was rapidly made acquainted with the mission which had brought them there. Deeply impressed with the circumstance, and a sense of her own importance, the good soul entered heartily into the matter, saying, with the pious simplicity of her race, —

"De ways ob de Lord is 'mazing 'sterious! but we's boun' to b'lieve dat He'll take special kere ob dat dear chile, elseways we shouldn't hab ben brung togedder so cur'us. I tole de blessed gen'l'man I'd 'member him, and I has; I prayed ter be spared ter see his kine face agin, an' I was."

"Where? when? Oh, Juno, you were surely sent to me in my last extremity," cried Rose, now trembling with interest and impatience.

"It was dis way, missy. When dat dear gen'l'man lef me I creeped on a piece, but was tuk sick, an' a kind fam'ly kep' me a long time. Den I come on agin bery slow, an' one day as I was gwine fru a town, — I'se los' de name, but it don't matter, — as I was gwine fru dat town, dere come a lot ob pris'ners frum Gettysbury, or some place like dat, a gwine to Richmun. Dear heart, honey, dey was an orfle sight, all lame, an' rags, an' hungry, an' de folks run out into de street wid bread ter feed um. De guard was bery ugly, and wouldn't let de folks come nigh ter do it, so dey jes' fell back and frowed de vittles ober de heads of dem rebs, and de pore souls cotched it as ef it was de manny dey tells of in de Bible. I helped um; yes, missy, I couldn't stay still noways, so I runned into a bake-shop wid some more women, and we stood in de winders and hev de bread down to de starvin' creeters in de street mighty hearty, you'm be shore ob dat. I had a big loaf in my han', and was lookin' roun' for de starvinest man dar, when I saw de bery face dat looked so kine inter mine yonder by de spring. I tank de Lord I'd kep de name handy, for I screeched right out, 'Oh, Massa Stirlin'! Massa Stirlin'! dis yere's for you wid my lub.' He looked up, he 'membered me, he larfed all over his pore thin face, jes' as he done de day I gib him de rose. Oh, missy! he was hurted bad; dey had tuk away his hat, and coat, and shoes, and I saw his heal was tied up, and dere was a great red stain on de bosom ob his shirt, and he looked so weak and wore down dat I jes bus out cryin', and forgot all 'bout de bread till I was gwine to wipe my eyes wid it. Den I got my wits togedder and gib de loaf such a great chuck dat I mos' fell out a winder, but he got it; I sawed him break it in bits and gib em roun' to de pore boys side ob him, some wid no arms to grab wid, some too hurted to fight and run for it like de res. Den I'se fraid he won't had nuf for his self, so I gets more and fros it far, and he larfs out hearty like a boy, and calls to me, 'I tank yer, ma'am. God bless yer!' Dat set me cryin' agin, like a ole fool as I is, and when I come to dey was movin' on agin, and de las I see ob dat dear soul he was marchin' brave, wid de sun beatin' down on his pore head, de hot sand burnin' his pore feet, and a sick boy hangin' on his arm. But fer all dat he kep lookin' back, noddin' and smilin' till dey was clean gone, and dere was nuffin left but prayers and sobbin' all dat day for me."

"It is certain then that he has gone to Richmond; I must follow. Jupe, what message did Mr. Norton send me?" asked Rose, remembering her unanswered inquiry at last.

"He bery busy, Missis, elseways he come down and see yer; but he says dere's no gittin' any passes, and de only 'vice he can gib, is dat you goes to 'Napolis and looks dere, kase dere's ben some pris'ners fetched dere frum Belle Island, and dere's jes one chance dat Massa Stirlin' mought be 'mong em."

"I'll go! Jupe, order the man back to the hotel. There's not a moment to be lost," said Rose.

"Oh, missy, lem me go wid you!" implored Juno. "I knows I don't look bery spectable, but I'll follow on hind yer some ways: I'se good at nussin', I can pry roun' in places whar a lady couldn't, and if dat bressed gen'l'man ain't dar, I'll jes go back and try to fetch him out ob de lan' ob bondage like I did myself."

"You shall go, Juno, for without you I should still be groping in the dark. Surely Heaven helps me, and I feel that I shall find him now."

She did find him, but how? She went to Annapolis, where a hundred and eighty exchanged prisoners had just arrived, and entering the hospital, stood aghast at the sight before her. Men who for weeks had been confined on that desert waste, Belle Island, without shelter or clothing, almost without food, and no help, sick or well, lay there dead or dying from starvation and neglect. Nurses, inured to many forms of suffering, seemed dismayed at the awful spectacle of living skeletons famishing for food, yet too weak to taste when eager hands tried to minister to them. Some were raving in the last stage of their long agony; some were hopelessly insane; many had died unconscious that they were among friends; and others were too far gone to speak, yet dumbly grateful for the help that came too late.

Heart-wrung and horror-stricken, Rose could only pray that she might not find Richard among these victims of a barbarous revenge which made her disown and denounce the cause she had clung to until then, and oppressed her with a bitter sense of remorse for ever giving it her allegiance. As she stood struggling with a flood of thoughts and feelings too strong for utterance, old Juno, who had pressed on before her, beckoned with an eager hand. Going to her, Rose found her bending over the mournful ghost of a man who lay there like one dead, with hollow eyes fast shut, the pinched mouth breathless, the wasted limbs stiff and cold, and no trace of Richard Stirling visible for the frightful emaciation, the long, neglected hair and beard, so changed him that his own mother might have passed by without a glance of recognition.

"It is not he, Juno. Poor soul, poor soul! cover his face, and let him rest," sighed Rose, with tremulous lips, bending to lay her delicate handkerchief over the piteous face, one glance at which had made her eyes too dim for seeing, and seemed to utter a mute reproach, as if the loss of this life lay at her door.

"It is de dear boy, missy; I'se shore ob it, fer see what I foun' in dis faded little bag dat lay on his heart, when I feeled to see if dere was any beat lef. Here's a bit ob gray hair in a paper wid somefin wrote on it, an' here's de flower I gib him. I knows it by de red string I pulled out ob my old shawl to tie de posy wid. Ah, honey, I specks he smiled so when he tuk de rose, an' kep it, kase he tort ob you, and bibbed you bery dear."

The little case and the dead flower fell from Rose's hand, as she read these words upon the worn paper that held the gray curl: "For Rick from mother, May 10, 1863"; and she laid her warm cheek down beside that chilly one, crying through the heartiest, happiest tears she ever shed.

"Oh, Richard, have I come too late?"

Something in the touch of tender lips, the magnetism of a living, loving heart, seemed to arrest the weary spirit in its flight, and call it back to life by the power of that passion which outlives death.

"De heart's a beatin', and de bref's a comin', shore. Lif up his head, honey! Jupe, fan him bery kereful, while I gets a drop ob brandy down his frote, an' rubs dese pore hans dat is all bones. Dear boy, we's got yer. Def may go 'way now!"

Juno both worked and spoke as if the young man were her son; for she forgot all differences of rank, color, and condition, in her glad gratitude to nurse him like a mother. Rose laid the unconscious head upon his bosom, and, brushing back the tangled hair, watched the faint flutter of the eyelids, as life came creeping back, and hope dawned again for both of them; for she felt that Richard's restoration would win Robert's pardon, and be her best atonement for the past.

It was long before he was himself again, but Juno never left him, day or night; Jupe was a sleepless, tireless guard, and Rose ministered to him with heart as well as hand, seeming to hold death at bay by the sheer force of an indomitable will. He knew the forms about him, at last; and the happiest moment of Rose's life was that in which he looked up in her face with eyes that blessed her for her care, and whispered feebly, "I thought I had suffered much, but this atones for all!"

After that, every hour brought fresh strength, and renewed assurances that the danger had gone by. At this point Juno discovered that her soul was stronger than her body, for the latter gave out, and Rose commanded her to rest.

"I need you no longer, for my work is nearly done," she said. "Jupe, I told you that if you served me well you should be rewarded, and I will keep my word. This paper assures your freedom, and your wife's, forever; this purse contains a little fortune, to keep you above want while you live. Take the late gift, my good old friends, and forgive me for the wrong I have done you all these years."

Rose's subdued yet earnest manner, and the magnitude of the gift, restrained the rapture of the old pair, which found vent only in a demonstration that touched Rose more than a stream of thanks and blessings. Holding fast the precious paper that gave them freedom only at life's close, they put back the money, feeling too rich in that other gift to fear want, and, taking one of the white hands in their black ones, they kissed them, wet them with grateful tears, and clung to them, imploring to be allowed to stay with her, to serve her, love her, and be her faithful followers to the end.

Much moved, she gave the promise; and happier than any fabled king and queen of Olympus were the old freedman and his wife, when they went away to nurse each other for a little while, at their mistress's desire, leaving her to tend the "General," as Jupe insisted upon calling Richard, laboring under a delusion that, because he had suffered much, he must have received honor and promotion.

Very quiet, useful hours were those that followed, and these proved the sincerity of her amendment, by the zeal with which she performed many a distasteful duty for Richard and his companions in misfortune, the patience with which she bore many discomforts, the energy with which she met and conquered all obstacles to the fulfilment of her purpose. Unconsciously Richard did more for her than she for him: because, though unseen, his work was both more difficult and more enduring than her own. She nursed and nourished an exhausted body; he, by the influence of character, soothed and sustained an anxious soul, helped Rose to find her better self, and, through the force of a fair example, inspired her with noble emulation. They talked much, at first: Rose was the speaker, and an eloquent one; for Richard was very like his brother, as she had last seen him, and she felt the charm of that resemblance. Then, as Richard gained strength, he loved to lie conversing upon many themes, too happy in her presence to remember the sad past, or to cherish a fear for the unknown future. Having lived a deep and earnest life of late, Rose found herself fitted to comprehend the deep and earnest thoughts that found expression in those confidential hours; for if ever men and women are their simplest, sincerest selves, it is when suffering softens the one, and sympathy strengthens the other.

Often Rose caught a wistful look fixed on her face, as she read or worked beside her patient, in the little room now set apart for him, and she could not but interpret it aright, since the story of the rose had given her a key to that locked heart. Poor Richard loved her still, and was beginning to hope that Juno's wish might be fulfilled, for Rose seldom spoke of Rob, had shivered and turner pale when she told his great misfortune, and, man-like, Richard believed that her love had changed to pity, and might, in time, be given to Robert's unmarred counterpart. He was very slow to receive this hope, very remorseful when he thought of Rob, and very careful not to betray the troubled joy that was doing more toward his recovery than any cordial that passed his lips. But, when the time came for them to think of turning homeward, he felt that he could not meet his brother with any secret hidden in his heart; and, with the courage that was as natural to him as his patience, he ended his suspense, and manfully went to meet his fate.

Rose had been reading him to sleep one night, and fancying, from his stillness, that she had succeeded, she closed her book, and sat watching the thin face that looked so pale and peaceful in the shaded light that filled the room. Not long did she study it, for suddenly the clear eyes opened, and, as if some persistent thought found utterance, almost against his will, he asked, "Rose, why did you come to find me?"

She divined the true meaning of the look, the words, with a woman's instinct, and answered both with the perfect truth which they deserved.

"Because your brother wanted you."

"For his sake you came for me?"

"Yes, Richard."

"Then, Rose, you — you love him still?"

"How can I help it, when he needs me more than ever? "

For a moment Richard's face changed terribly; then something seemed to gush warm across his heart, sending a generous glow to check and forehead, banishing the despair from his eyes, and lending to his voice a heartiness unheard before. —

"Forgive me, Rose; you are a nobler woman than I thought you. He does need you more than ever; give him your whole heart, and help me to make his hard life happy."

"I will — God bless my brother Rick!" and, bending, Rose kissed him softly on the forehead, the only token that ever betrayed her knowledge of his love, the atonement she had it in her power to make him for his loss.

Richard held the beautiful, beloved face close to his own an instant, then turned his head away, and Rose heard one strong, deep sob, but never any word of lamentation or reproach. Too much moved to speak, yet too full of sympathy to leave him, she leaned her head upon the arm of the cushioned chair in which she sat, and soon forgot the lapse of time in thoughts both sweet and bitter. A light rustle and a faint perfume recalled her to the present; and looking, without moving, she saw Richard's almost transparent hand hold the dead rose in the flame of the lamp until its ashes fluttered to the ground; she saw him watch the last spark fade, and shiver as he glanced drearily about the room, as if all the warmth and beauty had died out of his life, leaving it very desolate and dark; she saw him turn toward her while his face grew clear and calm again, and, believing himself unseen, he lifted a little fold of her dress to his lips, as if he bade the woman whom he loved a long farewell; then he lay down like one spent with some sore struggle, which, though hardly fought, had been wholly won.

At that sight Rose's tears fell fast; and, long after Richard slept the sleep of utter weariness, she still sat there, with her head pillowed on her arms, keeping a vigil in which she consecrated her whole life to the service of that cause which, through many trials, had taught her a truer loyalty, a purer love.

IN THE RUDDY GLOW OF an October sunset, Rose led Richard across the threshold of the dear old home, and gave him to his mother's arms. At first, a joyful tumult reigned; then, as the wonder, gratitude, and joy subsided, all turned to Rose. She stood apart, silently receiving her reward; and, though worn and weary with her long labor, never had she seemed so beautiful as then; for the once proud eyes were grown sweetly humble, the serenity of a great content shone in her face, and a fine blending of gentleness and strength gave the crowning grace to one who was now, in truth, a "right noble woman."

The mother and her sons regarded her in silence for a moment, and silently she looked back at them with a glance, a gesture that said more eloquently than any words: "Forgive me, love me, and forget the past." Mrs. Stirling opened her arms, and Rose clung to that motherly bosom, feeling that no daughter could be dearer than she was now, that all her pain and penitence was known, and her reward secure at last.

"Rose, I have but one thing precious enough to give you in return for the great service you have so beautifully conferred upon me. If I read your heart aright, this is the prize for which you have striven and suffered; and, loving you the dearer for your constancy, I freely give one-half my treasure to your keeping, sure that you will find life richer, happier, and better for your devotion to the man you love."

Rose understood her, — felt that the mother wished to prove the woman's pride, the lover's truth, — and well she stood the test; for going straight to Robert, who had scarcely spoken, but whose eye had never left her since she came, she said, clearly and steadily, — too earnest for maiden shame, too humble for false pride, too hopeful for any fear, "Robert, you once said you would never ask either pity or love of me. Will you accept both when I offer them humbly, heartily, and tell you that all my happiness, my hopes, my peace, are now bound up in you?"

Poor Rob! he had no arms in which to receive her, no words wherewith to welcome her, for speech failed him when those tender eyes looked up into his own, and she so generously gave him the desire of his life. He only bowed his head before her, deliciously oppressed with the happiness this double gift conferred. Rose read his heart, and with a loving woman's skill robbed the moment of all its bitterness and left only its sweetness; for, putting both arms about his neck, she whispered like a pleading child, "Dear, let me stay; I am so happy here!"

There was but one answer to that appeal; and as it was given, Mrs. Stirling turned to beckon Richard from the room, glad to have him all her own again. He had already stolen out, and standing in the autumn sunshine, looked across the quiet river with a countenance as cheerful as the sunshine, as tranquil as the stream. His mother scanned his face with a searching yet sorrowful eye, that dimmed with sudden dew as, reading its significance, her son met it with a glance that set her anxiety at rest.

"Have no fears for me, mother; I have fought my double fight, and am freed from my double captivity. The lost love is not dead, but sleeping, never to waken in this world, and its grave is growing green."

"Ah, my good son, the world will see Rob's sacrifice, and honor him for it, but yours is the greater one, for through many temptations you have been loyal, both to your country and yourself. God and your mother love and honor you for that, although to other eyes you seem to stand forgotten and alone."

But Richard drew the gray head tenderly, reverently down upon his breast, and answered, with the cheerful smile unchanged, —

"Never alone while I have you, mother."

Colored Soldiers' Letters

DEAR COMMONWEALTH: —

As every one is, or ought to be, interested in the efforts now being made for the education of colored persons, old and young, I venture to think that the accompanying letters from several members of one of the colored regiments lately in camp at Readville, will prove interesting to some of your readers as proofs of what a few months of faithful teaching can do for the men, who, with Testament and Primer in their knapsacks, cheerfully shoulder their muskets and march away to fight for a country that disowns them and grudgingly pays for the lives they give in the defence of our liberties as well as their own.

The young lady to whom the letters were written by grateful ex-pupils, tells me that none of them could read, write or spell, when the class was formed; when it was broken up by orders to march, all could read more or less fluently, many could spell as correctly as half our so-called educated boys and girls, and I can testify that the handwriting of the half dozen letters in my possession is in some cases excellent, in no case as unreadable as certain specimens of illustrious illegibility with which most of us are familiar. All errors of spelling, punctuation and grammar have been preserved for the truth's sake, because a few months of care, however heartily bestowed, cannot repair the neglect of years, while the inaccuracies and inelegancies contrasting with the honest and manly sentiments of a great need, but prove how deep a wrong is committed in denying the black man an equal education with the white.

The first letter is dated

"IN CAMP NEAR CITTY POINT.

"Dear Lady:—I have just Come off pickit duty in the woods and altho very tired and sleepy I feel so happy at receiving your kind letter that I can

First published in the *Commonwealth* 3, no. 44 (1 July 1864)

take no rest untill I have written you a few lines to inform you that we are mostly well. we have only one man that is very sick and he is S. P. one of your scholars. he has bin made sick by lying on the ground. We had a small fight on Sunday the 29th of may. it was not very much but anough to let the Rebs or any one Else know that the —— Man is not to be fooled with. no indeed we came from the old Bay state & we are not going to do any thing that will make the blush of shame come upon the face of dear Good Governor Andrews or any of our Good friends at home sweet home the name never had such a sweet sound before as it has now but enough of sentement. now is the time for action. we are as buzzy as bees throughing up Earth works as the Rebs are very near. the firing this morning was very heavy we could see the flush of Guns and the Bomb shells flying through the air like lighted candles. I am sorry to say that Company—has lost one of their corporals. he was on pickit duty and got outside the lines by some means or other & was mistaken for a Reb by the sentinel on that post who fired on him and shot him through the thigh of which wound he died this morning. I rejoice with Miss C for the safe return of her brother home from the wars will my poor sister ever have the same cause to rejoice that she has—God knows best—I hope you and yours are all injoying the greatest of all Earthly blessings good health. that you are is the cincear wish of your very humble servant. H. C.

"Excuse this poor appology for a letter but the fact is there is so much firing bugles sounding men running to and from that a person cannot compose his mind to write. T. M. sends his respects to you and all his teachers."

The next letter is a most imposing document in the original, well written on a sheet of fools'-cap, expressed with some elegance, and scaled with a thick splash of red wax evidently stamped with a thumb. Not a bad device for a man whose first and perhaps only chance of winning a name lies in the speed and accuracy with which that stout thumb can pull a trigger.

"Dear Madam: —Through the politeness of my first sergeant, I sit down to fulfill a promise made you on the eve of my departure from Readville.

"The evening of the day we left found us embarked on board of a boat at New London, Conn. The next morning we were in New York where we re-embarked for Amboy, N.J. Arrived there about three P.M. we proceeded by rail to Washington, Via Philadelphia and Baltimore. We were sent to Camp

Stoneman, six miles from Washington, where we remained for a few days. We were soon dismounted and sent to Camp Casey, located on old General Lee's farm. One night there and we were ordered to report to Gen. Butler, City Point. We started at once by water and were two days and three nights on the journey.

"We found ourselves in the vicinity of rebeldom on the 14th inst., and had not been there two hours before we were drawn up in line of battle. It appeared that our pickets had been driven in by the rebels inconsiderable force, and it was presumed that they might be in sufficient numbers to make an attack upon us with a promise of success. No demonstration was made, however, and although the troops have been chafing for battle their desire has not yet been gratified.

"We are within hearing of Gen. Butler's guns against Fort Darling and can frequently see the shells burst. We were aroused from our slumbers on the night of the 21st by heavy cannonading up the river and were drawn up in line of battle and remained there till morning. I found that rebels were attempting to send a flat down the river for the purpose of attacking us, but were caught by some of Gen. Butler's gunboats and repulsed with a loss of fifteen hundred killed and wounded. Our loss was two killed and three wounded.

"We are drawn up every morning in line of battle and remain so from three A.M. till seven P.M. Our position is well defended by both nature and art. We are protected on two sides by the James River, and on the greater part of the remaining sides by a deep marshy ravine, filled with fallen trees and other obstructions, and exposed to the fire of the Union gunboat fleet, would make our position almost inaccessible from that direction.

"But I have not the time to give you a description of all I see that interests me, but you may expect to hear from the pen of Sergeant P. some correspondence in some of the popular journals that will post you upon the more minute details.

"I have been in good health and fine spirits ever since I left Readville; but even during our most exciting moments I frequently think of those whom I left behind me, whose images, as my imagination pictures them, always recall pleasant moments. I shall be highly gratified to hear from you as often as convenient, and shall write as often as opportunity will allow.

"I have grown heavier and larger since I left Mass, and am impressed with the belief that this climate will do much toward my physical development. Give my love to Miss N. and reserve a share for yourself.

Yours, truly, S. J."

If space permitted I should be strongly tempted to add, as a pendant to this letter, one lately received from a white soldier, now a student in one of our Western colleges, which has refused to grant a colored student the honors he had won. In which case the white man would be worsted, for "S. J." with his "troops chafing for battle," his positions "well defended by both nature and art," and his impressions regarding his "physical development" entirely outdoes his more fortunate countryman.

The last letter begins in a somewhat novel manner.

"Miss, Permit me through the columns of this letter to write you a few lines to inform you that I am well and hopping this may find you in the same. This present finds me on the sackred soil of Virginia. We are only twenty-six miles from Richmond on the James River. The first day we arrived we thought we would have a battle but we did not; but they are fighting about fifteen miles from here, and we can hear heavy firing almost every minute.

"I am almost through my primer. I say my lesson in my Testament when I have time. We have to sleep on our muskets with our equipments on, and have to git up at three o'clock. If I send you a hundred dollars will you take care of it for me? C. A. sends his respects and said he has not done much toward his book, but has done all he could. Miss W., I hope I may have a chance to come back and have you to teach me some more. I will send you this gold dollar for a present, perhaps when I come home I will be able to give you something worth while speaking of. No more at present, but I have the honor to subscribe your most obedient servant.

T. M."

No, good and grateful "T. M." I think you will find nothing more precious to offer your teacher than the little gold dollar, because the gratitude, affection and respect of which it is the symbol, make it one of those treasures which do not take to themselves wings and fly away. Nor is the ill-spelt but hearty letter valueless, for though sleeping on the "sackred soil of Virginia" with his musket for a pillow, this book-loving "T. M." finds time to get almost through his primer, to read his Testament when he can, and say a friendly word for poor C. A., who has not been able "to do much toward the book" which has been so long in doing anything "toward" him. Let us hope that both may prosper in the double battle they must fight against treason and ignorance, and "have a chance to come back" to the same gentle teaching which has already done so much for them.

Many touching incidents might be related of these men; the hunger for learning which kept some of them poring over books by fire light when the day's duties were done; the eagerness with which an especial gift for mathematics was pursued till its possessor outstripped his accomplished teacher; the pathetic patience with which the dullest plodded on till kindly sympathy and perseverance warmed the benumbed intellect into life and made the soldier twice a man; and more than all, the beautiful respect, the native courtesy, the unspeakable gratitude which found expression in acts that both surprised and touched the receiver. To any who find time hangs heavy on their hands, who have a prejudice to conquer, or who long to help on the great transition, we would say, become a teacher in the Readville barracks and earn a lasting satisfaction through the duties and the pleasures of a just work generously performed.

Nelly's Hospital

NELLY SAT BESIDE HER MOTHER picking lint; but while her fingers flew, her eyes often looked wistfully out into the meadow, golden with buttercups and bright with sunshine. Presently she said, rather bashfully, but very earnestly, "Mamma, I want to tell you a little plan I've made, if you'll please not laugh."

"I think I can safely promise that, my dear," said her mother, putting down her work that she might listen quite respectfully.

Nelly looked pleased, and went on confidingly. "Since brother Will came home with his lame foot, and I've helped you tend him, I've heard a great deal about hospitals, and liked it very much. To-day I said I wanted to go and be a nurse, like Aunt Mercy; but Will laughed, and told me I'd better begin by nursing sick birds and butterflies and pussies before I tried to take care of men. I did not like to be made fun of, but I've been thinking that it would be very pleasant to have a little hospital all my own, and be a nurse in it, because, if I took pains, so many pretty creatures might be made well, perhaps. Could I, mamma?"

Her mother wanted to smile at the idea, but did not, for Nelly looked up with her heart and eyes so full of tender compassion, both for the unknown men for whom her little hands had done their best, and for the smaller sufferers nearer home, that she stroked the shining head, and answered readily: "Yes, Nelly, it will be a proper charity for such a young Samaritan, and you may learn much if you are in earnest. You must study how to feed and nurse your little patients, else your pity will do no good, and your hospital become a prison. I will help you, and Tony shall be your surgeon."

First published in *Our Young Folks,* 1, no. 4 (April 1865).

"O mamma, how good you always are to me! Indeed, I am in truly earnest; I will learn, I will be kind, and may I go now and begin?"

"You may, but tell me first where will you have your hospital?"

"In my room, mamma; it is so snug and sunny, and I never should forget it there," said Nelly.

"You must not forget it anywhere. I think that plan will not do. How would you like to find caterpillars walking in your bed, to hear sick pussies mewing in the night, to have beetles clinging to your clothes, or see mice, bugs, and birds tumbling down stairs whenever the door was open?" said her mother.

Nelly laughed at that thought a minute, then clapped her hands, and cried: "Let us have the old summer-house! My doves only use the upper part, and it would be so like Frank in the story-book. Please say yes again, mamma."

Her mother did say yes, and, snatching up her hat, Nelly ran to find Tony, the gardener's son, a pleasant lad of twelve, who was Nelly's favorite playmate. Tony pronounced the plan a "jolly" one, and, leaving his work, followed his young mistress to the summer-house, for she could not wait one minute.

"What must we do first?" she asked, as they stood looking in at the dim, dusty room, full of garden tools, bags of seeds, old flower-pots, and watering cans.

"Clear out the rubbish, miss," answered Tony.

"Here it goes, then," and Nelly began bundling everything out in such haste that she broke two flower-pots, scattered all the squash-seeds, and brought a pile of rakes and hoes clattering down about her ears.

"Just wait a bit, and let me take the lead, miss. You hand me things, I'll pile 'em in the barrow and wheel 'em off to the barn; then it will save time, and be finished up tidy."

Nelly did as he advised, and very soon nothing but dust remained.

"What next?" she asked, not knowing in the least.

"I'll sweep up while you see if Polly can come and scrub the room out. It ought to be done before you stay here, let alone the patients."

"So it had," said Nelly, looking very wise all of a sudden. "Will says the wards—that means the rooms, Tony—are scrubbed every day or two, and kept very clean, and well venti—something—I can't say it; but it means having a plenty of air come in. I can clean windows while Polly mops, and then we shall soon be done."

Away she ran, feeling very busy and important. Polly came, and very soon the room looked like another place. The four latticed windows were set wide open, so the sunshine came dancing through the vines that grew outside, and curious roses peeped in to see what frolic was afoot. The walls shone white again, for not a spider dared to stay; the wide seat which encircled the room was dustless now,—the floor as nice as willing hands could make it; and the south wind blew away all musty odors with its fragrant breath.

"How fine it looks!" cried Nelly, dancing on the doorstep, lest a footprint should mar the still damp floor.

"I'd almost like to fall sick for the sake of staying here," said Tony, admiringly. "Now, what sort of beds are you going to have, miss?"

"I suppose it won't do to put butterflies and toads and worms into beds like the real soldiers where Will was?" answered Nelly, looking anxious.

Tony could hardly help shouting at the idea; but, rather than trouble his little mistress, he said very soberly: "I'm afraid they wouldn't lay easy, not being used to it. Tucking up a butterfly would about kill him; the worms would be apt to get lost among the bed-clothes; and the toads would tumble out the first thing."

"I shall have to ask mamma about it. What will you do while I'm gone?" said Nelly, unwilling that a moment should be lost.

"I'll make frames for nettings to the window, else the doves will come in and eat up the sick people."

"I think they will know that it is a hospital, and be too kind to hurt or frighten their neighbors," began Nelly; but as she spoke, a plump white dove walked in, looked about with its red-ringed eyes, and quietly pecked up a tiny bug that had just ventured out from the crack where it had taken refuge when the deluge came.

"Yes, we must have the nettings. I'll ask mamma for some lace," said Nelly, when she saw that; and, taking, her pet dove on her shoulder, told it about her hospital as she went toward the house; for, loving all little creatures as she did, it grieved her to have any harm befall even the least or plainest of them. She had a sweet child-fancy that her playmates understood her language as she did theirs, and that birds, flowers, animals, and insects felt for her the same affection which she felt for them. Love always makes friends, and nothing seemed to fear the gentle child; but welcomed her like a little sun who shone alike on all, and never suffered an eclipse.

She was gone some time, and when she came back her mind was full of new plans, one hand full of rushes, the other of books, while over her head floated the lace, and a bright green ribbon hung across her arm.

"Mamma says that the best beds will be little baskets, boxes, cages, and any sort of thing that suits the patient; for each will need different care and food and medicine. I have not baskets enough, so, as I cannot have pretty white beds, I am going to braid pretty green nests for my patients, and, while I do it, mamma thought you'd read to me the pages she has marked, so that we may begin right."

"Yes, miss; I like that. But what is the ribbon for?" asked Tony.

"O, that's for you. Will says that, if you are to be an army surgeon, you must have a green band on your arm; so I got this to tie on when we play hospital."

Tony let her decorate the sleeve of his gray jacket, and when the nettings were done, the welcome books were opened and enjoyed. It was a happy time, sitting in the sunshine with leaves pleasantly astir all about them, doves cooing overhead, and flowers sweetly gossiping together through the summer afternoon. Nelly wove her smooth, green rushes. Tony pored over his pages, and both found something better than fairy legends in the family histories of insects, birds, and beasts. All manner of wonders appeared, and were explained to them, till Nelly felt as if a new world had been given her, so full of beauty, interest, and pleasure that she never could be tired of studying it. Many of these things were not strange to Tony, because, born among plants, he had grown up with them as if they were brothers and sisters, and the sturdy, brown-faced boy had learned many lessons which no poet or philosopher could have taught him, unless he had become as childlike as himself, and studied from the same great book.

When the baskets were done, the marked pages all read, and the sun began to draw his rosy curtains round him before smiling "Good night," Nelly ranged the green beds round the room. Tony put in the screens, and the hospital was ready. The little nurse was so excited that she could hardly eat her supper, and directly afterwards ran up to tell Will how well she had succeeded with the first part of her enterprise. Now brother Will was a brave young officer, who had fought stoutly and done his duty like a man. But when lying weak and wounded at home the cheerful courage which had led him safely through many dangers seemed to have deserted him, and he was often gloomy, sad, or fretful, because he longed to be at his post again, and time passed very slowly. This troubled his mother, and made Nelly wonder why he found lying in a pleasant room so much harder than fighting battles or making weary marches. Anything that interested and amused him was very welcome, and when Nelly, climbing on the arm of his sofa, told her plans, mishaps, and successes, he laughed out more heartily than he had done for many a day, and his thin face began to twinkle with fun as it used to do so long ago. That pleased Nelly, and she chatted like any affectionate little magpie, till Will was really interested; for when one is ill, small things amuse.

"Do you expect your patients to come to you, Nelly?" he asked.

"No, I shall go and look for them. I often see poor things suffering in the garden, and the wood, and always feel as if they ought to be taken care of, as people are."

"You won't like to carry insane bugs, lame toads, and convulsive kittens in your hands, and they would not stay on a stretcher if you had one. You should have an ambulance and be a branch of the Sanitary Commission," said Will.

Nelly had often heard the words, but did not quite understand what they meant. So Will told her of that great and never-failing charity, to which thousands owe their lives; and the child listened with lips apart, eyes often full, and so much love and admiration in her heart that she could find no words in which to tell it. When her brother paused, she said earnestly: "Yes, I will be a Sanitary. This little cart of mine shall be my amb'lance, and I'll never let my water-barrels go empty, never drive too fast, or be rough with my poor passengers, like some of the men you tell about. Does this look like an ambulance, Will?"

"Not a bit, but it shall, if you and mamma like to help me. I want four long bits of cane, a square of white cloth, some pieces of thin wood, and the gum-pot," said Will, sitting up to examine the little cart, feeling like a boy again as he took out his knife and began to whittle.

Up stairs and down stairs ran Nelly till all necessary materials were collected, and almost breathlessly she watched her brother arch the canes over the cart, cover them with the cloth, and fit in an upper shelf of small compartments, each lined with cotton-wool to serve as beds for wound insects, lest they should hurt one another or jostle out. The lower part was left free for any larger creatures which Nelly might find. Among her toys she had a tiny cask which only needed a peg to be water-tight; this was filled and fitted in before, because, as the small sufferers needed no seats, there was no place for it behind, and, as Nelly was both horse and driver, it was more convenient in front. On each side of it stood a box of stores. In one were minute rollers, as bandages are called, a few bottles not yet filled, and a wee doll's jar of cold-cream, because Nelly could not feel that her outfit was complete without a medicine-chest. The other box was full of crumbs, bits of sugar, bird-seed, and grains of wheat and corn, lest any famished stranger should die for want of food before she got it home. Then mamma painted "U. S. San. Com." in bright letters on the cover, and Nelly received her charitable plaything with a long sigh of satisfaction.

"Nine o'clock already. Bless me, what a short evening this has been," exclaimed Will, as Nelly came to give him her good-night kiss.

"And such a happy one," she answered. "Thank you very, very much, dear Will. I only wish my little amb'lance was big enough for you to go in,—I'd so like to give you the first ride."

"Nothing I should like better, if it were possible, though I've a prejudice against ambulances in general. But as I cannot ride, I'll try and hop out to your hospital to-morrow, and see how you get on,"—which was a great deal for Captain Will to say, because he had been too listless to leave his sofa for several days.

That promise sent Nelly happily away to bed, only stopping to pop her head out of the window to see if it was likely to be a fair day to-morrow, and to tell Tony about the new plan as he passed below.

"Where shall you go to look for your first load of sick folks, miss?" he asked.

"All round the garden first, then through the grove, and home across the brook. Do you think I can find any patients so?" said Nelly.

"I know you will. Good night, miss," and Tony walked away with a merry look on his face, that Nelly would not have understood if she had seen it.

Up rose the sun bright and early, and up rose Nurse Nelly almost as early and as bright. Breakfast was taken in a great hurry, and before the dew was off the grass this branch of the S. C. was all astir. Papa, mamma, big brother and baby sister, men and maids, all looked out to see the funny little ambulance depart, and nowhere in all the summer fields was there a happier child than Nelly, as she went smiling down the garden path, where tall flowers kissed her as she passed and every blithe bird seemed singing a "Good speed!"

"How I wonder what I shall find first," she thought, looking sharply on all sides as she went. Crickets chirped, grasshoppers leaped, ants worked busily at their subterranean houses, spiders spun shining webs from twig to twig, bees were coming for their bags of gold, and butterflies had just begun their holiday. A large white one alighted on the top of the ambulance, walked over the inscription as if spelling it letter by letter, then floated away from flower to flower, like one carrying the good news far and wide.

"Now every one will know about the hospital and be glad to see me coming," thought Nelly. And indeed it seemed so, for just then a blackbird, sitting on the garden wall, burst out with a song full of musical joy, Nelly's kitten came running after to stare at the wagon and rub her soft side against it, a bright-eyed toad looked out from his cool bower among the lily-leaves, and at that minute Nelly found her first patient. In one of the dewy cobwebs hanging from a shrub near by sat a fat black and yellow spider, watching a fly whose delicate wings were just caught in the net. The poor fly buzzed pitifully, and struggled so hard that the whole web shook; but the more he struggled, the more he entangled himself, and the fierce spider was preparing to descend that it might weave a shroud about its prey, when a little finger broke the threads and lifted the fly safely into the palm of a hand where he lay faintly humming his thanks.

Nelly had heard much about contrabands, knew who they were, and was very much interested in them; so, when she freed the poor black fly, she played he was her contraband, and felt glad that her first patient was one that needed help so much. Carefully brushing away as much of the web as she could, she left small Pompey, as she named him, to free his own legs, lest her clumsy fingers should hurt him; then she laid him in one of the soft beds with a grain or two of sugar if he needed refreshment, and bade him rest and recover from his fright, remembering that he was at liberty to fly away whenever he liked, because she had no wish to make a slave of him

Feeling very happy over this new friend, Nelly went on singing softly she walked, and presently she found a pretty caterpillar dressed in brown fur although the day was warm. He lay so still she thought him dead, till he rolled himself into a ball as she touched him.

"I think you are either faint from the heat of this thick coat of yours, or that you are going to make a cocoon of yourself, Mr. Fuzz," said Nelly.

"Now I want to see you turn into a butterfly, so I shall take you, and if you get lively again I will let you go. I shall play that you have given out on a march, as the soldiers sometimes do, and been left behind for the Sanitary people to see to."

In went sulky Mr. Fuzz, and on trundled the ambulance till a golden green rose-beetle was discovered, lying on his back kicking as if in a fit.

"Dear me, what shall I do for him?" thought Kelly. "He acts as baby did when she was so ill, and mamma put her in a warm bath. I haven't got my little tub here, or any hot water, and I'm afraid the beetle would not like it if I had. Perhaps he has pain in his stomach; I'll turn him over, and pat his back, as nurse does baby's when she cries for pain like that."

She set the beetle on his legs, and did her best to comfort him; but he was evidently in great distress, for he could not walk, and instead of lifting his emerald overcoat, and spreading the wings that lay underneath, he turned again, and kicked more violently than before. Not knowing what to do, Nelly put him into one of her soft nests for Tony to cure if possible. She found no more patients in the garden except a dead bee, which she wrapped in a leaf, and took home to bury. When she came to the grove, it was so green and cool she longed to sit and listen to the whisper of the pines, and watch the larch-tassels wave in the wind. But, recollecting her charitable errand, she went rustling along the pleasant path till she came to another patient, over which she stood considering several minutes before she could decide whether it was best to take it to her hospital, because it was a little gray snake, with a bruised tail. She knew it would not hurt her, yet she was afraid of it; she thought it pretty, yet could not like it; she pitied its pain, yet shrunk from helping it, for it had a fiery eye, and a keep quivering tongue, that looked as if longing to bite.

"He is a rebel, I wonder if I ought to be good to him," thought Nelly, watching the reptile writhe with pain. "Will said there were sick rebels in his hospital, and one was very kind to him. It says, too, in my little book, 'Love your enemies.' I think snakes are mine, but I guess I'll try and love him because God made him. Some boy will kill him if I leave him here, and then perhaps his mother will be very sad about it. Come, poor worm, I wish to help you, so be patient, and don't frighten me."

Then Nelly laid her little handkerchief on the ground, and with a stick gently lifted the wounded snake upon it, and, folding it together, laid it in the ambulance. She was thoughtful after that, and so busy puzzling her young head about the duty of loving those who hate us, and being kind to those who are disagreeable or unkind, that she went through the rest of the wood quite forgetful of her work. A soft "Queek, queek!" made her look up and listen. The sound came from the long meadow-grass, and, bending it carefully back, she found a half-fledged bird, with one wing trailing on the ground, and its eyes dim with pain or hunger.

"You darling thing, did you fall out of your nest and hurt your wing?" cried Nelly, looking up into the single tree that stood near by. No nest was to be seen, no parent birds hovered overhead, and little Robin could only tell its troubles in that mournful "Queek, queek, queek!"

Nelly ran to get both her chests, and, sitting down beside the bird, tried to feed it. To her great joy it ate crumb after crumb as if it were half starved, and soon fluttered nearer with a confiding fearlessness that made her very proud. Soon baby Robin seemed quite comfortable, his eye brightened, he "queeked" no more, and but for the drooping wing would have been himself again. With one of her bandages Nelly bound both wings closely to his sides for fear he should hurt himself by trying to fly; and though he seemed amazed at her proceedings, he behaved very well, only staring her, and ruffling up his few feathers in a funny way that made her laugh. Then she had to discover some way of accommodating, her two large patients so that neither should hurt nor alarm the other. A bright thought came to her after much pondering. Carefully lifting the handkerchief, she pinned the two ends to the roof of the cart, and there swung little Forked tongue, while Rob lay easily below.

By this time Nelly began to wonder how it happened that she found so many more injured things than ever before. But it never entered her innocent head that Tony had searched the wood and meadow before she was up and laid most of these creatures ready to her hands, that she might not be disappointed. She had not yet lost her faith in fairies, so she fancied they too belonged to her small sisterhood, and presently it did really seem impossible to doubt that the good folk had been at work.

Coming to the bridge that crossed the brook, she stopped a moment to watch the water ripple over the bright pebbles, the ferns bend down to drink and the funny tadpoles frolic in quieter nooks, where the sun shone, and the dragon-flies swung among the rushes. When Nelly turned to go on her blue eyes opened wide, and the handle of the ambulance dropped with a noise

that caused a stout frog to skip into the water heels over head. Directly in the middle of the bridge was a pretty green tent, made of two tall burdock leaves. The stems were stuck into cracks between the boards, the tips were pinned together with a thorn, and one great buttercup nodded in the doorway like a sleepy sentinel. Nelly stared and smiled, listened, and looked about on every side. Nothing was seen but the quiet meadow and the shady grove nothing was heard but the babble of the brook and the cheery music of the bobolinks.

"Yes," said Nelly softly to herself, "that is a fairy tent, and in it I may find a baby elf sick with whooping-cough or scarlet-fever. How splendid it would be! only I could never nurse such a dainty thing."

Stooping eagerly, she peeped over the buttercup's drowsy head, and what seemed a tiny cock of hay. She had no time to feel disappointed for the haycock began to stir, and, looking nearer, she beheld two silvery gray mites, who wagged wee tails, and stretched themselves as if they has just waked up. Nelly knew that they were young field-mice, and rejoiced over them, feeling rather relieved that no fairy had appeared, though she still believed them to have had a hand in the matter.

"I shall call the mice my Babes in the Wood, because they are lost and covered up with leaves," said Nelly, as she laid them in her snuggest bed where they nestled close together, and fell fast asleep again.

Being very anxious to get home, that she might tell her adventures and show how great was the need of a sanitary commission in that region. Nelly marched proudly up the avenue, and, having displayed her load, hurried to the hospital, where another applicant was waiting for her. On the step of the door lay a large turtle, with one claw gone, and on his back was pasted a bit of paper, with his name,—"Commodore Waddle, U.S.N." Nelly knew this was a joke of Will's, but welcomed the ancient mariner, and called Tony to help her get him in.

All that morning they were very busy settling the new-comers, for both people and books had to be consulted before they could decide what diet and treatment was best for each. The winged contraband had taken Nelly at her word, and flown away on the journey home. Little Rob was put in a large cage, where he could use his legs, yet not injure his lame wing. Forked-tongue lay under a wire cover, on sprigs of fennel, for the gardener said that snakes were fond of it. The Babes in the Wood were put to bed in one of the rush baskets, under a cotton-wool coverlet. Greenback, the beetle, found ease for his unknown aches in the warm heart of a rose, where he sunned himself all day. The Commodore was made happy in a tub of water, grass, and stones, and Mr. Fuzz was put in a well-ventilated glass box to decide whether he would be a cocoon or not.

Tony had not been idle while his mistress was away, and he showed her the hospital garden he had made close by, in which were cabbage, nettle, and mignonette plants for the butterflies, flowering herbs for the bees, chickweed and hemp for the birds, catnip for the pussies, and plenty of room left for whatever other patients might need. In the afternoon, while Nelly did her task at lint-picking, talking busily to Will as she worked, and interesting him in her affairs, Tony cleared a pretty spot in the grove for the burying-ground, and made ready some small bits of slate on which to write the names of those who died. He did not have it ready an hour too soon, for at sunset two little graves were needed, and Nurse Nelly shed tender tears for her first losses as she laid the motherless mice in one smooth hollow, and the gray-coated rebel in the other. She had learned to care for him already, and when she found him dead, was very glad she had been kind to him, hoping that he knew it, and died happier in her hospital than all alone in the shadowy wood.

The rest of Nelly's patients prospered, and of the many added afterward few died, because of Tony's skilful treatment and her own faithful care. Every morning when the day proved fair the little ambulance went out upon its charitable errand; every afternoon Nelly worked for the human sufferers whom she loved; and every evening brother Will read aloud to her from useful books, showed her wonders with his microscope, or prescribed remedies for the patients, whom he soon knew by name and took much interest in. It was Nelly's holiday; but, though she studied no lessons, she learned much, and unconsciously made her pretty play both an example and a rebuke for others.

At first it seemed a childish pastime, and people laughed. But there was something in the familiar words "Sanitary," "hospital," and "ambulance" that made them pleasant sounds to many ears. As reports of Nelly's work went through the neighborhood, other children came to see and copy her design. Rough lads looked ashamed when in her wards they found harmless creatures hurt by them, and going out they said among themselves, "We won't stone birds, chase butterflies, and drown the girls' little cats any more, though we won't tell them so." And most of the lads kept their word so well that people said there never had been so many birds before as all that summer haunted wood and field. Tender-hearted playmates brought their pets to be cured; even busy fathers had a friendly word for the small charity which reminded them so sweetly of the great one which should never be fogotten; lonely mothers sometimes looked out with wet eyes as the little ambulance went by, recalling thoughts of absent sons who might be journeying painfully to some far-off hospital, where brave women waited to tend them with hands as willing, hearts as tender, as those the gentle child gave to her self-appointed task.

At home the charm worked also. No more idle days for Nelly, or fretful ones for Will, because the little sister would not neglect the helpless creatures so dependent upon her, and the big brother was ashamed to complain after watching the patience of these lesser sufferers, and merrily said he would try to bear his own wound as quietly and bravely as the "Commodore" bore his. Nelly never knew how much good she had done Captain Will till he went away again in the early autumn. Then he thanked her for it, and though she cried for joy and sorrow, she never forgot it, because he left something behind him which always pleasantly reminded her of the double success her little hospital had won.

When Will was gone and she had prayed softly in her heart that God would keep him safe and bring him home again, she dried her tears and went away to find comfort in the place where he had spent so many happy hours with her. She had not been there before that day, and when she reached the door she stood quite still and wanted very much to cry again, for something beautiful had happened. She had often asked Will for a motto for her hospital, and he had promised to find her one. She thought he had forgotten it; but even in the hurry of that busy day he had found time to do more than keep his word, while Nelly sat indoors, lovingly brightening the tarnished buttons on the blue coat that had seen so many battles.

Above the roof, where the doves cooed in the sun, now rustled a white flag with the golden "S. C." shining on it as the west wind tossed it to and fro. Below, on the smooth panel of the door, a skilful pencil had drawn two arching ferns, in whose soft shadow, poised upon a mushroom, stood a little figure of Nurse Nelly, and underneath it another of Dr. Tony bottling medicine, with spectacles upon his nose. Both hands of the miniature Nelly were outstretched, as if beckoning to a train of insects, birds, and beasts, which was so long that it not only circled round the lower rim of this fine sketch, but dwindled in the distance to mere dots and lines. Such merry conceits as one found there! A mouse bringing the tail it had lost in some cruel trap, a dor-bug with a shade over its eyes, an invalid butterfly carried in a tiny litter by long-legged spiders, a fat frog with gouty feet hopping upon crutches, Jenny Wren sobbing in a nice handkerchief, as she brought dead Cock Robin to be restored to life. Rabbits, lambs, cats, calves and turtles, all came trooping up to be healed by the benevolent little maid who welcomed them so heartily.

Nelly laughed at these comical mites till the tears ran down her cheeks, and thought she never could be tired of looking at them. But presently she saw four lines clearly printed underneath her picture, and her childish face grew sweetly serious as she read the words of a great poet, which Will had made both compliment and motto:

"He prayeth best who loveth best
All things, both great and small;
For the dear God who loveth us,
He made and loveth all."

The Blue and the Gray

"DON'T BRING HIM IN HERE; every corner is full — and I'm glad of it," added the nurse under her breath, eyeing with strong disfavor the gaunt figure lying on the stretcher in the doorway.

"Where shall we put him, then? They won't have him in either of the other wards on this floor. He's ordered up here, and here he must stay if he's put in the hall — poor devil!" said the foremost bearer, looking around the crowded room in despair.

The nurse's eye followed his, and both saw a thin hand beckoning from the end of the long ward.

"It's Murry; I'll see what he wants;" and Miss Mercy went to him with her quick, noiseless step, and the smile her grave face always wore for him.

"There's room here, if you turn my bed 'round, you see. Don't let them leave him in the hall," said Murry, lifting his great eyes to hers. Brilliant with the fever burning his strength away, and pathetic with the silent protest of life against death.

"It's like you to think of it; but he's a rebel," began Miss Mercy.

"So much more reason to take him in. I don't mind having him here; but it will distress me dreadfully to know that any poor soul was turned away, from the comfort of this ward especially."

The look he gave her made the words an eloquent compliment, and his pity for a fallen enemy reproached her for her own lack of it. Her face softened as she nodded, and glanced about the recess.

"You will have the light in your eyes, and only the little table between you and a very disagreeable neighbor," she said.

Published anonymously in *Putnam's Magazine*, 1, no. 6 (June 1868).

"I can shut my eyes if the light troubles them; I've nothing else to do now," he answered, with a faint laugh. "I was too comfortable before; I'd more than my share of luxuries; so bring him along, and it will be all right."

The order was given, and, after a brief bustle, the two narrow beds stood side by side in the recess under the organ-loft — for the hospital had been a church. Left alone for a moment, the two men eyed each other silently. Murry saw a tall, sallow man, with fierce black eyes, wild hair and beard, and a thin-lipped, cruel mouth. A ragged gray uniform was visible under the blanket thrown over him; and in strange contrast to the squalor of his dress, and the neglect of his person, was the diamond ring that shone on his unwounded hand. The right arm was bound up, the right leg amputated at the knee; and though the man's face was white and haggard with suffering, not a sound escaped him as he lay with his bold eyes fixed defiantly upon his neighbor.

John Clay, the new-comer, saw opposite him a small, wasted figure, and a plain face; yet both face and figure were singularly attractive, for suffering seemed to have refined away all the grosser elements, and left the spiritual very visible through that frail tenement of flesh. Pale-brown hair streaked the hollow temples and white forehead. A deep color burned in the thin cheeks still tanned by the wind and weather of along campaign. The mouth was grave and sweet, and in the gray eyes lay an infinite patience touched with melancholy. He wore a dressing-gown, but across his feet lay a faded coat of army-blue. As the other watched him, he saw a shadow pass across his tranquil face, and for a moment he laid his wasted hand over the eyes that had been so full of pity. Then he gently pushed a mug of fresh water, and the last of a bunch of grapes, toward the exhausted rebel, saying, in a cordial tone,

"You look faint and thirsty; have 'em."

Clay's lips were parched, and his hand went involuntarily toward the cup; but he caught it back, and leaning forward, asked in a shrill whisper,

"Where are you hurt?"

"A shot in the side," answered Murry, visibly surprised at the man's manner.

"What battle?"

"The Wilderness."

"Is it bad?"

"I'm dying of wound-fever; there's no hope, they say."

That reply, so simple, so serenely given, would have touched almost any hearer; but Clay smiled grimly, and lay down as if satisfied, with his one hand clenched, and an exulting glitter in his eyes, muttering, to himself,

"The loss of my leg comes easier after hearing that."

Murry saw his lips move, but caught no sound, and asked with friendly solicitude,

"Do you want any thing, neighbor?"

"Yes — to be let alone," was the curt reply, with a savage frown.

"That's easily done. I sha'n't trouble you very long, any way;" and, with a sigh, Murry turned his face away, and lay silent till the surgeon came up on his morning round.

"Oh, you're here, are you? It's like Mercy Carrol to take you in," said Dr. Fitz Hugh as he surveyed the rebel with a slight frown; for, in spite of his benevolence and skill, he was a stanch loyalist, and hated the South as he did sin.

"Don't praise me; he never would have been here but for Murry," answered Miss Mercy, as she approached with her dressing-tray in her hand.

"Bless the lad! he'll give up his bed next, and feel offended if he's thanked for it. How are you, my good fellow?" and the doctor turned to press the hot hand with a friendly face.

"Much easier and stronger, thank you, doctor," was the cheerful answer.

"Less fever, pulse better, breath freer — good symptoms. Keep on so for twenty-four hours, and by my soul, I believe you'll have a chance for your life, Murry," cried the doctor, as his experienced eye took note of a hopeful change.

"In spite of the opinion of three good surgeons to the contrary?" asked Murry, with a wistful smile.

"Hang every body's opinion! We are but mortal men, and the best of us make mistakes in spite of science and experience. There's Parker; we all gave him up, and the rascal is larking 'round Washington as well as ever to-day. While there's life, there's hope; so cheer up, my lad, and do your best for the little girl at home."

"Do you really think I may hope?" cried Murry, white with the joy of this unexpected reprieve.

"Hope is a capital medicine, and I prescribe it for a day at least. Don't build on this change too much, but if you are as well to-morrow as this morning, I give you my word I think you'll pull through."

Murry laid his hands over his face with a broken "Thank God for that!" and the doctor turned away with a sonorous "Hem!" and an air of intense satisfaction.

During this conversation Miss Mercy had been watching the rebel, who looked and listened to the others so intently that he forgot her presence. She saw an expression of rage and disappointment gather in his face as the doctor spoke; and when Murry accepted the hope held out to him, Clay set his teeth with an evil look, that would have boded ill for his neighbor had he not been helpless.

"Ungrateful traitor! I'll watch him, for he'll do mischief if he can," she thought, and reluctantly began to unbind his arm for the doctor's inspection.

"Only a flesh-wound — no bones broken — a good syringing, rubber cushion, plenty of water, and it will soon heal. You'll attend to that Miss Mercy; this stump is more in my line;" and Dr. Fitz Hugh turned to the leg, leaving the arm to the nurse's skilful care.

"Evidently amputated in a hurry, and neglected since. If you're not careful, young man, you'll change places with your neighbor here."

"Damn him!" muttered Clay in his beard, with an emphasis which caused the doctor to glance at his vengeful face.

"Don't be a brute, if you can help it. But for him, you'd have fared ill," began the doctor.

"But for him, I never should have been here," muttered the man in French, with a furtive glance about the room.

"You owe this to him?" asked the doctor, touching the wound, and speaking in the same tongue.

"Yes; but he paid for it — at least, I thought he had."

"By the Lord! if you are the sneaking rascal that shot him as he lay wounded in the ambulance, I shall be tempted to leave you to your fate!" cried the doctor, with a wrathful flash in his keen eyes.

"Do it, then, for it was I," answered the man defiantly; adding as if anxious to explain, "We had a tussle, and each got hurt in the thick of the skirmish. He was put in the ambulance afterward, and I was left to live or die, as luck would have it. I was hurt the worst; they should have taken me too; it made me mad to see him chosen, and I fired my last shot as he drove away. I didn't know whether I hit him or not; but when they told me I must lose my leg, I hoped I had, and now I am satisfied."

He spoke rapidly, with clenched hand and fiery eyes, and the two listeners watched him with a sort of fascination as he hissed out the last words, glancing at the occupant of the next bed. Murry evidently did not understand French; he lay with averted face, closed eyes, and a hopeful smile still on his lips, quite unconscious of the meaning of the fierce words uttered close beside him. Dr. Fitz Hugh had laid down his instruments and knit his black brows irefully while he listened. But as the man paused, the doctor looked at Miss Mercy, who was quietly going on with her work, though there was an expression about her handsome mouth that made her womanly face look almost grim. Taking up his tools, the doctor followed her example, saying slowly,

"If I didn't believe Murry was mending, I'd turn you over to Roberts, whom the patients dread as they do the devil. I must do my duty, and you may thank Murry for it."

"Does he know you are the man who shot him?" asked Mercy, still in French.

"No; I shouldn't stay here long if he did," answered Clay, with a short laugh.

"Don't tell him, then — at least, till after you are moved," she said, in a tone of command.

"Where am I going?" demanded the man.

"Anywhere out of my ward," was the brief answer, with a look that made the black eyes waver and fall.

In silence nurse and doctor did their work, and passed on. In silence Murry lay hour after hour, and silently did Clay watch and wait, till, utterly exhausted by the suffering he was too proud to confess, he sank into a stupor, oblivious alike of hatred, defeat, and pain. Finding him in this pitiable condition, Mercy relented, and, woman-like, forgot her contempt in pity. He was not moved, but tended carefully all that day and night; and when he woke from a heavy sleep, the morning sun shone again on two pale faces in the beds, and flashed on the buttons of two army-coats hanging side by side on the recess wall, on loyalist and rebel, on the blue and the gray.

Dr. Fitz Hugh stood beside Murry's cot, saying cheerily, "You are doing well, my lad — better than I hoped. Keep calm and cool, and, if all goes right, we'll have little Mary here to pet you in a week."

"Who's Mary?" whispered the rebel to the attendant who was washing his face.

"His sweetheart; he left her for the war, and she's waitin' for him back — poor soul!" answered the man, with a somewhat vicious scrub across the sallow cheek he was wiping.

"So he'll get well, and go home and marry the girl he left behind him, will he?" sneered Clay, fingering a little case that hung about his neck, and was now visible as his rough valet unbuttoned his collar.

"What's that — your sweetheart's picter?" asked Ben, the attendant, eyeing the gold chain anxiously.

"I've got none," was the gruff answer.

"So much the wus for you, then. Small chance of gettin' one here; our girls won't look at you, and you a'n't likely to see any of your own sort for a long spell, I reckon," added Ben, rasping away at the rebel's long-neglected hair.

Clay lay looking at Mercy Carrol as she went to and fro among the men, leaving a smile behind her, and carrying comfort wherever she turned, — a right womanly woman, lovely and lovable, strong yet tender, patient yet decided, skilful, kind, and tireless in the discharge of duties that would have daunted most women. It was in vain she wore the plain gray gown and long apron, for neither could hide the grace of her figure. It was in vain she brushed her luxuriant hair back into a net, for the wavy locks would fall on her forehead, and stray curls would creep out or glisten like gold under the meshes meant to conceal them. Busy days and watchful nights had not faded the beautiful bloom on her cheeks, or dimmed the brightness of her hazel eyes. Always ready, fresh, and fair, Mercy Carrol was regarded as the good angel of the hospital, and not a man in it, sick or well, but was a loyal friend to her. None dared to be a lover, for her little romance was known; and, though still a maid, she was a widow in their eyes, for she had sent her lover to his death, and over the brave man's grave had said, "Well done."

Ben watched Clay as his eye followed the one female figure there, and, observing that he clutched the case still tighter, asked again,

"What is that — a charm?"

"Yes — against pain, captivity, and shame."

"Strikes me it a'n't kep' you from any one of 'em," said Ben, with a laugh.

"I haven't tried it yet."

"How does it work?" Ben asked more respectfully, being impressed by something in the rebel's manner.

"You will see when I use it. Now let me alone," and Clay turned impatiently away.

"You've got p'ison, or some deviltry, in that thing. If you don't let me look, I swear I'll have it took away from you," and Ben put his big hand on the slender chain with a resolute air.

Clay smiled a scornful smile, and offered the trinket, saying coolly,

"I only fooled you. Look as much as you like; you'll find nothing dangerous."

Ben opened the pocket, saw a curl of gray hair, and nothing more.

"Is that your mother's?"

"Yes; my dead mother's."

It was strange to see the instantaneous change that passed over the two men as each uttered that dearest word in all tongues. Rough Ben gently reclosed and returned the case, saying kindly,

"Keep it; I wouldn't rob you on't for no money."

Clay thrust it jealously into his breast, and the first trace of emotion he had shown softened his dark face, as he answered, with a grateful tremor in his voice,

"Thank you. I wouldn't lose it for the world."

"May I say good morning, neighbor?" asked a feeble voice, as Murry turned a very wan but cheerful face toward him, when Ben moved on with his basin and towel.

"If you like," returned Clay, looking at him with those quick, suspicious eyes of his.

"Well, I do like; so I say it, and hope you are better," returned the cordial voice.

"Are you?"

"Yes, thank God!"

"Is it sure?"

"Nothing is sure, in a case like mine, till I'm on my legs again; but I'm certainly better. I don't expect you to be glad, but I hope you don't regret it very much."

"I don't." The smile that accompanied the words surprised Murry as much as the reply, for both seemed honest, and his kind heart warmed toward his suffering enemy.

"I hope you'll be exchanged as soon as you are able. Till then, you can go to one of the other hospitals, where there are many reb — I would say, Southerners. If you'd like, I'll speak to Dr. Fitz Hugh, and he'll see you moved," said Murry, in his friendly way.

"I'd rather stay here, thank you." Clay smiled again as he spoke in the mild tone that surprised Murry as much as it pleased him.

"You like to be in my corner, then?" he said, with a boyish laugh.

"Very much — for a while."

"I'm very glad. Do you suffer much?"

"I shall suffer more by and by, if I go on; but I'll risk it," answered Clay, fixing his feverish eyes on Murry's placid face.

"You expect to have a hard time with your leg?" said Murry, compassionately.

"With my soul."

It was an odd answer, and given with such an odd expression, as Clay turned his face away, that Murry said no more, fancying his brain a little touched by the fever evidently coming on.

They spoke but seldom to each other that day, for Clay lay apparently asleep, with a flushed cheek and restless head, and Murry tranquilly dreamed waking dreams of home and little Mary. That night, after all was still, Miss Mercy went up into the organ-loft to get fresh rollers for the morrow — the boxes of old linen, and such matters, being kept there. As she stood looking down on the thirty pale sleepers, she remembered that she had not played a hymn on the little organ for Murry, as she had promised that day. Stealing softly to the front, she peeped over the gallery, to see if he was asleep; if not, she would keep her word, for he was her favorite.

A screen had been drawn before the recess where the two beds stood, shutting their occupants from the sight of the other men. Murry lay sleeping, but Clay was awake, and a quick thrill tingled along the young woman's nerves as she saw his face. Leaning on one arm, he peered about the place with an eager, watchful air, and glanced up at the dark gallery, but did not see the startled face behind the central pillar. Pausing an instant, he shook his one clenched hand at the unconscious sleeper, and then drew out the locket cautiously. Two white mugs just alike stood on the little table between the beds, water in each. With another furtive glance about him, Clay suddenly stretched out his long arm, and dropped something from the locket into

Murry's cup. An instant he remained motionless, with a sinister smile on his face; then, as Ben's step sounded beyond the screen, he threw his arm over his face, and lay, breathing heavily, as if asleep.

Mercy's first impulse was to cry out; her next, to fly down and seize the cup. No time was to be lost, for Murry might wake, and drink at any moment. What was in the cup? Poison, doubtless; that was the charm Clay carried to free himself from "pain, captivity, and shame," when all other hopes of escape vanished. This hidden helper he gave up to destroy his enemy, who was to outlive his shot, it seemed. Like a shadow, Mercy glided down, forming her plan as she went. A dozen mugs stood about the room, all alike in size and color; catching up one, she partly filled it, and, concealing it under the clean sheet hanging on her arm, went toward the recess, saying audibly,

"I want some fresh water, Ben."

Thus warned of her approach, Clay lay with carefully-averted face as she came in, and never stirred as she bent over him, while she dexterously changed Murry's mug for the one she carried. Hiding the poisoned cup, she went away, saying aloud,

"Never mind the water, now, Ben. Murry is asleep, and so is Clay; they'll not need it yet."

Straight to Dr. Fitz Hugh's room she went, and gave the cup into his keeping, with the story of what she had seen. A man was dying, and there was no time to test the water then; but putting it carefully away, he promised to set her fears at rest in the morning. To quiet her impatience, Mercy went back to watch over Murry till day dawned. As she sat down, she caught the glimmer of a satisfied smile on Clay's lips, and looking into the cup she had left, she saw that it was empty.

"He is satisfied, for he thinks his horrible revenge is secure. Sleep in peace, my poor boy! you are safe while I am here."

As she thought this, she put her hand on the broad, pale forehead of the sleeper with a motherly caress, but started to feel how damp and cold it was. Looking nearer, she saw that a change had passed over Murry, for dark shadows showed about his sunken eyes, his once quiet breath was faint and fitful now, his hand deathly cold, and a chilly dampness had gathered on his face. She looked at her watch; it was past twelve, and her heart sunk within her, for she had so often seen that solemn change come over men's faces then, that the hour was doubly weird and woeful to her. Sending a message to Dr. Fitz Hugh, she waited anxiously, trying to believe that she deceived herself.

The doctor came at once, and a single look convinced him that he had left one death-bed for another.

"As I feared," he said; "that sudden rally was but a last effort of nature. There was just one chance for him, and he has missed it. Poor lad! I can do nothing; he'll sink rapidly, and go without pain."

"Can I do nothing?" asked Mercy, with dim eyes, as she held the cold hand close in both her own with tender pressure.

"Give him stimulants as long as he can swallow, and, if he's conscious, take any messages he may have. Poor Hall is dying hard, and I can help him; I'll come again in an hour and say good-by."

The kind doctor choked, touched the pale sleeper with a gentle caress, and went away to help Hall die.

Murry slept on for an hour, then woke, and knew without words that his brief hope was gone. He looked up wistfully, and whispered, as Mercy tried to smile with trembling lips that refused to tell the heavy truth.

"I know, I feel it; don't grieve yourself by trying to tell me, dear friend. It's best so; I can bear it, but I did want to live."

"Have you any word for Mary, dear?" asked Mercy, for he seemed but a boy to her since she had nursed him.

One look of sharp anguish and dark despair passed over his face, as he wrung his thin hands and shut his eyes, finding death terrible. It passed in a moment, and his pallid countenance grew beautiful with the pathetic patience of one who submits without complaint to the inevitable.

"Tell her I was ready, and the only bitterness was leaving her. I shall remember, and wait until she comes. My little Mary! oh, be kind to her, for my sake, when you tell her this."

"I will, Murry, as God hears me. I will be a sister to her while I live."

As Mercy spoke with fervent voice, he laid the hand that had ministered to him so faithfully against his cheek, and lay silent, as if content.

"What else? let me do something more. Is there no other friend to be comforted?"

"No; she is all I have in the world. I hoped to make her so happy, to be so much to her, for she's a lonely little thing; but God says 'No,' and I submit."

A long pause, as he lay breathing heavily, with eyes that were dimming fast fixed on the gentle face beside him.

"Give Ben my clothes; send Mary a bit of my hair, and — may I give you this? It's a poor thing, but all I have to leave you, best and kindest of women.

He tried to draw off a slender ring, but the strength had gone out of his wasted fingers, and she helped him, thanking him with the first tears he had seen her shed. He seemed satisfied, but suddenly turned his eyes on Clay, who lay as if asleep. A sigh broke from Murry, and Mercy caught the words,

"How could he do it, and I so helpless!"

"Do you know him?" she whispered, eagerly, as she remembered Clay's own words.

"I knew he was the man who shot me, when he came. I forgive him; but I wish he had spared me, for Mary's sake," he answered sorrowfully, not angrily.

"Can you really pardon him?" cried Mercy, wondering, yet touched by the words.

"I can. He will be sorry one day, perhaps; at any rate, he did what he thought his duty; and war makes brutes of us all sometimes, I fear. I'd like to say good-by; but he's asleep after a weary day, so don't wake him. Tell him I'm glad he is to live, and that I forgive him heartily."

Although uttered between long pauses, these words seemed to have exhausted Murry, and he spoke no more till Dr. Fitz Hugh came. To him he feebly returned thanks, and whispered his farewell — then sank into a stupor, during which life ebbed fast. Both nurse and doctor forgot Clay as they hung over Murry, and neither saw the strange intentness of his face, the half awe-struck, half remorseful look he bent upon the dying man.

As the sun rose, sending its ruddy beams across the silent ward, Murry looked up and smiled, for the bright ray fell athwart the two coats hanging on the wall beside him. Some passerby had brushed one sleeve of the blue coat across the gray, as if the inanimate things were shaking hands.

"It should be so — love our enemies; we should be brothers," he murmured faintly; and, with the last impulse of a noble nature, stretched his hand toward the man who had murdered him.

But Clay shrunk back, and covered his face without a word. When he ventured to look up, Murry was no longer there. A pale, peaceful figure lay on the narrow bed, and Mercy was smoothing the brown locks as she cut a curl for Mary and herself. Clay could not take his eyes away; as if fascinated by its serenity, he watched the dead face with gloomy eyes, till Mercy, having done her part, stooped and kissed the cold lips tenderly as she left him to his sleep. Then, as if afraid to be alone with the dead, he bid Ben put the screen between the beds, and bring him a book. His order was obeyed, but he never turned his pages, and lay with muffled head trying to shut out little Watts' sobs, as the wounded drummer-boy mourned for Murry.

Death, in a hospital, makes no stir, and in an hour no trace of the departed remained but the coat upon the wall, for Ben would not take it down, though it was his now. The empty bed stood freshly made, the clean cup and worn Bible lay ready for other hands, and the card at the bed's head hung blank for a new-comer's name. In the hurry of this event, Clay's attempted crime was forgotten for a time. But that evening Dr. Fitz Hugh told Mercy that her suspicions were correct, for the water was poisoned.

"How horrible! What shall we do?" she cried, with a gesture full of energetic indignation.

"Leave him to remorse," replied the doctor, sternly. "I've thought over the matter, and believe this to be the only thing we can do. I fancy the man won't live a week; his leg is in a bad way, and he is such a fiery devil, he gives himself no chance. Let him believe he killed poor Murry, at least for a few days. He thinks so now, and tries to rejoice; but if he has a human heart, he will repent."

"But he may not. Should we not tell of this? Can he not be punished?"

"Law won't hang a dying man, and I'll not denounce him. Let remorse punish him while he lives, and God judge him when he dies. Murry pardoned him; can we do less?"

Mercy's indignant face softened at the name, and for Murry's sake she yielded. Neither spoke of what they tried to think the act of a half-delirious man; and soon they could not refuse to pity him, for the doctor's prophecy proved true.

Clay was a haunted man, and remorse gnawed like a worm at his heart. Day and night he saw that tranquil face on the pillow opposite; day and night he saw the pale hand outstretched to him; day and night he heard the faint voice murmuring kindly, regretfully, "I forgive him; but I wish he had spared me, for Mary's sake."

As the days passed, and his strength visibly declined, he began to suspect that he must soon follow Murry. No one told him; for, though both doctor and nurse did their duty faithfully, neither lingered long at his bedside, and not one of the men showed any interest in him. No new patient occupied the other bed, and he lay alone in the recess with his own gloomy thoughts.

"It will be all up with me in a few days, won't it?" he asked abruptly, as Ben made his toilet one morning with unusual care, and such visible pity in his rough face that Clay could not but observe it.

"I heard the doctor say you wouldn't suffer much more. Is there any one you'd like to see, or leave a message for?" answered Ben, smoothing the long locks as gently as a woman.

"There isn't a soul in the world that cares whether I live or die, except the man who wants my money," said Clay, bitterly, as his dark face grew a shade paler at this confirmation of his fear.

"Can't you head him off some way, and leave your money to some one that's been kind to you? Here's the doctor — or, better still, Miss Carrol. Neither on 'em is rich, and both on 'em has been good friends to you, or you'd 'a' fared a deal wus than you have," said Ben, not without the hope that, in saying a good word for them, he might say one for himself also.

Clay lay thinking for a moment as his face clouded over, and then brightened again.

"Miss Mercy wouldn't take it, nor the doctor either; but I know who will, and by G—d, I'll do it!" he exclaimed, with sudden energy.

His eye happened to rest on Ben as he spoke, and, feeling sure that he was to be the heir, Ben retired to send Miss Mercy, that the matter might be settled before Clay's mood changed. Miss Carrol came, and began to cut the buttons off Murry's coat while she waited for Clay to speak.

"What's that for?" he asked, restlessly.

"The men want them, and Ben is willing, for the coat is very old and ragged, you see. Murry gave his good one away to a sicker comrade, and took this instead. It was like him — my poor boy!"

"I'd like to speak to you, if you have a minute to spare," began Clay, after a pause, during which he watched her with a wistful. almost tender expression unseen by her.

"I have time; what can I do for you?" Very gentle was Mercy's voice, very pitiful her glance, as she sat down by him, for the change in his manner, and the thought of his approaching death, touched her heart.

Trying to resume his former gruffness, and cold facial expression, Clay said, as he picked nervously at the blanket,

"I've a little property that I put into the care of a friend going North. He's kept it safe; and now, as I'll never want it myself, I'd like to leave it to — " He paused an instant, glanced quickly at Mercy's face, and seeing only womanly compassion there, added with an irrepressible tremble in his voice — "to little Mary."

If he had expected any reward for the act, any comfort for his lonely death-bed, he received both in fullest measure when he saw Mercy's beautiful face flush with surprise and pleasure, her eyes fill with sudden tears, and heard her cordial voice, as she pressed his hand warmly in her own.

"I wish I could tell you how glad I am for this! I thought you were better than you seemed; I was sure you had both heart and conscience, and that you would repent before you died."

"Repent of what?" he asked, with a startled look.

"Need I tell you?" and her eye went from the empty bed to his face.

"You mean that shot? But it was only fair, after all; we killed each other, and war is nothing but wholesale murder, any way." He spoke easily, but his eyes were full of trouble, and other words seemed to tremble on his lips.

Leaning nearer, Mercy whispered in his ear,

"I mean the other murder, which you would have committed when you poisoned the cup of water he offered you, his enemy."

Every vestige of color faded out of Clay's thin face, and his haggard eyes seemed fascinated by some spectre opposite, as he muttered slowly,

"How do you know?"

"I saw you;" and she told him all the truth.

A look of intense relief passed over Clay's countenance, and the remorseful shadow lifted as he murmured brokenly,

"Thank God, I didn't kill him! Now, dying isn't so hard; now I can have a little peace."

Neither spoke for several minutes; Mercy had no words for such a time, and Clay forgot her presence as the tears dropped from between the wasted fingers spread before his face.

Presently he looked up, saying eagerly, as if his fluttering breath and rapidly failing strength warned him of approaching death,

"Will you write down a few words for me, so Mary can have the money? She needn't know any thing about me, only that I was one to whom Murry was kind, and so I gave her all I had."

"I'll get my pen and paper; rest, now, my poor fellow," said Mercy, wiping the unheeded tears away for him.

"How good it seems to hear you speak so to me! How can you do it?" he whispered, with such grateful wonder in his dim eyes that Mercy's heart smote her for the past.

"I do it for Murry's sake, and because I sincerely pity you."

Timidly turning his lips to that kind hand, he kissed it, and then hid his face in his pillow. When Mercy returned, she observed that there were but seven tarnished buttons where she had left eight. She guessed who had taken it, but said nothing, and endeavored to render poor Clay's last hours as happy as sympathy and care could make them. The letter and will were prepared as well as they could be, and none too soon; for, as if that secret was the burden that bound Clay's spirit to the shattered body, no sooner was it lifted off, than the diviner part seemed ready to be gone.

"You'll stay with me; you'll help me die; and — oh, if I dared to ask it, I'd beg you to kiss me once when I am dead, as you did Murry. I think I could rest then, and be fitter to meet him, if the Lord lets me," he cried imploringly, as the last night gathered around him. and the coming change seemed awful to a soul that possessed no inward peace, and no firm hope to lean on through the valley of the shadow.

"I will — I will! Hold fast to me, and believe in the eternal mercy of God," whispered Miss Carrol, with her firm hand in his, her tender face bending over him as the long struggle began.

"Mercy," he murmured, catching that word, and smiling feebly as he repeated it lingeringly. "Mercy! yes, I believe in her; she'll save me, if any one can. Lord, bless and keep her forever and forever."

There was no morning sunshine to gladden his dim eyes as they looked their last, but the pale glimmer of the lamp shone full on the blue and the gray coats hanging side by side. As if the sight recalled that other death-bed, that last act of brotherly love and pardon, Clay rose up in his bed, and, while one hand clutched the button hidden in his breast, the other was outstretched toward the empty bed, as his last breath parted in a cry of remorseful longing,

"I will! I will! Forgive me, Murry, and let me say good-by!"

My Red Cap

I.

IT WAS UNDER A BLUE cap that I first saw the honest face of Joe Collins. In the third year of the late war a Maine regiment was passing through Boston, on its way to Washington. The Common was all alive with troops and the spectators who clustered round them to say God-speed, as the brave fellows marched away to meet danger and death for our sakes.

Every one was eager to do something; and, as the men stood at ease, the people mingled freely with them, offering gifts, hearty grips of the hand, and hopeful prophecies of victory in the end. Irresistibly attracted, my boy Tom and I drew near, and soon, becoming excited by the scene, ravaged the fruit-stands in our neighborhood for tokens of our regard, mingling candy and congratulations, peanuts and prayers, apples and applause, in one enthusiastic jumble.

While Tom was off on his third raid, my attention was attracted by a man who stood a little apart, looking as if his thoughts were far away. All the men were fine, stalwart fellows, as Maine men usually are; but this one overtopped his comrades, standing straight and tall as a Norway pine, with a face full of the mingled shrewdness, sobriety, and self-possession of the typical New Englander. I liked the look of him; and, seeing that he seemed solitary, even in a crowd, I offered him my last apple with a word of interest. The keen blue eyes met mine gratefully, and the apple began to vanish in vigorous bites as we talked; for no one thought of ceremony at such a time.

"Where are you from?"

First published in *The Sword and Pen*, Boston, Massachusetts (7-10 December 1881).

"Woolidge, ma'am."

"Are you glad to go?"

"Wal, there's two sides to that question. I calk'late to do my duty, and do it hearty: but it is rough on a feller leavin' his folks, for good, maybe."

There was a sudden huskiness in the man's voice that was not apple-skins, though he tried to make believe that it was. I knew a word about home would comfort him, so I went on with my questions.

"It is very hard. Do you leave a family?"

"My old mother, a sick brother, — and Lucindy."

The last word was uttered in a tone of intense regret, and his brown cheek reddened as he added hastily, to hide some embarrassment. —

"You see, Jim went last year, and got pretty well used up; so I felt as if I'd ought to take my turn now. Mother was a regular old hero about it and I dropped everything, and come off. Lucindy didn't think it was my duty; and that made it awful hard, I tell you."

"Wives are less patriotic than mothers," I began; but he would not hear Lucindy blamed, and said quickly, —

"She ain't my wife yet, but we calk'lated to be married in a month or so; and it was wus for her than for me, women lot so on not being disappointed. I couldn't shirk, and here I be. When I git to work, I shall be all right: the first wrench is the tryin' part."

Here he straightened his broad shoulders, and turned his face toward the flags fluttering far in front, as if no backward look should betray the longing of his heart for mother, home, and wife. I liked that little glimpse of character; and when Tom returned with empty hands, reporting that every stall was exhausted, I told him to find out what the man would like best, then run across the street and get it.

"I know without asking. Give us your purse, and I'll make him as happy as a king," said the boy, laughing, as he looked up admiringly at our tall friend, who looked down on him with an elder-brotherly air pleasant to see. While Tom was gone, I found out Joe's name and business, promised to write and tell his mother how finely the regiment went off, and was just expressing a hope that we might meet again, for I too was going to the war as nurse, when the order to "Fall in!" came rolling down the ranks, and the talk was over. Fearing Tom would miss our man in the confusion, I kept my eye on him till the boy came rushing up with a packet of tobacco in one hand and a good supply of cigars in the other. Not a romantic offering, certainly, but a very acceptable one, as Joe's face proved, as we scrambled these treasures into his pockets, all laughing at the flurry, while less fortunate comrades helped us, with an eye to a share of these fragrant luxuries by and by. There was just time for this, a hearty shake of the big hand, and a grateful "Good-by, ma'am;" then the word was given, and they were off. Bent on seeing the last of them, Tom and I took a short cut, and came out on the wide street down which so many troops marched that year; and, mounting some high steps, we watched for our man, as we already called him.

As the inspiring music, the grand tramp, drew near, the old thrill went through the crowd, the old cheer broke out. But it was a different scene now than in the first enthusiastic, hopeful days. Young men and ardent boys filled the ranks then, brave by instinct, burning with loyal zeal, and blissfully unconscious of all that lay before them. Now the blue coats were worn by mature men, some gray, all grave and resolute: husbands and fathers, with the memory of wives and children tugging at their heart-strings; homes left desolate behind them, and before them the grim certainty of danger, hardship, and perhaps the lifelong helplessness worse than death. Little of the glamour of romance about the war now: they saw it as it was, a long, hard task; and here were the men to do it well. Even the lookers-on were different now. Once all was wild enthusiasm and glad uproar; now men's lips were set, and women's smileless as they cheered; fewer handkerchiefs whitened the air, for wet eyes needed them; and sudden lulls, almost solemn in their stillness, followed the acclamations of the crowd. All watched with quickened breath and brave souls that living wave, blue below, and bright with a steely glitter above, as it flowed down the street and away to distant battle-fields already stained with precious blood.

"There he is! The outside man, and tallest of the lot. Give him a cheer, auntie: he sees us, and remembers!" cried Tom, nearly tumbling off his perch, as he waved his hat, and pointed out Joe Collins.

Yes, there he was, looking up, with a smile on his brave brown face, my little nosegay in his button-hole, a suspicious bulge in the pocket close by, and doubtless a comfortable quid in his mouth, to cheer the weary march. How like an old friend he looked, though we had only met fifteen minutes ago; how glad we were to be there to smile back at him, and send him on his way feeling that, even in a strange city, there was some one to say, "God bless you, Joe!" We watched the tallest blue cap till it vanished, and then went home in a glow of patriotism, — Tom to long for his turn to come, I to sew vigorously on the gray gown the new nurse burned to wear as soon as possible, and both of us to think and speak often of poor Joe Collins and his Lucindy. All this happened long ago; but it is well to recall those stirring times, — to keep fresh the memory of sacrifices made for us by men like these; to see to it that the debt we owe them is honestly, gladly paid; and, while we decorate the graves of those who died, to remember also those who still live to deserve our grateful care.

II.

I never expected to see Joe again; but, six months later, we did meet in a Washington hospital one winter's night. A train of ambulances had left their sad freight at our door, and we were hurrying to get the poor fellows into much needed beds, after a week of hunger, cold, and unavoidable neglect. All forms of pain were in my ward that night, and all borne with the pathetic patience which was a daily marvel to those who saw it.

Trying to bring order out of chaos, I was rushing up and down the narrow aisle between the rows of rapidly filling beds, and, after brushing several times against a pair of the largest and muddiest boots I ever saw, I paused at last to inquire why they were impeding the passageway. I found they belonged to a very tall man who seemed to be already asleep or dead, so white and still and utterly worn out he looked as he lay there, without a coat, a great patch on his forehead, and the right arm rudely bundled up. Stooping to cover him, I saw that he was unconscious, and, whipping out my brandy-bottle and salts, soon brought him round, for it was only exhaustion.

"Can you eat?" I asked, as he said, "Thanky, ma'am," after a long draught of water and a dizzy stare.

"Eat! I'm starvin'!" he answered, with such a ravenous glance at a fat nurse who happened to be passing, that I trembled for her, and hastened to take a bowl of soup from her tray.

As I fed him, his gaunt, weather-beaten face had a familiar look; but so many such faces had passed before me that winter, I did not recall this one till the ward-master came to put up the cards with the new-comers' names above their beds. My man seemed absorbed in his food; but I naturally glanced at the card, and there was the name "Joseph Collins" to give me an additional interest in my new patient.

"Why, Joe! is it really you?" I exclaimed, pouring the last spoonful of soup down his throat so hastily that I choked him.

"All that's left of me. Wal, ain't this luck, now?" gasped Joe, as gratefully as if that hospital-cot was a bed of roses.

"What is the matter? A wound in the head and arm?" I asked, feeling sure that no slight affliction had brought Joe there.

"Right arm gone. Shot off as slick as a whistle. I tell you, it's a sing'lar kind of a feelin' to see a piece of your own body go flyin' away, with no prospect of ever coming back again," said Joe, trying to make light of one of the greatest misfortunes a man can suffer.

"That is bad, but it might have been worse. Keep up your spirits, Joe; and we will soon have you fitted out with a new arm almost as good as new."

"I guess it won't do much lumberin', so that trade is done for. I s'pose there's things left-handed fellers can do, and I must learn 'em as soon as possible, since my fightin' days are over," and Joe looked at his one arm with a sigh that was almost a groan, helplessness is such a trial to a manly man, — and he was eminently so.

"What can I do to comfort you most, Joe? I'll send my good Ben to help you to bed, and will be here myself when the surgeon goes his rounds. Is there anything else that would make you more easy?"

"If you could just drop a line to mother to let her know I'm alive, it would be a sight of comfort to both of us. I guess I'm in for a long spell of hospital, and I'd lay easier if I knew mother and Lucindy warn't frettin' about me."

He must have been suffering terribly, but he thought of the women who loved him before himself, and, busy as I was, I snatched a moment to send a few words of hope to the old mother. Then I left him "layin' easy," though the prospect of some months of wearing pain would have daunted most men. If I had needed anything to increase my regard for Joe, it would have been the courage with which he bore a very bad quarter of an hour with the surgeons; for his arm was in a dangerous state, the wound in the head feverish for want of care; and a heavy cold on the lungs suggested pneumonia as an added trial to his list of ills.

"He will have a hard time of it, but I think he will pull through, as he is a temperate fellow, with a splendid constitution," was the doctor's verdict, as he left us for the next man, who was past help, with a bullet through his lungs.

"I don'no as I hanker to live, and be a burden. If Jim was able to do for mother, I feel as if I wouldn't mind steppin' out now I'm so fur along. As he ain't, I s'pose I must brace up, and do the best I can," said Joe, as I wiped the drops from his forehead, and tried to look as if his prospect was a bright one.

"You will have Lucindy to help you, you know; and that will make things easier for all."

"Think so? 'Pears to me I couldn't ask her to take care of three invalids for my sake. She ain't no folks of her own, nor much means, and ought to marry a man who can make things easy for her. Guess I'll have to wait a spell longer before I say anything to Lucindy about marryin' now;" and a look of resolute resignation settled on Joe's haggard face as he gave up his dearest hope.

"I think Lucindy will have something to say, if she is like most women, and you will find the burdens much lighter, for sharing them between you. Don't worry about that, but get well, and go home as soon as you can."

"All right, ma'am;" and Joe proved himself a good soldier by obeying orders, and falling asleep like a tired child, as the first step toward recovery.

For two months I saw Joe daily, and learned to like him very much, he was so honest, genuine, and kind-hearted. So did his mates, for he made friends with them all by sharing such small luxuries as came to him, for he was a favorite; and, better still, he made sunshine in that sad place by the brave patience with which he bore his own troubles, the cheerful consolation he always gave to others. A droll fellow was Joe at times, for under his sobriety lay much humor; and I soon discovered that a visit from him was more efficacious than other cordials in cases of despondency and discontent. Roars of laughter sometimes greeted me as I went into his ward, and Joe's jokes were passed round as eagerly as the water-pitcher.

Yet he had much to try him, not only in the ills that vexed his flesh, but the cares that tried his spirit, and the future that lay before him, full of anxieties and responsibilities which seemed so heavy now when the strong right arm, that had cleared all obstacles away before, was gone. The letters I wrote for him, and those he received, told the little story very plainly; for he read them to me, and found much comfort in talking over his affairs, as most men do when illness makes them dependent on a woman. Jim was evidently sick and selfish. Lucindy, to judge from the photograph cherished so tenderly under Joe's pillow, was a pretty, weak sort of a girl, with little character or courage to help poor Joe with his burdens. The old mother was very like her son, and stood by him "like a hero," as he said, but was evidently failing, and begged him to come home as soon as he was able, that she might see him comfortably settled before she must leave him. Her courage sustained his, and the longing to see her hastened his departure as soon as it was safe to let him go; for Lucindy's letters were always of a dismal sort, and made him anxious to put his shoulder to the wheel.

"She always set consider'ble by me, mother did, bein' the oldest; and I wouldn't miss makin' her last days happy, not if it cost me all the arms and legs I've got," said Joe, as he awkwardly struggled into the big boots an hour after leave to go home was given him.

It was pleasant to see his comrades gather round him with such hearty adieus that his one hand must have tingled; to hear the good wishes and the thanks called after him by pale creatures in their beds; and to find tears in many eyes beside my own when he was gone, and nothing was left of him but the empty cot, the old gray wrapper, and the name upon the wall.

I kept that card among my other relics, and hoped to meet Joe again somewhere in the world. He sent me one or two letters, then I went home; the war ended soon after, time passed, and the little story of my Maine lumberman was laid away with many other experiences which made that part of my life a very memorable one.

III.

Some years later, as I looked out of my window one dull November day, the only cheerful thing I saw was the red cap of a messenger who was examining the slate that hung on a wall opposite my hotel. A tall man with gray hair and beard, one arm, and a blue army-coat. I always salute, figuratively at least, when I see that familiar blue, especially if one sleeve of the coat is empty; so I watched the messenger with interest as he trudged away on some new errand, wishing he had a better day and a thicker pair of boots. He was an unusually large, well-made man, and reminded me of a fine building going to ruin before its time; for the broad shoulders were bent, there was a stiffness about the long legs suggestive of wounds or rheumatism, and the curly hair looked as if snow had fallen on it too soon. Sitting at work in my window, I fell into the way of watching my Red Cap, as I called him, with more interest than I did the fat doves on the roof opposite, or the pert sparrows hopping in the mud below. I liked the steady way in which he plodded on through fair weather or foul, as if intent on doing well the one small service he had found to do. I liked his cheerful whistle as he stood waiting for a job under the porch of the public building where his slate hung, watching the luxurious carriages roll by, and the well-to-do gentlemen who daily passed him to their comfortable homes, with a steady, patient sort of face, as if wondering at the inequalities of fortune, yet neither melancholy nor morose over the small share of prosperity which had fallen to his lot.

I often planned to give him a job, that I might see him nearer; but I had few errands, and little Bob, the hall-boy, depended on doing those: so the winter was nearly over before I found out that my Red Cap was an old friend.

A parcel came for me one day, and bidding the man wait for an answer, I sat down to write it, while the messenger stood just inside the door like a sentinel on duty. When I looked up to give my note and directions, I found the man staring at me with a beaming yet bashful face, as he nodded, saying heartily, —

"I mistrusted it was you, ma'am, soon's I see the name on the bundle, and I guess I ain't wrong. It's a number of years sence we met, and you don't remember Joe Collins as well as he does you, I reckon?"

"Why, how you have changed! I've been seeing you every day all winter, and never knew you," I said, shaking hands with my old patient, and very glad to see him.

"Nigh on to twenty years makes consid'able of a change in folks, 'specially if they have a pretty hard row to hoe."

"Sit down and warm yourself while you tell me all about it; there is no hurry for this answer, and I'll pay for your time."

Joe laughed as if that was a good joke, and sat down as if the fire was quite as welcome as the friend.

"How are they all at home?" I asked, as he sat turning his cap round, not quite knowing where to begin.

"I haven't got any home nor any folks neither;" and the melancholy words banished the brightness from his rough face like a cloud. "Mother died soon after I got back. Suddin', but she was ready, and I was there, so she was happy. Jim lived a number of years, and was a sight of care, poor feller; but we managed to rub along, though we had to sell the farm: for I couldn't do much with one arm, and doctor's bills right along stiddy take a heap of money. He was as comfortable as he could be; and, when he was gone, it wasn't no great matter, for there was only me, and I don't mind roughin' it."

"But Lucindy, where was she?" I asked very naturally.

"Oh! she married another man long ago. Couldn't expect her to take me and my misfortins. She's doin' well, I hear, and that's a comfort anyway."

There was a look on Joe's face, a tone in Joe's voice as he spoke, that plainly showed how much he had needed comfort when left to bear his misfortunes all alone. But he made no complaint, uttered no reproach, and loyally excused Lucindy's desertion with a simple sort of dignity that made it impossible to express pity or condemnation.

"How came you here, Joe?" I asked, making a sudden leap from past to present.

"I had to scratch for a livin', and can't do much: so, after tryin' a number of things, I found this. My old wounds pester me a good deal, and rheumatism is bad winters; but, while my legs hold out, I can git on. A man can't set down and starve; so I keep waggin' as long as I can. When I can't do no more, I s'pose there's almshouse and hospital ready for me."

"That is a dismal prospect, Joe. There ought to be a comfortable place for such as you to spend your last days in. I am sure you have earned it."

"Wal, it does seem ruther hard on us when we've give all we had, and give it free and hearty, to be left to knock about in our old age. But there's so many poor folks to be took care of, we don't get much of a chance, for we ain't the beggin' sort," said Joe, with a wistful look at the wintry world outside, as if it would be better to lie quiet under the snow, than to drag out his last painful years, friendless and forgotten, in some refuge of the poor.

"Some kind people have been talking of a home for soldiers, and I hope the plan will be carried out. It will take time; but, if it comes to pass, you shall be one of the first men to enter that home, Joe, if I can get you there."

"That sounds mighty cheerin' and comfortable, thanky, ma'am. Idleness is dreadful tryin' to me, and I'd rather wear out than rust out; so I guess I can weather it a spell longer. But it will be pleasant to look forrard to a snug harbor bymeby. I feel a sight better just hearin' tell about it." He certainly looked so, faint as the hope was; for the melancholy eyes brightened as if they already saw a happier refuge in the future than almshouse, hospital, or grave, and, when he trudged away upon my errand, he went as briskly as if every step took him nearer to the promised home.

After that day it was all up with Bob, for I told my neighbors Joe's story, and we kept him trotting busily, adding little gifts, and taking the sort of interest in him that comforted the lonely fellow, and made him feel that he had not outlived his usefulness. I never looked out when he was at his post that he did not smile back at me; I never passed him in the street that the red cap was not touched with a military flourish; and, when any of us beckoned to him, no twinge of rheumatism was too sharp to keep him from hurrying to do our errands, as if he had Mercury's winged feet.

Now and then he came in for a chat, and always asked how the Soldiers' Home was prospering; expressing his opinion that "Boston was the charitablest city under the sun, and he was sure he and his mates would be took care of somehow."

When we parted in the spring, I told him things looked hopeful, bade him be ready for a good long rest as soon as the hospitable doors were open, and left him nodding cheerfully.

IV.

But in the autumn I looked in vain for Joe. The slate was in its old place, and a messenger came and went on his beat; but a strange face was under the red cap, and this man had two arms and one eye. I asked for Collins, but the new-comer had only a vague idea that he was dead; and the same answer was given me at headquarters, though none of the busy people seemed to know when or where he died. So I mourned for Joe, and felt that it was very hard he could not have lived to enjoy the promised refuge; for, relying upon the charity that never fails, the Home was an actual fact now, just beginning its beneficent career. People were waking up to this duty, money was coming in, meetings were being held, and already a few poor fellows were in the refuge, feeling themselves no longer paupers, but invalid soldiers honorably supported by the State they had served. Talking it over one day with a friend, who spent her life working for the Associated Charities, she said, —

"By the way, there is a man boarding with one of my poor women, who ought to be got into the Home, if he will go. I don't know much about him, except that he was in the army, has been very ill with rheumatic fever, and is friendless. I asked Mrs. Flanagin how she managed to keep him, and she said she had help while he was sick, and now he is able to hobble about, he takes care of the children, so she is able to go out to work. He won't go to his own town, because there is nothing for him there but the almshouse, and he dreads a hospital; so struggles along, trying to earn his bread tending babies with his one arm. A sad case, and in your line; I wish you'd look into it."

"That sounds like my Joe, one arm and all. I'll go and see him; I've a weakness for soldiers, sick or well."

I went, and never shall forget the pathetic little tableau I saw as I opened Mrs. Flanagin's dingy door; for she was out, and no one heard my tap. The room was redolent of suds, and in a grove of damp clothes hung on lines sat a man with a crying baby laid across his lap, while he fed three small children standing at his knee with bread and molasses. How he managed with one arm to keep the baby from squirming on to the floor, the plate from upsetting, and to feed the hungry urchins who stood in a row with open mouths, like young birds, was past my comprehension. But he did, trotting baby gently, dealing out sweet morsels patiently, and whistling to himself, as if to beguile his labors cheerfully.

The broad back, the long legs, the faded coat, the low whistle were all familiar; and, dodging a wet sheet, I faced the man to find it was indeed my Joe! A mere shadow of his former self, after months of suffering that had crippled him for life, but brave and patient still; trying to help himself, and not ask aid though brought so low.

For an instant I could not speak to him, and, encumbered with baby, dish, spoon, and children, he could only stare at me with a sudden brightening of the altered face that made it full of welcome before a word was uttered.

"They told me you were dead, and I only heard of you by accident, not knowing I should find my old friend alive, but not well, I'm afraid?"

"There ain't much left of me but bones and pain, ma'am. I'm powerful glad to see you all the same. Dust off a chair, Patsey, and let the lady set down. You go in the corner, and take turns lickin' the dish, while I see company," said Joe, disbanding his small troop, and shouldering the baby as if presenting arms in honor of his guest.

"Why didn't you let me know how sick you were? And how came they to think you dead?" I asked, as he festooned the wet linen out of the way, and prepared to enjoy himself as best he could.

"I did send once, when things was at the wust; but you hadn't got back, and then somehow I thought I was goin' to be mustered out for good, and so wouldn't trouble nobody. But my orders ain't come yet, and I am doing the fust thing that come along. It ain't much, but the good soul stood by me, and I ain't ashamed to pay my debts this way, sence I can't do it in no other;" and Joe cradled the chubby baby in his one arm as tenderly as if it had been his own, though little Biddy was not an inviting infant.

"That is very beautiful and right, Joe, and I honor you for it; but you were not meant to tend babies, so sing your last lullabies, and be ready to go to the Home as soon as I can get you there."

"Really, ma'am? I used to lay and kind of dream about it when I couldn't stir without yellin' out; but I never thought it would ever come to happen. I see a piece in the paper describing it, and it sounded dreadful nice. Shouldn't wonder if I found some of my mates there. They were a good lot, and deservin' of all that could be done for 'em," said Joe, trotting the baby briskly, as if the prospect excited him, as well it might, for the change from that damp nursery to the comfortable quarters prepared for him would be like going from Purgatory to Paradise.

"I don't wonder you don't get well living in such a place, Joe. You should have gone home to Woolwich, and let your friends help you," I said, feeling provoked with him for hiding himself.

"No, ma'am!" he answered, with a look I never shall forget, it was so full of mingled patience, pride, and pain. "I haven't a relation in the world but a couple of poor old aunts, and they couldn't do anything for me. As for asking help of folks I used to know, I couldn't do it; and if you think I'd go to Lucindy, though she is wal off, you don't know Joe Collins. I'd die fust! If she was poor and I rich, I'd do for her like a brother; but I couldn't ask no favors of her, not if I begged my vittles in the street, or starved. I forgive, but I don't forgit in a hurry; and the woman that stood by me when I was down is the woman I believe in, and can take my bread from without shame. Hooray for Biddy Flanagin! God bless her!" and, as if to find a vent for the emotion that filled his eyes with grateful tears, Joe led off the cheer, which the children shrilly echoed, and I joined heartily.

"I shall come for you in a few days; so cuddle the baby and make much of the children before you part. It won't take you long to pack up, will it?" I asked, as we subsided with a general laugh.

"I reckon not as I don't own any clothes but what I set in, except a couple of old shirts and them socks. My hat's stoppin' up the winder, and my old coat is my bed-cover. I'm awful shabby, ma'am, and that's one reason I don't go out more. I can hobble some, but I ain't got used to bein' a scarecrow yet," and Joe glanced from the hose without heels that hung on the line to the ragged suit he wore, with a resigned expression that made me long to rush out and buy up half the contents of Oak Hall on the spot.

Curbing this wild impulse I presently departed with promises of speedy transportation for Joe, and unlimited oranges to assuage the pangs of parting for the young Flanagins, who escorted me to the door, while Joe waved the baby like a triumphal banner till I got round the corner.

There was such a beautiful absence of red tape about the new institution that it only needed a word in the right ear to set things going; and then, with a long pull, a strong pull, and a pull all together, Joe Collins was taken up and safely landed in the Home he so much needed and so well deserved.

A happier man or a more grateful one it would be hard to find, and if a visitor wants an enthusiastic guide about the place, Joe is the one to take, for all is comfort, sunshine, and good-will to him; and he unconsciously shows how great the need of this refuge is, as he hobbles about on his lame feet, pointing out its beauties, conveniences, and delights with his one arm, while his face shines, and his voice quavers a little as he says gratefully, —

"The State don't forget us, you see, and this is a Home wuth havin'. Long life to it!"

CREDITS

ILLUSTRATIONS

Front cover: Louisa May Alcott, 1862. *National Library of Medicine*
Back cover: "A Ward in Armory Square Hospital". *Library of Congress*
Frontispiece: *On Picket Duty and Other Tales* (Boston: James Redpath, 1864)
Pages 79 and 96, *Hospital Sketches* (Boston: Roberts Brothers, 1881)
Page 232, *Our Young Folks*, 1, no. 4 (April 1865)

ORCHARD HOUSE

We encourage you to support the Orchard House, home of the Alcotts. This historic house museum is owned and operated by the Louisa May Alcott Memorial Association. The Louisa May Alcott Memorial Association is a private, not-for-profit corporation, founded in 1911. The Association provides the financial and human resources required to conduct public tours, special programs, exhibits and the curatorial work that continue the tradition of the Alcotts, a unique nineteenth century family.

Orchard House, Home of the Alcotts
399 Lexington Road
P. O. Box 343
Concord, MA 01742-0343
978-369-4118